ROADS

ROADS

A NOVEL

MARINA ANTROPOW CRAMER

ACADEMY

CHICAGO

Copyright © 2017 by Marina Antropow Cramer
All rights reserved
Published by Academy Chicago Publishers
An imprint of Chicago Review Press Incorporated
814 North Franklin Street
Chicago, Illinois 60610
ISBN 978-1-61373-556-5

Library of Congress Cataloging-in-Publication Data
Is available from the Library of Congress.

Cover design: Joan Sommers Design
Cover image: Photo by Sovfoto/UIG via Getty Images
Typesetting: Nord Compo

Printed in the United States of America
5 4 3 2 1

For Baba Lena

Но вечно жалок мне изгнанник,
Как заключенный, как больной.
Темна твоя дорога, странник,
Полынью пахнет хлеб чужой.

But to me the exile is forever pitiful,
Like a prisoner, like someone ill.
Dark is your road, wanderer,
Like wormwood smells the bread of strangers.

—Anna Akhmatova, "I Am Not with Those Who Abandoned Their Land," trans. Judith Hemshemeyer

———————

All those you really loved
Will always be alive for you.

—Anna Akhmatova, "And All Those Whom My Heart Won't Forget," trans. Judith Hemshemeyer

PROLOGUE

Germany, 1945

IN THE END, getting away was easy.

They set off across the field through ankle-high summer-browned grass, heading for the road, Filip's shovel swinging by his side. Ilya set the pace, purposeful but not too fast. They walked abreast, heads down.

"Keep walking," Ilya said softly, glancing sideways at his son-in-law. "Don't look back. He'll think we're going to work on the road."

With a rucksack and all our belongings? Filip thought, but merely grunted in reply, refusing to look at the older man, expecting at any moment a shout, a bullet in the back. The old man had to be crazy, thinking two Russian men in German uniform, ROA insignia on their sleeves, could expect to survive in this alien land, even if the war was over. Wasn't the American camp they had just left behind their best hope?

When they reached the shade of the linden trees that lined the road, the men stopped and turned. Across the field they had just crossed, the camp looked small, a forlorn grouping of gray barracks, a dusty yard, a neglected watchtower, a wisp of smoke rising from the kitchen chimney, where even now the next meal they would not eat was being prepared.

And there was Anneliese, carrying a basket of laundry to the officers' quarters, throwing her brash laugh over her shoulder at a passing remark. His eye caught the glint of sunlight on her cropped auburn hair, hair he knew to be fine and smooth and smelling of almonds.

Filip suffered a momentary twinge of regret, a little ache at the back of the throat. Did Anneliese care that he had not said good-bye?

A few men milled around the yard with no apparent purpose. Some stood in small groups or squatted in a circle where, Filip knew, there would be dice or a card game in progress. The lone sentry stood with his back against a fence post, one leg bent back at the knee, the sole of his booted foot resting against the fence. He lit a cigarette, tossed the match into the scrubby grass. *That's what I want,* thought Filip. *An American cigarette.*

PART I

Yalta

Friends

1

SHE HAD WANTED to be a nun. As a young child, Zoya had studied them, marveling at their ageless appearance. Their faces were either smooth as eggshells, as if their very skin had absorbed the translucent glow of the thousands of candles with which they marked their days, or so finely wrinkled, fragile and deeply etched like a fallen leaf, that she could not imagine they had ever looked otherwise.

When she was older, she admired their bearing, the dignified humility, austere gentleness. Mysterious virginal passion. Awestruck, she never dared talk to them, only nodding reverentially if their glances happened to fall in her direction.

She saw them only at church. They would come from the nearby convent on service days—Saturday evening, Sunday Mass, holidays, and, if asked, weddings, christenings, and funerals—to sing the hymns and responses and read the Psalter selections while the priest carried out his secret duties inside the curtained altar. "To help you forget about everyday things, and think about being a good person," Father Yefim had explained when she once asked about the reason for these interludes of monotonous recitation when nothing seemed to be happening.

She wanted to ask, *Isn't it just the opposite?* The cool, semidark interior, the hypnotic, melodious drone of archaic Slavonic words whose full meaning was only revealed after years of arduous study, did these really make you think about your soul? But she did not dare contradict the priest; perhaps when she was older, she would understand.

Zoya loved the nuns' thin voices, the way they seemed to reach only half volume, chanting almost to themselves, conversing with their God. She wanted to be like them, to wear the severe robes that hid their bodies, not only from the eyes of the world but even from themselves. At seven, after making her first Communion, she was permitted to tend the candles, gathering the burnt-down stubs into small buckets placed discreetly along the walls, delivering them, when nearly full, to the sacristan, who passed them on to the nuns to melt down into new candles. Father Yefim warned her against taking pride in her small task, but she knew it was important, a vital part of the cycle that placed her, however indirectly, in touch with the holy women.

By the time she turned twelve, Zoya had taken to wearing a scarf, draped to cover every strand of her glossy black hair, and tied modestly at the nape of her neck. While she grew through adolescence and into young womanhood, it made her even lovelier, setting off her perfect Grecian features, the fine straight nose, deep black eyes, perfectly proportioned mouth.

"Why hide yourself away?" her mother had protested. "How will you ever be a bride if you never go dancing?"

"I will be a bride of Jesus. Dancing does not interest me."

The day she fell in love with opera it was raining. It had always been there, the music, in her home, on the records her father played evenings or Sunday afternoons while her mother napped or gossiped with neighbors. Zoya paid little attention at first, absorbing the music as naturally as breathing, humming along with favorite passages while dressing her doll, leafing through a picture book, daydreaming. Then, with the rain beading down the parlor window, the air serenely gray, she was suddenly listening. She was entranced with the sound, the harmonies that pleased her ear, the purity that pierced her heart.

When he noticed her interest, her father told her the stories. It all began to make sense. She did not need to understand the words; as with church, she could absorb the sonorities and follow the narrative, gleaning more and more meaning with repeated listening. It was secular, yes, but it carried the clearest of moral messages: evildoers were punished, the selfish or guilty suffered the consequences of their transgressions, the clean of heart received their reward. More often than not, they had to die for it, transported by sacrifice to ecstatic salvation. She wept, filled with desire to suffer, to *be* Gilda, Marguerite, Mimì, Tatiana.

And the spectacle! She would never forget traveling with her father to Kiev to visit relatives, going with them to the opera house to see *Carmen*. She was thirteen.

It was glorious. She tried reminding herself it was entertainment, the devil's way of distracting her from pure thoughts, as Father Yefim would say. But from the overture's opening chords, she was bewitched by the blazing lights and splendid, colorful costumes, her resistance defeated by the powerful emotions playing out onstage.

Thinking about it later, she told herself, *Carmen dies with no hope of redemption because she is wicked and self-indulgent, unlike the virtuous Micaela, who is faithful and good. And dull.* Secretly, Zoya cherished the high drama of Carmen's story, her valiant death at the hands of the jealous Don José a fitting testament to the honesty of her private outlaw creed. Would she, Zoya, be capable of such intense integrity? It was a dangerous, troubling question, implying layers of interpretation behind the superficial concepts of right and wrong she had so far accepted on faith. She pushed it out of her mind.

And what was the Orthodox church service if not spectacle? The ornate vestments, gold vessels encrusted with precious stones, candlelight and incense; the chanting in strictly ordained cadences; the beautiful singing, the call-and-response between priest and choir—all in observance of rituals hundreds of years old that engaged all the senses while requiring little active participation. You just had to be

there and pay attention. Take heed. Absorb what you had witnessed
in your own way.

Back home in Yalta, she finished the tenth grade at eighteen and
received her teaching certificate. She taught first grade and loved it.
She lived with her parents, went to church, observed days of Lent and
fasting and, with a few colleagues from school, attended every opera
and play that opened in the city. She gave most of her modest salary
to her parents, and, except for inexpensive balcony seats, spent almost
none on things for herself.

It was this, embracing theater and recognizing the vital part that
music and the performing arts had come to play in her life, that finally
turned her away from dreams of the cloistered life. At sixteen, she had
stopped wearing the head scarf, except in church. She would be good.
She would not drink or gamble or use profane language. She would
not know a man before marriage. But she would live in the world,
and she would go to the opera whenever possible.

———————

Vadim, a postal clerk six years older than Zoya, had recently arrived
in Yalta to serve as assistant to the postmaster. A distant cousin of
one of her theater friends, he joined their circle, and soon focused his
attention on her.

They made an incongruous couple. She was diminutive, fine-boned,
with straight black hair she wore braided and unadorned. Her ward-
robe consisted of simple dresses in plain colors: blue, gray, brown,
with lace collars she crocheted herself, and a single cameo brooch she
saved for special occasions. Vadim was tall, sandy-haired, blue-eyed.
At twenty-five he was still gangly but was beginning to show the first
signs of future corpulence: a little slackening of the chin, some soften-
ing around the middle.

They met at a concert performance of Tchaikovsky opera arias and songs. At intermission, both stood aside until the crush of people at the buffet had eased, rather than fight their way to the front of the hungry throng.

To her own surprise, Zoya spoke first, sensing the young man's discomfort as a stranger in their midst. "Are you enjoying the performance, Vadim . . ." She hesitated, not knowing his father's name.

"Nikitich," he supplied. "But please just call me Vadim. Patronymics are for old folks and college professors." Smiling, he steered her toward an opening in the crowd around the table. "Come, or we will get no *pirozhki*."

"I suppose we are old-fashioned here in the south. Now that I am finally old enough to be called Stepanovna, the customs seem to be changing. What is the filling?" she addressed the kerchiefed woman behind the table, pointing to the last few buns in the basket. "Mushroom and onion? Yes, please."

"Why so particular?" Vadim paid, over her protest, and they took their punch and pastries toward the mezzanine railing.

"It's still Lent," she explained. "I should not even be here, at the theater. But at least I can refrain from eating meat."

"Surely Tchaikovsky is good for the soul. And yes, I am enjoying the performance, but I find these disembodied arias a frustration. In my head, the music continues to the next scene, while on the stage, they are already singing something completely different. 'From another opera,' as my father used to say whenever I tried to change the subject in one of our discussions."

She smiled at the familiar expression. "But the concert songs are lovely, so lyrical—" Zoya broke off, turning to greet some friends, just as the light flashed for the beginning of the program's second half, and they returned to their seats.

I like this young man, she thought. He seemed different from the other men she knew, with none of the austerity of her distant father, or the benign severity of Father Yefim, whose stern words, softened by the kindness in his eyes, had been falling into her child's heart all her life. Vadim had a self-confidence that was new to her, an air of developing authority that seemed to take its strength from some inner source, some intellectual center quite unlike her own emotional compass.

When she got to know him better, she learned that he did not sing or play the guitar, like some of her other friends, he did not joke and he did not drink. She came to admire the way his face lit up when the conversation turned to serious matters—questions of philosophy or history, or the bewildering recent events that frightened her into silence because she did not understand them.

"Change is coming," Vadim said, his voice firm and self-assured. "We are that change." *He is the sturdy oak to my bending willow*, she thought, echoing the words of a folk song. She did not know where he was going, but feared getting left behind.

"What do you see in me?" she asked when his courteous attentions crossed the line into undeniable courtship. "I am such a mouse next to your lively friends. I have nothing to say that would interest them."

"Even a mouse has a worldview. Yours may encompass only this apartment, but within it there is certainty and peace. I love your quiet charm, and the glimpses of passion you reveal at the opera, like sunlight glinting through cool summer foliage." He stopped, blushed deeply. "I don't know what came over me. I don't usually wax poetic. But that's exactly what I mean."

"My charm?" Zoya colored slightly, genuinely perplexed.

"Yes. You are so serene. My friends may shout their opinions, convinced they see the truth at last, the solution to our country's difficult problems. You bring calm into the room. Into my life." As if mindful of her modesty, he did not say, *And you are beautiful. I love looking at you.*

When the revolution came, in 1917, it left her convictions relatively untouched. She had never delved into political matters; the Tsarist system had given her enough food and education, respectable work, access to refined entertainment and to sustaining religious practice. She did not understand, when she read about workers' demands for bread, or peasants clamoring for land, who were these workers, these peasants? Russia was a vast country, rich in land and resources, as she had learned at school, and taught her pupils. Wasn't there enough for everyone?

Not so, Vadim, now her husband, explained. "We can only be happy if the least fortunate among us bear their burden in silence, to paraphrase Anton Chekhov," he said solemnly over their morning tea. "This can't go on. Soldiers who suffer brutal punishment and starvation rations instead of pay are banding with oppressed factory workers, joining our infamously ignorant peasants. Their demand for reform can no longer be ignored. It's time for change, my dear." He kissed the top of her head and patted her shoulder.

"He treats me like a child," Zoya said aloud when Vadim had left for work, her resentment just short of anger. "Well, when it comes to politics and *change*, I suppose I am."

Curious, she reread Chekhov, and found herself of two minds about her country's greatest storyteller. She admired his vivid characters and the easy flow of his words across the page, capturing moments in nineteenth-century Russian life with a vibrant quality that would, she was sure, continue to delight readers for years to come. But why did he dwell so much on the sordid side of life? His stories lulled you with their eloquence while showing you the very worst in human nature: lies, deceptions, cruelties, and bitter twists of fate. Even love, so prominent a theme in almost every piece, was tainted. Those few characters who loved truly, wholeheartedly, invariably came to a bad end, never understanding how their own naive view of grand emotions led to their downfall.

"There is going to be a child." She released the words into the dark above the bed, not sure whether she wanted Vadim to hear her whispered news.

He heard, and turned to her. "Is there? Are you sure?"

"Oh, yes. In mid-May, the doctor said."

She did not know how to interpret his silence.

"I will need some knitting wool." *Are you not glad?* She wanted to ask, but feared the answer and kept the thought to herself. They had talked little about starting a family; in the six years of their marriage, in contrast to the country's turmoil, their home was a refuge, quiet and safe.

Now she could leave her teaching position with dignity. She had begun to feel out of step in the classroom, where portraits of the imperial family had been replaced with Lenin's grave countenance. Reference to God was forbidden, and it seemed more and more of her job involved leading the children toward involvement in Young Pioneers. Now, she could walk away before her loyalty to the new order could be called into question.

When Filip came, he hollowed her out, taking with him the sheltering contents of her womb. His breech birth left her uterus so damaged that the doctor and attending midwife removed it, telling the exhausted young mother only after she regained consciousness.

The baby was surprisingly small, for all the pain and disruption of his arrival. Zoya peered at the little wizened face, marveled at the blankness of its expression, except for a hint of smugness around the tiny puckered mouth. *I am your child*, it seemed to say. *There will be no other.*

It took time for Zoya to see this child as a gift from God. The entire experience, the interminable pregnancy, punctuated with episodes of unaccountable bleeding that sent her to bed for days at a time; the hellish birth, which left her lying in her own sweat and blood, barely aware, before the blessed relief of deep sleep, that the moans still reverberating in the overheated room had been her own.

Father Yefim came, held her hand and encouraged her to pray. But her mind felt numb, her body violated; she could not force the words out of her desiccated mouth.

"God allows us to suffer so we will cherish our children. He will not send more pain than we can bear." Eyes closed, he recited phrases meant to give her comfort, but she could not fathom their relevance and soon fell asleep, lulled by the rhythmic droning of his familiar voice.

"I have no quarrel with God," she would reply when she awoke and he was gone. "But there was no *we* in this event, was there?" She covered her mouth with the edge of the sheet, even though no one but the sleeping baby was there to hear the impertinent words. This child, why did he have to announce his arrival with such wrenching ferocity, the memory of which convulsed her with fresh waves of dread? If God had done anything, it was to guarantee that she would never go through this again. She was grateful for this proof of divine mercy, but felt vaguely ill at ease, as if she had misunderstood an important lesson, failed to grasp the kernel of truth in a complicated parable. It was too much to think about. She slept.

There was no one to help her with the child. In spite of the best efforts of the sanatorium and the healing effects of the Black Sea climate, Zoya's mother had succumbed to tuberculosis the previous year. Travel was difficult, requiring special passports even within the same district; no other female relatives from either side of the family lived close enough to make the journey, or want to. Only her father was nearby, and he knew nothing about babies.

He was a beaten man, her father. Accused of being a monarchist and White Army sympathizer, he was stripped of his upper-grade teaching position and now worked as a janitor at the elementary school. "I was lucky," he said. "Some of the teachers were hounded to the point of madness." He reached a tentative finger into the basket where his grandson lay, quiet and watchful, dark eyes scanning the limits of his visible world. "Is there more tea?"

Refilling his cup, Zoya did not ask about her father's colleagues. She knew there had been hasty interrogations, People's Court trials convened on the spot, followed by swift executions. She preferred not to hear how rough, unschooled hands reviewed the scanty evidence of treasonous leanings, based, sometimes, on a lazy student's personal grudge against a stern teacher.

Even at home, it was best not to talk about patriotism; the word's meaning shifted constantly from one week to the next, as nascent political parties scrabbled for power in a government as raw as it was chaotic. When the civil war ended, Lenin died, and Stalin emerged victorious, she felt, frankly, indifferent. What did it matter? They were all guilty, in her view. All of them, whatever they called themselves, were complicit in the murder of the tsar and his radiant family.

"It was unfortunate, but necessary," Vadim said on the one occasion when the topic came up between them. "And they are still a threat, even in death. As martyrs, they will continue to attract support, particularly abroad. Comrade Stalin is right to be vigilant."

Zoya flushed deeply, surprised by the vehemence of her feelings. "It was barbaric. Are we pagan Pechenegs, or ancient Romans, who thought nothing of removing their fathers, their own brothers, just to have a turn at sitting on the throne a few years? They are assassins. Tsar Nicholas was a gentle man. He loved peace and family life."

"No doubt some hundred years from now he will be elevated to sainthood," Vadim predicted. "In the meantime, please keep these views to yourself, my dear." He filled a pipe with Turkish tobacco and lit it, leaning back in his chair, watching his wife through half-closed eyes.

"As he should be," she muttered, returning to the mending in her lap. Even a Communist Party member, it seemed, could never have enough good shirts.

2

NASTYA WAS A TALL, gaunt woman who brought vegetables to Yalta's open-air bazaar from her small tenant plot in the Ukrainian countryside.

"Not much there. *Ne mnogo,*" Vadim observed, peering into her roughly woven basket, the straw dark as strong tea, stained by many years' use.

"*Shto Bog dayot.* What the Lord provides," she answered unsmiling, squinting up at him from her mat, her bronzed face rugged as the land.

"And the kolkhoz? Doesn't the collective distribute the goods fairly?"

She glanced up sharply, meeting and holding his gaze for an instant before shifting her eyes to one side. For a while, in the first flush of postrevolutionary euphoria, it had been possible to speak one's mind, to criticize officials and policies openly in letters to the myriad newspapers that sprang up like mushrooms after rain. That time had passed; the dissident presses were closed down, and one wrote such letters at one's own peril. "The kolkhoz? It's the same *barin,* only this landlord wears a cap with a red star instead of a frock coat. These are my vegetables. I grew them myself."

"Govern your tongue, woman," Vadim warned. "What of the citizens' council, and the Komsomol? Aren't the young people making sure everyone has their say?"

"*Da, da.*" Nastya waved a hand. "Yes, of course. The beets are fresh, sir. I pulled them early this morning," she addressed a middle-aged man in a summer coat and dusty boots. She brushed a clod of dirt off the vegetables and cradled them in her hands for the customer to see. The man shook his head and moved on.

Vadim, too, was ready to walk on, but something about the woman held him. Was it the strong hands, with flat, stony palms, hands so unlike Zoya's smooth long fingered ones? Or the hint of insolence in her knowing eyes? "Listen—what are you called?"

She hesitated. "Nastya," she finally answered.

"Nastya. I would buy your beets, but I brought no bag to carry them home."

The woman turned her head to one side. "Masha!" she called, and a child of three years or so stepped out from behind her back. In one swift gesture, Nastya removed the oversized yellow kerchief from the girl's head, shook it briskly, and wrapped the beets, tying the corners together in a neat package. "Bring it back, if you please, next market day," she said, pocketing the coins while the child stood in silent acquiescence, doe eyes unblinking in her placid face.

Vadim was halfway down the row of vendors when he stopped, turned, and came back. He liked this woman, her quick thinking, her serious demeanor and sturdy practicality. "How many more do you have at home?" he asked, nodding at little Masha.

"She is my last. I gave my man and two sons to the motherland"— she crossed herself—"and the older daughters all found husbands, thank the Lord. *Slava Bogu.* Even if one is a cripple and the other a drunkard."

"Nastya. My wife is sick. She needs someone to help her with the baby until, you know, she gets back on her feet. I'm not a wealthy man, but I can pay you more than you get for your vegetables."

"How long?"

"I don't know. Two months, three? She is very weak, and the baby cries . . ."

"Does she have milk?"

Vadim reddened. "I—I think so. These are women's matters. You must ask her yourself. I'll arrange the temporary travel permit. You can bring the little one, too," he added, regaining his composure.

So Nastya came, leaving Masha in her sister's care, because a city, no matter how beautiful, was no place to raise a healthy child.

Filip thrived under Nastya's care. From the first day, in spite of his undernourished frailty, she handled the infant fearlessly—not without affection, but with the assurance of a woman with no time to waste.

"*Ai!*" Zoya half-rose from her seat at the kitchen table. "You'll drop him!"

Nastya passed the pale squirming body from one hand to the other, balancing him over the basin while ladling warm water over his head. "I raised six brothers while my mother worked in the fields, then my own five. I never dropped one of them, not that you'd see any damage."

She placed the now quiet baby on a towel, rolled him gently but firmly from side to side. *Like a yeast bun,* Zoya thought, but said nothing. In no time at all, the new mother was holding the bundle, deftly diapered and swaddled, in her arms.

"I will bring you milk, and *tvorog,* farmer cheese, from the country, if I can," Nastya said, submerging the baby's spare blanket and tiny shirts under the tepid bathwater. "You can't feed a baby with smiles. Where is your laundry pot?"

"Behind the stove," Zoya said, her gaze fixed on her ravenous son. Expressions of tenderness, amazement, and curiosity passed in quick succession over her face, then dissolved into a momentary wince of pain as Filip latched on. Within minutes, they both settled into the rhythm of his sucking, and she was overcome with a hypnotic tiredness, a bone-melting fatigue so insistent she felt her arms relax and her head swirl with fog. *I will be the one to drop him,* she thought. She tightened her grip and forced herself to focus, watching Nastya rinse a handful of soiled diapers in the last of the bathwater. Humming to herself, Nastya wrung out the diapers and added them to the clothes in the laundry pot, filled it with fresh water, sprinkled in some washing soda, and pushed the vessel to the back of the stove.

"After it has boiled, I can hang the laundry in the courtyard?" Nastya asked, taking the sated infant from his mother and tucking him into his basket. "And you must sleep now, too."

Zoya allowed herself to be led to bed. "That tune you were humming—what was it? I know it but can't remember . . ."

"Just something that popped into my head. My mother used to sing it." Nastya closed the curtains against the afternoon light.

"Yes . . . yes." Zoya drifted off, becoming aware, just before sleep took her, of the words. It was a Christmas hymn, coming to her in the pure sweetness of nuns' voices, reminding her that, with the birth of her child and slow recovery, she had not been to church in many weeks, and of how much she missed it.

She could not have gone to church, as she well knew, until the requisite forty days had passed after the birth of her child. She was not sure how becoming a mother made her unclean, or why the natural cycles of a woman's body made her less worthy.

"It has to do with original sin, Zoya Stepanovna," Nastya reminded her. They walked, Nastya restraining her longer, quicker stride to match Zoya's slow progress. In the baby carriage, Filip slept, his tiny fists clenched above his head, his face bathed in a dewy sheen of perspiration. Vadim had stayed home, claiming to be suffering from indigestion.

"You mean Adam and Eve and the Garden of Eden?"

"I don't understand it myself. In the village, we think of the forty-day ceremony as bringing the baby into the fold, for everyone to see."

"Isn't that what baptism is for?"

"Baptism makes you a Christian, and it can be done in secret. This tradition is more . . . public."

"Jesus spent forty days wandering in the wilderness," Zoya observed.

"Yes, and Noah floated in his ark for forty days before landing on Mount Ararat," Nastya added. "But I don't know what any of it has to do with the birth of a child."

They fell silent, each keenly aware of the precarious status of their religious observances. There was no need to talk about the escalating church and monastery closings, or the diminishing number of priests still able to serve the remaining believers.

"Sit here a moment." Nastya indicated the wide limestone church steps. "I will have them tell Father Yefim you have come *za molitvoy*—to receive a prayer for your son."

Zoya sat, choosing the end of the step shaded by a spreading acacia tree. The walk had wearied her. She closed her eyes against the wild array of colors shifting and swimming around her, not even able to remember what all these familiar flowers were called. Filip was still sleeping, with the barest shadow of a smile hovering around his lips. Watching him, she suddenly felt completely alone, as if they had all disappeared—her father, Vadim, Nastya—and she was left with the burden of survival, with this young life entrusted to her keeping. What if it happened? What then?

It was no idle question. People were here one day and gone the next. Would these prayers protect her then? Who could know? Zoya leaned her head against the baby carriage and surrendered to panic, its grip sending shivers down her arms and legs in spite of the warmth of the midmorning sun.

Filip woke up and wailed just as Nastya came out to tell her they were ready for the ceremony. Standing at the front of the sanctuary, Father Yefim beckoned for her to approach. He took the child from her and held him up, his firm hands easily encircling the little body. Zoya noticed the frayed edge of the priest's cassock, the shiny, worn patches on his brocaded vestments, then forgot everything when her son disappeared through the altar gates, out of her sight. She knew it was a privilege given only to boys, that girl babies, while receiving the same prayers, were forbidden to pass the gates. Minutes later Filip, still crying, was back in her arms, but the separation, however brief, had seemed unbearable.

The service resumed, with Zoya first in line for Communion. When Father Yefim placed a drop of sacramental wine in the child's mouth, Filip protested lustily, squirming and screaming. Zoya lowered her head and retreated to the back of the church in tears.

She was ashamed—of the priest's evident shabbiness, of her own fears, of the church itself, which held fewer than half the usual number of people, of her son's unequivocal rejection of his first taste of ceremonial wine. She had imagined it all so differently, each of them playing a part in this sacred pageant with the solemn dignity it deserved.

She barely heard Father Yefim's abbreviated sermon and final benediction: "God willing, we'll meet again next week"—words that offered scant hope and little comfort. After the service, everyone scattered as if eager to return to their harried lives. No neighborly chatting, no family news, no impromptu invitations to tea.

Two elderly nuns were the last to leave. Zoya watched them close the carved oak doors and walk briskly away, one carrying a bundle of vestments to launder, the other a pail of burnt-down stubs to melt down into new candles. She followed them with her eyes until the last glimpse of their black billowing robes disappeared around the corner of the deserted street.

"Come, Zoya Stepanovna," Nastya said firmly, pushing the baby carriage in the opposite direction. "*Pora domoi.* Time to go home."

3

FILIP KICKED OFF his sandals as soon as he turned the corner, pushing them deep under the neighbor's azalea bush. A few of the petals clung to his hands and he paused to admire them. He liked the way the deep-pink flowers glowed against his tanned skin; their velvety weightlessness intrigued him. He wanted to go home, right now, take out his watercolors, and paint. Maybe he could capture their fragile beauty if he mixed the colors just right. Even now he could see an overlay of white over the pink base, a tinge of palest yellow around the edges, a hint of almost-red at the stem end.

But Mama was waiting for the flour to make his birthday cake, and Avram might be busy with other customers, so he had to hurry. Filip jammed the petals into the pocket of his shorts and ran barefoot the rest of the way to the grocer's shop. He ran in the road—its cobblestones were smoother than the rough-hewn sidewalk, and had better puddles. He jumped the puddles, but not always far enough to clear them, the satisfying splash of rainwater drenching his feet and legs. Filip laughed out loud at the cool joyous delight of it.

Avram's shop was in the front room of his squat two-story house. He and his wife, Laila, lived in a small apartment in back, and rented the upstairs rooms to a succession of students from the university. They charged very little rent, and treated their young tenants to home-cooked meals and Yalta's copious fresh fruit. "God gave us no children," Laila would say, tying a clean apron around her slender waist. "But he sends us these fine young men. Jewish or not, it makes no difference. They need a home."

The shop was stocked with every kind of kitchen necessity; floor-to-ceiling shelves lined the walls, and bins, crates, and barrels crowded into the floor space, spilling out onto the sidewalk in good weather. From sugar, salt, and rice, to dried fruit, marinated herring, and fresh butter—Avram had it all, with the exception of meat and bread. He left those essentials to the butcher across the road, and Nikos the Greek baked enough bread to fill the neighborhood's daily needs. One wall of the shop was devoted to basic implements—pots, bowls, everyday dishes, wooden spoons, inexpensive cutlery, knives, flour sack towels, even thimbles and sewing needles and scissors.

Filip burst through the open door at a full run, stopping short at the counter, his hands in front of his chest to brake the momentum. "It's my birthday, Avram," he announced. "Mama needs flour for the cake."

Avram put down his newspaper. "Your birthday," he said, his voice a slow, thunderous rumble. "And how old?"

"Seven. Now I can start school." Filip bounced from foot to foot.

No need to tell Avram the other milestone this birthday represented: he would be old enough to have dour old Father Yefim hear his confession. Father Yefim was bearded, like Avram, but with mournful eyes and a downtrodden look that made children avoid him. Some women, like Zoya, Filip's mama, attended the clandestine Orthodox church services he held in the basement of his tailor shop, but Filip could see no possible way this privilege of confession—of telling a stern adult what he had done wrong—could be good for him. Better to keep your mistakes to yourself, he thought, say you're sorry if you must, and work harder at not getting caught.

"Seven." The shopkeeper tapped the pitted countertop with a thick index finger. "Seven. Do you know, this is the most important birthday you will ever have? School changes everything in your life. You will now become an educated man."

Filip giggled. "I can already do adding up. Papa showed me on the abacus." He touched the beads on Avram's ancient calculator, pushing them randomly back and forth on their thin wire rods, their surfaces burnished to a rich shine by constant use.

"But now you must learn adding up with a pencil. So, you will need this." Avram reached up to a shelf behind him and took down a pencil box. "A present, for your birthday."

The box was pale wood, big enough for half a dozen pencils, the top painted with Yalta's most famous landscape—the cliffs over the Black Sea, a castle's outline etched against a pale-blue sky perched precariously on the very edge. The lid slid back easily under Filip's tentative finger, moving silently along the grooved edges of the box. "Oh," he exhaled, raising wide brown eyes to the grocer's solemn face. "Oh."

Avram measured flour into a paper sack, weighed it, and folded down the top. He jotted down the transaction in the tattered account book with a stubby pencil. "Here," he said, handing it to the boy. "Better get home, or there will be no cake."

Filip was out the door before he found his voice, and his manners. "Thank you, Avram," he said, then shouted it from the street. "Thank you!" He ran home, skirting the puddles, holding the gift close to his chest, barely remembering to stop for his sandals, the wilted azalea petals crushed, forgotten, in his pocket.

4

"PAPA, CAN WE GO to the dock? There's a ship coming in right now." Galina stood very still; only her dancing eyes revealed anticipation. As if on cue, a ship's horn wailed its throaty announcement, waves of sound stirring the air with vibrations she could feel from the pit of her stomach down to her knees.

"Not today, *dochenka*, my daughter." Ilya replied without taking his eyes from the wire he was bending with small sharp-nosed pliers. Under his fingers, the Russian letters *ya* and *l* were already formed. He turned the pin around, looping the wire deftly to form the *t* and *a*, then added a decorative flourish before starting on the date—1935.

Galina never tired of watching him work. Her earliest memories included the silhouette of her father bent over his worktable, framed by yellow lamplight, humming and occasionally talking to himself: "Careful, the antlers are tricky" or "Just a few more leaves" or "*Vot*. Finished." She would fall asleep to the whisper of his chisel scraping against polished ivory, wake up to examine with delight the newest bracelet or brooch. Deer grazing in leafy meadows, birds in flight, exquisite flowers framed by impossibly delicate fern fronds—each unique, each, to her admiring eye, priceless.

Ilya spent his days clerking at the government procurement office in the harbor. Seeing a ship come in was entirely routine, requiring a flurry of paperwork that had long ago blunted for him the novelty or excitement of any arrival. Saturdays were spent outdoors in one of the city's parks, or down by the quay, offering his work for sale, making up wire mementos on the spot for those who had money to buy them. These were mostly Party members on holiday, or traveling artists—film and theater actors, circus performers, members of opera companies or ballet troupes, who enjoyed more travel privileges than the average Soviet citizen.

Galina loved these weekend outings with her father. School was interesting, but she did not share, or understand, her friend Filip's thirst for knowledge. She could see the value of knowing how to read, and learning arithmetic seemed practical enough, but in the end school was something you had to do until you were old enough to step into the stream of life.

Her brother Maksim was the studious one. Already, at thirteen, he talked about medical school. Galina was convinced that he spent hours at the library at least in part to avoid the household duties that fell, more and more, to her hands. But he was a boy, and the only son; more was expected of him. Her own reality of daily tasks was brightened by the singing that started and ended each school day, and by the time she spent with her father outdoors, away from their crowded rooms and the unavoidable intrusions of other people's family dramas.

Family drama was common fare in the tenement, where every argument floated out into the open courtyard, unrestrained by thin walls, aided by the perpetually open windows. No arrival or departure escaped notice, though sudden disappearances tended to remain unasked about and unexplained. But ordinary gossip was fair game, especially when fueled by Uncle Zhora's potent *samagon*, the fiery vodka he distilled from potato peels and exchanged freely for anything edible.

Uncle Zhora was a loner, and no one's relation. He had been a corporal in the tsar's imperial army as a young man, ending his service in the 1905 Russo-Japanese War with no particular distinction, but had suffered a leg wound that left him with a permanent limp and a cantankerous disposition. He lived at the rear of one of the apartments in a single small room that he never cleaned, coming and going through the back door that led, by way of a dark hallway, directly into one of the city's narrow alleys. Along with the *sama-gon*, he supplemented his meager and irregular pension with sales of kvass, the tangy yeasty beer fermented from black bread crusts and a handful of raisins.

Except for one or two steadfast drinking companions, no one particularly liked the old man. He was short, unkempt, and taciturn, given to shouting obscenities at children who disturbed his morning sleep. He kept odd hours. Sometimes, late at night, his neighbors would hear him playing the *bandura*, strumming passable renditions of old Ukrainian love songs on its worn-out strings. "Who knows," someone would sigh, "how much he has to remember, or regret? We are all strangers to one another." So Uncle Zhora was tolerated, whether from a sense of charity toward the less fortunate, simple compassion, or the more practical desire to maintain a ready source of cheap intoxication.

Galina had wandered away while her father worked, up to the sanatorium—it was as far as she was allowed to go by herself. She took the wide marble staircase at a run, descending in skips syncopated to a private rhythm inside her head. She loved the grand old sandstone building, with its tall windows and red tiled roof, famous throughout Europe for its mineral baths.

Once, according to her teacher, Leonid Petrovich, it had served only the rich, who could afford to travel to Russia's riviera and partake of its legendary attractions. Now, the benefits of its healing waters were available to all who could take the time to enjoy them. It was an example, Leonid Petrovich said, of socialism at work, caring for the health needs of all the people, not just a privileged few.

She had never been inside, her mama always too busy for this kind of self-indulgence. Her father, who did go from time to time, described the palatial interiors beginning to show signs of neglect, the mats and towels growing ever more dingy and threadbare. The few remaining attendants had become efficient to the point of rudeness, as though it was now less important to serve the clientele than to guard the premises against looting.

But the steps were magnificent, and she ran up and danced down them again and again, until forced to sit on the cool cypress-shaded stone pediment, out of breath and panting with exhaustion. Then she was running with renewed energy down the path lined with cherry trees, dodging the strolling couples and babushkas with small children, skirting wandering groups of soldiers on leave, coming to rest under a sapling festooned with its first or second year's blossoms.

Galina wrapped her hands around the slender trunk and shook the tree with all the strength in her nine-year-old body, covering her head and shoulders with a shower of petals. She ignored a passing elderly woman's disapproving glance and ran again, leaving a trail of cherry blossoms in her wake, reaching her father's side just as he finished the wire pin.

"Papa, is Uncle Zhora a wood-carver, too?" She picked up an oblong cherry wood plaque from Ilya's tray, ran her fingers over the paper-thin rounded edges carved in an undulating design reminiscent of ocean waves.

"Uncle Zhora? That old goat? I doubt he has ever carved anything but the crusts off his bread rations. Why?" He put down his pliers and started polishing the YALTA pin with a scrap of chamois cloth.

"Oh, I don't know. Will you put something in the middle here? HAPPY BIRTHDAY or something?" She stroked the plaque's burnished center, vacant except for the subtly grained patina of the wood.

"Whatever the customer wants. You have something in your hair," Ilya replied, reaching out to remove a petal nestled above her ear. Galina pulled back, cowering, her breath coming quick and sharp, surprising them both with the violence of her reaction.

"*Shto s toboi?* What is it? Have I ever hit you, even once?"

She stood still while he smoothed her hair, plucking out the petal and an errant leaf or two. "There," he said, smiling the radiant smile that never failed to warm her heart. "A little less wild now."

Galina turned away, blushing deeply, and fixed her eyes on the horizon, where the Black Sea breathed against the cloudless sky with a barely perceptible shimmer. "That's what Uncle Zhora said," she mumbled. "'You have something in your hair.'"

Ilya laid the shiny pin in the tray, turned his daughter firmly by the shoulders to face him. "When?"

"The other day, when Mama sent me with a bowl of soup for him, to get kvass for your dinner." She kept her head down, forcing him to lean closer to hear her words.

"And then? He touched your hair?" Ilya lifted her chin. "Look at me."

"He . . . he said, 'You have something in your hair.' Then I felt the wood in his pants pocket, against my—here," she said, touching her stomach. "Papa, he smelled so bad, and his eyes were all crazy. I was afraid." Galina began to cry, leaning into her father, her face turned against his chest. Ilya embraced the shuddering child, holding her close until she stopped sobbing.

"Does your mother know?" His voice took on a hard edge.

"Nobody knows, only you. Mama will say I am too lazy, or that I don't want to go because his room is so dirty. She says we should feel sorry for him because he was hurt in the war. But I don't want to go there anymore."

Ilya wiped her face with his handkerchief. "Blow your nose," he said. "You will never go there again. I promise."

He packed his things, and they walked down to the embankment, where they sat on a bench facing the sea, talking of this and that, until a passing commercial photographer came by and took their picture, which Ilya paid for even though he had sold nothing that day.

The picture showed Ilya seated on the bench in his white summer suit, one long leg crossed casually over the other at the knee, his captain's cap pushed back to reveal a becoming disarray of dark hair.

He is not smiling, but his face looks pleasant, relaxed. Galina sits at his side, hands in her lap, bony shoulders and skinny legs protruding from a simple sundress, her braided hair glowing in the last of the afternoon sun. She, too, does not smile, but looks contented, the traces of tears all but imperceptible on her solemn face.

5

IF HE TILTED his notebook just a few centimeters to the right, Filip thought Galina might be able to read his answers. She had never asked for his help, not even in history, where he knew she struggled with the dates and battles that seemed so important to Leonid Petrovich. But just in case, if it helped her get a better grade, at least on this written part of the exam, Filip wanted to make it easier for her. He couldn't do much for her in the orals, but maybe her sweet disposition and pretty face would charm the old curmudgeon of a teacher enough to get her through.

Galina and Filip had been deskmates from the first day of school, apparently purely by chance. For one thing, from the age of seven until now, when they were both twelve, they had been almost exactly the same height. They did not know if this mattered, or if the placement followed some other arcane logic. In any case, fate or administrative will had given them a place halfway down the row of double desks nearest the wall, under the faded map of the world, and so it had stayed through a succession of teachers with only a change in fourth grade to a room with bigger desks.

The world map looked old and dull next to the bright new one of the USSR, which showed the changed city names and boldly outlined the borders with Europe, Asia, and the Arab countries, like a vast net holding in the nations of the Soviet Union against encroachment by unenlightened or aggressive neighbors. Filip had dutifully learned the names—Ossetia, Azerbaijan, Chechnya, Kazakhstan, the dreaded Siberia; he memorized the new cities, too—Leningrad, Murmansk, Gorky, Engels, Svobodny. Often, though, he found his eyes wandering with fascination into the forbidden shadowy West.

It was a world he could only access through classic literature and his growing stamp collection. He sank into all the European novels he could find: Dumas, Stendhal, Goethe, Cervantes. He devoured Shakespeare's plays and anything else in translation that had evaded the censor's hand. The stamps he bought from an outdoor stall at the weekly market, with pocket money his indulgent mother slipped him whenever she could. He especially prized the occasional stamp from France, Germany, even America, that his father, who worked for the postal service, was able to bring home from confiscated mail.

"What happens to the letters?" Filip asked once, admiring a new South American stamp: a woven cornucopia, representing fruit farming, with oranges, pears, peaches, cherries, a fine-looking melon, succulent grapes, all etched in muted blue, framed with a russet geometric border. *Fruticultura*, he read the inscription to himself, savoring the strangeness of the foreign words. *Republica Argentina.*

"The inspector takes them away," his father replied, sipping his morning tea. He had the fine-boned fingers, keen intelligence, and taste for sweet treats that Filip had inherited. The dark eyes, olive complexion, and slight build Filip had from Zoya, his Greek mother, along with her capricious temperament.

"What if there's money inside, or photographs?"

His father turned the page of the book he was reading. Filip knew the conversation was over. *No loose talk* was the law of survival in their world, especially in government matters. Questions about the reasons for repressive edicts were best kept buried deep in one's own mind, like the little icon of the Virgin Mary his mother hid in the lining of her handbag, wrapped in a hand-embroidered handkerchief with delicate crocheted edges.

"*Mat' moya*," his mother would say whenever some unpleasant situation arose: an uncommonly long line for bread, or the sharklike appearance of a black sedan at the end of their street, gliding silent and ominous, as if the car itself were endowed with superior powers of detection, capable of seeing into the shuttered rooms of your very soul. It was a common enough expression—Mother mine. Filip knew she was not invoking the grandmother who had died before he was born, but calling on the divine protector whose presence no edict could excise from Zoya's life.

Filip looked on this outmoded obsession with amused indulgence, like a harmless if annoying habit that had nothing to do with his own life. He had long since refused to accompany Zoya to her secret meetings with other Orthodox celebrants, where they lit candles and chanted ancient prayers in whispered tones. It was no more than a witches' Sabbath to him, a pointless throwback to bygone times that had kept the Russian people humble and penitent for centuries. He thought the promise of eventual reward in some other life a dubious prospect. Where was the evidence? If Jesus had indeed decreed that people must endure the harsh burden of farm or factory labor and embrace their poverty, while elegant, listless intelligentsia played their lives away in Finland, Monaco, Tuscany, and Paris, then he had no use for Jesus.

He was a modern boy. He washed and ironed his red scarf with meticulous care, its vibrant glow reflecting his own pride in being part of the ascendant Soviet future.

"I want to be a Young Pioneer," he had told his parents shortly after his eighth birthday. "My friend Borya and just about all the other kids belong. They sing songs and march in parades, and wear a red scarf around their necks. I want a red scarf." He spoke breathlessly, the words rushing from him in a single stream, not to be stopped by the look of horror on his mother's face.

"*Mat' moya!*" she had exclaimed, hurriedly crossing herself against this specter of evil in her house. "What are you saying?"

"It might be a good idea, Zoya," his father had cut in. "Just last week a postal clerk at our office was let go for exhibiting 'monarchist nostalgia.' It seems he spoke a little too warmly about old times."

"So you think this might help you keep your job? By sacrificing our son, our only child?" She had laid a protective hand on Filip's shoulder.

"It is not sacrifice. It may be survival, ours and his." He had looked at his son with a sympathetic smile. "What do they do, the Pioneers?"

"They meet after school. They sing songs and march in parades," Filip repeated, not knowing what else to say.

He had been sent to bed without an answer. He lay sleepless on his cot, straining to hear the conversation in the kitchen, trying to decipher, if not the words, then at least the direction of the argument. But his parents were adept at keeping adult matters from his curious ears, a skill honed by cramped postrevolutionary living conditions. He had caught the occasional word—*club . . . no harm . . . children*—in his father's even tone. His mother's voice was higher, more agitated, lapsing into a whiny drone that signaled, to Filip, her extreme distress. And then, a breakthrough; a whole sentence rang out, clear and sharp in the evening stillness: "They teach them to be godless informers!" Zoya had exclaimed, each word distinct as hail in a storm. It got quiet then, with only his mother's soft sobbing, his father repeating *"Dovol'no, dovol'no,"* in an effort to calm her down. Enough.

Was that what worried her? That he would tell someone she prayed to God and the Virgin Mary? *How silly*, Filip thought, finally letting sleep take him. As if he cared about her secrets and incantations; as if they caused him anything but embarrassment.

"Well, you can join, for your father's sake," his mother had assented with obvious reluctance the next evening, and added, in a whisper, "as long as you don't believe."

But he did believe. He sang "The International" with something like missionary passion, believing in the anthem's promise of a world ruled by peace and brotherhood. Never mind that his singing was wildly off-key; he made up for it in volume and enthusiasm. Russia's youth would rise and lead the world toward the new dawn and he, Filip, would be among them.

It bothered him, though, when on Thursday mornings the Young Pioneers wore their scarves to school in preparation for the afternoon's meeting, and Galina was one of the few children in his class whose neck remained bare. He had tried his best to persuade her to join. She had even asked her parents, timidly, for their permission and met with her mother's fierce unequivocal refusal. "I will die first," Ksenia had pronounced, the subject closed.

"I don't want my mother to die," Galina told Filip with sadness in her brown eyes. "Please don't ask me anymore."

And yet, in spite of his burgeoning patriotism, his fascination with the West remained undiminished. Filip saw no contradiction in this. Did not Peter the Great, the history of whose reign was the subject of the day's exam, travel widely and bring back progressive ideas to raise eighteenth-century Russia out of her dark, superstitious morass, shoving the reluctant nation into a scientific future where knowledge ruled and merit was rewarded? Perhaps it was the richness of the international literature or the intriguing variety of the world's stamps that ignited his curiosity. And now Soviet Russia had a message to share with the world, a kind of reversal of Peter's accomplishment, a giving back, letting enlightenment flow in reverse for the liberation of people everywhere.

Filip wrote furiously, confident in his grasp of the material. He did not notice that Galina, who never once looked at the page slanted her way, had long ago laid down her pen and closed her exam booklet. She sat twirling her fingers around the end of the single braid she wore draped over one shoulder, the pale-blue ribbon woven through the amber strands reaching almost to her waist.

6

"WHAT IS THIS, GALINA?" Ksenia emerged from the kitchen holding a partly filled glass jar.

"Rice," the girl said simply, her placid demeanor belied by the color rising from her neck, spilling across her face and under the roots of her hair.

She was standing behind Ilya, who sat shirtless, reading a newspaper in the tiny yard behind their rooms. Gently, she peeled her father's sunburned shoulders. Her hand stopped in midair at her mother's words, a longish translucent piece of dry skin clinging to her fingers until an erratic summer breeze lifted it away.

They had played this game, she and her father, since she was very small, no bigger than a toddler. Then, Ilya would lie on the beach, the sun drying the seawater on his burnished back while she picked away, exposing odd-shaped patches of new skin to bake and start the process all over again. Ksenia would shake her head, amused but mystified by this intimate ritual. She found it silly, but said nothing; there was no harm in something that gave both father and daughter so much pleasure.

But on this day everything was different. Ilya had refused to join the Communist Party, and had lost his job at the shipping office. He did whatever day work came along—any kind of painting, carpentry, or roadwork—for cash wages or extra food coupons, no questions asked. Between jobs, he started traveling to nearby towns along the coast, setting up his portable workshop anywhere people congregated: in market squares, near government buildings, along roads leading to the beach. He needed the travel time, he told his family, to reach new markets, and to recover from the effects of physical labor. "You know this digging and hammering make my hands tremble. If I do it all the time, I cannot practice my craft. One slip of the chisel and the piece is ruined. And new materials are hard to come by."

Ilya used almost anything that came his way; even a broken Bakelite box could be cut up to become inexpensive jewelry. His eye grew quick at spotting bits of wire, beads, cord, anything that might be turned into a keepsake or gift. There was real satisfaction in this scrounging, turning discards into durable, and saleable, art. He enjoyed sifting through the trash of the newly privileged *apparatchiks* and committee members, finding scraps to resell to them as ornaments tweaking the noses of the same authorities who denied him legitimate livelihood.

But beach outings were rare now, all but forgotten in the daily scramble for a little money, something to trade, a meager share of the less and less available food. Ilya's sunburn was now a hard-earned badge of his exertions, the feathery touch of his daughter's cool fingers a balm to his wounded sensibilities, and a concrete reminder, if one was needed, of her steadfast love.

Looking now, speechless, from Ksenia's icy gray eyes to Galina's shamefaced expression, he waited for an explanation. Clearly, this was a grave matter; no crumb of food in the house escaped his wife's frugal management.

"I can see that," she said, giving the jar an ominous shake, the grains dancing against each other in a chilling parody of a baby's rattle. "You will tell me now where it came from, and why it was in your dresser drawer."

"It's—I—you . . . Oh, Mama." Galina dropped her arms to her sides, hung her head, and sobbed. Tears soaked the front of her dress and ran down her father's bare back. For several minutes, no one moved. The depth of her distress was so unquestionably genuine, so touching, that no words of comfort or reproach seemed fitting. When the flood subsided, they moved into the kitchen to sit at the table and talk, away from the ever-present eyes and ears all too eager to know everybody's business.

And so it all came out. How Ksenia, sick with the recurring bronchitis that had plagued her since childhood, too feverish to leave her bed, had sent Galina to the grocer with the family's monthly rice coupon. How Nina Mihailovna, standing behind the girl in line had said, "Take mine too. They have children's shoes across town, my little one needs them."

"Nina Mihailovna is such a good neighbor, the way you sometimes combine your rations—her tea and sugar, your pie—to sit together and talk. I was sure she meant for us to have her rice, after I had told her how sick you were." Galina wiped her face with a kitchen towel. "And I came home and made the soup that day. It was good, Mama. Didn't you say it was good?" She twisted the towel into a thick rope around her slender wrist, then dropped it into her lap.

Ksenia's voice rose in disbelief. "You used Nina Mihailovna's rice? How—"

"Let her finish," Ilya interrupted, raising a conciliatory hand. "Then what?"

"Well, a few days later, I saw her in the courtyard, at the water pump. 'Did you get my rice, Galya? Was there enough to go around?' What could I say? I could not lie to her. I told her I would return her ration to her myself, from our share."

"But you could lie to me," Ksenia said quietly, her voice a cold sharp knife.

"I did not lie! I took a little from our rations and put it away; there is almost enough now," she picked up the jar and put it down again, pushing the silent witness to her crime away from herself, toward her mother. "In another week, everything would be all right. Nina Mihailovna would have her rice, and you would have no reason to be angry. But now everything is ruined, and I am the stupidest girl in the world, and everyone will know it." She buried her face in the sodden towel, bony shoulders shaking with fresh sobs.

"Galya, *dochenka*." Ilya moved toward the child, but this time Ksenia stopped him, a firm hand restraining his arm.

"You did not tell the truth. That is the same as lying. No different. If you go to confession and do not tell the priest all your transgressions, does that mean you did not commit them? No, the sin is on your head and in your heart until you make it right." She pointed an unforgiving finger at her daughter.

Then her face softened, just a bit; the clench of her jaw relaxed a little. She lowered her hand and leaned forward, her voice a whisper. "We live in a sea of falsehoods, child. This godless regime steals from the people and lies with every breath. How can we survive as a family if we do not tell each other the truth?"

"Mama, I am so sorry. It was my mistake, but I thought I could fix everything, and no one would have to know. You were so sick!" Galina stopped talking, remembering her mother's face, drained and drawn, her tall thin frame racked by deep fits of bronchial coughing. *Please, please don't die*, Galina had begged, repeating the silent mantra while she cooked the soup. Only a carrot and some wild parsley, but thickened with the extra rice, it had a comforting texture that reminded her of better times. She had inhaled the starchy aroma with almost sensual pleasure, ladled the soup into Ksenia's bowl like a healing potion, taking care not to spill a drop, watching her mother eat, then lean back on her pillow and sleep.

And it had worked, hadn't it? Within two days, Ksenia was up, the fever gone, the rumbling cough a lingering annoyance, the household back in her strong hands.

They were interrupted by Maksim bursting into the kitchen from the front room, flushed and breathless. "I have passed the entrance examination, Mama," he announced, ignoring his sister and father. "I start university in September." He looked around, catching the tension in the room. "What has happened?"

Ksenia rose. "Nothing, son, we were just talking. Galina, take this rice to Nina Mihailovna right now. Tell her she will have the rest next week. Ilya, where is your shirt?" She turned to Maksim. "Tell me everything."

Ilya walked his daughter through the front room to the apartment door. "Hurry back," he winked. "I have an itchy spot between my shoulder blades."

7

"MY BROTHER IS the most boring person alive," Galina said. "He keeps his nose in a book and his head in the clouds."

She loved her brother. Of course she did. Even if Maksim, four years her senior, was a stranger to her. From a young age he had grand plans for his own future: he would be a doctor. He would wear a white coat, heal the sick, make a contribution to the science of medicine, advance the knowledge of disease. People would treat him with respect.

If he had political opinions, he kept them to himself; his only focus was on how to take advantage of the new opportunities the Soviet educational system offered young people. You no longer had to be well born or a landowner to realize your potential. It helped to have connections to powerful people, but if you had ability and managed to steer the right course through the bureaucratic maze of tests and forms, you received your reward—an education second to none in Europe, based on recognition of your gifts.

In spite of his gifts, or maybe because of them, Galina could not recall a single interesting conversation with him. He found her so intellectually inferior that they simply dismissed each other, occupying the same cramped space but living utterly separate lives.

The living space had been a point of conflict between them for years. Try as she might to obey his demand for privacy, his side of the room drew her like a magnet. The seashells in his collection looked no different from any she had picked up and discarded on the beach. Why had he chosen these? He kept insects in another box, with little cardboard dividers between them, and labels inked in a precise hand, as if anyone didn't know this was a cicada, this a moth or a bee.

No matter how careful she was to put things back where they belonged, Maksim always knew when she had trespassed on his side of the room, as if her eyes had left tracks along the shelves.

Still, things remained cordial between them, until the day she dropped the mouse skeleton. She had only wanted to see it better, reaching in among the skulls ranged along the back edge of his desk. Weasel, squirrel, rabbit, vole, sheep—each carefully labeled, frightening with their vacant eye sockets and bared teeth. The mouse was on a little paper tray, partially obscured by the tail of a faded translucent snakeskin.

She had picked it up, daring to touch, ever so carefully, the minuscule head, imagining the weightless spine covered with sleek gray fur, the rib cage concealing a tiny beating heart.

"Galya," her mother had called from the kitchen, "come help me with this." Galina had turned, startled and guilty; the mouse slipped from her hand, landing on the floor with no more than a whisper of impact.

"What have I done?" she wailed softly, scooping the mangled remains up into their tray, her fingers coated with bone dust. "What have I done?"

Maksim had been beside himself, of course, harboring a cold fury that degenerated into contempt only after many weeks had passed. At first, she understood, accepting the burden of fault her carelessness had caused. As time wore on, though, and no detente seemed possible, she lost her patience.

"I'm your sister," she reminded him. "The only one you have. There might not be much food, but there are still plenty of mice."

"That's true," he conceded. "Though one of you is more than enough. Just stay out of my things, will you, while I'm away at school."

✻

When Maksim entered university, and Galina was nearly fifteen, he persuaded his parents of his need for a private room. "I need more than a curtain separating my cot from hers. When I'm at home, I need a place to study," he maintained, "and a place to keep my books away from prying eyes. Mama, forgive me for showing you such things, but do you want Galya exposed to this? Look." He opened a medical textbook and flipped through the pages, slowly enough to allow Ksenia to glimpse the graphic anatomical cutaways and diseased body parts rendered more gruesome by stark unretouched photography.

Together, mother and son added a small room to their apartment, stealing a corner of the already tiny inner courtyard, scrounging for scrap building materials through the neighboring streets.

Ilya could not help with the work. His one attempt at framing the outside wall made him unable to complete a jewelry order by the promised delivery date. In the days it took for his hand tremors to subside, the general's daughter's birthday passed, and Ilya was forced to accept reduced payment for the lovely brooch carved meticulously with the girl's name.

"It looks like the rest of you must do the hammering if I'm to continue working." He smiled ruefully at his assembled family, stirring the weak tea in his glass as if there were sugar in it.

"You've already done enough, Father," Maksim replied. "I never expected my new room would have a window."

"Yes, imagine that! A window!" Galina chimed in, ignoring the look of pained annoyance that crossed her brother's face when she began to speak. She scooped a teaspoonful of mulberry jam onto stale bread, then scraped most of it off before Ksenia could voice the disapproval evident on her face. Galina tapped the excess jam back into the jar but could not resist licking the spoon.

By the end of the week, the room was done. Ilya, with his aesthetic sense, advised them on the best way to fit the disparate pieces into firm, solid-looking walls. He took his toolbox downtown and set up his traveling workbench near a building repair project. In two days, he looped wire into YALTA 1940, and enough ANNA, ELISAVETA, and MARIA pins for the workmen to trade for a small bucket of fresh plaster. They could have used two, but with Ksenia's careful hand it covered the three inside walls enough to seal any spaces between planks and give the room a fresh, cheerful appearance.

"Good thing we live in a mild climate," she said, nailing a decorative rug over the fourth wall to conceal the rough exterior surface of the main house. "With the roof in one piece, you and your books will be safe and dry here. And for most of the winter months, you will be in Kharkov, at university."

"Is there snow in Kharkov?" Galina asked. She had come in through the new outside door, carrying her brother's desk chair. When no one bothered to reply, she left the room, coming back with a stack of notebooks.

"Is there snow in Kharkov? More than the few flakes we see here— blink and it has melted away?" She poked Maksim in the back with the corners of the books in her arms.

"What a nuisance. Snow, yes," he started to say, then spun around. "Give me those! *Ai*, Mama, when will she learn not to touch my things?"

Galina relinquished the notebooks, raised her arms in surrender. "Just trying to help. Tell me about snow."

"Cold and wet. Walk in it without galoshes and you ruin your shoes. Turns to filthy slush in the road, ice on the sidewalks. Causes train wrecks." He placed the notebooks on his desk, aligning the corners with methodical precision. "You would tire of it in a week."

"Well, you can have it. I like the beach, the sun, the sea birds. What do you have in Kharkov, pigeons?"

"Who cares? I'm not there to look at birds. Besides, pigeons are tastier than seagulls, and much easier to catch." He turned away from her, began arranging books on the shelf his mother had nailed above his narrow desk.

"As if you have ever tried," Galina muttered. She watched him slide the books this way and that, shifting them in an exacting order known only to himself.

"You must have something else to do," he said without looking at her. "We are finished here."

"Thank you, dear sister, for all your help," she prompted, mimicking his cool tone.

He sighed, took off his glasses, polished their already clean lenses on his shirt sleeve. "Thank you. Now go."

8

Kharkov, 4 October 1940

Dear Mama,

I have moved out of the dormitory, where there are simply too many distractions. You know I do not care to discuss politics, or the war in Europe, or the state of the world, especially with people I barely know. Too much chatter gets in the way of my studies, even if people talk among themselves and not to me.

Professor Zorkin, my anatomy instructor, helped me find a room in a private apartment, very close to the university. My landlady is a widow, about your age, I would guess, with two sons in the service: one in the army, the other a sailor. In exchange for my weekly meat ration, I receive a plate of soup for my daily dinner and the use of a very small but quiet room. Along with my full bread and tea rations, which I keep for myself, I get by well enough.

Please send some warm clothing and socks, if possible.

Your loving son,
Maksim

PS: My greetings to Father and Galya. I trust you are all well.

Kharkov, 10 December 1940

Dear Mama,

Thank you for the package. Miraculously, it arrived intact just this morning, along with your letter. The coat, alas, was too small, but I was able to trade it for a proper fur-lined *shapka*, with earflaps—a little moth-eaten but quite serviceable. At least my head will be warm and dry.

Please thank Galya for the socks. It was clever of her to unravel my old blue vest and reuse the yarn. They are a little snug, and I might have chosen a different color, but I can see they are well made and I am grateful for her efforts.

I have secured a little employment, tutoring the young son of a prominent Party member. The boy has fallen behind in mathematics and his family is afraid he will not pass his exams. I will do what I can, but he is lazy and not too bright. The army may turn out to be the best place for him. But the money is welcome, so tell Father not to worry about me on that account.

Do not respond to this letter; I am not likely to receive your reply before the holiday recess, when I expect to be home with you.

Your son,
Maksim

9

UNLIKE FILIP, WHOSE FAMILY lived just two streets in from the sea in a government-issued three-room apartment, Galina's home was inland, too far to walk. In the last year, they had started to spend time together, strolling down to the embankment after school if the weather was clear, watching the waves break against the concrete seawall, talking or not, as the mood struck them.

"Why do they call it Black?" Galina wondered aloud, leaning over the iron guardrail to peer into the water. She had been singing "Chernoye Morye" softly to herself. The new sentimental ballad about the Black Sea had quickly become a popular hit. "It's so blue, blue, blue."

"You have to go out on a boat, where the water is deeper," Filip replied seriously. "Then it looks black."

"How do you know?" she challenged him, laughing.

"My uncle took me once, on a fishing trip."

"But that's not allowed! My papa says no one can sail or fish without special permission."

"It was a few years ago, when I was small. Maybe he had permission, or maybe it was not required then. I don't know." Filip shrugged, impatient with the question. "We went out at sunrise, with a couple of my older cousins."

"Did you catch anything?"

"Not me. I did not like the fishing. Too messy and smelly, and kind of boring." He made a face, remembering the ingrained odors that permeated the weathered wood, odors unrelieved by the steady breeze that seemed to blow from all directions at once. "But I liked being on the boat," he added. "One day I want to really go somewhere, have an adventure, see more than our own shoreline from an inland sea."

"Let me know when you're ready to sail to America. I will come see you off." Galina laughed again, her hair and lashes adorned with beads of sea spray, making her look magically iridescent.

Filip smiled. "How beautiful you are," he blurted, amazed at his own courage.

"I have to go now." She was suddenly serious. "It's washing day. I have to help Mama with the laundry."

They walked in silence through the shopping district, looking absently in nearly empty store windows. The famine years were over, but since Hitler's invasion of Poland, Belarus, and Ukraine, goods had become scarce; strict rationing was a fact of daily life. What merchandise there was—toys, household goods, books—seemed to be for the benefit of Yalta's visitors, who still trickled in, drawn by the salt air and sunny climate. They, and the newly arrived German troops, were the ones who had money to spend in shops.

After Galina boarded the tram that would take her home, Filip walked aimlessly, his hands deep in his pants pockets. His senses were filled with Galina—the open, spirited look of her, the way she smelled faintly of starch and rosewater, the little joyous skip in her step, the curve of her neck when she bent her head over her schoolwork. Filip had stopped offering to help her; she was not troubled by her mediocre grades, moving from one class to the next with just enough effort to get by. "You want to go to university, to be an architect. I only want to sing," she would say. "Do I need geometry to sing?"

And she sang at every opportunity: traditional folk songs and the new jazzy tunes and romances introduced by popular performers at Sunday bandstand dances in the park. Her voice was pure and sweet; it never failed to tug at his heart. It had an ephemeral beauty but also a concrete quality, as if you could pluck it from the air and hold it in your hand, sift it through your fingers like fine sand. Even now, the fading refrain of "Chernoye Morye" lingered in his ears.

Not knowing quite how he got there, he found himself in front of Avram's shop. The usual crates of cherries and apricots rested on rough wooden trestles beside the open door, but something was different. The battered, peeling sign (HOUSEHOLD GOODS, PRODUCE, FLOUR, TEA), with its hand-painted whimsical teapot, was gone. In its place hung a garish red board, THE PEOPLE'S STORE spelled out in large white letters. A short, round-faced woman in a dingy brown smock leaned against the doorway, cracking sunflower seeds with her teeth.

"*Shto nado?*" she asked brusquely, popping the last few seeds into her mouth and brushing her large square hands down over an ample stomach. "What do you need?"

"I—I," Filip stuttered. "Where is Avram?"

"No more Jew store," the woman said, spitting sunflower shells onto the sidewalk and crossing arms plump as unbaked dough across her bosom. "No more Jew boardinghouse. Rooms for officers only."

"But where is Avram?" Filip repeated dumbly. "I—I owe him some money."

"Gone," she shrugged. "I don't know where, and I don't care. Nor should you," she added, nodding at the Young Pioneer pin on his collar. "If you owe money, you can pay me. The motherland needs you, young man."

"I . . . don't have it with me." Filip backed away, feeling assaulted by the slogan; it sounded glib and hollow coming from this peasant. Who was this *baba* anyway? The Pioneers were young and energetic, led by schoolteachers and government clerks. Even the factory workers' children among them were striving for a better future. *From each according to ability, to each according to need.* He had repeated the words countless times, thinking he knew their meaning: you serve your country, make your contribution to society, you receive education, wages, housing, food, a pension when you retire. That made sense. But this woman, this crude, seed-crunching uneducated usurper, who was she? She must be the embodiment of "the people," an amorphous, faceless entity Filip had always assumed had nothing to do with himself and his world. Then where did Avram fit in, and Laila? They had served the neighborhood since before Filip was born, making a modest living in exchange for tireless and cheerful labor. There was room in the Soviet future for them, too. Wasn't there?

10

FILIP HURRIED. It had not been easy to slip out of the house with his mother's favorite records; even finding a spare pillowcase to hide them in had taken some doing. But the clubhouse door was not locked, and he was able to hide his package under a table in the vestibule, concealed by a red cloth someone had draped over it in honor of the holiday.

What holiday was it again? He could not remember which fearless leader's birthday or pivotal struggle was being celebrated. Now he was late for the Young Pioneer meeting at school, and was sure to catch a reprimand from the unit leader. The reprimand did not matter to him as much as the attention—he dreaded being singled out before the group, everyone a witness to his shame.

". . . and this is why we have called a special meeting today. Good morning, Comrade! Did you sleep well?" Every head turned to watch Filip, red-faced, sink into the nearest seat amid general laughter.

The leader, a young schoolteacher, held up a restraining hand. "Some may think that a patriotic holiday is a time for personal relaxation. Not so. What the motherland expects of you is personal *reflection* and ever-greater vigilance. What have you observed this week?" She scanned the room expectantly.

"My mother was up very early to iron a fresh blouse for the ceremony. But my grandfather grumbled, saying he would miss his walk in the park," a girl in the third row offered.

"Good work. We must help our older citizens to overcome their outdated thought habits. You must do this. And remember, we are all here to help you, to help one another recognize the greater good, and to fight against weakness and negativity."

Filip squirmed in his seat. When had things changed? He missed the innocence of the earlier meetings, the stories of valor and leadership, the lessons from history. He had loved hearing about the downfall of Napoleon's prideful exploits, about the heroes of the French Revolution, unafraid to spill the blood of aristocrats in the streets along with their own. He had loved learning how, even in America, the fearless revolutionary George Washington had triumphed against imperialist evil, only to see his efforts sabotaged by greedy capitalist interests. And had not the great Abraham Lincoln, a humble man of the people, laid down his life to lift his black brethren out of bondage? Most of all, Filip missed the songs of his childhood, the songs of brotherhood and hope in a shiny new future, a future as unequivocally pure, true, and logical as a mathematical equation.

Now the meetings had acquired a different character. There would still be a song or two, but the words were harsh, impatient, militant. The rest of the hour was given to sharing—what have you heard in your neighborhood, your building, your home? Who has extra rations, and how did they get them? Every bit of information, no matter how small, was praiseworthy. One child after another rose to report on intimate domestic activities, ridiculously harmless in themselves, that took on a sinister cast in the leader's cynical suspicious interpretation.

In this, Filip's efforts were deemed to be nearly worthless. He could see no danger to the state from his mother's love of opera, even if some of the recordings she treasured were sung in decadent foreign languages. If his own father, a Party member, could tolerate her participation in clandestine religious meetings, from which she returned calm and visibly happy, he could see no reason to expose her to ridicule or punishment. By his early adolescent years, he had gained a reputation as the least observant of dreamers, content to spend his time with books and stamps, deaf to any amount of increased pressure to do his share of reporting on the activities of others.

So he kept quiet, or, when pressed to the limit, made his remarks so vague as to be entirely useless.

"I heard someone say the Bolsheviks were becoming as bad as the old regime," he'd disclosed at an earlier meeting.

"Where did you hear this? At home?"

"No, in the street."

"Who said it?"

"I don't know."

"A man or a woman?"

"It was a gruff voice. I can't be sure."

"You did not see them?"

"No, it was dark, and they were a few people behind me in the bread line."

"When was this?"

"Last Tuesday, or maybe the week before . . ."

Dismissed, finally, with a disgusted wave of the hand, he knew he would be safe from questioning for some time to come.

Soon, when he turned sixteen, he would be too old for Young Pioneers. He had already decided not to sign up for membership in the Komsomol, the next level of youth service intended to complete the process of indoctrination, turning out fully formed Soviet citizens ready for Party work. Instead, he would focus his energies on his studies, making his grades so brilliant that his entrance to university would be assured.

After the meeting, there was a short procession around the schoolyard, a few enthusiastic speeches, two or three songs. Then they were free to spend the afternoon at leisure, following a final reminder to think, always, of the good of the nation.

The clubhouse had once been a restaurant and had a working kitchen. There was no extra food, of course, but every one of the twenty or so young people who were regular members tried to contribute a pinch of tea to brew in the communal pot. Lemons grew abundantly in Yalta's Mediterranean climate, and sometimes, if anyone brought sugar, there would be lemonade.

Here young people could play games, listen to music, dance, and enjoy each other's company. Except for the obligatory portraits of Lenin and Stalin on the wall, the club was not politically oriented and was free and open to all. Someone had found a used phonograph. The city, for the time being, charged no rent, as long as the premises were kept clean and undamaged. Whether the motivation was to provide young people a safe place to be together, or a way for authorities to know where they gathered, was open to interpretation.

Making his way toward the clubhouse after the Pioneer meeting, Filip hoped Galina would come. She had promised, but he knew that her mother could override any plans they made, requiring Galina to help in the house or simply not allowing her to go out at all. Today was an important day, not because of the patriotic holiday, but because he so very much wanted her to hear the records he had brought. He was welcome to visit in her home, but there was no phonograph there, and it was entirely unseemly for her to come to his parents' apartment, as they all knew. And he did not think he could "borrow" the records a second time.

Immersed in these thoughts, he barely noticed the change in activity around him. People were moving faster, some were running, carrying small children or dragging them by the hand. Had something happened? Filip stopped, bewildered.

He did not register the drone of the engines until the airplane was almost directly over his head. It was a sleek slate-gray apparition, emblazoned with black swastikas. Dark as a storm cloud, it sliced through the sunlit afternoon sky like a fish through water. He was struck by the power of its inescapable presence; it seemed indestructible, commanding the space around it with total authority.

It was magnificent.

How must it feel to be a young man, not much older than his own fifteen years, in control of such a splendid machine, for all the world to see? He stood rooted, unable to take his eyes off the plane, mystified by the dark cylindrical object that emerged from an open hatch in its belly. What kind of odd robotic birth was he witnessing? What did it all mean? How like a scene from a Jules Verne novel, where strange and wonderful things happened in vaguely futuristic settings created by the author's prodigious imagination. Only this was real, the object now falling rapidly toward the ground.

"Filip!" He felt a hand on his arm, looked down to see Galina's flushed face, contorted with anxiety. "What are you gaping at? Take shelter!" The air filled with a piercing whine, moving over and past them like an otherworldly siren. Galina yanked at him; they followed a middle-aged woman into a nearby building, down a steep flight of stairs into the basement. "Have you never seen a bomber before?"

"No," he admitted. "Only in pictures and on stamps." Becoming aware of other people around him in the murky room, he dropped his voice to a whisper. "It was beautiful."

Galina stared at him, speechless. She shook her head and sat down on some kind of trunk or crate. In the dim light her eyes glowed like a cat's in a coal bin.

"It's all right if you hear them," a voice from the other end of the room observed to no one in particular. "If you hear the whine, the bomb has already passed. The one that kills you is the one you never hear."

There was no more conversation after that, only the uneven breathing of twenty or thirty people and, somewhere in the dark recess of the dusty cellar, a quavery voice reciting the Lord's Prayer. Then silence, punctured by another muffled explosion, the sound of glass breaking, and, somewhere outside, the frenetic barking of a dog. After a few minutes the barking stopped, and the howling began, one dog joined by a chorus of others in a weird call-and-response of raw animal terror. Filip felt Galina shudder beside him at the primal, eerie sound; the hair on the back of his neck prickled at its unearthly timbre.

Someone at the top of the stairs opened the door, and everyone filed out, avoiding each other's eyes as if they had shared a guilty secret. Outside, a bony black mutt still howled, its muzzle raised to the now empty sky in a classic folkloric silhouette.

"*Molchi, Satanah,*" a man's rough voice broke the spell. "Shut up, son of Satan. It's all over." He picked up a loose stone and lobbed it at the dog. The stone caught the beast in its emaciated hindquarters, making it yelp and slink away.

"Is that your dog?" someone asked.

"Who can afford to keep a dog? This one looks too skinny to eat and too mean to die. Lucky, in its own way."

The air smelled acrid. Yellowish smoke, licked with receding flames, circled and spiraled up from a shallow crater in the sidewalk. The street had turned to rubble where the bomb had hit, missing a furniture warehouse but damaging the facade on several limestone government buildings. Galina held the back of her hand against her mouth and nose, trying to avoid breathing in the fine ochre dust that seemed to float on the sunbeams of a heedlessly fine Yalta afternoon.

"Watch the glass," Filip said, his voice muffled by the edge of the Pioneer scarf he had pulled up to mask his face. "Do you want this?" He offered her the immaculately pressed handkerchief his mother had left on his dresser just that morning.

She shook her head, crossed the street to where the air seemed to have cleared a little, and faced him. "Have you no sense? To stand there gaping like a country fool on his first trip to the city, watching a bomb"—she stamped her foot, repeating "a *bomb*" in a voice edged with total exasperation—"fall on your head. You would be dead now!"

"I . . . ," he started, but found he had nothing to say. To admit that he had not recognized the bomb for what it was sounded too stupid, even to his own ears. He shrugged, pressing his lips together, then took the scarf off his neck, folded it neatly, and tucked it, along with the pristine handkerchief, into his pocket. "I thought my father said the Germans are north of here, near Moscow," he finally managed by way of explanation. "Can we still go to the clubhouse?"

"It's not the first time they have turned to fly in our direction. You must have had your head buried in your stamp collection," Galina said grimly, but with the hint of an indulgent smile. "We may as well go to the clubhouse. It may be gone tomorrow."

The clubhouse was buzzing with excitement. Those who had witnessed the bombing took center stage, describing the experience to the less fortunate ones, who had only heard the explosion. The room resonated with questions and speculations. Why was there only one bomber? Why not a squadron? Was this an isolated incident, or a warning? Maybe it was just an inexperienced pilot who had lost his bearings and needed to lighten his aircraft to conserve fuel so he could get back home. *Well, what are we, then? Pieces on a game board?* Filip thought. *What does it matter whether the attack is deliberate or accidental, to a dead man?*

"My uncle says the Germans have moved south, through Czechoslovakia and Ukraine. Crimea could be next, Odessa and Yalta, while most of our troops are engaged to the north, defending the cities," one boy said soberly.

"Why would the Nazis want Yalta? For the mineral baths, or the figs and melons?" another challenged.

"*Durak.* For access to the Black Sea, you fool, with Turkey on the other side."

A dark-haired girl in a faded blue dress jumped up and cranked the phonograph. "Let's dance. *Pomirat' tak s mouzikoy.* If we must die, let's at least have music."

It was a sentiment everyone agreed with. Soon the room was alive with energetic bodies moving to a jazzy polka beat, laughing and twirling, making up new steps, singing along with mindless lyrics that spoke of love and hope and more love and love again. They moved in the moment, their joy as irrepressibly desperate as it was spontaneous.

They took turns cranking the machine, playing tune after tune without stopping, changing partners midstep, as if the only thing that mattered was to keep moving until they dropped, exhausted and happy, into the nearest chair. No one spoke while the music wound down, the last notes contorted into a weird, slow rendition of the original sprightly tempo.

After a few minutes, two girls went to the kitchen to brew tea; through the open door, the others could hear them talking as girls do, in easy camaraderie, assembling the mismatched cups and saucers each young person had contributed to the communal cupboard.

"A game of chess?" Filip's friend and frequent game adversary Borya inquired lazily, brushing damp, sandy hair out of his eyes.

"Maybe later. I want to play something for Galya," Filip slid one of his mother's records out of its cardboard sleeve.

"What?" Galina glanced at the cover. "*Yevgeniy Onegin*? It's by Pushkin. We read it in school. We even listened to some of the music, remember? All about love, what else?" She raised her eyes to the ceiling and recited in an expressionless voice: "Onegin scorns the young Tatiana, kills her sister's fiancé in a stupid duel, then finds, years later, that Tatiana is the only woman he can ever love. But she is married, of course, and refuses to betray her aged husband by indulging the undeniable passion she has felt for Onegin since their first meeting." She sighed. "It *is* a good story. I'm just not sure it needs to be an opera."

"*Chai gotov*," one of the girls sang out from the kitchen. "Come get your tea. And we have mulberry jam, too, thanks to Galya's mother."

"Where's the cake?" Borya joked, filling a chipped cup and stirring in a generous spoonful of jam. "You know I never have tea without cake."

"You forgot to bring it, *balda*. You numbskull, who even remembers what cake tastes like?" someone quipped, and everyone laughed.

"Galya, I know you don't love opera, but listen to this one aria," Filip pleaded in an urgent whisper, ignoring the general banter.

Galina turned away from the group, still laughing. "All right, then. I can see you will give me no peace. Let's hear your *ahhhria*," she stretched out the word, rolling her eyes, setting off a new wave of hilarity.

"No, really, play it for me," she relented, noting the stricken look on his face, the faint quiver of his smooth cheek, the hurt in his eyes. "You know we're all friends here."

Filip hesitated. Was it worth the risk, the possibility of ridicule? But these were his friends, after all, his only friends. He placed the record gingerly on the turntable. With infinite care and complete accuracy, he brought the needle down about halfway across its glossy, spinning surface.

Galina's face lit up with the first notes. "*Kouda, kouda? Kouda vy oudalilis'*," she sang along softly. "Why, this is Lenski's aria, lamenting the loss of the innocent days of his youth. Then Onegin shoots him. Dead. So sad and beautiful. Everyone knows this."

"Yes, yes. It is beautiful," Filip agreed impatiently. "But listen, now. This is Onegin, expressing his own thoughts about what is about to happen. Do we have to do this? Is there a way out? Why do good friends have to threaten each other's lives over a silly jealous dispute, a meaningless party prank?"

"I know this, too, I have heard it before . . ."

"But here, here . . . ," he emphasized as Lenski's limpid tenor mingled with Onegin's baritone, the lines crossing from unison to harmony. "Do you see? In weaving the voices together, it is Tchaikovsky's subtle rendering of Pushkin's brilliant idea. In creating these two characters, these friends and country neighbors, isn't he revealing two sides of his own nature? He is both Lenski, the soulful sensitive poet suffering the throes of romantic love, and Onegin, the cosmopolitan sophisticate trapped in the suffocating boredom of provincial life. He, Pushkin, is both!"

"Hey! I'm soulful and sensitive, and bored with life in this provincial town," Borya cut in, striking a theatrical pose. "Does that make me a poet?"

Filip ignored him. "I picture this scene with the two men back-to-back, each lost in his own thoughts, refusing to bend to the bonds of friendship, unable to see a way out of the imminent tragedy. When Lenski dies, it is the victory of arrogance over decency, not just onstage but also in Pushkin the man, himself. It is brilliant, you see?"

"I . . . think so. I never thought about it like that," Galina said, her interest aroused by his enthusiasm. *In truth, I never thought about it at all,* crossed her mind, but remained unspoken, out of respect for the passion of her friend's revelations. She did not know if what he was saying was true, but she could see how deeply he had thought about it.

"And then Pushkin the poet gets killed in a ridiculous duel over his wife's flirtation with a French officer. So you could say it's prophetic, too," added a voice out of the group who had gathered around, almost in spite of themselves, to hear what was going on.

"Yes. And Tchaikovsky knows that, and of course, we know it too, so it adds another layer of meaning." Filip's head bobbed up and down.

"Or maybe Pushkin just couldn't resist playing a part in his own drama," Borya drawled. "I'm sure he never imagined he would be the one to die. It wasn't in the script."

"I guess none of us do," Filip mused, seeing again the bomb backlit by sunlight and feeling, for the first time, a shudder of fear run down his spine in an icy stream. The others must have felt it, too. They grew silent, avoiding each other's eyes.

"Well, thank you, Professor." The dark-haired girl jumped up and rummaged through the pile of records strewn across the table. "How about one more dance before we go home?"

The group moved away, began dancing almost before the music started. Filip took out his handkerchief and wiped invisible dust off his mother's record with care, replacing it gently in its sleeve.

"Come," Galina said, cupping his elbow and peering into his face. He was still flushed with excitement at the audacity of his performance. "I'll show you how to fox-trot."

PART II

Enemies

1

THE LITTLE THEATER GROUP came together almost out of desperation. They were only eight people, local residents who gave their time to this artistic pursuit in affirmation of some measure of free will. Their offerings were modest, of necessity—no one had much money or time, and productions had to be restricted to plays with few characters onstage at the same time. Promotion consisted of two or three small hand-lettered signs placed at news kiosks. But people came, packing the abandoned storage shed for every performance, paying what they could, escaping for an hour or two the rigors and uncertainties of life in time of war.

Three of them had professional training. Fyodor, a grand old man with the abundant white hair and aristocratic bearing of Leopold Stokowski, was director and impresario, drawing on his many years in legitimate theater, on both sides of the lights, to shape the troupe's efforts into a presentable performance. Luyba, whose promising film career had faded with the loss of her good looks and the genetically inevitable thickening of her ingenue's figure, could still interpret any female character with convincing and only slightly overplayed finesse. And Mishka, who supported himself with petty thievery and personal-scale black marketeering; he used his native gifts to play a comic role like nobody's business, counting on his expressive face and beer barrel body for the full range of physical humor while peeling off clever lines

65

as if his life depended on it. As, no doubt, in his frequent brushes with law enforcement and competing operators, it sometimes did.

The others were amateurs, drawn to this activity for their own reasons: exhibitionism, self-delusion, missed opportunity, emotional escape, intellectual curiosity. Filip was among these, introduced to the group by a colleague of his father's.

"Your boy has talent," the man had opined, admiring the watercolor landscapes Zoya had displayed on every available wall of their little flat. "The set man they have now at the theater group is an art teacher at the *gymnasium* who needs to spend more time on paying work to support his family. Filip could paint scenery and learn a thing or two from him while also helping out."

This time there were no objections from either parent. "Just keep up your schoolwork," his father admonished with a stern look.

"And don't stay out too late," Zoya added, smiling in relief at this nonpolitical use of Filip's time. It had nothing to do with Young Pioneers, and mirrored her own lifelong passion for theater.

Filip had no interest in performing. In the two years he stayed with the troupe, he successfully resisted most of Fyodor's attempts to draft him into a speaking part onstage. He would do the occasional walk-on servant or messenger if pressed to the limit, but knew that any lines he spoke would be wooden and unconvincing. He was best as stagehand, moving with feline quickness across the floor, arranging furniture and props with silent efficiency.

"It is the best job," he told his mother over the late-night cup of tea they often enjoyed together alone, his father having gone to bed to rise early for work. "Every play needs a set—you can't just have people walking around talking—what kind of theater would that be? So my job is really important. Even if I make a mistake, the actors can fix it by moving something or changing the dialogue on the spot. I don't have to worry about humiliating myself by forgetting my lines or tripping over a chair."

"And the painting?" Zoya asked, glancing wistfully at the glass sugar bowl, half-filled with diminutive cubes she had long since denied herself, saving the precious rationed commodity for her husband and son. It was a sacrifice that she suffered with secret satisfaction. Neither husband nor son was aware of her yearning for sweetness as she sipped her bitter tea.

"Oh, Mama, the painting is excellent. I learn more every day. Sometimes I imagine I'm like our famous Ivan Shishkin, painting in the forest." Filip colored slightly at this immodest comparison; he knew full well that his cardboard trees with their randomly stippled leaves were a far cry from Shishkin's lush Russian landscapes. "Not that I can ever be that good," he amended, feeling the need for at least a show of humility.

They talked on a while, until an irritated cough from the other room reminded them that it was time for sleeping. "And I love building the backdrops, too," he added, rising and pushing his chair against the oilcloth-covered table. He popped a sugar cube into his mouth, washed it down with a last sip of cold tea. "I love to see how things fit together, what makes them stand up, how lines and angles can fool the observer's eye into seeing what I want them to see."

Zoya rose, too. She kissed his downy cheek, his face still flushed with adolescent enthusiasm. Who knew what obstacles lay in the path of his youthful ambition? For now, it was enough that he was too young for military service. In a city overrun with German occupation troops, she nurtured the hope that soon it would all be over, Stalin and Hitler would somehow cancel each other out, and life would go on like before, or better. She would be free to go to church, and her boy would attend university and blossom into the influential man his aspirations promised he should become.

She covered the sugar bowl. "Good night, son," she said quietly to his retreating back.

The question of music came up at the planning meeting for the summer season. The only music they had used, to this point, was an occasional medley of folk tunes Mishka cranked out on his accordion during scene changes, if he was not cast in a major role in the production. For the new season, the group had planned an evening of one-act plays: a serious, if sentimental, emotional piece, and a popular farce bordering on burlesque. Mishka was featured prominently in both, and would be too busy with costume changes to play at intermission.

"In any case, accordion music is not suitable here," Fyodor mused, raising his teacup to his lips and setting it down again with deliberate grace. "We have a major shift in mood between the two pieces. We need a palate cleanser to help the audience make the transition."

"You mean like bread and butter between vodka shots?" Mishka pulled on the homemade cherry brandy in his own teacup. "A bit of marinated herring?"

"More or less." Fyodor smiled indulgently, remembering evenings in Paris and St. Petersburg, the frosty elegance of sherbet between courses of exquisitely prepared food, the company of lovely ladies, the belief that this enchanted life would never end.

"We could use a gramophone," Luyba suggested. She leaned back in her chair and laid her lacy knitted shawl across her generous knees. "I have some very fine Chaliapin records. I met him once . . ." She stroked the shawl absently with pudgy fingers, as if it were a favorite lapdog.

"Hm. Chaliapin is very fine, of course, but his basso may be too heavy for our program. I think we need something else. Something light and charming that the audience can get caught up in, to clear the emotional residue and prepare them to receive the second play."

"I know just the thing," Filip said, jumping to his feet. "But I have to arrange it." He had been sitting quietly at the corner of the rickety table they used for their conferences. He wasn't sure what he could add to the process of decision making, didn't quite understand what was expected of him, but he had an idea. "I should know by tomorrow afternoon, Fyodor Andreevich."

*

It was the last week of school. Eighth grade final exams were over; those who passed would have satisfied the mandatory minimal educational requirement and would soon be free to enter the workforce or join the army. Galina was among these. Her father, Ilya, had arranged for her to start working in a toy store downtown in time for the summer season that still brought a few intrepid travelers to this world-famous resort. Some food items were in short supply, and strictly rationed, but toys could be bought for money, and people wanted them. The growing number of German occupation troops quickly became regular customers, too, buying wind-up dancing bears and rosy-cheeked country dolls for children back home.

"You start at the *gymnasium* in September," Galina said, a wistful tremor in her voice. "We will no longer see each other."

"I may need to buy a toy from time to time," Filip replied, his eyes fixed on the ground. They were strolling in the park, the air thick with competing aromas of honeysuckle and lilac. He stirred the pebbles on the path with one sandaled foot.

"That's silly. There are no children in your family."

"I have cousins," he protested. "Some of them quite small. They need toys. And we can still meet here, for Sunday dances."

"You know my mother doesn't approve of dancing in public," Galina reminded him. "She only lets me come to hear the songs."

They walked a while in silence, while birds sang lustily, concealed in flowering fruit trees. "Galya, listen." Filip stopped at an ornate wrought-iron bench. He perched on the edge of the seat, pulling her down to sit beside him. "You know the troupe, Fyodor Andreevich and his theater players?"

"Of course. I admired your trees in *The Cherry Orchard* last winter, even if they did need more green paint."

"We can't always get what we need, so we make do. I'm learning new ways to mix colors. It can be challenging," Filip admitted. "But here is what I wanted to say. We need a singer for the summer season, someone to engage the audience while we change sets between plays. What do you think? Would you do it?"

Galina stared at him, wide-eyed. "Me? Onstage?"

"Why not? Your voice is so fine. People would love to hear you sing."

Galina gazed into the near distance, where a family of ducks paddled around the lily pond, the fuzzy youngsters following their mother like beads on a string. "Mama would never allow it," she said decisively. "Why even think about it?"

"Well, what if I . . . you know . . . if I were to ask her, to explain . . ." Filip's voice trailed off, breaking up into a hoarse crackle he thought he had outgrown. He coughed, twice. "It might help," he continued, back in control of his vocal cords.

Galina said nothing. She watched the ducks dive in unison for tasty tidbits under the water's surface, their tail feathers wagging in the air like a line of folk dancers' scarves. A tall thin man walking a large thin mutt passed their bench, casting a questioning glance at the tense silence between the young people. *How does he manage to feed that dog?* Galina wondered. *He must give it all his meat rations.*

She pushed away the irrelevant thought, waited until the man and his dog had moved on down the path, and turned to face Filip, her fingers laced tightly together in her lap. "*Horosho.* All right. We can ask. But don't be surprised at the answer."

They boarded the tram at Pushkinskaya Street, found a seat at the rear, facing the back of the car. They sat straight as soldiers on parade, their bodies not touching but close enough to feel the heat radiating from each other's sunbaked skin. "Look at those tracks," Galina giggled, watching the car glide along its prescribed course through a web of city streets, the parallel silver rails stretching behind as if spun out by the rhythmically clicking wheels. "Like a pair of snail trails in Mama's garden."

Filip smiled absently, his attention focused on the people in the street. Some hurried by with paper-wrapped parcels or string shopping bags, in which he spotted the occasional bunch of carrots or beets. Most people, though, were not moving. They stood in long lines that snaked through the streets and around corners, waiting for a loaf of bread, a half kilo of sausage, a pair of ill-fitting shoes, a small measure of rice. Why was that? He knew there were war shortages, that the nation's defenders had to be fed and that their needs came first. He had heard, too, that the German occupation troops often commandeered shipments of food and supplies to send to their own homeland, now under attack from both east and west. But wasn't Ukraine a region of limitless resources and efficient collective farms? The newspapers printed photographs of strong, cheerful women, hair tied back with head scarves, filling vacancies in factories and operating farm equipment while the men served in the armed forces, defending the nation against yet another intruder who had not learned the lesson of Napoleon's ignominious defeat.

Filip understood the need to make sure basic goods were fairly distributed among the people, to discourage greedy hoarding for personal capitalist gain, but was it really necessary to have these lines? He hated waiting, standing in place in all kinds of weather; more and more, these days, he had to perform this deadening duty while his mother stood in another line for another commodity. With school nearly out and summer approaching, he knew he would be spending precious time at this boring activity, taking time from his painting, his stamps, his books, and his theater work.

"We get off here," Galina said, tapping his arm. Out on the street, she led him briskly through a maze of alleys, skirting groups of playing children. Pairs of old men sat on overturned crates, absorbed in games of chess or dominoes, while lines of washing snapped overhead, strung between second-story windows.

Filip had never seen this part of the city. Away from the vintage architecture of hotels and elegant tourist guesthouses, the shops and government buildings he passed every day going to and from school, here was life as he had never imagined it. He followed Galina into a short cobblestone alley that ended in a small open courtyard, the earth packed down hard by years of daily use, a water pump and shallow trough in the center. The yard was bordered on four sides with identical two-story brick-front houses; a narrow wooden balcony ringed the upper level.

All around him were signs of life—chickens scratched gravely in the dirt, children squatted over a game of marbles. A woman filled battered tin buckets at the pump; a baby wailed; an old man's voice raised in querulous anger floated on the afternoon air. Filip's nose was assaulted with an intensity of smells: harsh laundry soap mingled with cooked cabbage, fried fish, baked goods, the sweetness of rotting fruit.

"How many families live here?" he asked, trying to cover his amazement at this concentration of human activity, its messy intensity completely unlike his own quiet neighborhood.

"Eight," Galina replied. "About forty people, more or less. Someone is always leaving or coming to stay awhile with relatives." She led him across the yard and stopped in front of an open door. "Wait here a minute. I'll get Mama."

Filip listened with growing apprehension to the kitchen sounds drifting out the open window—a lid clanged against a cooking pot, an oven door creaked shut, releasing the tantalizing aroma of baking dough.

He wanted to run, to be anywhere but here. This cauldron of humanity had no relevance at all to his mission. The errand he had invented, which had appeared so inspired in the sanctuary of the group's wishful discussion, now seemed foolish and impetuous. What did any of this have to do with Galina singing at the theater? He had new stamps to sort, a Victor Hugo novel to finish reading. His mother, back from the day's shopping expeditions, would be putting down her crochet hook, or pausing in a game of solitaire, beginning to wonder why he was late. He wanted to run, but felt trapped by the maze of streets and did not know the way out. There was nothing to do but wait.

He became aware, through the ceaseless overlay of noise, of a faint rustling off to the left of the door. Turning, he gave an involuntary shudder, then stepped closer, overcome by curiosity, for a better look. A small oblong table placed against the wall of the house held several rough wooden trays covered with wire mesh. The trays were alive with glossy dark-green leaves and white grubs thick as his little finger. He watched, fascinated, while the revolting mass writhed in an orgy of feeding, like maggots in rotting meat.

"Silkworms." In his absorption, he had not heard Galina come out of the house. "We take the cocoons to a cloth manufacturer in the Tatar settlement, outside of town, in exchange for food and household stuff. They have horse meat and fine leather things, the Tatars. Sometimes my father carves the belts and little boxes with ornamental designs and sells them in the bazaar. Germans pay good money for them, along with Papa's carved ivory brooches and Yalta mementos."

"I had no idea," Filip said, bemused.

"Of what? Where silk comes from, or of how we get by? The worms are not much trouble, as long as we can get mulberry leaves for them to eat, and keep the birds away. Come inside," she instructed. "Mama would rather not talk in the courtyard."

"I had no idea," he repeated. His head buzzed, bombarded by impressions, his eyes opened to a complexity of survival tactics far beyond the scope of government programs or Pioneer guidelines. Here, just beyond the reach of the orderly officialdom that ruled his own household, was another way to live, trading worms for food. It was too much.

Galina led him through a small sitting room crowded with old furniture. In passing, his eye caught a faded upholstered chair, a simple lamp on a low cloth-covered table, a sewing machine set on a vintage desk in front of the only window, a narrow daybed against the opposite wall, draped with an ornamental rug, several small embroidered cushions piled at one end. Another rug hung on the wall, a troika speeding through a wooded winter landscape. Filip stopped in front of the tapestry, admiring the realistically rendered horses, manes flying, breath steaming from flared nostrils, a wild look in the single eye turned toward the viewer.

"It's been in the family for years," Galina said. "My grandfather was a merchant. He brought it from the Caucasus, along with these others." She gestured vaguely, taking in the spread and the floral rug beneath their feet.

"And the icon? Are you not afraid to have it on display?" He pointed to the holy image on a high corner shelf, a votive candle reflected in the protective glass.

"Mama is not afraid. She says Saint Nicholas—that's him, in the icon—will protect us. He has been her family's patron saint for generations. So far, it seems to be working. Come. Now. Mama has to finish the wood."

They passed quickly through a doorway draped with floor-length curtains separating the living area from the tiny kitchen. A freshly baked pie cooled on the cast-iron stove, filling his senses with its savory blend of potatoes, onions, and pastry, provoking a gnawing, instantaneous hunger. At home, there would be grape leaves stuffed with rice—he had seen the leaves soaking in a basin when he left for school—and maybe a thin soup for supper, depending on what rations his mother would have received that day. Good, but nothing like this. Was there any hope of getting even a little taste?

Filip was so distracted he did not notice how he and Galina had ended up in the little yard behind the house, where he could see garden tools in a tiny rough-built shed next to a flourishing kitchen garden. A tall, large-boned woman was splitting logs for firewood, stacking the finished pieces under a corrugated metal canopy next to the back door.

He would always remember his first meeting with Ksenia, the indelible impression of bare, powerful arms wielding an ax with as much skill as any man. She had the preoccupied appearance of a woman with too much to do. Her hair, cropped to just below the ears, for convenience rather than any concession to style, was a fine light brown streaked with silver. Her features had none of the radiant beauty Galina so innocently displayed; only a slight resemblance around the mouth revealed the relationship.

"Mama, this is Filip." Galina raised her voice to be heard above the crack of splintering wood.

Ksenia buried the ax in the chopping block and looked at him with unsmiling gray eyes. "Ksenia Semyonovna," she introduced herself.

"Pleased to make your acquaintance," Filip answered formally. "I am sorry to intrude on you. I can see you are busy."

"There is always work to do." The words echoed similar pronouncements he had heard repeated in Pioneer meetings and noticed on billboards around the city, but sounded decidedly different coming from this formidable woman. This was no ideology expressed for the good of the people. This was a fact of life.

"Yes. Well, I am involved in another kind of work. Well, not work, exactly, but . . . still important, in its own way . . . you know . . ." Filip floundered, feeling the sure ground of his idea give way in the face of this undeniable practicality. "Galina and I . . ."

"I know. You have been deskmates for years. You start at the *gymnasium* in the fall. You want to be an architect, yes? Galya chatters about you endlessly." Ksenia glanced at her daughter, who stood meekly next to her earnest friend, twisting the end of her braid with nervous fingers.

"Oh, yes, I do. Unless I am called to serve the motherland."

"Like my Maksim," she said, offering no further explanation. Filip knew Galina's brother was studying medicine at university, but felt too much a stranger to the household to ask for more details.

"Well. I work with the Theater Players. We are trying to keep our cultural heritage alive for future generations." The words sounded condescending and grandiose even to his own ears, and he wished he had not spoken them.

Galina tittered. "Go on." She punched his arm. "Future generations!"

He ignored her. There was nothing to do but continue. "And provide entertainment, of course. A rest from the routine . . . Anyway, we need a singer for the next production, the summer series. I know how your daughter loves to sing. I thought . . ." He trailed off, his courage ebbing with each word.

"And you want her to sing? To exhibit herself on the stage?" Ksenia faced her daughter. "Galya, do you want to do this, in front of all those people? People who may know you? And German soldiers, too?"

The young people both spoke at once, their words mixing in a chorus of enthusiasm the older woman found endearing in spite of her reservations.

"Yes, Mama, I do want to sing."

"Her voice is so fine; it would be perfect for our program. The audience would be uplifted by its beauty. Don't we all need some beauty now, in these hard times?" Filip finished bravely. If the cause was hopeless, he had nothing to lose.

"And how long?" Ksenia turned her head to one side, studying their flushed faces.

"Oh, just the summer, Ksenia Semyonovna. We perform Thursday through Sunday evenings, at seven o'clock, so everyone can be home before curfew."

"No Sundays. Sunday is the Lord's day."

"Very well. *Ladno.*" Filip rocked on his feet, elated. Was she really giving in? "No Sundays. I will arrange it with Fyodor Andreevich."

"So I can do it? Yes? And Papa will not mind?" Galina hopped in place, just stopping herself from clapping her hands.

"I will explain it to Papa. He will not mind." Ksenia's voice was firm. "My husband is often away, selling his jewelry and crafts in nearby towns," she explained to Filip. "I cannot wait for him with every question." He nodded, but sensed that making decisions came naturally to this forceful woman; unlike his own mother, she seemed likely to have the last word in any situation.

"Come inside," she added. "Have some pie before you go."

2

Kharkov, 4 February 1941

Dearest Mama,

I trust this letter finds you well. I know that life in Yalta is hard, but you are strong. And you have Galya to help you. She is good at practical matters. You know I am not.

About her singing—do not worry about the exposure giving her romantic ideas of a theatrical career. She has been wailing one song or another practically since birth, and I suppose she has a pleasing enough voice, but she lacks the discipline required of professionals, and is probably too old to begin formal training. Well, perhaps not. I really know little about the artistic world, especially of singers. I do know that with the real threat of escalation of the war, many have put aside pursuing personal ambitions until after the conflict ends. So let her sing if it pleases her and people want to listen. Soon enough she will marry and her life will take its course.

The theaters and concert halls are filled to capacity for every performance here. The other day, *Uncle Vanya* was interrupted by an air raid. Everyone just filed into the bomb shelter, then came back for the final act. You could say we love Chekhov more than life itself. Recently, the Moscow circus was in town, and the performers say it is the same there, even though the German threat is advancing and many shops are out of food by eleven in the morning. I cannot say I truly understand this madness for theater, film, and ballet, except that we as a people have always loved the arts and appear to need this release, pretending for an hour or two that life is normal and all is well. Psychology is not my specialty.

My studies are going well. I have begun to see some patients at the hospital, under a senior doctor's supervision. Once the initial shock of dealing with the flesh-and-blood application of theoretical knowledge is past, things begin to fall into place. This is the work I was meant to do.

With regards to the family,
Maksim

Kharkov, 16 May 1941

Dearest Mama,

You do not complain, but I can hear the strain behind your cheerful words. I know that life is difficult for you, especially now that Father has lost his job and is away so much, traveling with his wares. I know he always comes back with money and goods, and that your situation is not as desperate as it is with many here, farther north. Surely, part of the reason is climate; you do not have to survive the harsh, killing winters or the mud-swamped spring and autumn that make life miserable for people here.

Is Father aware of the daily threats and privations you suffer? Does he appreciate your boundless ingenuity, your trading trips to the Tatar villages and the endless waiting for rations which may run out before you reach the head of the queue? The increasing presence of the enemy among us must make a difficult situation almost unbearable for you.

Without you, I would not have a room to come home to. Neither Father nor Galya, with all their best intentions, could have done that for me. It was your arm that swung the hammer, your determination that drove in the nails. I will never forget this.

I will be home before your reply reaches me. Looking forward to your warm embrace.

Your loving son,
Maksim

Kharkov, 18 September 1941

Dear Galya,

Thank you for the birthday greeting.

Professor Zorkin has recommended I go to Moscow, to complete my studies with an eminent doctor at the university there. He has arranged the transfer and the travel pass, but suggests I bring as much warm clothing and extra food as I can carry. There are rumors of increased enemy activity north of us, but life cannot wait for rumors, and there are too many conflicting reports. Tell Mama I will come home to collect anything she can find. A good pair of boots would be most welcome, if she can manage it.

It will be a brief visit, one night only. Train travel is difficult and there is no time to waste. At least the weather is still good; the first hard frost has not yet come, followed by the inevitable thaw—the *rasputitsa* that drowns everything in mud and makes moving about a misery for man and beast, not to mention machinery. It makes one wish for the true start of our infamously brutal Russian winter.

I will see you soon.

Your brother,
Maksim

PS: Help our mother every way you can.

3

"I SO ADMIRE your singing, Fräulein Galina," the officer said in heavily accented Russian, taking her hand and bowing formally from the waist. He hesitated as if looking for words, then lapsed into his native German. *"Das ist sehr herrlich. Lovely."*

She had not observed him working his way to the front of the knot of well-wishers surrounding the cast of the evening's play. Only when he had elbowed past the last row of theatergoers did she recognize the young man who had stood conspicuously on his chair near the back of the hall while she sang. Everyone had seen him, she thought, flattered but also embarrassed at his bold attentiveness to her performance.

He was a short, slender man, with dark-brown hair cut close to a round, boyish head that reached just past Galina's chin. She could not help noticing how young he was—surely not more than twenty-two or so—and how smoothly the fitted German uniform, with its junior officers' insignia, set off his toned and compact form.

"What is the song called, the last one?" he asked politely.

"'Belaya Akatzyia,'" she replied shyly. "'White Acacia.' A love song, very sad."

"All the best love songs are sad, *nicht wahr?*" He smiled and released her hand. "I am Franz. I hope I may hear you sing again."

"Yes," she said, not sure which part of his statement she had agreed with. Not sure, too, how to interpret the warmth in his voice, and whether to look for meaning in the hot flush flooding her face and neck.

Many Germans came to the little theater's performances now; word had spread since summer, and the hall was frequently packed to capacity. "We may be at war," Fyodor had remarked at one of the recent rehearsals. "But these occupation troops need something to do in their spare time. And most of them actually pay for their tickets."

"The Germans are a refined, cultured people," Luyba had said in her best leading-lady stage whisper. "Our company may be small and impoverished, but I am sure they recognize the quality of our professional training."

"*Da.* And what a convenient way to look for Gypsies and Jews," Mishka, whose training was in a decidedly different profession, had growled. "Or haven't you seen them checking papers during intermission?"

Remembering this conversation, Galina became aware of the people around her. Fyodor and Luyba stood talking to an elderly couple, glancing discreetly in her direction. Mishka, always on his guard, laughing with a few of his buddies, his accordion on the floor at his feet, keeping a wary eye on her. And Filip near the door, at the edge of the crowd, waiting to walk her home.

They made their way through the familiar streets in silence. Filip walked with his shoulders hunched, head down, as if studying the pattern of the lightly falling winter rain on the sidewalk in front of him. Galina kept pace with him easily with quick, short steps, one hand pulling her thin sweater closed against the chill evening breeze.

"What did he say to you?"

"It went well tonight—" They spoke at the same time, not looking at one another, the usual tension of being out in the city after dark magnified by a new awkwardness neither could identify or explain.

"Not bad—" and "Nothing much—" they said together again, their eyes meeting this time. Both laughed spontaneously, relieved and suddenly happy.

"*Papiere, bitte.*" The sentry had stepped out of the shadows, catching the young pair by surprise, blocking their way. They produced the necessary documents at once. No one ventured out without their identity papers; it was now as natural as breathing. They stood meekly side by side, but not too close together, while the middle-aged soldier examined the papers, lifting his gaze to rest brazenly on Galina's features for several interminable moments. She pulled at her head scarf, shielding her face from the now steadily falling rain as much as from the penetrating intrusion of his stare.

He pushed his cap back, laid one finger along her cheek, moving her face from side to side like a photographer looking for a subject's best angle. Galina froze. *Filip!* The name filled her head, but her mouth, dry with dread, made no sound. She felt her friend at her side, wooden, useless, dumb. What did she want from him? Any heroic rescue attempt was likely to end badly for them both. They were entirely at the man's mercy, helpless against his superior strength, and the power evidenced by the pistol at his side. He could do anything he wanted to, with absolute impunity, here on this deserted street corner.

"*Ja . . . ,*" he said, drawing out the syllable with palpable menace. She closed her eyes against the sight of her tormentor's unshaven jowls, holding her breath against the stale, nauseating smell of cigarette smoke and wet wool, hoping he had not seen her fear. Knowing, too, that fear was the one thing she could not conceal, that it was written indelibly on her and that the soldier fed on it, violating her even if he released her unharmed.

"How old are you, boy?" The soldier addressed them in a hodge-podge of German and Russian so clumsy it might have been comical under different circumstances. He shifted his eyes to Filip without moving his head, his hand now resting heavily on Galina's shoulder. "Wait . . . I can work it out . . . 1925 . . . May . . . so, seventeen, *ja?*

Almost ready to serve der Führer. You don't look like you could do much work, though, skinny kid like you." He made a strange sound, something between a snort, a laugh, and a whinny, something animal and chilling.

Perhaps it was the weather that saved them, the sky now lit with intermittent lightning, the rain hard and cold. Or maybe the presence of the boy, who, though clearly unable to protect his companion against the older man, could have been enough of a nuisance to make the enterprise not worth the trouble. The soldier could have shot him, of course, but just this week the *Kommandant* had impressed on the men in his unit the need to supply the fatherland with a steady stream of "recruits" to work in factories and mines—labor essential to Germany's war effort. This kid was no Hercules, but even he could be made useful, soon enough. Besides, the new austerity measures extended to munitions; every bullet had to be accounted for.

He let them go, but not before the back of his hand brushed against Galina's neck and slithered over her breast, coming to rest for several interminable heartbeats at her waist. "Forty minutes to curfew," he said curtly, shooing them away like bothersome flies. "*Vierzig Minuten.*"

They hurried on, Galina in front now, her head down, arms wrapped tightly around herself.

"Galya, I—I—" Filip stuttered, running to catch up to her.

"What?" She turned on him, feet planted wide, the icy fury in her eyes catching the weak reflection of a single ineffectual streetlight. "You what?"

They stopped talking to let an old woman by, her net shopping bag distended with several small paper-wrapped parcels, scuffed house slippers slapping against her bare heels. She eyed the young people with guarded curiosity. "Make peace with one another, children," she muttered in passing. "For God's sake, make peace."

Filip looked away. "I was afraid," he confessed once the woman was out of earshot. How to begin to explain his failure even to make a sound while the person he cared about most in the world faced imminent danger? And what about the threat to himself? He had no words to describe the utter paralysis that had gripped his every muscle, a paralysis now released with spasms of violent shivering. He jammed his fists into his pockets to hide the trembling of his fingers.

Galina looked at him, seeing the boy, the sheltered child that he was. Her stance relaxed a bit, her voice softened. "I know," she said.

They did not speak again until they turned onto Galina's street. There was nothing to say; it had been the first direct threat to their safety, but surely, in this city crawling with invading troops, not the last.

"My friend Vova, you remember him from school?" Filip asked.

"Vova the joker, who put toads into Leonid Petrovich's briefcase?" she recalled, her tone lighter but still strained.

Filip nodded. "He ran off yesterday, looking for a Red Army unit to join."

"Vova's eighteen? It doesn't seem possible." Galina shook her head. "But the Reds are retreating. How will he find them?"

"Papa says they are north of here, heading toward Moscow."

"What will he do? Vova, I mean."

"Fly. He said he would rather die in a blaze of glory from the sky than be shot like a rat in a muddy maze of trenches. And anything is better than working for the Germans."

"*Ai*," she exclaimed softly. "Is no one safe?"

"Men under eighteen and over forty-five, and some university students, though I hear they will be next. And married men are exempt for now, I think."

The rain had all but stopped. Galina took off her kerchief and shook it briskly, the wet cloth flapping sharp as a gunshot in the stillness of the night. "I know several families whose fathers are at the front."

"So do I. But I don't understand why they went."

"And you a Young Pioneer! Have you forgotten your lessons? Patriotism, defending the motherland, doing your part? *A Pioneer honors the memory of those who gave their lives in battle for the freedom and glory of the*

Soviet homeland." She recited the slogan so solemnly that he could not be sure she didn't believe it. "Some went for the pay, too. You know there's practically no work here."

"Not much sense in it if they are killed. Or worse, captured. The Nazis are not known for humane treatment of prisoners. I was never a model Pioneer. You know I'm no good at informing on family and neighbors. I can't even sing properly." They turned into the alley leading to Galina's courtyard, walking quickly now, aware of the passing time.

"I will be eighteen in two months." Filip stopped at the door to Galina's flat, speaking in an urgent whisper. "There is no university exam until the end of May."

"What will you do?" She leaned into him, her breath sending a shiver down his spine.

"I cannot fight. It's just not in me. I can do something, 'my part,' as you say. But not fight. And the thought of working in Germany makes me sick." He looked up, watching the turbid sky clear to reveal its wintry arrangement of stars, the rain clouds moving south in the direction of the Black Sea.

"Then we must marry." She kissed him, quick as a bird, and disappeared behind the door, shutting it rapidly behind her.

Filip ran. Was it possible for so many monumental things to happen at one time? He was grateful for the night's cover, hiding his confusion, his delight overshadowed with uncertainty and fear. It was overwhelming—the young officer's gallant advances to Galina, followed by the ugly threat to their personal safety, the frightening prospect of forced service in Germany. His cowardice. No other word would do. He had been tested, and failed to behave with courage or even simple dignity. How could he be expected to defend his country, to fight and kill, if he could not even protect his dearest friend from danger?

His mind shifted tracks, like a streetcar jolting off in an unexpected direction, heedless of its beleaguered passengers. If he secured his ticket for the university exam before his birthday, he might be able to defer his German labor obligation. No war lasts forever. Things could change.

And if he did not pass the exam? The new entrance requirements were more rigorous than ever, making a student exemption from service nearly impossible to come by.

Could marriage save him? The thought was so bold, so completely new, it stunned him just to consider it. He tried to picture life wedded to Galina, setting up a household, scrounging for scarce commodities, sipping tea together in the evening before retiring to the murky mysteries of the bedroom. It was almost too much to think about. *But she kissed me*, he thought, reaching the entrance to his apartment building with a few minutes to spare before the siren blast announcing curfew. "Galya kissed me, a coward," he said aloud, dizzy at the wonder of it.

Galina turned off the little tabletop lamp her mother had lit in expectation of her arrival, and leaned her back against the closed street door. She liked the dark, liked the softer outlines of her familiar surroundings; things took on a comforting presence while concealing some of their blatant daylight shabbiness.

She could hear muted voices in the kitchen. She knew her father was on the road, following the warmer weather along the coast, selling his wares. When he returned, he was sure to bring something—a little money, some fresh fruit, a piece of clothing to use, alter, or trade. Tonight, Mama and their neighbor, Nina Mihailovna, would be having their evening tea together.

She could hear her mother talking. "You know my Maksim is at university, studying to be a doctor." Galina felt a familiar twinge of envy at the unconcealed pride in Ksenia's voice. *Why is there no letter from him, your beloved, since September?* she wanted to say. *Is he too busy, studying to be a doctor, to leave his mother with no news all these months?* But her complaint withered and died almost as soon as her mind formed the hurtful thought. Who was she to stifle her mother's only hope? What source of comfort could she offer instead? The postal service was erratic at best, as everybody knew only too well.

Galina was in no hurry to join them in the kitchen. She felt no special closeness to her brother. Maksim had always treated her with an impatience bordering on contempt; she was only a girl, a younger sister whose opinions were of no consequence, whose gift of song was, to his mind, no gift at all. A second-year medical student with poor eyesight, he had avoided Soviet military service; his course of study was considered vital for the good of the nation.

He was lucky, too, her brother, with a cool, quick wit, capable of reasoning like a diplomat, getting himself out of any number of difficult situations. "You can find plenty of rough hands among us for labor," he had brazenly told the German officer who had marked him for inclusion in a recent transport. "I can serve your country better as a doctor, no? Once I finish my studies." And the officer had, miraculously, agreed, granting Maksim the coveted deferment.

But Filip—what would happen to him? Galina loved the gentle side of his nature, the quiet ways and dreamy aspirations that were sure to mark him as sacrificial fodder for the war cause. Even if he passed the university entrance exams, she knew her country, in its struggle against the Fascist invasion, needed soldiers more than it needed architects. If, like Vova, he managed to join the Red Army, he was surely doomed to suffer and probably die.

That left only the shadowy world of the Partisan resisters, tough, energetic men and women committed to frustrating the enemy with acts of sabotage and home-baked espionage missions. No, she decided, Filip could not do that, either. He lacked the unique blend of recklessness and stealth these patriotic fighters required. And, she admitted, he lacked the courage.

She thought of Franz, of the way he radiated confidence, free, it seemed to her, of the arrogance one would expect of the aggressor.

And yet—what acts of exemplary service had he performed to earn his junior officer's rank at such a tender age? Service to his country against its enemies. Against her people. He seemed educated, perhaps even sensitive. Yet how different could he be, really, from the oaf of an enlisted man whose loathsome pawing she had just escaped? Galina shuddered, rubbing at her face with her wet scarf as if to remove any trace his coarse touch might have left on her skin.

People were different from one another, though, even if they were committed to the same merciless cause. That was the point, and the source of her confusion. She knew that any stirring of attraction toward a young, appealing enemy officer was entirely inappropriate, just as she knew that Filip was no soldier, that he could never cultivate the poise that, for some men, came with the uniform. And Filip was the one she needed to save.

She took off her shoes, slid her feet, still cold and wet from the storm, into house slippers kept by the door, and made her way through the darkened front room toward the warmth of the kitchen.

4

Near Moscow, 22 October 1941

Dearest Mama,

I hope this letter reaches you. Things are so chaotic here, there are simply no guarantees. My journey north was harrowing. Twice we had to leave the train and take shelter in the woods to escape enemy bombers. Several cars were damaged; a military commander (I do not know his rank) formed us into work details to detach the shattered wagons, push them off the tracks, and reattach the sound ones so the train could proceed. It was very hard; you know I am not accustomed to such work. Afterward, the shortened train was so crowded, we traveled most of the way standing up. Sleeping was out of the question.

The next air attack blew up the engine. We gathered our things and walked for several days, keeping to wooded areas as much as possible. Along the way we passed a few deserted burned-out villages. In one of them, the charred house timbers were still smoldering, giving off a pungent, acrid smell for miles. The roads were choked up with people, some dragging carts or herding farm animals. They told us that things were far worse up north; Moscow was under constant attack, day and night. Most of the fires had been started by our Partisans, to make the enemy's inevitable retreat more difficult. Just like Napoleon in 1812, forced to go back the way he came, unprepared for our winter and demoralized by failure. Many seem sure the German retreat is yet to come, but as of now the Nazis are still advancing on Moscow and people are fleeing any way they can.

I met a group of nurses on their way to a field hospital and decided to travel with them. I don't think I can resume my studies until the fighting dies down, so I might as well help care for the wounded. The nurses told me that whole factories, along with all their workers, have been evacuated to the east, so they could continue to manufacture munitions and other military necessities.

Theatrical companies, the Bolshoi Ballet, and many thousands of ordinary citizens have also been moved out of range of enemy air raids, although enough remained to continue mounting performances and showing films to determined, appreciative audiences. It sounds crazy, but I heard it first-hand from people who had experienced this phenomenon—actors in their overcoats (it is now seriously cold), performing French comedies in unheated theaters to amuse frightened, hungry Muscovites and military personnel.

Somewhere in the confusion, I lost the bundle of clothing you had so lovingly prepared for me. I can only hope that it will help save the life of some other person; the need is universal and immeasurably desperate. My documents were safe in my breast pocket, though, and I kept my dwindling food supplies with me at all times. I wore the boots, too, and have bleeding blisters to prove it, after all this unexpected hiking.

I will write again, when I have an address to receive your letters. Be strong, Mama, be strong.

Your son,
Maksim

18 November 1941

Dearest Mama,

Here is what happened. On my arrival at the field hospital, I was immediately inducted into the army. Like every conscript, I was given a few days' rifle and grenade training and a military regulations manual to study. Since I am medical personnel, though not officially a doctor, I was not issued a weapon. Truly, I am not sure that I could use one against another human being, no matter what his national allegiance.

I cannot begin to describe the horror of this place, the young men who come here with maimed and broken bodies, the innocence I still see in their dying eyes. There is no real medicine practiced here; we have a drastic shortage of medication and supplies. We patch up the ones we can and send them back into the inferno. And they go, for the most part, resigned to their fate in the service of their homeland. We have heard stories of desertion, both individuals and entire units, frustrated by poor communication, conflicting orders, and debilitating lack of food and supplies. They say many thousands have been taken prisoner, their future now uncertain. Even if liberated, their actions will remain suspect, tainted by perceived lack of courage and contact with the enemy.

Winter is here in full force, with no thaw expected until March. The patient barracks are mostly unheated. The sick huddle under blankets and greatcoats, their heads and feet wrapped in rags. Clothing from fatalities is immediately snatched up by survivors, with savage fights breaking out over a fur cap or decent pair of felt boots.

Do not send packages; they will not arrive. All I ask for is a letter from you, to warm my heart. You can write care of my regiment. I hope to receive your letter eventually, even if the hospital is moved. I long for news of home and my dear family.

In my dreams, I sit with you in our clean, orderly kitchen, drinking tea, waiting for Father's return from his travels. Galya is there, too, singing her sentimental songs, interrupting our conversation in her usual mindless manner. I see now that it is only a sign of her inexperience. She knows nothing of life, nothing at all.

I send you all my love.

Your son,
Maksim

5

ZINAIDA GRIGORYEVNA KNEW how fortunate she was. If it were not for her father's status as a beribboned hero of the revolution, there would have been no toy shop to occupy the time of her now certain spinsterhood. She had long since stopped asking exactly what his function was; she only knew that he traveled freely and extensively throughout the Soviet Union and, occasionally, abroad. Something to do with industry, visiting factories, submitting reports, attending conferences in Kostroma, Stalingrad, Vladivostok.

He had served with enough distinction to earn a spacious Moscow apartment and the privilege to call on an Italian tailor from time to time. If his luggage held two or three carefully wrapped porcelain dolls or a fairy-tale marionette (for the grandchildren he would never have), no customs clerk would presume to question their presence, any more than they would cast more than a passing glance at his doeskin gloves or hand-sewn shoes.

Zinaida Grigoryevna was not politically inclined; she did not delve into questions of economic models or political ideologies. Her personal needs were modest, and running the shop had never been about money. She simply loved toys.

And she loved Yalta. Her father's Party status and her mother's poor health had created the opportunity for her to visit the renowned resort several times while growing up. When her mother's advanced condition had reached a stage beyond the help of salt air, healing

mineral baths, and a climate as close to paradise as one could find in
the northern hemisphere, the two of them stayed on, away from the
capital's dark bone-chilling winters. Her father visited them when he
could, dividing his time between Moscow, his bureaucratic obligations,
and his sad little family.

When Zinaida Grigoryevna was twenty-six her mother died. A large,
ungainly, plain young woman with close-set eyes, a small mouth, and
big feet, she claimed to have no interest in marriage at all, especially
since no likely candidates seemed to be forthcoming. She convinced
her doting father to help her turn a lifelong passion for playthings
into a livelihood, securing a choice spot on the broad avenue facing
the picturesque seawall.

It turned out to be a wise decision. The new nation struggled to
define itself, putting the turmoil of the revolution and civil war behind,
looking ahead to an uncertain future marked by agrarian mismanage-
ment and political infighting. In the famine years of the 1930s, life
was hard, bread was scarce, meat almost nonexistent. Toys were, and
always had been, universal—harmless and, in their own way, necessary. Enjoying the protection of a prominent Party member had its
advantages. It was good for business when, inevitably, some comrades
proved to be more equal than others.

Before long, Stalin's isolationist policies made access to imports
all but impossible, even for Party members. Official rhetoric worked
hard to convince the people that desire for foreign goods was not only
decadent but also dangerously unpatriotic. If domestic windup toys or
music boxes did not perform as well as their Swiss or Austrian counter-
parts, blame fell on the perpetual shortage of quality materials and the
collective failure to meet production standards. *Roll up your sleeves, work
harder, show the capitalist enemy what Soviet society can do*, went the official line.

When World War II started, factories adapted. Die-cast cars became
shell casings; real tanks took precedence over toy models. Undeterred,
Zinaida Grigoryevna turned her attention to local artisans.

The toy shop was small, only a single room in one of the still-elegant prerevolutionary two-story houses that lined the main boulevard in Yalta's business district. Convenient to all the resort attractions—the health spas, the beach, the guest cottages, and the once grand hotels—it continued, even in wartime, to attract a modestly reliable level of trade. The tourists were gone, naturally, but some people still had a little money, no matter how bad things were, and a few seemed to have quite a bit.

Unlike food and clothing, toys were not rationed. The Red Army had been good for business for a while. Now they were in retreat, replaced by homesick German occupation troops with time on their hands and money in their pockets.

"These figurines are well made," Zinaida Grigoryevna told Ilya, fingering his menagerie of miniature carved bears, squirrels, rabbits, and foxes. "But the rag dolls, no. Tell your wife to sell them in the bazaar."

Ilya gathered up the unwanted dolls, saying nothing about his young daughter's, not his wife's, painstaking work. Who cared about her little hoard of cloth scraps, pieces too small for any other purpose except maybe patchwork, which she did not enjoy doing? The child in her still wanted to play, to lose herself in a world of her own making, singing to herself while she shirred and gathered a bright bit of cloth into a traditional *sarafan*, adding a wide contrasting hem, pulling a colorful thread to use for embroidery.

Galina's dolls looked unquestionably homemade, but her work was neat, the little hand-stitched faces sweet in their simplicity. "I could never do this," Ksenia said, turning her daughter's handiwork this way and that in her broad hands. "I was always clumsy with a needle. I'd rather chop wood." She took the dolls to the market, along with her wild berry jam, to sell or trade. And Galina, through her father's introduction, went to work at the toy shop.

The figurines sold well. People liked their uniqueness, the carefully carved details, the way Ilya's skilled hand made a scrap of wood look like fur or feathers, adding a realistic eye, an inscrutable expression, with a touch of his knife.

"Can you make toys that move?" Zinaida Grigoryevna asked him, paying now in advance for another delivery of forest creatures. "You know, bears sawing wood, chickens pecking? Peasant toys. The Germans like to send them home to their families."

—————

The first time Franz came into the toy shop, Galina was dusting the nearly immaculate shelves, her back to the door. She was half-singing a new song she had heard in the park, filling in the spaces between words with uncertain humming. *My heart, it is not peace you want . . . hmm hmm my heart . . .*

"*Spasibo, siertze,*" he prompted, causing her to spin around in surprise, the dust cloth clutched to her chest. One of Ilya's carved squirrels fell to the floor behind her.

"*Ai,*" she said, "it's broken. Zinaida Grigoryevna will be angry."

"May I see it?" Franz took the pieces from her hand and examined the break, tentatively fitting the tail back onto the plump body. "It is nothing. A little glue only is needed. I will buy it, Fräulein."

"But—"

"My grandfather says squirrels are just rats with fluffy tails, because they chew everything and do much damage. I will send it to him. It will be amusing."

After he left, the figurine pieces tucked securely in his shirt pocket, she stood a moment, recalling the touch of his fingers against her palm, and the way he nodded politely at the door, waiting until he stepped outside to put the cap back on his head. *Siertze, kak horosho na svete zhit'.* The lyrics rushed in from some recess of her memory.

"What nonsense," she said aloud. *How good it is to be alive, indeed. Try to remember that when in line for a half-kilo ration of worm-eaten potatoes, the skins creased like walnuts and about the same size, too.*

✻

He came again, always when Galina was working alone.

"The shop is too small to need two attendants at one time," Zinaida Grigoryevna had declared, conceding that the younger woman's charm was good for business. "I will open in the mornings; you come later and stay until closing."

The merchandise was displayed, one of each item, in polished pre-war cabinets placed against two walls and the front window. Additional stock was kept on shelves behind the counter, in a haphazard order whose logic was known only to the eccentric owner. But Galina caught on quickly, handling the simple housekeeping and occasional customer with ease.

"When this war ends . . . ," Zinaida Grigoryevna would sigh, picking up the previous day's receipts or bringing in a few more handmade toys. She never finished that sentence, to Galina's growing irritation. Things will return to the way they were? People will have time to play? Children will stop pointing sticks at one another in mock battle and return to the innocent joys of spinning tops and long-haired dolls? She found it increasingly hard to imagine a world without troops in the street, shortages in the shops, fear, and the dull reality of perpetual hunger.

None of this seemed to affect Zinaida Grigoryevna, who had lately discovered the solitary pleasure of writing poetry. In her airy room above the shop, she filled page after page of her old school notebooks, gazing at the familiar view of the Caucasus Mountains sheltering the inland sea. She marveled at the play of light on the Black Sea, watching the sun, wind, and clouds arrange themselves in a stunning infinity of variations.

She composed everywhere, repeating phrases in her head while standing in line for chicken, birds so scrawny some suspected their allotments consisted of the rapidly diminishing pigeon population. She used the rough butcher paper to jot down the words before she lost them. Never stopping to consider whether the work had any value, she contemplated and wrote, day after day, leaving Galina more and more to run the shop alone.

"Will you sing again soon, Fräulein Galina?" Franz put down the bear he'd been playing with, its brightly painted teacup raised halfway to its open mouth, a diminutive samovar resting on a tree stump table. She finished wrapping another soldier's purchase before turning to answer him.

"Friday evening. We have a new play, a comedy. I will sing before it begins."

"*Ach*, I am on duty until ten o'clock. A pity." He walked around the small room, examining the contents of the cabinets as if for the first time. "If you will permit me a very"—he paused, searching for the word—"humble suggestion."

"About my singing?"

"*Nein, nein*, the singing, it is perfect. It is about the merchandise, the—how do you say it—the stock." He studied the disorganized shelves behind the sales counter. "How do you know where things are?"

Galina reddened. "I know where things are," she shot back. "It's my job to know."

"Forgive me, Fräulein. I did not mean . . ." Franz stepped back, holding both hands palm outward before his chest as if to deflect her protest. "If you had only a little tag, perhaps, with each toy on display, and a number that you could match on the shelf behind you . . . it would be a system, you see?" He spoke softly, but his voice had a firm edge, a certitude she found irritating. *What next?* she thought. *Numbers on people, maybe, eliminating the need to carry flimsy pieces of paper that could be lost, destroyed, or forged? Is that where this kind of thinking will end?*

"We are a country at war, sir. Under enemy occupation. We need food and work and peace. We do not, right now, need a system for arranging toys." She stopped, shocked by her own foolish audacity, as if she had forgotten that this man, this suave, innocent admirer, could have her detained, arrested, and executed.

"*Ach*, you are angry. Forgive me. I want only to help a little. In my country, too, things are hard. People suffer, and many have died. *Auf Wiedersehen*," he started to say, then caught himself. "*Do svidanya*." Franz backed out of the shop, his face showing confusion and a hint of regret.

But she was not looking at him. She closed the door, drew the shade, flipped the sign to CLOSED, and turned off the light. Out in the street, she locked up, deposited the key in Zinaida Grigoryevna's mailbox, and turned to leave.

He was still there, his back against the building, cap in hand. "May I walk with you?" he asked.

"No!" Did he not understand what kind of girls walked with enemy soldiers, especially with officers? Everyone knew them, the girls who traded the comfort of their bodies for a box of chocolates or a piece of cloth or a pair of stockings only the most daring "companions" had the nerve to wear in the street.

"Please, *bitte*, I just want to say . . ." He looked away, as if studying the purple evening sky was the most important thing he needed to be doing at that moment.

"Well?" Galina glanced around. The few people about seemed not to notice them, hurrying to finish their errands in the gathering dusk. She heard the rudeness in her own voice, regretted it. But this was no time or place for polite conversation.

"You are a fine young woman, hardworking and talented, and so beautiful." Franz brought his gaze back to her face and spoke faster, as if aware of her growing discomfort. "I can get papers for you and your family. Work papers. Germany needs help with farming. Here." He took a photograph from the black leather billfold in his breast pocket. "Look. *Das ist meine Mutti*. My mother. She is alone now, with my grandfather. She needs some help."

Galina started to walk away, then, her curiosity piqued, stopped to glance at the picture. A short, pretty, youthful woman looked back at her, unsmiling, her face framed with tendrils of light wavy hair. "It is a small farm," he went on. "Near Munich. My father was an engineer before he was killed in the fighting. Now everyone with even a little land must grow some vegetables or grain to help for the war. My mother has little experience of farming, but the need for food is great in my country, too."

Not just here. Galina decided to ignore the implication.

For the first time since their meeting at the theater, she noticed how young he was, how like a boy, far from home, holding a picture of his mother for her to see. She looked at it again, this time taking in the whitewashed cottage with lace curtains at the window and roses, yes, roses, blooming on a trellis near the open door. Something in her rankled at the bucolic cliché the scene portrayed. This was no picture of need or hardship; it had no relevance to the bleakness of her life at all. She shook her head, took a step back.

Franz seemed to read her unspoken reaction. "This was three years ago, before the Russian bombing. It is not so lovely now. But listen, please. After the war we can marry. I am in love with you, Galina."

He still held his hat in his hand, like a supplicant, but he looked at her with unwavering confidence, the blue of his eyes clear as morning light. She did not question the honesty of his admiration, and his love of music was clearly genuine. But how did those things translate into love?

These boys—Filip, Franz, Borya, even Vova, the reckless soldier— they seemed to play at everything, their games growing more complicated, with higher stakes and greater risks as they grew older. When would they become men? How did that happen? She wondered what incident, what irrefutable knowledge would turn them into stalwart, dependable people capable of tenderness. Like her father.

Surely Franz could see that she would never be more than an indentured servant to the woman in the picture. His idea was no more than a dreamy vision that had nothing to do with anyone's happiness but his own. She, Galina, was the answer to several of the pressing problems in his life. How fortunate for him, she thought, that he also found her appealing enough to love.

Maybe he imagined a placid domestic scene, playing chess with his grandfather, his *Mutti* sipping her coffee while she, his wife, sang the babies to sleep before washing the dinner dishes and making sure the chickens were safe in their coop for the night. Or maybe his world was full of easy camaraderie, frequent gatherings, boisterous card games. *Bring more beer for our friends, Galina. And sing for us!* And where, exactly, did her family, with their own customs and expectations, fit into either picture? She was ashamed, now, of ever having harbored the beginnings of affection for his open, naive, overconfident nature.

She had also moved toward her own solutions.

"Thank you, but this is no proposal, Franz," she said, meeting his eyes with a flash of her own, matching his lapse into the familiar form of address. "This is a plan. I cannot help you feed your people while mine starve at the hands of your government. And I am already married."

She moved off to stand with her back to him, ready to board the approaching streetcar, her face raised to catch the fading rays of the setting sun. From her seat by the window, she saw Franz put his cap on, using both hands to center it properly on his head. He squared his shoulders, spun on his heel, and walked away in the opposite direction.

6

SHE MIGHT AS WELL make it true, now that the words were spoken. It was as if Galina had needed the release, the confessing out loud to someone other than Filip what had weighed on her mind since her impetuous pronouncement. *Then we must marry.* So why not marry Filip?

She knew him better than any of her friends. Galina had never been one to trade secrets with other girls. She preferred the anonymity of social gatherings, being one of the group without having to reveal many of her thoughts or expose the details of her life. With Filip, there was no need of much talk; they had been the closest of friends since early childhood. They understood each other.

She knew his bookish nature. He could bury himself in his stamp collection to the point of oblivion—an occupation for which, admittedly, she had little patience. He was self-centered but also deeply sensitive to beauty; she had learned to see art, music, literature in new ways through his eyes. If he was inept at solving problems of daily living, well, they were both young. They would mature together. She had enough practicality for them both.

If marriage would save Filip from forced labor, what was the harm in it for her? It was just a matter of living together, sharing meals and obligations. The other thought, the one about the bedroom, frightened her. She banished it from her mind. Eventually, she would know about that, too. But it could wait.

✦

Filip turned eighteen in mid-May. On his birthday, a Wednesday, they arranged to meet downtown early, skipping school for the first time in both their lives. "Don't forget your documents," Galina had admonished. "And bring a witness."

By nine o'clock they were outside the building, its limestone facade austere in its respectable solidity, an emblem of order and calm. Borya, their witness, was late. Out on the street, Filip stood rooted, an air of vague anxiety on his face, his shoulders slightly hunched.

Galina paced. "Did you tell him Wednesday? Are you sure?"

Filip nodded.

"What will we do if he doesn't come? And why won't you talk to me?"

"He will come. He promised," Filip answered dully after a lengthy pause, his voice hoarse. With a quick glance, he consulted a wristwatch pulled surreptitiously from his pants pocket. "It's only quarter past."

Galina stopped pacing. She could feel the day's warmth beginning to radiate from the building's rough-hewn exterior. "Is that yours? For your birthday? Let me see it." She admired the brushed silver case and elegant face. "Umm, nice," she said, holding the leather band up to her nose, then handing the watch back to Filip, who slipped it quickly back into his pants pocket.

They stood side by side in silence a few minutes. Along the Black Sea wall, the palm trees swayed in the breeze, waving their leafy fronds like handkerchiefs to unseen departing travelers.

"Do you want to do this?" she said finally, looking straight ahead, her voice low but steady. "Can you see me as your wife? I mean, we could just go to school, and only miss a class or two."

Filip lowered his head. He spoke softly. "It's not . . . yes . . . I'm sure you will be a fine wife. But this is not how it happens, is it? We are so young; we know nothing. I have no work. There are no rooms for us. It's just not . . . normal."

"Normal." Galina repeated the word as if considering it for the first time, trying to fathom its meaning. "Normal. And is it normal to stand in line for hours for paltry handouts? Is it normal to wonder what happened to your neighbors who were there yesterday and are gone today, without a word to anyone? Is it normal to share the streets and shops with bands of foreign soldiers who can do anything they please with us? What is normal now? Tell me."

"I know. And I know that I cannot join the army. It's not the politics. You know I'm neither a monarchist, like your parents, nor a Communist, like my father. I just can't see myself fighting, at all. And I know the risks if I stay single, the almost certain conscription to work in Germany." He took a deep breath, then raised his head and faced Galina. "But we haven't even asked our parents. How will we live? And where?"

"Is that what worries you?" She twisted her mouth into a crooked smile. "If we ask our parents, they will say no. So I think we should just do this, and stay where we are, each with our own parents, for now. Don't you? We are young, as you say, and there is nowhere we can go, but your legally married status will protect you from the work transport, at least for a while. Yes?" She placed a hand on his arm. The touch of her fingers, cool on his feverish skin, was feathery, tentative. Its intimacy sent a shiver through his entire body.

"Yes," he said, finally meeting her eyes. Then, firmly, "Yes. Here comes Borya."

They turned to watch their friend weave his way through the morning's pedestrian traffic, everyone intent on some urgent mission, some personal business or family matter of great immediate importance. People barely spoke to one another, embracing a new kind of rudeness that seemed to exclude all civility. Galina reflected how, even a few short years ago, it had all been different. Life had been hard, but people had stopped, exchanged a few words, smiled. Or was it only because a few years ago she had been a child, protected from the worst of the famine years by her mother's lifesaving frugality, her father's tireless industriousness?

Galina stroked the brooch pinned modestly at her throat: a swallow in flight, every detail of beak, feather, eye, neatly forked tail etched impeccably into the polished ivory, ringed with intricately carved miniature flowers. An Easter gift, the work of her father's hand. She knew he could easily have sold it, that someone else, a girl or woman far away, perhaps in another country, could be wearing it with casual pleasure, with no inkling of the dangers of life in an occupied city.

This premature marriage, this urgent mission, while it was clearly a desperate solution to an intolerable situation, surely there was something undeniably humane, something inevitable about it. *We two were meant to be together, sooner or later,* she thought. *So why not now?*

"Sorry to be so late," Borya panted, coming to a stop in front of the waiting couple. "I—"

"Don't tell me. You lost your papers," Filip interrupted, tapping his friend's shoulder playfully with the back of his hand.

"No. I . . . well, I overslept, actually," Borya admitted. He pushed a lock of unruly hair out of his eyes and dazzled them with a sheepish smile.

They laughed then, deeply and joyfully, relieved at this most mundane of all excuses, feeling for an unguarded moment like the children they still were. "You will never succeed in today's world if you persist in being so honest," Filip said, pulling a stern face before dissolving into a new fit of laughter.

Still smiling, they approached the desk clerk in the vestibule. "We would like to get married," Galina said, her confidence bolstered by good cheer.

The humorless matron behind the desk barely looked at the little group. "Which of you?"

"Filip—I mean, this . . . man and I," Galina replied, tripping over the alien-sounding word and pointing to her speechless fiancé.

"Your papers?" The clerk held out her hand, took the documents, moved her eyes rapidly over the text. She glanced up sharply to compare the applicants with their photographs. "And your witness?"

"Here." Borya placed his own document on the desk.

She studied the paper, folded it, and gave it back. "Due to wartime conditions, the Commissariat has permitted women to marry at seventeen," she pronounced, oozing self-importance. "But the witness must be eighteen years of age, which you, Comrade, are not." She skewered Borya with an accusing stare. "Therefore, your request is denied. Next?"

"But Madam, I mean Comrade," Galina persisted, flustered but not ready to give up, "he will be eighteen in only one month. Surely—"

"Then come back in one month. Please step away from the desk. You are interfering with the business of others."

Back in the street, they stood chastened, silent. What recourse did three adolescents have against this unfeeling bureaucracy?

Filip spoke first. "So we must wait. You may as well go, old man," he said to his friend. "Thanks just the same."

Yet no one moved; they didn't know how to take up the rhythm of this singular day. Go to school, as if they, like Borya, had simply overslept, forced by their parents to accept the consequences? Or spend several hours at the beach or in the park, hoping not to be seen by anyone they knew, or noticed by anyone with the authority to question their aimless behavior?

Galina brushed the thought aside. Why should anyone care what they were up to? Everyone had something to hide, avoiding each other's eyes whenever possible lest they give themselves away—from the merely shady to the fully illegal schemes and enterprises that kept people going from one day to the next.

She was no child. Even without chronological majority, she refused to surrender to helpless frustration. Something had changed in her when she told Franz, *I am already married.* Then, saying to the clerk this morning, *We would like to get married,* she had felt a strength rise in her, a buoyant sense of control that still simmered under the surface of her disappointment. It was as if, by voicing it, it was already done. She would not have her plan so easily thwarted.

"Next month, then?" Borya asked, ready to make his escape. "My birthday is on the twenty-seventh. At least I'll never forget your wedding anniversary." His smile, though still disarming, was more tentative now. His eyes held a question. Then he was gone, absorbed by the midmorning crowd.

"No," Galina said softly. "Filip. We can't wait. You cannot hide for six weeks. Any Fascist can check your papers, right now, today, and have you sent away." She scanned the street, pivoting in all directions with a dancer's grace. "All we need is a witness."

"Exactly," Filip started to say, "but—where are you going?"

Galina chose a clean-shaven middle-aged man wearing glasses and a gray fedora and carrying a scuffed leather briefcase. She was already deep in conversation with him when Filip approached them. He noticed the man's slightly wrinkled trousers; his shirt, while clean, was fraying at the cuffs, his mismatched black suit coat shiny with wear. He heard the words *war orphan . . . prisoner . . . disabled*. Just what was Galina up to?

"And this is my Filip," she said, extending her hand, drawing him closer. "My fiancé. He is quite alone in the world. No family left at all."

"I see," the man said, glancing from one to the other. The corners of his thin mouth twitched, as if not sure whether to be amused or suspicious. "That's quite a tale you're spinning here. But why the hurry? Why must it be today?"

"Well, *nu*, not today—maybe—but . . . soon." She bowed her head and blushed.

"So. Couldn't wait for the wedding day? Too much sorrow in your young lives?" He raised an ironic eyebrow, pushed his glasses down his nose with one finger, and appraised the young couple. "Well, what's it to me. And what have you got—"

"Oh. Here." Galina unpinned the brooch from her blouse. "It's ivory, hand carved. You can get a good price for it."

The man took the brooch, flipped it nonchalantly from hand to hand, squinting at the intricately wrought details, passing his thumb over the smooth surface of the back, still warm from contact with Galina's body. "I don't know. This is no small matter. It's a nice pin, but . . ."

"Filip," Galina said firmly, "give him your watch."

Stunned, Filip obeyed, handing over his father's birthday present as if in a trance, amazed at this audacious display of Galina's ingenuity. When had she become such an accomplished liar? "It's new," he offered weakly. "Austrian."

"Well, then." The man pocketed the items with a smirk. "And who am I, exactly?"

"My uncle, twice removed, from my mother's second marriage," Galina replied, with no hint of hesitation.

"*Tak*. We are all related now, *da*? Twice removed," their conspirator remarked, following them through the oak doors into the government building.

And so it was done.

7

ALL THAT WAS LEFT now was to tell the parents. *Simple enough*, Galina thought, ignoring the momentary dread that flashed through her like summer lightning. What could parents do to them now? She and Filip had taken charge of their own lives. She had the document to prove it.

They decided to see Ilya and Ksenia first. "My father should be home. He just came back from Sevastopol last night," Galina said.

"What was he doing in Sevastopol?" Filip asked, trying to match her rapid pace. "Slow down a little. Why do you walk so fast?"

"Listen to you! Not married ten minutes and finding fault already. I always walk fast. It's just a habit. It never bothered you before." She glanced at him, but he was looking the other way, where a convoy of open trucks had come into view, approaching at full speed. Filip took her arm and pulled her away from the curb, keeping a firm grip on her elbow while the trucks, each carrying four armed soldiers, a pile of axes and saws, and a stack of empty burlap sacks, rumbled past.

"I wonder what they do all day, the Germans," Galina mused when the trucks had disappeared around the corner. "There's no fighting here, no battles."

"They drill, I guess. Clean their rifles and pistols. Polish their boots. Go out and intimidate people," Filip speculated, guiding her now safely across the street.

"And spend money. My father was delivering orders, brooches and the little carved wooden boxes they like so much." Her hand went involuntarily to the bare neck of her blouse. Had Ilya seen her wearing the pin this morning? Would he notice it was gone? Even if he did not, she felt its loss in a moment of regret so keen, so physical, that she abruptly stopped walking. Like each of her father's creations, the pin was unique; there was no other in the world like it. Like innocence, once gone there was no way to replace it.

She leaned against Filip, one hand to her head as if to arrest the feelings spinning within. "What is it? Are you not well?" he inquired when he noticed her agitation.

"No. I mean, it's nothing. The sun . . . Will your father mind terribly about the watch?"

"Yes. He is not so very influential; he can't get things as easily as you might think. And I know he will not buy me another, even if he could." *And I mind about the watch,* Filip thought petulantly. *It was my birthday present.*

"When this war is over and you are a famous architect, you will have many watches, one for every day and two for Sundays," Galina said brightly, as though reading his mind. He, too, had lost something he valued. "Let's have ice cream, to celebrate."

They pooled their pocket change to buy one treat from the vender's cart, passing the little paper cup back and forth between them, Galina licking the last sweet drops off the rim with undisguised childish pleasure. "I will know that hard times are behind us," she pronounced, "when you always know what time it is, and there is ice cream every day."

Walking slowly, side by side but not touching, they talked easily, laughing at nothing in particular, zigzagging through the midmorning downtown crowd in the general direction of Galina's home.

"Look out!" someone shouted, and they turned to see the convoy return, slow down, then stop in the middle of the road. Several of the trucks now held, along with the guards, half a dozen or so civilians.

As soon as the trucks stopped, Galina felt Filip pull at her, moving deeper along the sidewalk, away from the curb. They stopped with their backs up against the buildings, with nowhere else to go. "Let go of me," she protested. Annoyed at his new bossiness, she yanked her arm free of his grasp, then stared at him in amazement.

Filip had somehow managed to shrink, as if he had reversed several years' growth and retreated into a younger version of himself. Shoulders hunched, face pale, he looked small, frail, childlike. Weak. *This is my husband*, she thought. *My man. And he is afraid.*

"*Achtung!*" she heard, her attention snapping back to the scene on the street. "*Halt!*"

She watched a young officer spring down from the passenger side of the first truck, barking orders at the soldiers, who blocked the street quickly and efficiently at both ends. *Franz?* she almost said out loud, clapping a hand to her mouth just in time to keep the word from slipping out. No need to reveal to everyone around her that she knew the enemy by name.

But this was a new Franz. This was not the homesick youth who liked carved toys and hummed romantic love songs. Gone was the gentle manner, the aesthetic sensitivity. This was a man in command—a *little* man, she saw—a martinet, strutting, issuing orders. "I need men for one or two days' work," he announced. "You will receive extra rations. You and you and you over there." He scanned the silent throng, pointing, while the soldiers rounded up the chosen ones and pushed them onto the waiting trucks.

When his eyes found her, she stopped breathing but did not lower her gaze. She felt Filip shrink even more at her side, as if deflated by Franz's piercing glance. "I will take women, also. Strong ones," he said, lifting his chin and smiling a little. "They can help the men."

This is it. We are finished. He will take his revenge. To her surprise, she felt not fear but a numbing, hopeless acceptance. She steeled herself for the inevitable mocking finger, resigned to the rough shove that would change her life, now, forever.

It did not come.

"We are finished," Franz echoed, climbing into his seat while the soldiers hustled the last workers, including several women, into the trucks. "*Schnell, schnell,*" he shouted. "Move faster. We are wasting time."

It was Galina's turn to feel deflated, while Filip slowly regained his full stature and touched her hand. "That was close," he said softly. "I thought he had me picked out for sure. Let's go, Galya." She walked with him, not trusting herself to speak. She felt—what did she feel? Relief, of course; they had both escaped who knew what unpleasant, perhaps dangerous outcome.

Betrayal. Not only Filip's. She already knew he did not have the strength to defend himself, let alone anyone else. In his hapless self-absorption, he was not remotely aware of the threat that had brushed so close to her, and she would never tell him. She had naively expected Franz to simply accept her refusal and fade gracefully into the past, becoming a nostalgic anecdote she might share with a granddaughter, perhaps, in the unimaginable future. Visiting her in the toy shop, listening to her performances, he had been sweet, almost tender, boyish and attentive.

Now, she had seen him at work, carrying out the duties delegated by his superiors. Which was the real Franz? How could a person change so completely, living like a chameleon, blending in with this twig, that leaf? She understood that the overarching issue for everyone, at every level, was survival. But even a chameleon has an essential nature, a basic chameleon-ness that defines its true state. With Franz, she saw that she knew nothing of what that true state might be.

But how dare he? How dare he play with her like that? Flaunting his power, choosing not to choose her, holding the threat over her like a blade arrested in midair, taunting her with his discretionary authority. She let the rage wash over her, burning away the last vestiges of sentimentality.

———

"What did you say?" Ksenia faced her daughter, her wide hands continuing to work the ball of dough as if of their own accord.

"I said, guess what we did today." Galina pulled Filip forward so they stood side by side. "We got married."

"Really? Hand me that towel. No, the clean one, over there. Is this a joke?" Ksenia stopped kneading. "I have enough to worry about without your schemes and pranks, like how to make bread with only half the yeast it needs to rise properly." She placed the dough gently into her favorite cracked bowl, covered it with the towel, and moved the bowl to the back of the stove.

"Mama," Galina said, blushing deeply and releasing Filip's hand. "We got married."

Ksenia brushed a floury hand over her thin graying hair, sat down slowly at the kitchen table. "Ilya? Come here. I need you," she called into the inner courtyard, from where they could hear the rhythmic sound of careful sawing.

"*Minutku.* One moment," he called back. After a few more whiny strokes, and the sharp *ping* of wood hitting the tabletop, he appeared at the door, brushing sawdust off his shirt before entering the room. "Galya, *shto s toboi?* What's wrong?" He stood behind Ksenia's chair. "Hello, Filip," he added, almost as an afterthought.

"Tell your father," Ksenia commanded.

"We . . . Filip turns eighteen today. He could be sent away, to work in Germany. So . . ." Galina hesitated, overcome with sudden shyness in the face of this cold questioning.

Filip moved forward. She felt his hand on her waist. "We are married, Ilya Nikolaevich," he said, looking at the older man directly, without fear.

Galina stiffened. She had been unprepared for that touch, that hand on her waist. It was so light she could barely feel it, but it was unmistakably intimate and proprietary. *What have I done? How much have I given away, no, lost?* She advanced into the room, moving out of the circle of Filip's arm. "It's just a formality, Papa," she said. "Nothing will change. I will still live here, and Filip with his parents, right? We just wanted him to be safe."

"Nothing, no one is safe in wartime," Ksenia said, her voice dull. "But this idea of yours, this living apart, it is childish. It will not do. The Germans are not fools. Do you think you are the first to try this ruse?" She looked squarely from one to the other, her gray eyes holding the question until both young people faltered and lowered their heads.

"No," Ksenia continued. "It will not do. If you are married, you must live as man and wife. But for me and for your father, Galina"—she gestured toward Ilya, who stood in stunned silence at her back—"there is no union until you receive the Church's blessing. So go home, Filip, and tell your parents. I will arrange things with Father Gennady." She stood up and moved toward the stove, lifting a corner of the towel to check the bread dough's progress. Filip turned to go, but Ilya's voice stopped him.

"Wait." Ilya grasped the back of the chair with both hands. "Wait a moment. What about love? This piece of paper means nothing, less than nothing, to me. It can be annulled. This is a fine gesture, Galya, a selfless, generous act. But marriage, as your mother says, is not a game. So tell me, is there enough love between you to understand each other, to live in harmony, and to forgive the mistakes you will both inevitably make? Is there enough love?"

Galina and Filip glanced at each other; each caught the same surprised expression on the other's face. "We never . . . that is, well . . . yes," she faltered, blushing fiercely. Then, regaining some composure, she spoke more firmly. "Yes, Papa, we are friends. Of course we love each other."

"Those are not the same thing, friendship and love, as you will see," Ilya replied kindly. "But it is a good beginning. And you?" he addressed his new son-in-law.

"Of course. Of course I love her, Ilya Nikolaevich. Since first grade, at school." He said it quietly, with confidence, but not without a trace of derision, as if stating something obvious to everyone that only Ilya could not see. Ilya caught the inference, raised his head, but let the challenge pass unanswered.

"All right. *Horosho.* I will make the arrangements," Ksenia said.

"But where . . . ," Galina began, sweeping her hand in an arc that included the kitchen, the front room, the tiny bedrooms, and the sheltered yard. She felt everything spinning away, the sense of control rapidly becoming an illusion, an imaginary exercise made real, to which she and Filip had come entirely unprepared.

"Here. You two can take your brother's room. Maksim is not likely to return from university before this occupation ends."

Urgent knocking at their door interrupted their conversation. "*Sosed!* Neighbor! Come quickly." Ilya went to answer the summons. In a moment, he returned with an older man who lived across the common yard on the other side of the compound.

"Such a tragedy," the man wailed, shaking his head in disbelief. "Such a tragedy."

"Tell us what you know," Ilya prompted.

"The bastards—excuse me, *sosedka.*" He nodded to Ksenia.

"What has happened?" She waved away his apology with an impatient gesture.

"They are cutting down the trees. I saw it with my own eyes." The man swayed from foot to foot, kneading his cap in his hands.

"Who?" "What trees?" "Where?" The choir of questions assaulted the distraught messenger from all sides, making him stop in maddening silence.

Galina was the first to react. "Here, Gavril Gavrilovich, sit down." She offered the man a chair and poured water into a glass from the ceramic pitcher they filled daily from the pump in the yard. He declined the chair but drank the water. "Thank you, my dear," he said, wiping his mouth with the back of his hand.

"Now please tell us, what trees?" Galina asked gently.

"The palms, along the seawall," he replied, his eyes filling with tears. "The pride of our beautiful city."

"Who?" Filip cut in. But they already knew the answer.

"The Germans," Gavril Gavrilovich whispered. "That is, our people are doing the work, but the Germans are giving the orders."

"But why?" Filip persisted. "Do they think we will climb the trees like monkeys and send distress signals to the Caucasus? Or pelt them with stones from above while they stroll on the beach?"

"Who knows why," Ilya said. "There may be some strategic reason, or it may just be an act of malice, a way to deface the enemy's homeland while keeping their own troops busy supervising the work." He paused, sighed deeply. "I am more worried about our people. Not everyone who serves on a work detail returns home when the job is done."

Ksenia crossed herself. "God's will. But maybe you should go see, Ilya. It may be possible to help someone. Now everybody out of my kitchen except you, Galya. Bread dough can't wait."

After the men left—Ilya and the neighbor to witness the destruction, and Filip home to inform his parents—the women worked in silence. Galina sliced vegetables for soup while Ksenia punched down the dough, which had risen nicely, in spite of the meager amount of yeast. She formed it into a loaf of respectable size and covered it with a towel, leaving it to rise once more before baking. "Here, let me finish with the soup. You do some of this mending. You know how I hate to sew," Ksenia said, pointing to a dilapidated wicker basket, itself so full of holes it was a wonder it could hold anything and still retain its shape.

"It is true, what your father said about love," she said. She opened a corner cupboard and took out a jar partly filled with barley. "When we were courting—we lived in Kostroma, where his family is from—we would go for walks along the river. Those were terrible times, worse than now, for everyone." She measured some grain into the palm of her hand.

"After the revolution?" Galina offered. She worked her deft needle around a hole in a pillowcase, joining the threadbare fabric to a bright patch of scrap cloth.

"Yes. I know in school they tell you it was glorious, freedom and brotherhood, work and bread and land for everyone. But it was a nightmare; people were angry, hungry, suspicious of each other, and no government in place with enough experience to restore order." She stirred the barley into the soup and covered the pot. Silently, she appraised the remaining grain with a calculating eye before returning the jar to its place on the shelf.

Galina went on sewing. Her mother almost never talked about her life. Oh, there were the childhood stories, the virtues of country life lived close to the soil under the blue skies of peace and merchant-class prosperity, stories tinted with nostalgia and prone to the pitfalls of selective memory. This was something different, something precious and personal, an intimacy with her mother she did not want to lose any more than she knew how to handle it. "Which river?" she ventured at last, hoping to keep the narrative going.

"The Volga. That's what your father called me, 'my Volga.' We had nothing to offer each other but the work of our own hands. He said, 'You are like this river to me, strong and constant and sure, ever flowing through me, dearer than my own blood.'"

"And so you are," Ilya said, coming in unexpectedly from the front room. "I forgot my cap," he apologized, smiling.

Galina did not know how to describe the thing that passed in that moment between her father and mother. It was something powerful and tender, silent and primal. She only knew that witnessing it had reduced her to insignificance. She was neither child nor woman, but something *becoming*, her essence submerged in some vague process she was only beginning to understand.

The wedding took place early one Tuesday morning, in one of the two churches still permitted to remain open. Filip's father, Vadim, had an urgent meeting at work; he sent his regrets and best wishes. His mother, Zoya, was there, along with Galina's parents and their neighbor, Nina Mihailovna, who served as witness.

Galina wore a borrowed white suit, wide in the shoulders and long in the skirt, but quite presentable if not exactly chic. Zoya had contributed a diminutive pillbox hat and veil. The bride carried a hastily picked bunch of virginal violets.

Filip was in a dark suit, only a little short in the sleeves, the trousers pressed so carefully that the hem marks hardly showed at all. Borya had insisted his friend wear his lucky green tie, even though Filip had two ties of his own to choose from. "I passed all my exams with this tie on," Borya said. "It will work for you, too." *This is not schoolwork,* Filip wanted to point out, but the difference seemed clear and it was simpler to just wear the tie.

The wedding ceremony was shorter than they used to be. Years ago, in a judicial edict that permitted him to keep his post, the Moscow Patriarch had excised all the prayers for the health and well-being of the imperial family, along with other sections deemed toxic to the Communist state. There were no ceremonial crowns for stalwart groomsmen to hold over the heads of the bridal couple. The crowns, along with every other gold object the church possessed, had been confiscated and melted down for the greater good of the state treasury. Filip and Galina held pencil-thin amber candles, spoke their vows, and exchanged rings: narrow brass bands procured by Vadim as his contribution to the festivities. The choir's part was sung by a lone nun from the convent at the outskirts of the city, the convent permitted to remain in existence solely because of the excellence of their winemaking.

After the ceremony, there was a party for all the courtyard residents and a handful of the couple's school friends. Even crusty old Uncle Zhora came, and brought his *bandura*; he consented to provide music as long as his glass of kvass was never less than half full. Never mind that the drink was of his own making; he had traded a small barrel of the bread beer to Ilya in exchange for a whole pack of German cigarettes. There was meat pie (what kind of meat was a question no one asked), pickled vegetables, beet and potato salad, fresh fruit, and whatever anyone else was able to add to the table. It was, after all, a wedding.

8

MAYBE IF Filip had not been so happy, nothing would have happened.

His married life settled into a succession of contented days. At school, preparing for the tenth grade examinations and the university entrance application to follow, he was as sure of himself as he had ever been.

Galina had no such ambitions. Once married, she had willingly dropped out of school and continued working at Zinaida Grigoryevna's toy shop. Her earnings made a significant contribution to the household, and her cheerful nature helped lighten the struggle of daily living for everyone in the family. She went about her tasks, sewing, sweeping, cooking, tending the silkworms and the little courtyard garden, humming or singing all the while, filling the house with peace, even if the songs she chose to sing were sad ones.

After school, Filip continued to volunteer with the theater group, sketching backdrops onto both sides of reclaimed cloth for scene changes. Mishka, the black marketeer, had disappeared. There were rumors of capture and execution, of double-dealing between one of the Partisan hideouts in the forest and the Nazi stronghold in town, but no one knew for sure.

A straitlaced woman with a guitar replaced him. Her repertoire was limited to simple tunes, and while she played well enough, she had none of the liveliness Mishka and his accordion provoked by his robust presence. And she had no feeling for comedy at all, only a thin, high voice that could not reach beyond the first few rows of the little hall. Jealous of her art, she refused to play for Galina's intermission songs. Galina sang without accompaniment, songs of love and betrayal, loss and longing, and people listened; her strong, clear voice filled their eyes with tears and their hearts with joy, in the paradoxical love of suffering that the Russian character is prone to.

Filip usually stood in the wings, listening, often with Borya at his side. Not involved, strictly speaking, with the theater, his friend liked to hang around, sometimes lending a hand with scenery or props.

"That's my wife," Filip said once, almost in disbelief, while Galina sang of faded chrysanthemums and of love gone cold.

"I know it. You're the envy of all the guys at school." Borya lit a cigarette.

"Including you?"

"Everybody loves Galya. Can you do this?" He inhaled deeply and blew out a perfect smoke ring. They watched it float, growing larger and thinner, its shape shifting this way and that before dissipating into the air.

"No. You'll have to show me how."

Most days, Borya would be at the house when Galina returned from work. She would find them playing chess in the yard or poring over Filip's stamp albums at the little table in the parlor, their heads, the dark and the fair, almost touching.

She envied them their bond, wished she, too, had a friend of the heart. But she had never been one to share girlish confidences; in the troubled times of their existence, everyone lived the same marginal, hardscrabble life. There was nothing to confide.

She was sure Filip and Borya never talked about their inmost feelings—what man would do that? Theirs was an easy, companionable friendship, born of shared interests and aspirations, unfettered by excess sentiment or unreasonable expectations.

Once, Borya brought firewood, dragging the roughly sawed logs from a young tree behind him like a sled on a rope. Filip, seated at the chess board, studying yesterday's unfinished game, looked up. "Why?" he said, his hand hovering over a pawn, then moving it decisively to block Borya's rook.

"To repay your mother-in-law for some of the meals you share with me."

"Huh. Where did you get it?"

"Where the trees grow." He stood at the board, took the pawn with his knight. "Check."

Filip groaned. "In the park?"

"No, city boy. In the forest. Trees grow in the forest."

Ksenia entered the yard from the kitchen, wiping her hands on her apron before reaching for the ax. "Let me do that, Ksenia Semyonovna." Borya took the ax from her hand. "You go have a cup of tea."

"How nice you are, Borya. No news?" They knew his parents had been arrested weeks ago, without a word of explanation.

Borya shook his head and went on chopping, expertly splitting the logs into stove-sized wedges. "Give me a hand here, Filip. Stack these over there."

Filip rose reluctantly from the game. He stacked the firewood near the door, handling the rough edges gingerly to avoid splinters. "*Ai, holera*," he swore, when the inevitable happened. He regarded the wobbly woodpile with malevolence, sucking the side of his thumb. "My queen took your knight. It's your move."

A month or so after Borya turned eighteen, his visits stopped, as did his school attendance. His name did not appear in the list of examination results posted on the announcement board. *Maybe he forgot to wear his lucky green tie*, Filip thought. He realized that with all the disruptions in his friend's life, he no longer knew where to look for him.

He missed his chess partner, the easy banter they had enjoyed. Galina was sweet, and he loved being married to her, but she was always busy. His in-laws treated him well enough, but he certainly couldn't talk to them. He saw his own mother two or three times a week, in the afternoons, and his father only on special occasions. *He'll turn up*, he told himself, trying not to imagine all the things that could have caused Borya to vanish. It was not an uncommon occurrence.

And then he saw him.

Filip had had an especially pleasant day. Rising late, he'd made his way to his mother's apartment. She gave him tea and baklava, then surprised him with a small square of Swiss chocolate.

"Mama, where did you get this? How?"

"Your father brought it. I don't ask," Zoya replied. "More tea?"

She gave him a little money, "for the house." He happily spent it on a tiny packet of Australian stamps. *Even Galya will like these*, he thought, eager to get home and examine his treasure, the animals in their curious exotic oddity, the sere desert landscape so alien to his own.

On the streetcar, he got a seat next to the open window, away from the crush of people, with their parcels and their children, in the aisle. He raised his face to the warm breeze and thought again about the chocolate, how it had felt on his tongue, how the melting richness had filled his mouth with something like ecstasy, leaving behind a nugget of hazelnut, a delicious surprise.

And then there Borya was, threading his way through the crowd on the sidewalk, wearing a dark shirt, looking a bit disheveled, his hair longer than Filip had ever seen it.

"Hey, Bor'ka!" Filip shouted, his joy at seeing his friend making him reckless. "Hey! How are things in the woods? Finding any mushrooms?"

Borya's head snapped back as if he'd been slapped. He froze, then ran, elbowing people out of his way, turning out of sight around the next corner.

Filip felt a sudden chill. *Nu, durak*, he scolded himself. *What a fool.* How could anyone know he'd been remembering the firewood Borya had brought, like Father Christmas dragging a tree through the streets to delight happy children? What a stupid, stupid thing to say.

He got off at the next stop and walked the rest of the way home, trying to shake off the echo of the hastily shouted words. "*Balda. Durak.* Idiot," he mumbled, then stopped. *I only wanted to talk to him,* he thought. *That's all.* Maybe no one had noticed; there were so many people, all busy with their own concerns. No doubt he was berating himself for nothing. *Forget it,* he decided, and told no one.

Two weeks passed. Filip and Galina, making their way home in the early evening, were caught in a roundup, herded along with dozens of others toward the main square.

"What do you think—" Galina started to say.

"More regulations. As if they don't already have us by the throat," he replied. "Be quiet."

In the square, backlit by the descending sun, two men hung from the lampposts, their necks broken, their bodies rotating slowly in the air. A gasp swept through the crowd, sharp and instinctive, followed by nervous, expectant silence.

"When did this happen?" Filip asked of no one in particular.

"About an hour ago," said a voice from the crowd. "They went away, but they won't let us leave until they're done with us. All the streets are blocked." This tragedy was clearly not over.

"*Kakoi uzhas,*" Galina whispered, blanched and trembling at the horror. But Filip did not hear, nor was he aware of her hand, the fingers digging into his arm in panicked recognition.

One of the men was short and stocky. He had Tatar features, with silky hair black as crow's feathers that glinted in the sun. He was dressed in green *sharivari,* the cloth of the loose trousers flapping in the evening air. The other one, long legs dangling closer to the ground, wearing scuffed and muddied cheap leather shoes, was Borya.

"No," Filip breathed, denying the evidence of his eyes. He felt the blood drain from his head, then rush back in, thundering in his ears; his body shuddered with ice and fire in a fever of contradictions. For a moment, all went black, but he did not fall, supported by helping hands of strangers on every side. He opened his eyes.

A dozen black-shirted SS men entered the square from a side street, swastikas emblazoned on the doors of their truck. The crowd parted to let them through. Two held the swaying body still while a sergeant, standing on the vehicle's roof, his legs spread wide for balance, lettered the word PARTISAN in thick, rough brushstrokes of red paint across their shirts, first on one and then on the other.

The rest of the men took up positions around the square, each cradling a semiautomatic weapon against his chest. No one doubted they needed only the slightest hint of a provocation to open fire.

The lieutenant surveyed the operation from the bed of the truck. He was tall and blond, his classic Aryan features contorted in a grimace of fury and contempt. He turned, sweeping his eyes over the crowd like an actor reaching out to every member of his audience; the sun, now low in a purplish-yellow sky, caught on the lightning bolt insignia pinned to his collar.

"If you fight against der Führer, we will find you," he shouted. He took the dripping brush from the sergeant and waved it in an arc, spraying drops of red paint over their heads like a ghoulish benediction. "We know who you are. Now go home."

In the morning, Filip went back. They had both had a restless night filled with disturbing dreams; Galina moaned and, once, cried out in her sleep, clutching his hand so tightly it hurt. Filip rose at first light, slipped quietly out of the house. The executed men were still there, swollen black tongues protruding from their parted lips; the damning word on their backs blazed like fresh blood in the rising sun.

Someone had taken their shoes. Filip stared numbly at the bare feet, the skin a ghastly greenish-gray threaded with ropy blue veins, toenails opaque as ram's horn.

He moved on, so as not to attract attention. He would not see his mother today. She would sense his rage, probe his ineffable sadness, understand his fear. He did not want to be understood. He walked to the sea, stood a long time at the retaining wall, watched the waves crash and recede until the rhythm calmed his mind a little. He tried to think of other things: the impending university exam, his father's birthday next week, the book of German verse he had left open on the floor near his and Galina's bed. Nothing could obscure the question he knew would nag him for the rest of his life, like an embedded splinter too deep under the skin to remove yet impossible to ignore. *Am I to blame?*

PART III

Maksim

1

THE FIRST THING Galina noticed was the limp. She watched him approach from the end of their street, bareheaded, a long heavy coat draped over his shoulders in spite of the warmth of the late May afternoon, his eyes cast down as if choosing his path with care. Yes, it was definitely her brother, and he was definitely limping, one foot dragging noticeably behind the other as he made his way in her direction.

"Maksim!" she shouted and ran to meet him, a string-tied parcel of dried beans dangling from her waving hand. "Maksim," she repeated, stopping in front of him, blocking his way forward.

"It's you," he said, raising his head. His look combined weariness, relief, and disappointment.

"You're so pale! We thought . . ."

"You thought I was dead. Well, perhaps I am."

"That's not funny," she said, even though his expression held no hint of humor. "We had no letter from you since early October. How could we know . . . Anyway, you're home. Kiss me." She giggled, surprised at her own impulsiveness. She leaned in closer and offered her cheek, trying not to flinch at his stale unwashed odor.

"Here, in the street?" He stepped back, as if afraid she might embrace him.

"You haven't changed. Give me your hand, then. No, not the left," she protested. "*Balda*. Never the left, you fool."

He withdrew the hand, concealed it under his coat, but didn't offer the right. "Is there food at home? I have not eaten since . . ."

"I will go and tell Mama. Come as fast as you can." She ran off, disappearing into the alley that led to the apartment courtyard.

"She has cut her hair," he said out loud, noting the absence of her maiden's braid. *Bah, that's a country custom,* he completed the thought. *Many girls cut their hair now, when they want to. It doesn't mean they're married.*

Ksenia was waiting just inside the door, her face wet with tears. "My son," she breathed when he entered the room. "*Syn moi, syn,*" she intoned, holding his face in both her hands, kissing the unshaven cheeks three times in the traditional Russian greeting. "So thin," she said. She embraced him, pushing the overcoat from his shoulders onto the floor.

From the kitchen doorway, they both heard Galina gasp, then burst into tears. When Ksenia stepped back, releasing Maksim, she saw the empty folded sleeve pinned to the right shoulder of his shirt. "*Bozhe moi.*" She crossed herself, then made the sign of the cross in the air between them. "My God. Your arm. How you have suffered."

Maksim bowed his head, accepting the blessing. When he looked at her, his own eyes were brimming. He whispered, "Mama, I am so hungry."

They sat with him while he ate bread, buckwheat kasha, briny salted cucumbers and onions. "We have heard nothing from you in more than seven months." Ksenia finally broke the silence, stacking the empty dishes in front of her. "Tell us what happened to you. Where are your things?"

"Then you don't know. I wrote to you after I left Kharkov, but you don't know. I have no things, only my papers, the clothes I'm wearing, and these *lapti.*" He pushed out his feet, showing them the straw slippers tied around his ankles with strips of rags. "A farmer gave them to me, out of pity for my bare feet."

"Where are your books?" Galina cut in, remembering his extreme possessiveness. "Your notebooks?"

"Who knows? I have no need of them now." His voice was dull, with no hint of his former irritation at her questions. "I served as a medic in an army field hospital near Moscow. There was heavy fighting. Many died." He paused. No one spoke. "Many died," he repeated.

"Where is your uniform, son, your boots?" Ksenia placed the dirty dishes in a washbasin, put water on for tea.

"I had no uniform, just an armband with a red cross on it. Everything was in short supply. Still is, I'm sure. So much confusion. The hospital was bombed in transit, moving from one location to another. I could not see the logic in it. How could it be in a safe place and still close enough to treat the frontline wounded? Anyway, we were bombed. I was hurt."

"That's it? 'We were bombed. I was hurt.'" Galina set a cup of tea in front of him, her tone rising with indignation. "As if it's an everyday occurrence."

Maksim stared at her with dead eyes. "It is an everyday occurrence."

"Never mind, children," Ksenia stepped in. "There will be time for talking, now you are home. Whatever happened, you survived."

"I survived," he echoed, his voice hollow.

They sat in silence for several minutes, the women's questions frustrated by his wooden expression. When his chin dropped to his chest in exhaustion, Ksenia stood up. "You need to sleep, son. Use our bed. Your father will not return until tomorrow."

Maksim rose. "I need to wash a little first. Is there a clean shirt I can use?"

"Filip has two or three, about your size," Galina offered. "We're married now. We took your room."

"I meant to ask you about the ring," he mumbled, "but it slipped my mind. Thank you, Mama. I can manage." He took the water bucket from his mother in his left hand, the towel draped over his shoulder, and headed for the inner courtyard. In the doorway, he turned. "My boots," he said. "I traded them to a band of Partisans in the woods, along with your socks, Galya, for some bread and fish. They had no use for a one-armed fighter with a limp."

2

LIFE TOOK ON a kind of routine, the kind of routine that makes ample allowances for the unexpected. Galina rose early to work more hours in the toy shop, and willingly took on a larger share of household duties.

After finishing tenth grade and receiving his diploma, Filip slept late every day; he had abandoned the pretense of looking for work after a few fruitless weeks, claiming the need to prepare for the upcoming university examinations. Most days, he spent an hour or two at the library before dropping in on his mother. She would be waiting with hot tea or fresh lemonade.

"How is it you always have sugar, Mama? We see it only rarely, and then my mother-in-law hoards every grain. Even when we use it, nothing tastes sweet."

"Every household has its own rules," Zoya said judiciously, dipping a stale bread crust into her tea. "And your father is fortunate. Party membership still has a few benefits."

"Hm." Filip preferred to remain noncommittal. It was not a matter of ideology. But what if the Germans won the war? The Soviet Partisans had spread the word of the victorious Red Army defense of Moscow, the Fascists beaten back at the city gates. But Ukraine was still firmly under occupation, both major cities, Kharkov and Kiev, now under enemy control. The war could end in a truce, with parts of the Soviet Union remaining under Nazi rule. He had read enough history to know that national boundaries were moveable and arbitrary, governed by shifting allegiances, secret agreements, games of chance played by the gods.

He said none of this to his mother, or to anyone. Zoya wanted only the return of religious freedom, so she could attend church services openly without fear of compromising her husband's position. Ksenia believed (and Ilya, too, he suspected), along with an ardent minority, in the restoration of the Romanov monarchy—a position he considered too ridiculous to warrant discussion. It was best to wait, see how things turned out.

What was it his friend Vova had said, just before running off to find a Red Army unit to join beyond the occupied territory? "Why, you're nothing but an opportunist! You believe in nothing."

"I believe in money in my pocket, meat for my dinner, sugar in my tea. And the right to be left alone," Filip had replied. "That's what I believe."

"Have you forgotten Borya? How many of us must die so that you may be 'left alone'? You are living a fantasy, my friend. Nothing comes without a price."

Forgotten. Could he, would he ever forget? Not just the sight, the spectacle of their friend and classmate strung up from a lamppost, turning in the wind like so much dirty laundry. The doubt, the agonizing flashes of conscience had cast an indelible shadow over Filip's life. Even if he was not guilty, he knew he would never again be innocent.

"I have forgotten nothing. But I can't help feeling it was a pointless death, brave as it was. He gained the status of a folk hero here in his hometown, but what has he accomplished? Whose life has been improved by his sacrifice?"

Vova had made an impatient sound, something between a grunt and a sigh. "Borya has earned his place among the saints of the new revolution. Many have died, die every day, out of the public eye, hunted like animals in the woods, fleeing the site of one last explosion, one final act of sabotage. His sacrifice will inspire fresh generations of fighters. He stood up for something. That's what I must do, too."

They'd parted with a firm handshake, neither convinced of the truth of the other's argument.

"So how is life for you with your new family, my son?" Zoya interrupted his ruminations. She pushed a small plate of baklava closer to his side of the table.

"All right. They are . . . hardworking, even if they lack Papa's sophistication and your good breeding. You know Ksenia Semyonovna is of humble stock. Her mother was a peasant, her father a merchant. She is uneducated, but not illiterate or stupid."

"And your father-in-law? He is clever with his hands, yes?"

"Well, yes, Ilya Nikolaevich is gifted," Filip conceded. "He is what you might call a good and righteous man. But I find him dull."

"And your bride, she is well?"

"She is the light of my life, Mama. She is so . . . so alive. I am happy just to look at her."

"Can she cook?"

"Well enough, I suppose, given the limited provisions available. Her mother is more capable that way, constantly trading and foraging. We do not often go to bed hungry. Still, I miss some of your dishes—the grape leaves, and that wonderful Greek soup you make. And this lovely baklava. If you could teach my wife to make it, I think I would be completely content." He lifted a spoonful of the confection to eye level, admiring its paper-thin layers interlaced with honey.

"It is not so difficult if you know how," Zoya dismissed the compliment, bristling a little at the comparison with the other household. "The dough requires no yeast, but does need some butter or lard, or it will not layer properly. This is a poor imitation. It should have more honey, and nuts, too, which I do not have."

"Let me see what I can do." Filip swallowed the pastry, drained his cup, and rose to go. "There must be hazelnuts in the woods. Galya will know."

"Don't go to any trouble for me," Zoya sighed, rising to see him to the door. "Just don't forget me."

"Filipok, wait," she called down after him, stopping his rapid descent. He looked up the stairwell at her, smiling.

"You have not called me that since I was five years old." He came back, obeying her beckoning finger.

"I forgot to ask you, how is Maksim? Any change?" Zoya whispered, pulling her son into the apartment vestibule even though the hallway was deserted, with no nosy neighbors in sight.

"Only for the worse. He used to try sweeping the yard now and then, but gave that up, saying it was too difficult with one hand. Now he does nothing. And he never goes out."

"What does he do, then? Read, like you?"

"Not anymore. He says nothing interests him. Most of the time, he just lies on his cot, staring at the ceiling."

"*Ai-ai-ai.*" Zoya shook her head, absorbing this last bit of news with the perverse pleasure only a confirmed gossip would understand. "He is a lost soul. A lost soul. His mother must be suffering so. I will pray for them to the Virgin Mary, and to Saint Nicholas, the worker of miracles."

That will surely help, Filip wanted to say, but stifled the sarcasm just in time and bent instead to kiss his mother's cheek.

"Go, son, go," she insisted. "And be kind to him. A lost soul," he heard her repeating behind the closed door.

Filip headed downtown, taking the long way through the park, stopping to buy a bag of cherries from a red-faced country woman's pushcart. He could bring them home; Ksenia would make compote or jam or her sweet-tart *kissel'* thickened with potato starch and served with rice cakes. He bit into the first one. Or he could eat them all, feel their juicy sweetness explode in his mouth, and no one would know. *Well, maybe not every last one*, he thought. *I'll save a few for Galya; she can enjoy them when I walk her home from work.*

From the park, he walked to the seawall, strolled along the esplanade, enjoying the cool spray, watching the rocking of the waves. He knew his mother meant well. She was sentimental, but even she understood the crucial difference between sentiment and true compassion. If everything was in God's hands, as she believed, then some of us were clearly meant to suffer more than others. Maybe it was enough to put some spare change in the poor box and say a hasty prayer. It was a facile argument, he knew. It lacked something about good works, personal responsibility, and the prospect of eternal salvation, but he had no patience with it one way or the other.

And Maksim, poor devil, what grievous sin had he committed to deserve his fate?

He had been arrogant, Maksim. So what? Filip could see no wrong in knowing your own worth, staying on the path to your chosen future. If anything, Maksim's mistake had been in caving in, accepting the patriotic rhetoric, losing sight of his own carefully laid out plans. He had been blinded by the illusion of the importance of service to others. "See where that gets you," Filip said, spitting the last cherry pit into the Black Sea.

Galina came out smiling, holding something half-concealed in her left hand. She locked up the shop, then opened her hand. "Look," she said brightly, "Zinaida Grigoryevna gave me this, for Maksim. What do you think?"

Filip glanced at the mechanical spinning top balanced on her palm. "I think Zinaida Grigoryevna has lost her mind," he replied. "Too much romantic poetry can do that to a person. What possible use is this . . . this trifle to a war veteran?"

"Well, the paint is chipping here and here. But the plunger you push in to make it spin, that works fine. She thought it might help him to, you know, exercise his good arm . . ." Her voice trailed off, as if no longer sure of the soundness of the idea.

"*Dura.* No, not you, Galya. That woman, she is a simpleton!" He reached for the toy, intending to toss it in the gutter, but Galina was quicker. She closed her hand and stuffed it into her pocket.

"I will give it to him anyway. It might cheer him up."

When they got home, Maksim was sitting on his cot, staring at the rug hanging on the opposite wall. It was a nature scene, a partridge and her chicks partially concealed in meadow grass, a fox watching them with interest from behind a bush, an eagle circling the panorama above the trees.

She sat down next to him. "What are you thinking about?"

"That picture. It's supposed to be peaceful, I think, but it's full of calamity about to happen. The forest food chain in tapestry. The only one who survives is the eagle. Until the hunter appears, that is."

"What a gloomy outlook. Not everything gets eaten all the time, not even in nature. Look, I brought you a present." She placed the top on his night table, pushed the plunger down to make it spin.

"What the—" He stared at the gyrating plaything, its stripes of blue, yellow, red blending into a blur of color. He looked up at his sister.

"It might help you strengthen your arm, and . . ."

"Is this one of your idiotic jokes?" he exploded, bringing Ksenia running in from the kitchen, Filip and Ilya from the yard. "What is wrong with all of you? Can you not see that I am worthless? No good to anyone? What is the point of 'strengthening my arm' if I can do nothing with it? *Ni cherta.* Not a damn thing." He flung the toy across the room; it bounced off the far wall and came to rest, still wobbling, under Ilya's worktable. Maksim stormed out, muttering, "Pardon my language, Mama," when he squeezed past her. "Just leave me alone," he said from the doorway through clenched teeth, his back to the room. "All of you."

When the evening meal was ready, Filip came in from the yard by himself. "Galya has a headache. I will bring her her food."

"I—" Ksenia rose, soup ladle in hand.

"No. I will do it." Filip took the plate from her, balanced the bread on the edge, and retreated, coming back after a few minutes to take his place at the table. They ate in silence.

3

"MAKSIM," KSENIA SAID SOFTLY, moving aside the curtain that separated his cot from the rest of the room, "are you sleeping?"

"No." He kept his eyes closed, his one arm shielding his face from the light.

"Go to the post office for me, *proshu tebya*. Please, I ask of you, do this for me. I have a letter for my sister, your aunt Varya, in Kostroma."

He faced her. "Why bother, Mama? She will not receive it. And if she does, you will never get her reply."

"We must try, son. She may not receive my letter, *kto znaet*? Who knows? But if she does, she will know we are still alive."

"Why me?" he asked peevishly. "It will take me forever to get there, and what if they're not open today? Or if there's a long line, with no way to rest my leg. I would not be home till sundown, and nothing will be accomplished. Send Filip; stamps are his special interest." He rolled onto his side, face to the wall. "Let me sleep."

Ksenia retreated to the kitchen. She stood, head down, hands grasping the back of a chair, for a long time. Finally, she raised her chin. *Nyet*, she decided. *No.*

She left the letter on the table and gathered a few things: a three-legged stool Ilya had fashioned from scraps, the legs cleverly carved to disguise imperfections in the wood; the last two painted teacups and matching saucers from her wedding set; a multicolored shawl

Galina had knitted from odd lengths of scavenged yarn. She tied everything in a bundle. As an afterthought, she tucked several cloth dolls and Maksim's discarded spinning top into one of her dress pockets and went out.

She took the streetcar north, to the city limits, then walked in an easterly direction, keeping to the wooded edge of the road. No one challenged her. She was just another *baba* lugging things around for who knows what purpose.

The day was clear and hot, the midsummer air still, the road nearly deserted. Somewhere far away, thunder rolled, approaching and receding in great invisible waves. Ksenia stopped to rest at the edge of a meadow. She listened. Yes, it was thunder. Not guns, not bombers. Thunder. "Jehovah's chariot," she observed, and smiled.

The road ended, turned into a dirt track through woods of pine and birch. Ksenia looked up. The sky above the treetops was still blue, the leaves high overhead barely disturbed by a breeze she did not feel. The storm was still some distance away. At the edge of the Tatar village she met a boy herding a few goats, brandishing a thin leafy branch. He waved it at her, as if taking pleasure in its supple motion; she raised a hand in return greeting. Later she would wonder if this had really happened. Or was it a dream, a vision of some bucolic paradise conjured by her need for relief from ugly, treacherous reality?

The first house she came to was small, the roof thatch in need of repair. The young woman who answered her knock shook her head, pointing to the small children clustered at her skirts, the baby in her arms. Outside, an older girl scattered a handful of kitchen scraps; Ksenia watched the two hens and lone rooster cluck and peck, devouring every trace within minutes.

She had not visited this particular village before, knowing that you could not keep coming back to the same people too often and expect good results. *Choose a bigger house*, she told herself, *one that looks more prosperous*. She found one near the village center, a solid structure with a painted flower trellis and shiny brass pump in the yard. The woman here was older, her tawny skin set off by large silver hoop earrings, a medallion necklace adorning her deep red caftan.

Ksenia untied her bundle and showed her wares, not in the aggressive manner she used on market days, but with simple dignity. Neither woman spoke much. They communicated with gestures and a few words that both understood in their respective languages. The Tatar examined the shawl from both sides, seemed to like its variegated colors and approve the workmanship. She turned the stool this way and that, tracing the carving with a slender finger. She held the teacups up to the light, looking for hairline cracks or imperfections. Finally, she nodded. She disappeared into the summer kitchen at the side of the house and came back with a small sack of flour, some carrots, and a few plums.

Ksenia nodded her appreciation, then gathered up her courage and said, "Do you have any meat? *Myaso?*"

The woman hesitated. She pressed her lips together, then took back the flour and produce and came back with a small paper-wrapped parcel and three eggs. "*Loshadina,*" she said. "Horse meat."

Ksenia bowed deeply, touched her hand to the ground at the woman's feet. She wrapped the eggs in her handkerchief, tying the corners with care, and slipped them into another dress pocket. She had turned to go, holding the meat parcel against her chest, when a lurid flash of lightning bisected the sky directly above, followed by a clap of thunder that sent both women back into the open doorway. Catching each other's eye, they both laughed at their instinctive reaction, then turned to watch the first heavy raindrops kick up puffs of dust in the yard, sending chickens into the sheltering branches of a nearby oak.

Within minutes, it was over; the furiously falling curtain of rain lifted as suddenly as it had descended. Ksenia stepped out, ready to leave, but the woman restrained her with a light touch on the arm. She went inside and reappeared with a cup. Ksenia drank. She did not care for koumiss, the pungent fermented mare's milk that had been a staple of the Tatars' nomadic ancestors for generations. But it would have been worse than rude to refuse, and she was hungry.

Leaving the village, she stopped again at the first house. Ignoring the look of annoyance on the young mother's face, she gave her the cloth dolls and spinning top without a word, and turned for home. She did not look back to see the speechless young woman, toys in hand, stare after her in open-mouthed amazement.

It was evening when Ksenia reached home. She was tired from the day's traveling, but knew she still had work to do before retiring to her bed. Ilya was at his worktable, bent over a bit of ivory he was carving with a fine-gauge tool, his face illuminated by the glow of the lamp at his elbow. *How handsome he is*, Ksenia thought. *His hair still dark and glossy, his tall body trim. And those hands, those beautiful, sensitive hands.*

"Good evening, my dear. *Dobryi vecher*," he said, without missing a stroke, looking up only when his tool reached the edge of the piece. "Was your expedition successful?"

"Yes. There will be meat pie tomorrow. How is . . ." She glanced toward the curtained corner of the room.

"Sleeping." Ilya picked up a wood-handled chisel, the blade fine as a scalpel, and set to work creating intricate flower petals. "Galya left you some food."

In the kitchen, Ksenia lifted the plate covering a small bowl of millet, two thin smoked smelts laid across the top. She ate one of the fish, grinding its tiny bones with her teeth, swallowing the head whole, licking her fingers one by one.

She untied the parcel and examined the meat. It looked fresh, with no greenish discoloration or brown curled edges, but who knew how long ago the animal had been slaughtered? Or died, more likely. Healthy horses were too valuable to kill for meat. She had to cook it now, tonight, taking no chances on spoilage from the summer heat.

If only I had an ice house, or a cool cellar, like in the country, she thought. *I could rest now.*

She sighed, added wood to the stove, covered the meat with water in the soup pot, peeled an onion from her kitchen garden. When the water boiled, she skimmed off the gray foam, added a dried bay leaf and the onion, along with two garlic cloves, and moved the pot to the back burner, where the heat was less intense and the soup would simmer, undisturbed, extracting as much essence from the meat as possible. She sat at the table, peeled the last of the month's potatoes, working expertly, her knife removing barely a shadow of the pulp. *This is my craft,* she thought. She savored the way the knife's handle fit her hand, the sharp blade worn paper-thin from many years' use. *My tools.*

She stirred the peels into the stockpot with a wooden spoon, put the potatoes on to boil in a separate pot. Tomorrow, she would shred the boiled meat, mix it with the fork-mashed potatoes and make a pie, using the potato water to enrich the dough. If there was enough flour, she would use one of the precious eggs to make *lapsha,* add the homemade noodles to the stock for a meal as satisfying as it was economical. The other eggs she would save for Maksim. They would give him strength, and perhaps, she fervently wished, a moment's joy.

Ksenia picked up the bowl of cold millet and ate it, slowly, standing up, chewing the swollen grains with deliberation. "Needs salt," she said to the empty room, but added none, scraping the last of the cooking liquid out with her spoon, finishing her supper with the second smoked fish.

From her kitchen window she could see into the room outside, a wisp of smoke rising from the kerosene lamp on what was now Filip's desk, his head bent over a stamp album, no doubt. She could not see Galina, but guessed she would be on the bed, sewing, working on one of the scrap projects that seemed to occupy all her spare time. And yes, singing. Ksenia could hear snatches of a popular melody—what was it? Ah, "Sinyi Platochek," "The Blue Scarf," another plaintive song of love and loss. Then Galina moved into her line of vision and

Ksenia stepped back; she felt a flicker of shame at her intrusion but was unable to avert her eyes. Filip rose and the two of them swayed together, dancing in the impossibly cramped space, Galina's mouth at his ear, still singing the haunting waltz. Ksenia saw the flush rise in Filip's cheeks, and then the light went out.

4

MAKSIM RESISTED SEEING the doctor. "What's the use? A doctor is not a magician, a wizard who can restore the past with a few incantations. Save your money, Mama. Let it be."

But Ksenia was adamant. "You may not know everything. An older doctor, with experience, may be able to help you, to improve your life."

"Improve my life?" He laughed, a strangely mirthless, bitter sound. "You mean equip me with a hook so I can tie my shoelaces and terrorize small children?"

"Do not mock your fate, son," she replied, stern and unyielding. "Do you think you are the only one who suffers?" she shamed him. "You owe a debt, because you have been spared. A debt to the many who have died, who are dying even now."

"A debt? What debt?"

"To live a productive life. To do what you can in the time you have. That is your obligation." He made no answer, his gaze fixed on a point between his feet, so she pushed on. "Let's see what comfort or relief medicine has to offer. Then we can talk about your future."

"These words: *comfort, relief, future*—they mean nothing to me. But I will see the doctor, Mama, because you want it so. I want to put these questions to rest for you."

"*Horosho,*" she said. "Good. Ilya? Fetch the doctor. I must finish this pie."

*

Toward evening, Ilya returned with a middle-aged woman. She was solid, gray-haired, businesslike. "Maria Kirilovna." She offered Ksenia a firm handshake, her own hand small and square. "I have been on staff at the sanatorium for the last twenty-two years. Many of my colleagues have been mobilized to treat the wounded at the front. The army determined that I could be spared to care for people here," she explained.

"This way, Doctor." Ksenia gestured toward the bedroom she shared with her husband. "My son sleeps here"—she indicated the curtained corner of the front room—"but our room will be more private for your examination." Maria Kirilovna nodded, followed Maksim into the room, and shut the door.

Ilya followed Ksenia into the kitchen. "Did you notice her limp?" he whispered. "That may be why she was passed over for service. That, and her age."

"As long as she knows doctoring." Ksenia removed the towel from the rising meat pie, pricked the smooth doughy surface at regular intervals with a fork, and slid the pan into the oven.

She had just removed the pie and set it on the table to cool, an hour or so later, when Maksim and the doctor emerged from the bedroom, just as Filip and Galina came through the front door. Ilya put down the book he was reading. Everyone stood a moment in silence, inhaling the incomparable aroma of baking, an aroma that filled the whole apartment with an essence so rich it seemed capable, almost, of satisfying the very hunger it provoked.

Several people sighed; someone grunted appreciatively. Maria Kirilovna spoke. "Maksim is an exceptionally fortunate young man. Any delay or carelessness in treating his wound would surely have been fatal. He would have died of infection or loss of blood, or both. But he did not." She sat down in the chair Ksenia offered, opposite Ilya. The pie steamed enticingly between them, Ksenia with a bread knife at the ready to cut into its burnished crust. The others stood around the kitchen, listening.

"The arm was amputated just above the elbow, as you know. It is possible, in my opinion, to have it fitted with a prosthesis, so that, with training, Maksim could regain some limited use of it. Unfortunately, unless you are members of the Politburo, that operation will have to wait; all medical resources are being focused on the war effort at present. Could I have some water, please?"

"*Ach*, forgive me. Galina, make some tea," Ksenia exclaimed. She put down the knife and reached for the teakettle.

"No, no. Water will do. Thank you. Now, the limp. My own condition is congenital; I was born with one shorter leg. But that is not the case here, correct? Your son did not limp before he left home. My examination revealed no wound or other trauma to the legs, hips, or back. I must conclude, then, that there is no physical obstacle preventing a natural walk. There is, however, the possibility of psychological shock, which can manifest itself in unpredictable ways. I am not expert in this area, but that is my suspicion."

Ksenia picked up the bread knife. Starting at the center of the pie and making the lightest tentative cuts, she marked off equal-sized portions along the edges of its rectangular surface at intervals so precise they would have stood up to mathematical measurement and been found accurate. She frowned. "What does this mean? That he is limping for no reason? He tells me there is pain."

"There is a reason, but it is not physical. There is a wound, of the mind and spirit. Until this wound is healed, I believe Maksim will continue to limp. The pain is caused by the unbalanced use of leg and back muscles—in other words, by the limp itself. That, too, will cease when the underlying cause is no longer present."

"So what can we do?" Ilya asked, his hands folded in front of him, fingers interlaced.

"I am not expert in this area," the doctor repeated, "but I believe . . ." She stopped speaking. Ksenia had begun to slice the pie, cutting deeply at each mark, through the firm upper crust, the aromatic layer of meat, onions, and potatoes, and the thinner bottom crust, her knife scraping along the metal pan. Everyone watched, entranced, completely absorbed in her actions. She turned the pan around, sliced in the other direction, then raised her head, signaling Galina with her eyes. Galina handed her a plate.

Maria Kirilovna cleared her throat. "I believe," she went on, "that the answer may lie in some meaningful activity. Maksim has suffered a grievous wound, it is true. But his heart is strong, and his intelligence is evident." Again she stopped, and everyone watched Ksenia lift each perfectly formed square onto the plate, stacking them in a pyramid four layers high. The pie seemed to breathe on the chipped platter, the air above it alive with vapor, heat from the savory filling radiating into the room.

"Please, eat," Ksenia invited, moving the plate closer to Maria Kirilovna. The doctor took a piece. Everyone followed suit. Ksenia watched them eat, her face aglow with intense satisfaction. After a moment, she also took a piece, crossed herself, and ate. *It is like a sacrament, this food,* she thought. *How little we need.*

Filip, standing near the door to the courtyard, wanted desperately to take a second piece, but did not dare. "What do you recommend, then, Doctor?" he said, trying to distract his attention from the pie and conclude the discussion. "What can he do?"

"Perhaps he can teach, or lead a youth group, give health and first aid instruction with someone else demonstrating the techniques. He has enough knowledge and experience to be useful at the sanatorium in some capacity. Or he could learn to use a typewriter and write for a journal or a newspaper."

"He could play chess," Filip suggested. "That only takes one hand." Maksim glared at him. Filip shrugged, watching with profound regret as Ksenia arranged the remaining pie pieces on a clean kitchen towel, folding the edges in to make a neat package.

"Thank you, Doctor," she said. "We can give you only a little money for your visit, and for your advice. But please also take this pie."

Maria Kirilovna stood up. "I will accept whatever you can manage. Your pie is delicious and I thank you for sharing it with me. But I live alone, and cannot take this bounty away from your family. Maksim, you are a fine young man. I wish you the best possible recovery, but you must take your life into your own hands." Realizing what she had said, she colored deeply and went quickly through the apartment and out into the night.

5

IN THE WEEKS FOLLOWING the doctor's visit, Maksim began to die. There was no sign of illness, no inexplicable cough, no sudden weakness or fever, just a profound crushing despair.

"Only a cup of tea, Mama," he said quietly, pushing away the food she had fortified with every nutritious ingredient she could find. "Thank you," he added with an anemic smile.

"Listen, we're doing a comedy tonight. Come with us," Galina encouraged. "Not much of a play, but you can see how Filip made a set out of practically nothing."

"I had help," Filip protested. "And people let us borrow things. Luyba's lamp steals the show, with its decadent fringed shade."

Maksim sighed. "No. Theater does not interest me. It never did, with or without lamps." He left the table, going out to the inner yard to smoke.

No one spoke. They finished the meal quickly; Galina jumped up from her seat. "I will wash the dishes, Mama, when I return."

She and Filip walked, stepping around freshly formed puddles with inordinate concentration, as if navigating a minefield. Finally, Galina said, "What will happen to my brother? He is so unhappy."

Filip said nothing, steering them clear of two German soldiers preoccupied with lighting their cigarettes in the evening breeze. But Galina wanted an answer. "Filip. How can we help him?"

"How do I know?" He spread his hands, palms up, and shrugged his shoulders. "He does nothing all day, sleeps and smokes, will not even try to help your mother in any way. Just smokes and stares into space."

"Do you talk to him? I know how you feel about idle conversation, but can you not talk as one man to another?"

"There is no common ground. What do I know of his experience? And he doesn't care about my life or interests."

"Common ground? Common ground?" Galina's voice held a rising note of sarcasm. "How much more common ground do we need? Are we not all in this, this . . . dreadful time together? Together," she repeated.

Filip had no answer. He had heard Ksenia say more than once how important it was for a family to stay together, mind its own business. *Keep your head down and your mouth shut.* All around them, people were disappearing, taken off the streets by patrolling troops, vanishing without a word. Their own little household was as if charmed, held together by the force of his mother-in-law's indomitable will. *Unless there's something we don't know about Ilya's frequent absences, and all those Germans who come to the door to pick up their purchases.* He shook his head, but the thought had struck him unawares and would not be banished.

Outside the theater entrance, Galina stopped and laid a hand on his arm. "Please. Please try."

A few days later, on a warm, clear afternoon when everyone was out of the house—Ilya to make and sell his crafts in the park, Galina to the toy shop, Ksenia to stand in line for whatever was available—Filip set his chess set up on a little folding table in the courtyard. At his elbow he had a book and a few sheets of paper he had cut and folded into a pocket-sized notebook. He studied the board intently, shifting the occasional piece, taking a pencil from behind his ear to record the move.

He was so absorbed in the game he did not notice his brother-in-law standing in the kitchen doorway until Maksim limped over to the bench by the wall and lit a cigarette. "Oh, hello," he said, glancing up. "I didn't know you were up."

"Mother does not like me to smoke in the house," Maksim replied, as if to justify his presence in the yard. He blew a fine plume of smoke, watching it dissipate in the sunlit air.

"But you do it anyway," Filip observed. "When it suits you. You have another? Mine are inside."

Maksim tucked the cigarette into the corner of his mouth, thumbed his case open, and passed it to Filip. The case was Ilya's work, two halves of scrap plastic joined with a wire hinge and latched with a diminutive hook. "Mother is a saint. We should not provoke her."

Filip said nothing. *Why bother?* he thought. His mother-in-law was frugal to a fault, and no one in the house went too hungry for long, yet he suspected there was always a little more, something extra held in reserve for the beloved invalid son and the husband returning from his travels. *Well, I have a saintly mother, too,* he thought, remembering the extra sugar cubes, the occasional tin of caviar Zoya saved for him—treats he devoured avidly, alone, with no shred of guilt.

They smoked in a silence if not exactly companionable, at least tolerant of the other's presence, each understanding the other's pleasure in the habit. "There's one advantage of your father's doing business with the Germans," Filip observed, stubbing out his cigarette and tossing the butt into a clay flowerpot kept for that purpose. "We never lack for smokes."

"*Pravda.* True enough." Maksim did the same.

"I mean, these European brands are far superior to our homegrown ones, right? Especially that stuff the peasants smoke. *Mahorka.* Have you tried it?" Filip warmed to his subject. He felt compelled to keep talking, egged on by his brother-in-law's monosyllabic reticence.

"I have. It is vile."

"When? With the army?"

"With the Partisans."

"Oh." It was the end of conversation. Not that Filip wasn't curious, but he feared belying his neutrality by knowing too much.

And Maksim would not talk about it. How to describe people whose patriotism suffered no compromise, who would fight to the death against self-serving invaders masquerading as liberators? People who were determined to protect the only country they had, however flawed and unjust? He could not talk about their fierce resolve, the acts of suicidal sabotage, the missions propelled by hard, hot fury. He could not. Not least because he knew that even if he had been whole, with two arms, and capable of rapid movement, he lacked the cold blind courage to do the necessary acts of violence. Mining roads, blowing up trains, burning villages—these actions caused people to die. He could not be a part of that; his mission was to save life, to heal.

I am a doctor, he thought, *or nearly. I cannot be an instrument of death.* So he had traded them his boots and socks, taking moldy bread, cold salted fish, and a handful of foul tobacco mixed with sawdust in exchange. How to describe the feeling of desolation and, yes, fear, when the Partisans moved off during the night, so quietly he never heard a twig snap, leaving him alone in a forest where even the predawn singing of birds had an ominous coded quality. They could have, should have, killed him, to guard against betrayal of their names and whereabouts. He would never know why they had not. He had picked up his piti-ful bundle and made his way home, relying on compassionate acts of strangers for his survival.

"Hey, friend," Filip tapped him on the shoulder. Maksim recoiled as if stung. "Why so jumpy? You know chess, yes? Could you move some pieces? You don't have to play seriously if you don't want to. It's so damn hard to work out these moves alone."

"I know how to move the pieces. But no one calls me friend." He half-turned on the bench, studied the board a moment, and advanced a black pawn.

Filip consulted his book, jotted something in his notebook. After some deliberation, he moved his knight into position, preparing to threaten the black queen in the next move. Maksim advanced another pawn and lost the queen.

They went on like this for another quarter hour, Maksim playing a quick, desultory game, Filip agonizing over every decision, chin in hand, pencil at the ready. "Ah, I understand!" he muttered. "It's all about the bishop, you see?"

Maksim stood, jarring the board, sending black and white pieces into an irretrievable jumble. "This is a waste of time," he announced, and retreated into the house.

"And what you do is not?" Filip flared up, unable to stop the words. *I tried, Galya,* he thought. *I tried. Who does he think he is?*

Soon after the chess incident, Maksim took to his bed, refusing nearly all food. Ksenia, too, ate less and less, as if in solidarity with her son's suffering. She moved silently about the house, wiping at invisible dust, straightening pristine coverlets, obsessively polishing her spotless stovetop. Some days, she sat at his bedside while he slept, interlacing the fingers of her large, restless hands, studying the ethereal beauty of his gaunt features, taking some small comfort in the regularity of his breathing.

She had not watched him sleep since he was a very small boy, a toddler in short pants. They had lived in the country then, in a little house of their own, with a kitchen garden, a few chickens and a goat in back, a fig tree at the front gate. He had slept with innocent abandon after a day of playing outside, his tousled hair smelling of sweat and earth and sunshine. As a young mother, she had inhaled this sweet, slightly rancid aroma with wonder and delight, marveling at the way this child's arrival had changed her status in the world. When the revolution finally reached them and everything changed, she and Ilya had their hands full just staying together and alive in a country they no longer recognized. No time then to indulge in the luxury of watching a child sleep.

She took the time now, whenever she could, her thoughts moving like summer wind over ripe grain, this way and that, stirring up memories. Once when he awoke she pleaded, "Tell me. I have lived through revolution, witnessed the execution of my father. When you were small, we suffered through the years of civil war and the horror of famine. I know these things, in my own mind and body; I will not forget them. But we survived all that; we are alive. We must have hope." She paused, placing her hand over his brittle fingers. "Share your sorrow with me. Your silence is breaking my heart."

"Tell you?" Maksim took his hand away, raising himself on his elbow. "Mama, what should I tell you? Shall I describe the mayhem of life at the front, the chaos of conflicting orders or breakdown of communication, the paralyzing fear of making a fatal mistake? Or would you like to hear about the swift, questionable justice of field executions, to stop the wave of desertion, neither the runners nor the shooters knowing what is right or wrong?" He took a sip of water from the glass Ksenia held out for him, and fell back heavily on his pillow.

"How can I tell you what it is like to be a medic with no supplies, no blankets, no safe or sanitary place to even try to save a life? I cannot make you hear the voices in my head, grown men crying for their mothers, boys who should be dancing with their sweethearts caught in the agony of slow, relentless death."

Ksenia closed her eyes but could not stop the tears. "We can pray," she said. "God will—"

"God will what? Erase the memory of mud, excrement, and blood, a stench for which there is no word? It permeates your clothing, your hair, clings to your skin; you eat it with your daily kasha and moldy bread, drink it with your foul water, breathe it in what passes for sleep. Is this the God we should pray to? The one who watches and allows such beastliness?" Maksim turned his face to the wall.

Ksenia wept. For the wasted lives, the needless stupid sacrifice, the crazed suffering from which there was no return to ordinary humanity. For the damaged, the broken, the shattered, the vanished. For the son she was losing, the son she had already, she knew, lost.

He lingered a few more days. One morning Galina sat with him, holding a cup of hot rice broth she knew he would not drink. Their parents were out; Filip was with his mother.

"Look." Maksim sat up abruptly. He pointed at the tapestry on the opposite wall. "There, do you see? There is a figure in that bush, a man, crouching. I never noticed it before."

"What man? Which bush?" Galina got up to examine the familiar woodland scene. "This one? I see nothing there."

"Yes, yes, you have your finger on it. But is he watching or hiding? I don't know." He sank back down on his cot, then turned to his sister, his eyes clear and bright. "I was hallucinating. It's the end," he said softly, as if some lucid corner of his brain remembered the sure signs of imminent death—the surge of energy, the visions, the momentary sharpened awareness.

"What? No," Galina said. "You're not hallucinating. There's just nothing there."

But he was no longer listening. His eyes dulled. His breath came quick and ragged, then stopped and resumed, knocking against his chest and throat like a trapped creature, and was still. "Death rattle," she said aloud to the empty room. "Gone."

Galina sat down carefully on the edge of the bedside chair. She sat a long time through the gathering dusk, still holding the cup, while evening fell all around her with crushing emptiness and the broth cooled in her hands.

PART IV

Germany

A New Life

1

"WHAT DO YOU DO with these doilies?" Filip stroked the latest addition Zoya had placed in her basket, this one with lacy scalloped edges and an intricate pineapple design.

She hesitated, colored slightly. "I sell them," she finally replied. "Or trade them for things we need."

"At the bazaar?" He couldn't imagine his demure, diminutive mother among the aggressive sellers hawking whatever goods they had in a cacophony of voices to rival the squawking of seagulls competing for a dead fish.

"No. No one would notice me there," she confirmed. "I just choose a street corner. Late afternoon and early evening seem to be the best times. People buy. I don't know why, but I'm grateful."

"Because your work is beautiful." He smoothed the piece, aligning the edges with the ones underneath. "Mother, what shall I do?"

Zoya looked up, struck by the anguish in her son's voice. She was not used to being so formally addressed, as if they were characters in an ancient Russian folk tale, in which the wise elders always had the answers. Filip slumped in his chair, unseeing eyes fixed on the book open on the table in front of him.

"What is it, son? You've become so gloomy. Has something happened?"

Yes, he wanted to say. *Yes. My best friend was hanged for defending his country, and I do nothing. Day after day, I do nothing, wondering if his death was my fault.* Had he ever held anything back from his mother, anything important? He didn't think so. But he knew she would find a way to bring God or the Virgin Mary into it, might try to persuade him to pray. That, to his mind, was no solution at all. He couldn't tell her.

"I've heard that young married men are to be taken to Germany now, with or without their wives. So no one will be exempt except small children and old people. The university exam has been postponed."

"Is there no work for you here?" Zoya's hands moved smoothly, her crochet hook darting in and out of the delicate piece taking shape under her fingers.

He had tried to find work, if only halfheartedly. And what, really, could he do? He thought the library might hire him, but in the end that opening went to someone older, with some experience. "No."

They sat silent for a while, she at her needlework, he turning pages without reading them.

"Ksenia Semyonovna—I can't call her 'Mama'—has proposed we go sign up for Germany. She says those who go voluntarily get better placements and are allowed to stay together." He spoke without looking at her.

Zoya glanced at her son, put her work down in her lap. "I have heard that, yes."

"You know my father-in-law was detained by the city police. Something about his travel permit. It turned out they were looking for someone else, a different Ilya—Ilya Zorin. Mistaken identity. So they let him go." He took a deep breath, held it a moment before exhaling, remembering the fear that had gripped the household; Ilya's release had only increased the sense of imminent danger. "We all know they didn't have to. They could have locked him up whether he was the right man or not."

"I know," Zoya said calmly. "Your father put a word in for him."

Filip stared at her, stunned. How much more was there he did not know? He was not a child. Yet it seemed he had no grasp at all of the ominous things going on around him every day. He felt adrift, incompetent. Maksim had died, sacrificed, however unwittingly, to the Soviet cause. Borya's execution was another casualty of the same struggle. Why did he, Filip, not feel part of that struggle? Where did he belong? If anything, the catastrophic events that brushed against his life filled him with ambivalence, a debilitating malaise that left him powerless to act.

Who was the enemy? It seemed clear enough that the invading forces of a foreign nation should be expelled at any cost, and yet . . . He remembered his father—was it just a few years ago?—a postal inspector with a fresh Communist Party card, refusing to talk at home about his work, even as his mother grew more secretive about her religious outings. This was in peacetime, he himself aglow in his Young Pioneer membership, until even he recoiled at the increasing pressure to tell on the activities within his home and neighborhood. Why was Stalin so afraid, the fear cascading in paranoid ripples through every aspect of everyone's life? It was far safer to take refuge in chess and stamps and music when the nation's leader was at war with his own people.

And now the Germans, like it or not, had brought a certain sense of order, along with their tanks and troops. There was a clarity in dealing with them. You overstepped, you died. But still, there were some rules. Or so it seemed. What he didn't know was whether their promises could be trusted, what, exactly, they meant by "better placement."

"Mama, I don't know what to do."

Zoya sighed deeply. "Your in-laws have decided on this desperate plan because Ilya Nikolaevich is being watched. His travels, his dealings with the Germans, however innocent they may be, do not sit well with the police." She picked up her crochet hook but did not resume her work. "And they are doing it for you. You are young, neither a student nor a worker; the Germans will surely take you for forced labor, if not this week or the next, then soon. By volunteering as a family, things may go better for you." She paused and looked at him, her gaze strong and kind. "And you must stay with your wife, son. It is your obligation, as a Christian and as a decent man."

"I may never see you and Papa again." He didn't need to add, *If we go with the Germans, there's no way back.* They both knew that well enough.

She put the hook down, letting the work slide off her knees and onto the floor, and took both his hands in hers. "It will be as God wills," she said. "I will pray for you every day."

For once, he felt no irritation at words that would have struck him as sanctimonious at any other time. The coolness of her fingers tempered the heat in his own hands, calming his mind a little but doing nothing to dispel his sadness.

They stayed together until the evening shadows began to fill the corners of the room. Filip paced, then threw himself into a chair, only to rise and stare out the window at the street below. Zoya wept from time to time, making no effort to conceal her silent tears.

When Vadim's key turned in the lock, neither one had heard his footsteps on the landing. "Why do you sit here in the dark?" He strode across the room, illuminating its familiar objects with lamplight: this polished table, that sofa with its brown plaid blanket laid across the back. The chair by the window, the black fringed flowered shawl draped carelessly over the armrest, the glass-globed lamp, the cups and plates in rows on shelves, the copper samovar, the sepia wedding portrait on the wall.

"Papa," Filip said, rising. "Oh, Papa."

2

HOW DO YOU PACK to leave your home?

Transport regulations allowed them one suitcase each and a small trunk for household items—cooking pots, dishes, bedding. Ksenia watched Galina fold her few dresses, underclothes, and nightshirt, tucking an extra pair of shoes in the corner and a light sweater on top.

"There," Galina said. "And I still have room for all the family pictures."

There were not so very many, but each picture was a treasure. Ksenia as a small child, with a soup-bowl haircut and a lacy old-fashioned smock; Ilya with his mother and sister, whom Galina barely knew; Ksenia unsmiling, but with the sparkle of youth and optimism in her adolescent eyes. Ksenia and Ilya's grave postrevolutionary wedding portrait, both gazing at the camera with a look of serious purpose.

And here was Maksim, first a sandy-haired toddler holding a bunch of droopy daisies, then a schoolboy, and finally, a university student, his open face a study of eagerness and hope. Galina remembered that session, Maksim impatient, his bags packed, ready to leave for the train station right from the photo studio, Ksenia trying to suppress her anxiety but letting the pride shine through tear-filled eyes while Galina and Ilya hovered in the background like the supporting players they were.

She packed the pictures of herself last, laying each one with care into the folio lined with tissue paper. Here, she is a baby, seated on

a white cotton coverlet, wearing a knitted dress and a halo of fine
wispy hair. This one, a school picture: dark dress, lace collar, holding
a book. And her favorite: she a gawky nine-year-old standing next to
her seated father. He is wearing his white summer trousers, his arm
draped casually along the back of the bench, his head thrown back, a
hint of a smile lighting up his face. She lingered over that one. *Will I
ever be so happy again? So sheltered, so contented, so loved?*

"Stop crying," Ksenia scolded. "Why take them if you ruin them
with your tears?"

Galina dried her eyes. She added her own wedding portrait, the
teenaged bride and groom side by side like children playing dress-up
in borrowed clothes. That went on top, along with extra copies of
everyone's official passport picture. And that was all. She closed the
cardboard folio, tied its brown silk ribbon, shut the suitcase.

"You have the travel permits, Ilya? The letters of introduction?"
Ksenia asked.

"Right here," he patted his breast pocket. "And my share of the
money."

"And I have mine," she replied. "In case we get separated."

Filip said nothing about the bills in his pocket, a parting contribution from his father. The photographs of his own family, which
Zoya had given him, were tucked safely in his suitcase under his stamp
albums.

"*Nu*, well then," Ksenia's glance swept the room. Was she taking
stock, noting the contents of her home, its abandoned furnishings,
its familiar floors and walls and windows, never to be seen again? Or
was she simply checking for forgotten necessities, making sure nothing
essential had been left behind? "Let's sit."

They all knew the ancient custom: when all the journey prepara-
tions were done, everything packed and waiting at the door, everyone
sits down and, after a moment of silence, all rise in unison and leave.
No last-minute farewells, no hesitation. Sit. Stand. Go.

Ksenia, Ilya, and Galina turned toward the east corner of the room, where until an hour ago the *ikona* of Saint Nicholas had hung, and crossed themselves. Filip stood behind, his hands at his sides; he refused to participate in the religious part of the ritual, but made sure no one noticed.

Galina stopped on the threshold for a last glance around the rooms, at the remaining furniture and rugs. "What will happen to our things?"

Her father laid a reassuring hand on her shoulder. "Someone will use them, or sell them. Don't trouble yourself over a few objects. We've had the use of them; now someone else can benefit. Is that suitcase heavy for you?"

"No, Papa. It's not heavy."

That wasn't what I meant, Galina wanted to say. She had no special attachment to these particular things, many of them already old before becoming part of her childhood home. Hers was a more specific curiosity: she wanted to know the people, to touch the coats they would hang on the hooks near the door, see them sleeping in the beds, feel the vibration of their footsteps across the front room carpet, hear their talk and laughter around the kitchen table, smell the food they cooked on the old iron stove. She felt unmoored, suspended between the yawning void that was their future and the unpeopled vacuum they were leaving behind. *Maybe we all feel this way,* she thought. *We just don't know how to talk about it.*

They passed through the courtyard and into the still-sleeping streets, the sun just rising over the distant mountains to the east. If anyone saw them leave, they gave no sign. No one called out a final greeting; no hand moved behind the curtained windows.

They took the early streetcar to the dock. The transport was to sail by barge to Odessa, they had been told, then travel by a succession of trains through Eastern Europe to its German destination. Papers checked, they sat on their luggage for hours in the open boat's dank interior, talking little, watching other passengers walk the shaky plank and find places for themselves. Waiting.

Galina grasped the side of the boat for balance against the swaying of the antiquated vessel. It smelled of stagnant seawater and rotten fish, underlaid with something industrial, a clinging oily stench that stung the nostrils, unrelieved by the steady breeze from the sea.

"Never mind," Ksenia said. "We are volunteers. We have good letters of introduction. Didn't the officer who signed them promise us a farm assignment? It's hard work, but it's not factory labor. At least we'll be in the country, in the fresh air."

She rose and walked toward the prow, Ilya following a moment later. They stood looking past the harbor at the Black Sea, the gulls gliding in widening circles over its placid waters, a scroll of smoke from a passing freighter unfurling slowly in the cloudless sky. Above them, perched on the edge of its cliff, the celebrated Gull's Nest Sanatorium kept vigil, the sea on one side and Yalta, their city, on the other. Ilya pushed his cap back, lit a cigarette. Ksenia tucked her hand under his arm. Neither spoke.

"What do I know of farm work?" Filip spat into the greenish foam lapping against the boat's edge. *I'm leaving all my hopes here, everything I love and wish for. Except . . .* He looked at Galina.

She sat motionless, perched on two suitcases, her back not quite touching the damp side of the barge. Only her hands moved, the fingers weaving around each other as if of their own will, composing and delivering mysterious messages. *My wife,* he thought. Filip studied her face, the radiant beauty of it muted by an expression of such wistfulness, such sorrow, that he felt something shift in him, as if his heart had suddenly disclosed a previously dormant chamber, even as his mind struggled with the enormity of this moment. As though his childhood fell away then, and life, in all its ugliness and random unrelenting progress, crowded in.

All at once, he had so much to say. "Galya . . ."

"What?" she acknowledged, her stare fixed to the decaying boards at her feet.

The trip passed in a blur. Two armed German guards stood at either end of the barge, smoking and laughing together over the huddled travelers' heads. Seasickness swept through the crowd, affecting most of the passengers; those who were not afflicted by the boat's motion were sickened by the spectacle. Vomit was everywhere, slimy underfoot, sticking to shoes and luggage, cascading down people's clothing in stinking patches that dried almost at once in the blazing afternoon sun.

Ilya was among the few who did not succumb; Ksenia held out longer than most by sheer force of will. Rocked by the slow progress of the barge through seas more turbulent than they appeared, Filip and Galina were able to retch over the side and avoid soiling their clothes.

They reached Odessa with the sun low in the sky, waited dockside while a dozen of their fellow passengers were put to work with buckets of seawater and stiff brooms, cleaning the boat for its return voyage. "*Schnell, russischen Schweine.* Pigs. Clean faster," the guards shouted, while the idle crew looked on, stony-faced, showing neither compassion nor contempt.

Then it was on to the train station, passing through the city's broad avenues, guards riding with semiautomatic weapons trained on the marching group. Like a grotesque parade that stopped traffic to let it through, ignored by pedestrians who thronged the wide sidewalks in their early evening rush to what? Home, dinner, family?

"If this is how they treat volunteers . . . ," Filip muttered, but no one replied or even looked at him.

And Odessa! He longed to break away from the humiliating transport march and have even one hour to explore this glittering city. There were no shortages here. The shops were full of goods. Their windows glowed and beckoned, spilling pools of yellow light into the streets filled with people. He watched their faces flicker, passing through light and shadow in a cinematic panorama, searched them in vain for the harried look everyone seemed to wear back home. *Why can't we stay here?* There was bread in the bakeries, and cakes, too; meat in the butcher shops. A haberdasher displayed hats and neckties; stylish creations draped on dress shop mannequins tempted the eye. There were toys, furniture, Turkish carpets, glassware, jewelry. *Why can't we stay?*

He wasn't the only one to notice. He listened, head down to catch the remarks circulating through the shuffling crowd.

"Why is this city different? Look at all the goods they have."

"It's the Romanians. They're in charge here."

"Romanians? Aren't they Nazis too?"

"Kind of. The Germans needed more troops in Europe, north and west of here, and on the Russian front, so they left the occupation of Odessa to their Eastern European allies."

"But they're just as bad! I've heard stories . . ."

"Was there ever a war without atrocities? Still, they run things here, not the Germans. Maybe they're lazier, not so crazy for absolute control."

"It can't last. Odessa is a big city, with mountains to the west, where people can hide, and the coast, the seaport. Our Soviet Navy could lock that up and then what? No shipping. No goods, no munitions."

"True, true. *Pravda.* But wouldn't I like to stay a while. A man can make a living here, war or no war."

Filip slowed down, shifted his suitcase to his other hand. He cast murderous glances at Ksenia's rigid retreating back, saw Ilya list to one side under the weight of the trunk it was his turn to carry, his toolbox tucked under the other arm. *Oh, yes. We can't stay because we're going to work on a farm. Isn't that a stroke of good luck.*

He wanted to forget the entire trip, couldn't wait for it to be over. How he and Ilya took turns with the trunk, which, though small, was cumbersome and knocked against their shins; how the locks on Ilya and Ksenia's suitcase gave way, and someone produced a length of rope to tie it closed, while the guards prodded the curious crowd and snapped insults and warnings. How they had all missed the evening train out of the city and had to spend the night at the station, propped up against each other, trying to sleep.

Leaving Odessa behind, the morning train took them past fields of wheat and rye, potatoes and cabbage, the country dotted with neat farmhouses alternating with dense stretches of deep loden evergreen forest. Factory smokestacks rose in the distance; warehouses, stone buildings, and churches flashed by the train windows.

It might have been idyllic, a picture of prosperity rising out of orderly, methodical practices and good management, but for the randomly cratered ground, fires smoldering here and there, the sight of women sifting through rubble, toting buckets of broken bricks, tugging at splintered boards. At the railroad stations, bands of boys hawked things taken from wrecked, abandoned houses, chased off by patrolling police only to reappear behind their backs. *Why do people have to suffer when their leaders can't agree?* Galina thought, passing a few coins to a skinny boy in an oversized cap in exchange for a pair of apples.

At the Czech border they changed trains, their escort replaced by an SS junior officer and several local police.

"*Juden?*" the SS man asked, watching the passengers descend to the platform, dragging their things, herding exhausted children before them.

"*Nein,*" the departing guard smirked. "*Ost. Arbeitslager.*"

Filip asked himself, *Why did they laugh? Ost.* East, that's where they had come from, of course. But *Arbeitslager?* Work camp? He had seen Ksenia's letters of introduction. They contained no mention of labor camps. The train must be making other stops along the way, if that's where some of these people were going. *And where is our train? How can we leave with these cattle cars blocking the tracks?*

"Filip, look." Galina tugged at his sleeve. "Those cars are full of people."

"No," he said, handing the guard his papers for inspection. "You must be mistaken. They are . . ."

He turned to look, and blanched. Those were not animal sounds coming from inside the windowless cars. They were words. "Water. Please, water." He stared in disbelief at fingers protruding between the slats, watched a policeman walk along the length of one wagon, crushing those fingers with his baton, to the amusement of the others.

"Stop!" Galina cried out.

Ksenia took her arm, saying, "Hush. You can't help them." Together, all four moved to the side of the platform, to the area designated for waiting.

"Where's this lot from?" one of the officers asked another, pointing at the crowded cattle cars with his chin.

"Prague. Four days ago."

"All right." The first one nodded. He unfurled the station's water hose, pointing the nozzle at the air space near the roof of the car. "Turn it on."

What followed, the wailing and keening fueled by panic but also by a desperate need for relief, was unlike the sound of any human voice Galina or Filip had ever heard. The captive bodies strained against the creaking sides of the wagon for what, in spite of the force of the flow, could not have been more than a few drops of water. After a few minutes, the first officer signaled to shut the hose off. "That's enough. They're only Jews," he said.

"There are children in there. Can't you hear them crying?" Galina whispered, tears running down her own face. Filip set down his suitcase and embraced her, holding her head firmly against his shoulder until she stopped sobbing.

Shuddering, she worked herself free of him, wiping her eyes on her sleeve. They watched the officer move along the tracks to an empty freight car. He raised his arm and, with theatrical flair, chalked the word OST in large capital letters on the side.

"Now you," he shouted at the Russians. "*Ostarbeiter*. In here." He angled a narrow board against the open freight car doors and shoved the first of the group up the makeshift ramp. Two policemen formed

the rest of the travelers into a ragged line, snorting impatiently while the
people struggled to keep their balance and hold on to their possessions.
At the foot of the ramp, the SS man handed each traveler a square
patch and a large safety pin. "Wear these on your coats at all times,"
he commanded. "Sew them on when you reach your destination."

Filip looked down at the roughly woven patch in his hand. OST,
it read, black letters on a whitish ground. "Where are we going?" he
asked aloud, of no one. No one answered.

3

ONCE LOADED, THE TRAIN traveled fast, speeding through Austria without incident. The wagon smelled of stale sweat and urine, but it was not especially crowded. Everyone found a spot, sitting on their trunks and cases; some stretched out on the grimy straw-covered floor and slept.

"I wish we could see out," Galina sighed, leaning her head against the wall, rocking with the motion of the train.

"I wish I had a cigarette." Filip closed his eyes. He had tried peering between the slats at the flickering landscape but gave up, feeling dizzy with the effort.

"Hmm," Ilya grunted, without clarifying which desire he shared. Perhaps both.

Sometime in the night, the train stopped, jolting the sleepers awake with a great screeching of wheels on metal tracks. It had grown colder. The car doors opened to let in more people, speaking other languages—Serbian, Czech, others Filip did not recognize—but with the same dazed look as the Russian travelers, the same scruffy luggage and OST patches on their coats.

"What day is it?" someone asked.

"November first if it's after midnight. Tuesday."

People shifted about, making room for the new occupants. Galina and her mother found themselves pushed to the car's open door. "Mama," Galina breathed. "Snow."

It fell gently. Huge flakes floated on the air as if chipped from a block of soap; they filled every crevice, covered each surface with a lacy, ever-changing pattern until all the spaces disappeared and everything dazzled against the dark.

What was it Maksim had said? *Cold and wet. You'd tire of it in a week.* The words rang clearly in her head, as if her brother had just spoken them. She could hear the disdain in his voice, see his hand pushing his glasses up the bridge of his nose. *Rest in peace,* she thought. *But you were wrong. Who could tire of such beauty?*

"Step back," a gruff voice commanded. The door slammed shut, a heavy bolt thudded into place. Galina closed her eyes to the murk, the ceaseless sighing and swaying of the human cargo, holding the image of pristine whiteness against her eyelids, until, still standing, she fell asleep.

A convoy of open trucks took them from the station to the outskirts of Munich, speeding through the city at sunrise. Filip admired the architecture, shocked by the signs of wanton destruction; he spotted the towering steeple of a Baroque church, a flock of birds rising through the gaping hole in its roof, the surrounding area reduced to rubble.

In the side streets, he glimpsed narrow passageways lined with squat two-story houses, small windows and painted doors, every roof covered with red tiles, wisps of translucent chimney smoke hinting at breakfast. Even with so much damage caused by enemy bombing, it was a medieval fairy-tale city, and he wished he could step in, even for a little while, and sample its daily routines, mingle with its residents. "Why are we at war with these people? What do we want from each other?" He said it under his breath, but Ilya, standing at his side, heard.

"If I were a younger man, I would be fighting them. But my lungs—" he stopped, his chest heaving in painful spasms of dry coughing.

"Don't let them hear you," Ksenia cautioned.

"What? Saying I would defend my home? There's no shame in that."

"No. Don't let them hear you cough."

"It's only the cold air." Ilya waved a dismissive hand.

They all knew it wasn't the cold air, that he *had* defended his country as a younger man, in the Great War, against this very enemy, that he'd soldiered through clouds of mustard gas that left him, along with thousands of other survivors, permanently, incurably impaired. "At least, you should not smoke," Ksenia persisted.

"*Ai, Mama.* Would you deny me every joy?"

Leaving the city behind, they watched the Bavarian countryside roll out: a cluster of painted cottages here, followed by a pine thicket, the cantilevered branches dusted with early snow. Then fields, farmhouses of stone and timber, barns, outbuildings. There was less bomb damage here; perhaps the area had fewer strategic targets.

They sped past an old man in a green cap leading an old horse pulling an even older wagon, saw him move to the side of the road to let the trucks pass. In the distance, stooped figures of women dotted the fields, digging the last of the year's potatoes. *Will there be enough farm work for us,* Ksenia wondered, *with winter coming?*

By afternoon, they had reached the work camp, its boundaries marked out with double rows of barbed wire enclosing some newly built barracks and several previously existing structures. Processing was rapid, methodical.

"We have letters, from your Lieutenant Berg, in Yalta," Ksenia held the documents out to the officer at the table. "For farm work. We volunteered."

"*Ja, klar.*" He glanced at the pages, dropped them onto a stack at his elbow. "Of course."

They were permitted to stay together, assigned, along with nine other families, to a low building that had once been a beer hall. The darkly paneled walls and wood floor still held a smoky, yeasty, not unpleasant aroma, though all counters and furnishings had been stripped out.

"Each family will stay in its own space," the escorting corporal decreed, pointing to a grid of white lines painted on the floor. Clotheslines above the lines crisscrossed the room from wall to wall. "No cooking. Lights out at ten. Up at six. Sharp."

"Are we to sleep on these?" Galina toed a stack of burlap-covered straw mattresses in the family's allotted space, some stained blankets folded on top.

"As you see," Ksenia said. "Help me with these blankets. It's good we have a corner space."

They draped the blankets on the clothesline, giving their "room" a semblance of privacy. Others were doing the same, talking in low voices among themselves. Children ran around the hall, weaving in and out of every grouping as if laying out the rules of a new game.

Supper, dispensed outside the kitchen door, was thin cabbage soup and a slice of grainy bread. For breakfast, the same bread, harder now, only made edible by soaking in bitter acorn "coffee" muddied with a bit of milk.

An open-bed truck took them and another thirty or so people, then, to an industrial area several kilometers away. The sun hung dully in a leaden sky that promised more snow.

"*Heraus, alle*," the guard commanded when the truck stopped in front of a large factory. "*Schnell*. Everybody out." It was a four-story rectangular building, not unlike a latter-day castle, with what looked like rounded grain silos at each corner for turrets and many tall, narrow windows cut into thick stone walls.

"What do they make here?" Filip asked the truck driver, who looked barely old enough to drive.

"*Zement*," the boy replied. He jumped into the cab and slammed the door. "Cement."

4

"SLOW DOWN." THE MAN at Filip's side plunged his shovel into the bin but came up with only half as much coal as it could hold.

"What?" Filip paused to wipe his face with his sleeve, then started in again, his shovel fully loaded, moving twice as fast as his wiry neighbor.

"Slow down. *Po malu*," the other said again after the overseer went by. "Unless you're eager to help the Fascists build more bunkers."

It didn't take Filip long to cultivate the illusion of working hard while producing little in the way of results; he quickly learned how to put his back into each shovel thrust but pitch fewer and fewer coals into the blazing furnace. Hadn't his father often chided him for laziness? Now, this natural inclination served him well.

It was a dangerous game. If the factory fell short of production quotas, if it failed to deliver the required amount of cement on time, everyone suffered the consequences. Shorter rations, longer hours, tighter, more vigilant supervision, and, of course, no end of verbal abuse seasoned with the occasional beating.

The violence was almost entirely arbitrary. Anyone, at any time, could feel the crack of a baton against his head or back; shoving and kicking were so commonplace as to be barely noticed, by workers and guards alike. Whether the misdeeds were real or imagined made no difference.

Some misdeeds, like the bucketful of steel shavings and rusted nails that found its way, bucket and all, into the stone crusher, were real enough. The sabotage went unnoticed until the metal, melted by the kiln's intense heat, fouled the morning's batch, requiring cooling down and thorough scrubbing of the machinery before work could resume. The entire workforce endured two days without food, then half rations for another week, while working sixteen-hour shifts with no days off for a month.

"We can survive this," the men said with grim satisfaction to one another. "But, damn, it feels good to slow them down, even a little."

Filip had gone to the infirmary with a high fever the day the guards took their revenge. He returned to work an hour later, dosed with aspirin, to find Savko, a young Macedonian, dead on the floor.

He started to ask, but read the warning in the other men's eyes, each going about his task with unaccustomed efficiency, stepping around the body with care. The guard shoved Filip's shoulder with the flat of his hand. "Take his boots off. Then get back to work. Your sick day is over."

Filip bent over the dead man, trying to ignore the blood pounding in his ears, willing his fingers to stop trembling. The boots were poorly made, the cheap leather scuffed and cracked; spots of mildew blossomed on them like buds on a vine. Jammed onto Savko's bare feet, they were a tight fit. The left came off without too much effort, but Filip struggled to work the right one free, rocking it from side to side, kneeling on the grimy floor to get a better grip. When it gave way, the edge caught and broke a blister on Savko's heel, oozing a snail's trail of pus onto Filip's hand.

The foot was still warm; the skin showed smooth and tawny between crusted patches of embedded dirt. Filip recoiled. He wiped his hand on the man's pant leg, suppressing the bile rising in his throat. He felt faint with fever. To steady himself, he glanced sideways at Savko's face. *He's only a boy,* Filip realized, shocked to see the first tendrils of an adolescent beard curled against a dimpled chin.

In the truck heading back to camp, the men started talking. "He was crazy, that Savko. They're all crazy, the *Makedon*. Wild," said one, referring to the mountain people from Macedonia

"Why crazy?" another man asked. "Aren't they all Yugoslav now?"

"Bah. Yugoslavia is not a country. Just a patched up mess of people the French and British couldn't tell apart, so they lumped them all together and washed their hands of the southern Slav problem. And mark my words: you'll see how the whole stew will disintegrate once their man Tito dies."

"Dictators have big heads but small shoes," the first man declared cryptically. "There's always another one ready to step in."

"But—" Filip tried to cut in, but the older men ignored him, caught up in their discussion, each eager to outdo the others in explaining his version of the world.

"Now the Serbians—" the first man started, shaking a calloused finger at the assembled circle, ready to make his point.

"Wait." Filip, his patience at an end, raised his voice. "What happened? Will someone tell me?"

"You don't know? Savko was up on the scaffolding, monitoring the paddles that stir the slurry. The guard was on the other side, his back turned, watching us worker ants below."

"They like to do that," someone observed.

"Yes. Well, he turned around just in time to see Savko pissing into the vat. Shot him in the head, on the spot."

Filip dropped his head into his hands. He had noticed Savko; there was something intriguing in his perpetual scowl, something that appealed to Filip's own guarded nature. They might have been about the same age, but Savko already had the outsized hands of a farmer or laborer, so unlike Filip's own. He looked at his hands now, revolted by the weeping scabs, the cracked nails, the skin caked with coal dust and grime, which no amount of washing seemed to remove.

I wish we could have talked. He thought he might have said the words aloud, but no one paid him any attention; the subject had moved from politics to the comparative qualities of the camp's women.

Savko had taken his midday meal with other men from his camp. Talking while working was nearly impossible, and what language would they speak? Russian, which the new Yugoslavs avoided with visceral hatred? Serbian, of which Filip knew only a few words, was even worse, sure to stir up ancient rivalries. German? It seemed absurd. Yet he was sure they could have found a common tongue. If only he had tried.

What pushed a man to this extreme, to commit an act so senseless? That cupful of urine in the vat was not sabotage; it made no difference whatever to the quality of the product, would make no wall crumble or foundation crack. It was either an irrepressible childish prank or simple, insane suicide.

Savko's body lay on the floor until the evening of the next day, gradually sifted over with a thick layer of stone dust that filled his open mouth and powdered his chestnut hair, leaving only his eyes to glisten, unseeing, in the gloom of the cavernous hall. Dust penetrated every crease of his stained brown shirt, the sleeves rolled up to reveal muscular hairless arms until they, too, were covered, along with his torn worker's pants and bare feet.

The task of removing the corpse fell to two of his campmates. "Where to?" they asked.

The SS captain never looked up from the evening roll call. "Into the furnace."

5

MORE WORKERS ARRIVED; the men from the new transport replaced most of the women at the plant. Ksenia and Galina were assigned to the camp kitchen. Ksenia was on familiar ground. Rising an hour before dawn to prepare the officers' breakfast was no hardship at all. A good cook, she knew how to work wonders with the simplest ingredients, how to compensate for shortages. Several of the guards noticed, and rewarded her on the sly: two extra potatoes here, a sliver of hard cheese, the uneaten crust of an officer's bread.

"Don't eat the workers' bread," she cautioned her family. "There's sawdust in it." She tried by sleight of hand, she told them, to avoid adding the pulverized wood shavings to the dough, but there were too many eyes and no one could be trusted. "It is indigestible," she said. "It will kill you, in time."

"Mama." Galina's voice was barely audible, her head lowered over a bucket of half-rotted potatoes she was peeling for the inmates' dinner. "They want me to go to the officers' club, to wait on tables. I would have better food and a bed in a special dormitory."

"That will never happen," her mother vowed, bringing her cleaver down on the mess of cabbage in front of her with enough force to make the table shake.

When they came for her, two men, one holding a frightened young woman by the arm, the other reaching for Galina, Ksenia put down her knife and stepped between them. "My daughter is a respectable married woman, with a husband in this camp. You will have to kill me before you take her."

"That would not be difficult," the younger guard sneered, reaching for his pistol.

"Wait," the older one said, remembering, perhaps, the previous day's turnips flavored with a hint of bacon and parsley. His own mother had never thought to do that. What other magic could this stubborn Russian woman do in the kitchen? "I saw livelier girls at the factory. All they need is a bath. But you"—he pointed at Galina—"you will report to Herr Doktor Blau. He has work for you."

————————————

The camp matron who escorted Galina to the dentist's house told her he'd been recently widowed, perhaps to explain his taciturn disposition. Herr Doktor Blau was well into middle age; his creased and jowly face was not unkind, although he seldom smiled. His wife had been much younger, Galina saw from the framed picture on his desk. They stood in front of a park carousel, she laughing, one hand holding a wide-brimmed straw hat to her head, the other pushing down the skirt of her summer dress against a playful breeze. The dentist, at her side, looking at her with bemused admiration, the painted eye of a carousel horse just above his head, two small girls aloft on the horse's back.

He said nothing about his wife's death, and Galina did not ask. The cottage stood a short distance from the camp, along the road the truck traveled to deliver workers to the factory, dropping her in the early morning and picking her up ten hours later. After a month spent toiling in the cement plant, and another laboring in the camp kitchen, this work was easy. She bathed the three-year-old twin girls, combed and braided their hair, helped them to dress, prepared their meals. Unless the weather was stormy, their father expected them to play outdoors, in the little fenced backyard, before they came in for a bowl of hot soup and a long afternoon nap. She cleaned the house and did the laundry, picked up their wet boots and soggy mittens with a smile, trying to decipher their cheerful chatter of southern German laced with baby talk.

"Listen for the siren," the dentist said on his way out to the black car waiting at the gate. He spoke to her in clear, slow German. "If there is an air raid, take the girls to the basement and stay there until all is clear. Understand?"

She understood, wondered where that black car took him several times a week—a vehicle that, as far as she knew, never portended anything good. Other days, he received patients at home, the whine of the drill from the examining room setting her own teeth on edge.

Afternoons, while the girls slept, she starched and ironed his shirts and their dresses. He wouldn't let her press his trousers, said he liked them just so, preferred to do them himself. It was amusing to watch him at the ironing board, bent close to his task, absorbed in placing each knife-edge crease with absolute precision. But she never dared laugh, just busied herself with the dinner they would eat after she had gone.

The morning the beggar came she was alone in the kitchen, washing the breakfast dishes. It had rained, a quick, drenching spring shower that left the yard too wet for the girls to go out until later. She could hear them twittering together like a pair of little birds, playing dolls in the dining room. Herr Doktor was out.

The man appeared out of nowhere, popping up at the open window like a circus performer on a trampoline. He was so close she could see the lice crawling in the stubble of his shaved head. He pulled a bundle from under the shirt of his striped pajamas, a yellow star hanging by a thread just below the collar. He held up a short-sleeved red dress with big white buttons, a clothespin dangling from one shoulder. "Nice, for you. You buy?" he croaked at her in rapid German. His voice was high, rasping, painful to hear.

Galina tried to scream, but no sound came. His collarbones were sharp as razor blades under the filthy cloth of his threadbare shirt. Huge scabby hands hung from his matchstick wrists; the toothless, gaping mouth smelled of rot. How could anyone so decimated still walk and talk? When had he last seen food? She reached for the nearest thing, the unwashed pan from this morning's oatmeal, several spoonfuls of cold cereal stuck to the bottom. She thrust it at the man and slammed the window shut.

She heard the pan crash to the ground. Footsteps, running. Dogs. A stifled wail. And silence, broken by the call of a crow, raucous in its sudden vulgarity.

She didn't know, for certain, that he was a Jew. She had heard some talk in the work camp, of other camps, much worse than this one. She remembered the closed cattle car, the muffled disembodied voices begging for water. Where did they go? What happened to them? And why? Did the barely human apparition at the window have some connection to such rumors? She did not know what to think.

Galina never again let the girls out by themselves, not even to the sheltered safety of the fenced yard. She took her mending or laundry tub outside, keeping her charges always in sight.

After she found the gold fillings, everything changed. The tin was not in the examining room; she was only allowed in there, to dust and sweep and clean the glass cabinets, when the dentist was present. It was on his bedroom bureau. She had never seen it before, an old cocoa tin with a smiling Bavarian *Mädchen* on the side, her hair a golden wreath of braids. The tin clattered to the floor with a swipe of her dust cloth, spilling its glittering contents on the polished boards, some of the nuggets still ringed with bits of black decaying teeth.

Her mind conjured an image of her father, in happier times, his head thrown back, a glass of tea in his hand, laughing, his gold teeth catching the light of the evening lamp. She had heard of widows asking for their departed husbands' fillings before burial, as a sentimental

memento or a hedge against impending poverty. But this, this could
be no fond remembrance. This was something dirty, a shameful hoard
wrenched from the mouths of what? Corpses? Whose? And if they
were inmates, didn't the gold belong to the captors, the Reich?

The noise brought the doctor in from the next room.

"I'm sorry, Herr Doktor. I am so clumsy." Galina was on her
hands and knees, gathering the evidence of her transgression into his
secret life.

He pushed her aside. It was the only time in her four months'
employment he had ever touched her. "Leave that," he said in a menacing voice icy with repressed rage. "Crying won't help. You think it's
easy serving these butchers? Yanking the fillings from the wretched
bastards' remaining teeth, the bodies not yet cold, the SS standing
around telling bawdy jokes." He scooped the fillings up with a quick
sweep and jammed the fistful of gold into the pocket of his immaculately pressed trousers. "They cannot pay me enough for what I do.
I have my daughters to think of, their future."

"I . . ." But there was nothing to say. *Will your daughters thank you
for a future bought with these gruesome wages of death?* Galina wiped her face
with her hands and backed out of the room.

The following week she was reassigned to the camp kitchen.

She told no one. Not her mother, working with her at the camp
kitchen stove. Not her father, assigned now to clean the infirmary,
his coughing, aggravated by the ever-present stone dust, making him
useless at the factory. And certainly not Filip, lying on the adjoining
mattress, waiting until the others were asleep before groping his way
onto hers, with urgent whispers and insistent hands.

6

SO IT WENT. Days of mind-numbing drudgery were relieved only by episodes of desperate resistance. Each careless blunder or show of independence was punished, the retribution that followed marked by wanton cruelty.

Day and night, there were Allied air raids. So often that, after the first few, work continued at the factory as if the disturbance was nothing more than a passing thunderstorm. Anyone who was outdoors when the bombers approached could seek shelter inside, but only until the danger passed. When one corner of the plant was hit, the storage silo split from top to bottom, every pair of hands went to work scooping up the dry stone clinker, transferring the salvaged material into the three remaining towers.

The work was so loathsome, so backbreaking and filthy, that when an officer entered the plant and demanded, "Who here speaks good German?" Filip stepped forward without the slightest hesitation.

The camp was filled beyond capacity, housing over three hundred workers in a space designed for half that number. No one was idle; the factory now operated twenty-four hours a day, with the same bunks and mattresses serving double duty for those returning from their shifts. Some preferred to take advantage of the milder weather and slept outside in hastily erected tents, hoping to avoid the bedbugs and disease that plagued the barracks in spite of regular fumigation.

With so many people and such demanding work schedules, there was plenty for an interpreter to do. Filip was busier than he had ever been, serving the communication needs of the camp administrators and factory managers at any time, day or night. But he never lacked for cigarettes, and his hands were clean.

The nighttime encounters perplexed Galina. Gradually, the dread she felt as bedtime approached gave way to resignation. Their corner was no different from any of the others, the darkness filled with grunts and whispers and, occasionally, muffled tears. She even heard, from time to time, a muted stirring from her parents' end of the room. "Men need this . . . this release," Ksenia had told her shortly after the wedding. "Women must endure, or lose their husbands."

She and Filip had known each other so long; it seemed natural for them to be together. But was it enough? She thought about romantic novels she had read as a girl, films she had seen. Where was the spark that passed, unspoken, between lovers, the caress that signaled a meeting of hearts? Filip had never so much as stroked her cheek. She wondered how that would feel, if it was different from her father's tenderness.

Galina remembered the clumsy fumbling of their early married nights, Filip awkward and self-conscious, angry with himself for not knowing quite what to do; she waiting, equally unschooled in the art of intimacy. Now, they grew adept at the love act (there were other words for it, she was sure, but in her innocence, she did not know them), with a furtive haste that reduced it to little more than coupling, leaving her wondering while Filip slept. What happened between them, was it love? She wanted to ask her mother, *How do we get to where you are, you and Papa? That place of harmony and understanding, one being with two hearts?* But she could not.

Once, not so long ago, her husband had looked at her with admiration. What was there to admire now? Since losing her job with Herr Doktor Blau, she had grown thinner, her hair dull as straw, her face pale and mottled, her hands roughened by kitchen work. He,

Filip, had bloomed on leaving the factory labor force; his work, while unpredictable in its demands, was far less taxing. He did not suffer the mindless exhaustion that, for her and so many others, marked the end of every working day.

And now, as May's last coolness gave way to the bright days of June, and even in this gray, depressing place some grass grew here and there in defiant clumps and violets appeared, followed by buttercups, and birds sang—now she was sick. "Mama, I can't eat this," she pushed her portion of greasy soup away. "You take it. I'll only throw it up."

Ksenia looked at her daughter as if seeing her bony body and sunken cheeks for the first time. "You're pregnant," she finally said. "Lord have mercy."

Summer changed to autumn. The bombing raids intensified. The factory continued to operate around the clock, blackout curtains over every window giving it a funereal aspect. It was, the men said, like working in hell, or some infernal tomb.

There was no way to conceal the smokestacks, to hide the sooty plume that hung perpetually overhead, sparks swirling into the night like ominous fireflies. As 1944 drew to a close, October was marked with frequent raids; November brought an onslaught so intense that even at the camp, several kilometers away, the ground quaked, walls shook, the air screamed and whistled with each explosive contact.

"Why don't they stop?" Galina's voice dissolved into a whine, her hands over her ears. "Don't they know we're not the enemy?"

Filip stared at her. How could anyone be so naive? She had never before been so prone to hysteria, so perpetually close to tears. *It must be the child*, he decided. *My child.* "We don't matter. To anyone." He lit a cigarette and sat, elbows on knees, to smoke it.

In the morning, the factory was gone. Several trucks were salvaged, and those people who were nearest the doors escaped outside, running for their lives as tons of stone, iron, and timber collapsed in a vast cloud of smoke and ash. Those inside, workers and guards alike, perished, their bodies crushed by falling slabs or incinerated beyond recognition in the ensuing fire.

The runners, too, were far from safe. Bombs rained randomly from the sky for another twenty minutes, until the planes swooped in a wide arc and disappeared into the night, leaving few survivors on the ground.

At the camp, no one knew why they had been spared. For hours after the attack, fires burned all around, lighting up the sky and obscuring a timid dawn. At the command house, there was a frenzy of activity. Telephone lines were down, telegraph communication intermittent. Confusion reigned until the highest-ranking surviving officer ordered all remaining inmates to the scene for rescue and salvage operations.

It was too soon. The rubble was still too hot to touch; dislodging any stone was likely to reignite the embers, causing new fires to spring up, fanned by the frosty air. More than once, moving a cooled piece made a fresh avalanche of debris descend on the would-be rescuers.

They worked for hours, shifting what could be moved, sorting what could be salvaged, all very much aware of the ultimate futility of the work. "They're waiting for orders," Filip clarified, helping a dozen or so men move a pile of rocks from one spot to another just like it. "They do nothing without orders."

By midafternoon, the orders came. The captain read the dispatch, conferred briefly with his staff, and turned to the expectant workers. He looked a moment at the blackened faces streaked with runnels of limestone dust, the impassive eyes like beacons in the smoke.

"*Halt*," he said, climbing onto a pile of charred timbers, his expression inscrutable. "Stop and listen. This *Arbeitslager* has been closed. You may return to gather your things. Everyone is to be gone by morning."

Gone? Gone where? The question buzzed through the crowd, the workers looking first to each other, then back at the German, who suddenly seemed smaller to them, less self-assured. Something that might have passed for compassion flickered in his eyes and disappeared.

"You all have work papers. Go where you want." He jumped to the ground and turned to Filip. "You, interpreter. You ride with us." He moved off in the direction of the waiting jeep.

Filip followed, pulling Galina by the hand. "Thank you, Herr Kommandant. But my wife, she is—"

"*Ja, ja.* I see. All right, then, but no one else."

But Galina broke away, refusing to ride while her parents walked.

They set off, a pathetic-looking crowd, filthy, hungry, thirsty, disheveled, confused. All knew they would not reach the camp before dark, and to have food, any food waiting for them was a miracle none expected to happen. They followed the dust of the retreating jeep until it disappeared around a bend in the road. Rounding the bend, they saw a man in the road, shoulders hunched, hands in his pockets, waiting.

No word was spoken. When they reached him Galina took her husband's arm, keeping her head down to conceal her tears. She had not meant to shame him, but was gratified to see that he, too, could not ride while the others walked.

As the trek wore on, the crowd spread out along the road, afraid at first to leave its relative safety for the unknown perils of scorched fields and denuded woods. Some stopped to rest; others, weighing the value of their paltry belongings against the chance to get an early start on their liberty, cut away, vanishing into pine thickets or turning onto roads leading who knows where.

The rest, walking as in a trance, watched the country come into view like images projected by a magic lantern onto a dusky sky: a village, people moving in blurry silhouette against still-burning buildings; a family sitting in a barren field, surrounded by scattered possessions including, inexplicably, a bed; a tractor, its rear wheels buried under a fallen tree, the smoldering engine gasping its last puffs of fumes. The desolate, eerie silence was broken by the sudden crash of a collapsing roof, or the mournful lowing of an abandoned cow. Now and then, a dog howled. Once, Filip was sure he heard the plaintive notes of a harmonica. He raised his head to listen, but the sound was gone; only a chill wind remained, carrying a prickling of early snow.

The family reached the camp well after midnight, among the last ones to arrive. Ilya's cough had worsened, aggravated by smoke and exertion. Time and again, they had stood with him while he struggled to regain his breath, unable to offer him help or comfort. Predictably, the barracks had been ransacked. In their haste, it seemed, the thieves had left—or overlooked—most of the things Ilya, Ksenia, Filip, and Galina cared about.

Galina examined the scattered contents of her suitcase. "They took my extra shoes and my green dress. But they didn't take our pictures."

"Why would they?" her father replied. "Here's a piece of luck— they missed my toolbox."

That thing is heavy as six bricks, Filip thought. *Who would want to lug it around?*

"Let's sleep a little now," Ksenia suggested. "We can pack up in the morning and decide what to do."

In the morning, early, they gathered in the camp kitchen. Filip took charge.

"We can't stay here. This area is too industrial; the Allies are sure to come back to finish the demolition job. As you see, most people are already gone. Berlin is out of the question. Do I have to explain why?"

"It's the seat of government, a primary target." Ilya sat back in his chair, arms crossed.

"Right. Frankfurt is a transportation center. Also not a good place to be."

"Where, then? And why go to a city?" Ksenia, rummaging in the bare pantry, emerged with half a jar of soured milk. "Aha. Breakfast."

"That's where the work is. And there are more people; it's easier to blend in."

"Maybe Herr Doktor Blau could help us." Galina held the cup her mother offered, sipped at the bitter stuff with unconcealed distaste.

"Blau? Blau's long gone. Don't ask me where. I don't know." Filip read the shock on his wife's face. "I thought you knew."

She turned pale, then burst into tears. "He was kind. And those sweet little girls . . ."

"Maybe they're safe somewhere, with relatives," Ilya said. But no one believed it.

"Well. So," Filip resumed, "the place to go is Dresden. They make porcelain and cigarettes. It's a cultural center, historic but not strategic. Even the Germans say it's a safe city."

"How do you know so much?" Galina, still sniffling, dried her eyes on her sleeve.

"I have ears. Germans may bark at us, but they like to talk among themselves."

"We go north, then, and east." Ilya rose to look out the window. The last few stragglers were at the gate, hoisting their bundles onto their backs, calling to their children not to fall behind. "It's as good a plan as any."

"Yes." Filip pushed his cup toward Galina. "You drink this. You need it more than I do."

7

FILIP WAS THE FIRST to reach the bridge.

"You wanted to see the world. There it is." Galina came up behind him, waved an open hand toward the city rising in stately grandeur on the far bank of the river.

Even the slight hill leading up to the bridge was enough to leave her puffing like a long-distance runner. She carried a bundle of clothes tied in a bed sheet across her back and shoulders, the ends secured in a knot under her breasts. She brought her right hand back to her chest to steady her breathing, while the left rested in its habitual place, on the small but unmistakable mound of her unborn child. Filip found this gesture, this mute confirmation of an experience only women could know, vaguely irritating and even embarrassing.

"To see the world? Yes. But not like this." He set down his suitcase as if wanting to deny any affiliation with its shabbiness. "Not as a beggar."

They stood, waiting for the rest of the ragged band of travelers to catch up. The sun, climbing in a cloudless February sky, caught on distant cathedral spires and laid a veneer of warmth onto the aged roughness of the stone parapet over the languidly flowing Elbe below.

After months of trudging through the German countryside, shunted from factory towns to village farms, wearing the degrading OST patch that marked them as conscripted laborers from the East, here was a city. Filip admired how the buildings of more recent construction, their limestone facades still to be tempered by time, fit seamlessly into the orderly design, lining the cobbled streets in harmony with their more weathered neighbors.

The place exuded history and culture. And possibility. Who knew what opportunities lay ahead there for a young man of nearly twenty with a quick wit and an adaptable mind? Even without formal education, he believed he understood how buildings were made. He felt ready to learn how to build an arch, construct a bridge, raise a spire, calculate the proper spacing for a staircase. His heart filled with desire to make something, something beautiful and grand, from wood, stone, iron, glass; something no one had imagined before in quite the same way. *I can, I will be an architect. Just give me a chance.*

From stamp collecting he had learned attention to detail, which translated readily into an aptitude for record keeping—an aptitude the Nazi camp managers seemed to value out of all proportion. His gift for languages had assured him of at least sporadic interpreter duties, sometimes resulting in extra rations.

And yet, since leaving Yalta, calling on these skills had amounted to nothing more than a kind of maneuvering, a way to evade the mindless degradation of hard labor. So far, it was only a way to stay alive without quite knowing for what purpose. But here, in this glowing city, with its trade schools, its university, its countless offices and ateliers, here a clever man who knew how to keep his eyes open and his mouth shut could find his chance, seize it, and begin to live.

He turned to his wife and was about to speak, then stopped. Was that a hint of mockery he had heard in her remark? *There it is.* He decided not to share his nascent hopes with her. He would surprise her. He would surprise them all, as soon as something concrete developed that would prove his worth beyond all doubt. "Where are the others?" he asked instead.

"Trading news with some people traveling from another town."

"And you didn't wait to hear the news?"

"We'll hear soon enough. I wanted to be with you." She said it simply, looking not at him but at the placid river, its path carved out of the land in broad curves, its blue-gray waters mirroring skeletal leafless trees growing along the banks. "I wonder what makes a river flow the way it does, moving this way and that. Is it just rocks and boulders the water can't move out of the way?"

Filip could not admit that he really did not know. "Taking the path of least resistance," he guessed. "Like us."

"Us?" She turned from the landscape to look at him with a quizzical smile.

"Yes. We are alive, and together."

"That's just luck, don't you think? We could have been separated, or died a hundred different ways."

He lit a cigarette and leaned forward, resting his elbows on the parapet. "Not just luck. It's knowing how to bend, like this river, when faced with obstacles or pushed around by forces we can't control."

"If you're saying we worked for the enemy, it was only to save our lives, and your child," Ksenia had come up soundlessly behind them. "But have we ever informed on or knowingly endangered another person? No."

The trunk they had brought from home had become too cumbersome for foot travel; they had sold it at a country bazaar along the way. A large wood-framed basket now contained their household items: two small pots, a frying pan, cutlery, a few plates, cups, and bowls, and some rudimentary supplies—salt, flour, rice. Ksenia sighed and sat down carefully on its edge, resting her head in her hands.

Filip went cold. He dragged deeply on his cigarette, hoping no one noticed the shudder that made his shoulders shift and fingers shake. Again, he saw the lamppost, Borya's body rotating slowly in the balmy breeze of a perfect Yalta afternoon, the damning word PARTISAN painted on his shirt, bare feet level with Filip's eyes. *Who would take a dead man's shoes?* he asked himself, outraged anew at the callousness, the disrespect for his young friend's extinguished life. *Anyone. Anyone would.* A dead man had no need of shoes.

Was I to blame? After months of dormancy, the question rose once again in his mind, surfacing like a drowned cadaver suddenly freed from weedy depths, rolling grotesquely with unseen underwater currents. What an idiotic thing to say—*How's life in the woods, Borya? Finding any mushrooms?*—on a crowded street in the middle of the day. But had anyone heard, or paid attention? "Surely not," he said out loud, as if in answer to Ksenia's question, forcing the thought away.

The day was bright and chilly. Patches of powdery snow lay here and there on the ground, sliding down the eaves of red-tiled roofs to trim their edges with lacy ice. A fine mist hung over the river, swirling and rising in gentle waves toward the same sun that made the ghostly vapor vanish into the morning air.

"A change in the weather," Ilya said. "Snow is coming."

"How do you know, Papa?" Galina challenged him, smiling. "What do any of us know about snow, except how beautiful it is, and how cold?"

"Well, the temperature is dropping, and my bones ache from the humidity," he replied, matching her smile. "And one of the other people said so."

"Then we must cross the bridge and see what we can see, right away." She took his arm and they set off, leading the rest of the group toward the sentry at the far end.

"*Papiere.*" The man was not young, and clearly bored with the monotony of his duties. He cast a disinterested glance at the passports and work papers each person proffered like a charitable offering, standing single file, not moving until passed through by a careless wave of the soldier's hand. "Twenty-four hours," he repeated, stamping each passport with a red-inked date. "Twenty-four hours."

Filip stopped. "What does that mean, twenty-four hours?"

"It means you transients cannot stay in Dresden more than one day." He looked up, frowning like an irritated schoolmaster. "One day, or there will be consequences."

"Where do we go then?"

"Go where you want. Back where you came from, but not here." The guard pushed them on, already reaching for the passport of the next person in line.

"Consequences," Filip muttered. "What the hell does that mean? Why would they care where we stay? Everyone knows the war is not going well for Germany."

"That's true," one of their traveling companions chimed in. "But between the Red Army approaching from the east and American and British air raids, where is a safe place for us if not here? It's just that there are too many of us for a city this size."

"Why safe? What makes Dresden different?" Galina turned to ask. They were standing at the foot of the bridge, at the top of wide stone stairs leading down to the main square, the city's streets laid out before them.

"No strategic targets. Why waste bombs on a cigarette factory or porcelain warehouse?"

"What about the river bridges? And the railroad," another man said. "They can't fight if they can't move."

"True enough. But see, the railroad station is still standing, and the tracks appear undamaged. If it was so important, the Allies would have hit it long ago."

By noon they had walked well into the town, down a wide avenue lined with shops, small hotels, and multistory apartment buildings, the cobblestones smooth as bread loaves beneath their feet. Some went to see about gallery seats for the afternoon circus performance; one couple headed for the art museum.

On the street, people moved briskly, with worried looks—the only sign, it seemed, that here, too, life was not entirely normal, touched by the war's shortages and anxieties. But there was still ersatz coffee and real tea, they saw in passing the glass doors of numerous cafés, and a tray of soft buns in a bakery window.

"Oh," Galina exclaimed, unable to ignore her hunger or to stifle her desire for the luxury of fresh bread.

"Wait." Ilya sat down on a bench facing the bakery door, pulled a small spool of wire and his ever-present pliers from his pocket. Within minutes, he had looped DRESDEN 1945 in fluid script out of the pliant coil, then added the name of the shop and a curlicue for garnish underneath. A few more snips and twists to attach a sharpened prong to the back, and the pin was done.

He entered the bakery, pin in hand, removed his cap and approached the woman at the counter. She looked up. They saw a shadow pass over her face when she took in his impoverished condition. She was pretty, past the bloom of youth but not yet middle-aged, with short curly hair and a large-breasted, well-proportioned figure. The group watched in silence, seeing the woman shake her head and begin to turn away, then stop, her head inclined attentively while Ilya worked the pliers on another length of wire.

"Give me a cup," he said to Ksenia, poking his head out of the shop, his expression triumphant. A few minutes later he emerged, holding a newspaper cone filled with buns. "Breakfast," he announced. "And this is for you, little mother." He handed Galina a cup filled with steaming milk.

"All this for a Dresden pin?" Galina held the cup with both hands, taking long, grateful sips.

"And her name. Also her sister's and two godchildren's. I will need to find more wire now."

They ate, chewing slowly to savor the bread's fresh goodness, knowing it would be gone all too soon, while the hunger, their constant companion, would reappear like a whiny stray dogging their existence with maddening regularity.

"Thank you, God, for this bounty," Ksenia said, crossing herself when she had done.

"And thank human vanity, too," Galina added, wiping the inside of the cup with the last of her bun.

"Where shall we go, then? We have only this day." Filip was glad he had not shared his thoughts with anyone. At least he was spared the humiliation of having his splendid plans fall apart for all to see.

"The circus?" Galina pointed to a colorful poster pasted to the outside wall of a news kiosk. Plumed horses shared the ring with dogs, acrobats, and clowns; a lone elephant held a young woman in the curve of its upturned trunk. "No, that would cost too much," she said quietly before anyone could object. "But there's a sign for the zoo."

"First we must see about the train, for tomorrow." Ksenia looked at her daughter kindly, with a shadow of a smile.

They pooled their money, hoping there would be enough to buy standing-room passage out of the city. "Maybe I can earn a little more," Ilya proposed, pocketing the sum. "The day is young."

They followed the stream of refugees to the train station—people with hungry eyes, bedraggled like themselves, sunken-cheeked and none too clean, clutching their pathetic bundles, their stuffed cardboard suitcases bulging with items too precious to leave behind.

What do you take on a journey into the unknown when the door to your homeland closes behind you, and the prospect of returning is more frightening than the flight? Your wedding *ikona*, with tarnished silver filigree around the Madonna's halo? Photographs, heirloom jewelry, no matter how gaudy, a favorite toy, your grandmother's shawl? Each bag a struggle between nostalgia and practicality, with an instinctive eye to items that can be traded or sold: these embroidered pillowcases, stitched by your mother's hand but also useful—a souvenir of home, a touch of beauty, a bargaining token against the difficulties of a hazardous meandering journey.

The cavernous waiting hall, full to bursting when they arrived at the railroad station, was a veritable Babel. The air was thick with languages: Russian, Polish, Czech, Serbian, Tatar, and other tongues they could

not name floated in a frenzy of communication, while children raised
the universal wail of the lost and confused. Galina took hold of Filip's
arm, her eyes wide. "*Skol'ko naroda!* How can so many people leave in
one day?"

Her question was answered when a train pulled in; passengers
thronged the platform, climbing into the empty cars before the
wheels had stopped turning, shoving and dragging their children
and belongings with them. In the momentary space that opened
with this departure, it was possible to see the railroad windows and
discern the lines of people queued up for tickets. "Where can we
go?" Ksenia asked.

"What difference does it make?" Filip loosened his wife's grip
on his arm, took a small tobacco pouch from his pocket, and rolled
himself a cigarette. She missed, or chose not to see, the way his lip
curled in disgust. *What difference does it make?*

"West," Ilya decided. "Away from the eastern border." And far
from the approaching Red Army, with its threat of forced repatriation,
they all understood at once.

Ksenia moved toward a cleared space near the open station doors.
"I will stay here with our things. You, Ilya, get in line for tickets. And
you two go, look around the city; we have enough time before our
permit expires. Try to find something to eat if you can. And don't
forget the curfew." She piled their cases and bundles together and sat
down on the sturdiest one.

It was a good plan. Without their things, the young couple could
blend more easily into the crowd, move around the city with less like-
lihood of being stopped at every turn to have their papers examined.
They wandered, looking in shop windows like newlyweds, admiring linens, furniture, glassware. A movie house marquee advertised an
Italian comedy; the concert hall promised an early evening chamber
music recital.

"Schubert? Who's Schubert?" Galina wondered.

"An Austrian composer, a little like Beethoven, but less"—Filip struggled for the right word—"forceful. You do know Beethoven, yes? His picture was on the wall of the music room at school."

"Yes. I never liked him. He looked like a beast." They spoke softly, lest their language attract unwanted attention.

"Well, speaking of beasts, it's this way to the zoo."

The zoo was quiet after the busyness of the street, the hubbub of the train station. A group of German schoolchildren crowded around a matronly guide, only half-listening to her talk about the lives and habits of sea lions. The still-energetic seals were starting to show the effects of war rationing, their otherwise shiny pelts dotted with dull, rusty patches and scabby lesions, which seemed to cause them some discomfort. They slithered about on the wet platform, scratching their necks with paddle flippers, filling the air with comical throaty barking.

Here and there, couples, almost invariably one or both of them in military uniform, strolled along the freshly swept paths, paying only cursory attention to the caged animals. Young mothers in groups of two of three pushed baby carriages; an old woman sat on a bench, scattering bread crumbs to a single peacock and his harem of hens. And everywhere there were refugees, dazed, pathetic-looking people moving mechanically from cage to cage, excited children in tow.

We look like that, Galina thought. *No wonder they don't want us here.* She straightened her shoulders, ran her hands down the sides of her thin coat, then took Filip's arm. "Where are the elephants? I can hear them, can't you?"

"Filip? Is it you?"

They turned, surprised and alarmed. Who would know them here? Was it wise to respond?

The man before them was young, and only a little older than they. He was almost impossibly handsome, his perfect features set off by smooth black hair swept back from his forehead, showing off high

Tatar cheekbones and piercing dark eyes. Galina did not recognize him. A face so beautiful was not easily forgotten.

"Musa," Filip said. "What the hell are you doing here?"

"Looking at the animals, just like you," the man smiled, his crooked stained teeth spoiling the overall effect. *What a shame*, Galina thought. She shot Filip a questioning glance. Did he really know this man? She shivered.

"Let's walk," Musa said. "It will be warmer than standing here in the wind. Still collecting?"

"Who has money for stamps?" Filip shook his head. "But I find one from time to time."

Musa was well dressed, in pressed trousers, good shoes, and a warm jacket, a fur cap in his hand. How had he come to be here? What gave him such a confident, secure air? Should they be talking to him? Was it simple acquaintance, friendship, that motivated his approach? Or was he an agent and, if so, for whom? What did he want?

Galina hung back, not wanting to appear suspicious, yet unsure how to respond to this dazzling young stranger from home. Filip seemed at ease, deep in conversation with Musa. They talked stamps, numbing detail about issues and watermarks, series and values—talk so specialized and mundane that she felt her fears dissipate. She turned her attention to the animals in their small but clean cages.

They walked through the monkey house, warm humid air heavy with a musky blend of fur and fruit, the occupants screeching invective at the passing spectators, pushing small leathery palms through the bars, demanding handouts. In the outdoor exhibits, a pair of black panthers, draped languidly on dead tree limbs near the top of their cage, appeared to be napping, ears flattened, tails gently twitching. There was a lone tiger measuring its confined space with endless pacing; a herd of gazelles, antelopes, and other hoofed creatures whose names Galina didn't know; a family of giraffes whose small heads and absurd necks made her laugh out loud.

"But where are the elephants?" She interrupted the men, who had moved on to other subjects, something about buildings or bicycles. "I want to see elephants." She stopped, a brown bear gnawing a large stick in the cage at her back. Musa took her arm and pulled her away just as the bear reared to its full height in a rapid movement that belied its shaggy bulk, baring fearsome tan teeth, waving furry paws the size of a man's head, claws extended, in their direction. Galina cried out, then covered her mouth, stifling a nervous laugh.

"He must be hungry," Filip observed, taking her arm and steering her away from the now indifferent bear.

"And so am I. Come have dinner with me," Musa said. "I insist," he added, seeing their hesitation. "I have plenty of food. After we see the elephants, of course." He smiled at Galina. To her own surprise, she smiled back.

The elephants were housed in a spacious cement compound surrounded on three sides by a deep dry moat. "Oh, look, they are chained!" Galina exclaimed. "How awful." Each creature was tethered to a thick iron post; the chains circling its hind leg had etched a deep groove into the skin.

"The chain is long enough for them to move around. See how they come right up to the edge of the moat? And most of them are born in captivity, so they have never known any other life," Musa explained in a tone that struck her as patronizing.

Filip, standing aside, hands in his coat pockets, turned to look at his companions. "Can you miss freedom if you have never known it?"

"That, my friend, is one for the philosophers, and I don't recommend we discuss it here in public." Musa bent to pluck a handful of dried grass from the frozen soil. "Here," he said to Galina. "Just stand near the fence and stretch out your arm. They can reach it."

First one, then all the elephants came to her, even the baby, trotting on its sturdy cylindrical legs, a stiff breeze stirring the wiry tuft of hair on its smooth gray head. She laughed to see them, waving their trunks, stretching across the moat to take the grass from her open palm. Musa and Filip moved along the path, looking for the last of the fallen leaves, brushing aside patches of snow to reveal clumps of grass underneath, plying her with these while she spun this way and that, trying to make sure each animal received at least one handful.

"Look how calm they are. No one is pushing or fighting to get more than the others. And, oh, Filip, you should try this! Their trunks feel like kisses in your hand, so warm and gentle." She was breathless with delight. "I just wish I could reach the baby."

"The baby is taking care of itself," Musa observed, handing her the last of the vegetation within reach. "Look." True enough, it had stopped shuffling from side to side and was sweeping its little trunk playfully along the ground, snuffling up bits of food the others had let fall. From time to time, this perfectly formed miniature replica of it gigantic elders would look up, holding the tip of its trunk in its mouth, which looked to be perpetually smiling.

When there was no more grass, the elephants moved off, dragging their chains, to huddle together at the far end of the compound, herding the baby into the middle of the group. Galina grew quiet. She moved both hands to her belly. The child turned inside her as if in response to the family scene before her. What kind of world would her little one know? Would she, Galina, be able to care for and protect this child the way these huge placid beasts cared for and protected theirs?

She had Filip, of course, yet however attentive he could sometimes be, he knew nothing, nothing at all. He and Musa were talking about stamps again. She felt more protective of him, she thought, than the other way around. Her mother was an anchor, indispensable to her survival in countless ways, and her father's tender love lay at the very center of her existence. They had all stayed together through the last harrowing months. She understood, from talking with other refugees, how rare that was.

What if they were separated? How would she manage?

The imminent birth of her child was an unimaginable ordeal; the prospect filled her with dread. Her fears were vague, unarticulated but powerful, chasing each other in an anxious jumble that made her feel suddenly weak. *Stay safe*—the words, rising out of her murky mood, had the fervent yearning of a prayer, encompassing her innocent child, the little elephant, and all the people she loved.

Galina shuddered. She turned to Musa. Eyes shining, she tucked a stray strand of hair behind her ear. "I will never forget this day."

"Nor I," Musa said quietly. He placed a hand on Filip's shoulder. "Your wife is cold. We should be going. There is a very good stamp dealer near my apartment. We can stop there on the way."

"I have no . . ." Filip faltered, torn between responsibility and desire.

"My treat, old man. For old times' sake."

While they walked, Musa filled them in; how, after leaving school, he had worked at one of Yalta's better seaside restaurants, learning the culinary craft and perfecting German in his spare time. They all knew that people from the Tatar villages were less likely to be taken to labor camps, those villages being a key source of provisions and information for the occupying forces. Through the restaurant, Musa had caught the eye of a Nazi colonel who took him on as his personal cook and interpreter, attached him to his staff, and arranged to keep him on when he received orders to return to Germany.

"Then you're a . . ." Galina could not get the word *traitor* out. She blushed deeply and lowered her eyes.

"Call it what you will. You Russians are in a tough spot there, caught between the monster at home and the tyrant who wants his land. Hitler's plan is to decimate the Slavic population, or reduce it to slavery, working for good Aryan colonizers, while he and his circle enjoy the heavenly Crimean climate and feast on your delectable fruit. Here, take some more of this." He served them veal schnitzel left over from the colonel's table, with fresh peas and wide buttered—buttered!—noodles. Galina could not be sure, after the rich dinner and half a glass of wine, whether his hand had brushed her arm by accident or by design. The gesture annoyed her, but she was too dulled by the welcome warmth of the room and the comfort of real food to give it much meaning. Somewhere in the recesses of her mind she felt a vague stirring of urgency; they had to get back to the train station, where she knew her parents would be worried about their long absence. But for the moment, she was blissfully content.

". . . the Ukrainians, the ones who work the land, raise the livestock and grow the food, they have it much, much worse," Musa was saying. He refilled Filip's wine glass, then his own. "It's ironic, don't you think? Persecuting the very people whose labor is most essential to your survival."

"And the Jews?" Filip ventured, no longer caring how safe it was to talk freely with this man of questionable allegiance. He was unable to stifle his own curiosity; there had been so little reliable information. And the wine had gone to his head.

"Well, yes, the Jews, of course. Unfortunately for them, Hitler has never considered their contribution as essential to society, nothing that can't be done as well, or better, by beautiful upstanding blue-eyed Christians. No, they can simply be disposed of." He sipped his wine, then added quickly, noticing how both his guests had gone pale. "I'm not saying I agree. History will sort it out. Right now, it's everyone for himself. Chocolates? They're very good. Made right here in Dresden."

"How do you mean, disposed of?" Filip reached for a bonbon but did not eat it, placing the square confection on the edge of his plate. "We were told they all got passage to Palestine."

"Palestine," Musa snorted. "They might be dreaming of Palestine, if the dead can dream."

"Avram . . ." Filip blinked rapidly, as if trying to erase the image of the kindly grocer, an echo of the gruff voice rumbling in his ears. "Surely not . . ."

"I don't know your Avram, but I doubt his fate was different from the others. Sadly, this is one area where Hitler and our Comrade Stalin were in agreement. I thought you knew. I'm sorry to have spoiled our pleasant evening like this."

Galina rose and began to clear the dishes. "We must go, Filip. How far is it to the train station?" The uneaten chocolate square fell off the edge of Filip's plate and rolled, like gambler's dice, several times before landing facedown on the tablecloth. For a moment, no one spoke.

Musa cleared his throat. "There is a curfew. Nine o'clock. The train station is too far for you to get there in time. The colonel has a car, but I could not use it to drive you there, even if it were available this evening."

"So let's go now, quickly!" Just then, the child flipped and kicked, forcing Galina to sit down heavily on her chair. Musa placed a light hand on her shoulder and ran it down her arm. "Don't touch me," she said, her eyes steely and her voice expressionless. *Coward* was the word in her mind, but she restrained herself. She could not wait to get away from this despicable man.

"It's better if you sleep here. I must leave early myself, to prepare the colonel's breakfast. I will show you the way."

They wasted more time arguing, Musa countering all her objections with calm, infuriating logic: "If you are stopped after curfew, you will be detained and miss your train. Your parents will be forced to leave without you." These last words defeated her; she had to concede there was no alternative. Through it all, Filip remained unaccountably silent.

They placed three chairs against the length of the narrow bed, pulling the mattress partly onto the seats, filling the gap with extra blankets. Galina lay down first, facing the wall, with Filip next to her and Musa on the chairs.

In the morning they took to the streets almost at a run, weaving among preoccupied people on their way to work or some equally pressing purpose. The train station turned out to be closer than Musa had suggested the night before.

"We could have left after dinner," Galina said. "Instead of worrying my parents and sleeping with that collaborator."

"Collaborator? You could call him that. More like an opportunist, I'd say. And what about your father, and all those Nazis coming to your apartment to pick up their pins and carved boxes?"

"How dare you! My father accepted their orders because he's a craftsman, and unlike our own people, those officers had money to spend. But he never served them breakfast or polished their boots. And he never told them anything."

"Don't be angry, Galya. I'm only saying he did business with the enemy, and took the food parcels they brought him while everyone else subsisted on rations. I never said he was a spy."

"Everyone else would have done the same, given the chance, and you know it. As if you ever turned down a bite of that extra food! And what about your work interpreting? What do you call that?"

"That was in a labor camp. I'm not much good at digging ditches or hauling rocks." He yawned. "That was the most uncomfortable night, but the food was good."

"I don't know why he was so generous. How well did you know him?"

"He's two or three years older. We met while buying stamps at a collectors' shop in town. Made some good trades, too. I don't know what came over him. Maybe he's homesick." He did not mention the hand resting on his waist, or the erection pressed against the back of his thigh, Musa whispering, "I know you're not asleep," his voice thick with wine. Filip first not breathing at all, then imitating the rhythm of deep slumber, until the older man's body went slack, his soft snoring hot on the back of Filip's neck. "Who knows why his colonel found him valuable enough to bring along? Forget him."

When they found the others, Galina broke down weeping into her father's arms. "*Nu, nu,*" he crooned, smoothing her hair. "Stop, now." Amid apologies and explanations, Ilya told them what he and Ksenia had learned.

"There are too many people. We are to leave our luggage here. Mama has the claim tickets. I've heard rumors that the Red Army is advancing, so they want to move us away from the border. Maybe they're afraid we'll join forces with our troops. I don't know."

"Where are we going?" Filip asked. "Must we leave everything here?"

"South and west." Ilya looked at his ticket. "Leipzig. Our things should be on the next train out."

"We are permitted to each take a small bundle or case," Ksenia added, spreading her hands apart to indicate the size. "No bigger than a woman's handbag."

They spent the next hour or so sorting through their belongings. All around them, clustered in tight family groups, people were doing the same, pulling on extra clothes, setting aside bulky items and household goods to reclaim later.

Ksenia focused on food supplies, tying a small article of clothing around each packet of rice, flour, and salt, finding room in her bundle to add two tin cups and some spoons. For Galina, she fashioned a flat backpack using a thin blanket rolled with underclothes and socks.

"*Ai*, Mama, I can hardly move," Galina complained. "I'm already wearing two dresses and a sweater under this coat."

Ksenia ignored her daughter's protests, crossed the ends of the blanket over Galina's shoulders, and tied them firmly in back. "Hush. Now sit here on this suitcase while we finish packing."

Filip refused to wear his second shirt. He wrapped it around his stamp albums, a notebook and pencils, and some photographs from home, jamming it all into the smallest suitcase they had. Ilya took only his workbox. "It may be bigger than a woman's handbag, but I'm not leaving it behind, not even for a day. I need my tools and materials. Where will I find ivory now?"

"Papa, do they hurt the elephants to get the ivory? How do they survive without their tusks?" Galina looked up from an open box filled with family memorabilia.

"No, *dochenka*, they harvest the tusks after the elephants die, or if they break them fighting with other males."

Galina nodded but thought, *How can you be sure?* "Can you fit these pictures into your box? There's your wedding photo, and Maksim, and you and me and Mama. And this—I really love these views." She handed him some photographs and a packet of souvenir postcards: Yalta, the Gem of the Black Sea.

They repacked their remaining things, making sure the identifying tags were clearly visible, then carried everything to the open area on the platform designated for luggage. The soldier on duty tossed their cases and baskets onto the growing pile, and shooed them away. "Your train leaves in an hour. Be ready," he growled.

Ready? Ready for what? Filip wondered. He was tired of this nomadic existence, his movements dictated by people who had not the slightest knowledge or interest in who he was or what he wanted, what he was capable of. He was ready to begin his own life, but when?

About midafternoon, the train pulled in. There were dark clouds in a sky the color of ashes. It snowed a little. Soldiers and civilians spilled out of dented passenger cars; the civilians formed into a mute line, waiting to have their papers checked and stamped. More soldiers appeared to unload the cargo wagons. The refugees watched them load large wooden crates marked with stenciled numerical codes onto waiting trucks and military vehicles. It all happened quickly, the men moving with grace and precision in virtual silence, like a latter-day ballet in combat boots.

"What do you think is inside?" Galina leaned heavily against Filip, tucking her hand under his arm. "Could it be food?" Last night's feast now seemed a distant memory. As if responding to her question, the baby tumbled inside her in a vigorous somersault. She bit her lip to keep from crying out.

"If so, it's not for us," he replied casually, not looking at her. "More likely ammunition or medical supplies or wine for the officers' table." He glanced at her then. "You look pale. Do you want to sit down?"

"I want a cup of tea, with sugar." She sighed.

Filip grunted at the impossibility of satisfying her yearning; she may as well have asked for claret with strawberries. But Ilya heard. He moved off quietly and soon returned, his hand covering a thick porcelain mug to keep the contents warm. "Drink it quickly, *dorogaya, my dear. I left a deposit for the cup.*" There was no sugar, but the weak brew was colored with a little milk, which tempered its bitterness, and she gratefully swallowed it.

A junior officer appeared, spoke a few words to the now idle soldiers, then turned to the mass of refugees. "You will now board the train," he commanded. "All of you." People looked at one another in confusion: *My ticket is for Frankfurt . . . Hamburg . . . Berlin—how can one train go in all directions at once?* "There has been a change of plan. Forget your tickets. You will all go to Plattling. Now *schnell,* hurry. Everyone on board. One parcel per person."

The soldiers moved to surround them, herding the throng past the passenger cars behind the steaming locomotive, toward the line of cargo wagons at the back of the train. "Not without Papa!" Galina shouted. She rose on her toes, craning her neck to find Ilya, who had gone to reclaim his deposit for the empty cup. "Mama, help me; we have to wait for him!" She clutched at Ksenia with one hand and held on to Filip with the other; together they formed a hard knot, struggling to hold their ground against the crowd surging and shoving all around.

"Not without Papa," she repeated, speaking directly into the face of a young soldier with short blond hair and a smooth chin. Their eyes locked. He was almost a schoolboy, surely still in his teens; she saw innocence there, and met it with her obstinate passion. The boy moved on, pressing the side of his rifle against a group of people bunched to their left.

By the time Ilya returned, most of the wagons were filled. The remaining crowd pressed toward the last one, a real passenger car, third class, with windows, benches along the walls, and doors at either end that opened out to a narrow railed platform. "No one sits! Children can stand on the benches. *Schnell, schnell,* everyone inside." The soldiers prodded at the backs of the heaving crowd, their shouts fueling the general panic.

Filip pushed forward using his suitcase as a wedge to maneuver through the crowd; the others followed closely in his wake. "You! That suitcase is too large. Give it to me." But Filip was already at the train, shoving the bag through the open window, where cooperative hands received it and passed it into the interior. "*Russische Idioten,*" the guard mumbled. "I'll be glad when you're all gone." Filip did not hear. He was working his way to the door, pulling Galina by the hand. Her scarf came loose, fluttered briefly above their heads, and fell to the ground, but he would not let her stoop to pick it up.

"It's the last car," he said urgently. "Stay with me, all of you." And then they were inside.

People tried to arrange themselves as best they could, but there were too many. Children wailed. Windows were quickly closed against the evening cold, and just as quickly reopened to let in some air. Packed one against the other, clutching their belongings, everyone grew quiet.

Still the train did not move. On the platform, the last of the refugees stood in a loose crowd. There was no more room, all the cars were packed beyond capacity. What would happen to them?

Then shouts: "All you men over here. Put your luggage down." The group of twenty or so men and boys disappeared around the side of the station. The women, left behind, stood in stunned silence, holding children by the hand. What now? What new indignity?

It was getting dark. Light snow was coating the heaped luggage with a sheen that glowed dimly in the pools of pale yellow light from the evenly spaced lampposts. Inside the wagon, it grew increasingly close, the air stale with unwashed skin and clothing, people pressed in so tightly that some slept, with no fear of falling down, their bundles and cases held firmly between their feet. "I can't breathe." Galina's face was drained of all color, her temples beaded with sweat. "Please . . ." She took large, yawning breaths. Her body trembled with a numbing fatigue. Unexpected tears trickled down her cheeks. Spots of light danced and flickered before her eyes.

"She needs air. Get her to the door, Filip," Ksenia instructed. "Nice people, please, let her through." Bit by bit, one tiny shuffling step at a time, Filip guided his wife toward the door at the back of the car. Some resisted, but most people tried to push even closer together in a slow undulation that gradually propelled the young couple to the edge of the throng.

Filip yanked at the door handle. *I could get shot for this.* The thought flitted across his mind, followed by another: *I could get shot for anything.* On the third try, with the effort of several hands, the door opened a crack.

Galina leaned her head against the door frame and let the air revive her, feeling the weakness ebb with every bracing gust. "Look," she said, peering through the crack to the outside.

Around a curve, the men and boys were returning, pushing a dusty-looking boxcar before them, its wheels creaking and grinding on the frigid tracks. Others had spotted the approaching wagon through the windows, giving rise to a chorus of speculation. "They really want us out of here." "We're already hours late." "You know the Germans and their schedules; lateness is a deadly sin."

A guard watched a few of the men hook the boxcar onto the end of the train. "This hitch is rusty," Galina heard one man say. "*Molchi,*" another growled. "Keep your mouth shut, or we'll be blamed for that, too."

Filip edged closer to the door, his voice a hoarse whisper. "What's the delay? We've been on this train for hours."

"Allied bombing to the west, I heard. Some track destroyed, fewer trains coming in. But they really want us gone. That's why we get to ride in this antique." The man outside inclined his head toward the now waiting boxcar.

"Must be why we're headed south, to Plattling," Filip mused. "Out of easy bomber range. The planes can't get there and back without refueling, maybe."

The boxcar filled up quickly, the last of the day's transport crammed into its windowless depths within minutes. Behind the mountain of luggage, new crowds of refugees were beginning to gather and mill about. *Exactly like us*, Filip observed. How many among them ready for a new life, now that returning to the old one was no longer possible? How many impatient to lead or even follow, using their abilities to transform a changing world, to heal the wounds inflicted by this endless war? How many artists, builders, writers, visionaries, scientists, who could have begun to make their contribution here, in this city, now, instead of being shunted to yet another place, guessing at a precarious future, their longing for stability once again postponed? *His* longing, *his* impatience to do something, to make a mark.

Instead, here they were on this train, again going who knows where to suffer whatever fresh travails were sure to be waiting there. The only certainty was the imminent birth of his and Galina's child, a thought that filled him with equal parts curiosity, bewilderment, and despair.

At least the train was moving now, after a long, deep tremor that rippled from car to car along its entire length, clouds of steam hissing in the night air, pluming backward as the engine pulled the train out of Dresden station.

The station clock read 10:10, Filip noted as they rolled by. He pulled the door open wider, stepped out onto the car's narrow platform, turning to help Galina follow. She leaned into the railing, holding on with one hand while pushing the hair out of her eyes with the other. "I wish I hadn't lost my scarf. Who knows when I'll get another."

"We'll find you a scarf. Germany is full of scarves."

"Just make sure it's blue, or has blue in it." She smiled.

But Filip was not smiling. He stared, open-mouthed, at the dark cloud-filled sky. "Hush," he said, as if any noise they could make would matter. "Bombers." He grasped her arm firmly and pulled her back against the wagon.

Then she heard the engines, and those inside the wagon heard, too, shouting in useless fearful commotion. Whatever happened, there was nowhere to go. The airplanes descended in a sweeping arc and began raining green flares onto the city, followed by the white flash of incendiary bombs, which burst everywhere into seething balls of blinding flame.

"Filip, the station! The railroad station is on fire! *Bozhe moi*, my God! All those people!" Galina screamed, her eyes wild with the horror of it.

"Hold on to the railing," Filip yelled in her ear. "I'll try to get us back inside the car." He tugged at the door with frantic urgency, but the crush of bodies against it was too great. It would not budge.

Absurdly, with an incongruity born of panic, his mind conjured an image of the chocolate bonbon rolling on Musa's tablecloth. *I should have eaten it.* It was a random, unbidden thought, baffling in its stupidity. He moved his head from side to side, as if to shake the nonsense out and return to the madness of reality.

The train picked up velocity, leaning into the incline leading out of the city as the next wave of bombers appeared in the west. With a sickening piercing metallic groan, the rusty hitch holding the boxcar onto the end of the train gave way. "*Ai, ai*, no, no!" Galina sobbed, letting go of the railing, reaching out as if to pull the loose car back with her own hands. From behind, Filip grasped her by the shoulders and held her tight against himself, while the train sped swaying into the night and the boxcar packed with desperate people rolled back into the flaming station, their screams rising like a lurid operatic chorus between the circling planes discharging their cargo of death and the infernal scene below.

"The animals . . . the zoo," Galina whispered. "Who will unchain the elephants?"

8

NO ONE SPOKE about Dresden. Not one person mentioned the things they had lost, though each still clearly saw the mountain of luggage consumed by flames, and pictured the ashes of their belongings fanning out over the ruined city, everything only so recently held to be precious or necessary to life now rendered frivolous, the remnants buried like ancient artifacts under the rubble of the train station.

Who could imagine the mayhem, people incinerated in their beds, or running, hair and clothing ablaze, while buildings crumbled like broken toys, the insatiable inferno engulfing everything in a wall of flame, sucking the air out of cellars, leaving those who sheltered there to die of suffocation? From the train now headed for undisclosed reasons to Plattling, they saw other fires along the way, burning in the distance, each a marker of death and destruction.

Dawn came slowly, a thin pearly light penetrating the edges of the eastern sky. Filip and Galina, now back inside the wagon with the others, watched the night lift away; a cold, mirthless sun pierced the shifting clouds. Villages half-concealed in swirls of soot and smoke flashed by the windows. People moved in the landscape as if under water, their gestures and poses arrested in gruesome tableaux by the motion of the train: several children huddled under a leafless tree near a farmhouse reduced to its doorframe and chimney, a bull, hindquarters crushed and bleeding, lowing in useless rage. Now and then, a house went by intact, as if protected by an unseen hand in a random act of mercy.

The morning of the third day, the train stopped within view of a demolished farmhouse. The refugees were, for the most part, alive. In the crush of bodies packed into the wagons, the dead could not fall down; their numbers would not be known until the doors were opened and people began to descend to the ground. Ahead, near the front of the train, rows of men were being marched forward to clear what looked like an obstruction on the tracks.

Filip was the last left on board. Squatting to tie his shoelace, he heard two guards from the other cars join the one standing at the steps. "How many dead?" one asked, his tone expressionless, as if inquiring about the weather.

"Three. No, four."

"Six in mine. I have the cattle car. One of them a boy, maybe ten years old. My son's age."

"Old enough to throw a grenade. Don't get soft, Corporal."

"What's their status? Any new orders?" The corporal stamped his feet. "Damn, it's cold."

"No orders. They're not DPs yet, just refugees with no camp assignment. The war's not over; we're still in charge. They'll want to keep the men separate, under closer guard so they don't join the Reds. But it's not our problem. We only have to get them to Plattling." Filip heard the officer pull on his cigarette, inhaled with longing the aromatic smoke drifting through the open door.

So that's it, he thought. *DPs. Displaced persons. That's who we are now, or nearly. But under whose protection?* Eavesdropping would get him killed, whether they knew he understood or not.

"Have them bring all the dead over here," the officer said, and the group moved off.

Filip waited to be sure, then stretched his muscles and slipped off the train just as a half dozen men were being deployed, under guard, to find anything suitable for a latrine. They came back with animal feeding troughs, bits of straw sticking out of the cracks between the weathered boards.

"*Ja,*" the ranking officer nodded. "This will do. Good enough. We have no time to dig trenches." Although time, it seemed to everyone, was one thing of which they had more than enough.

"What's that? Pig troughs? Perfect," another added.

"Now," the commander resumed. "Men here, women over there. Do your business, and be quick."

No one moved. As soon as their feet hit the ground, they had all stooped to scoop handfuls of snow, shoving it in their mouths to slake the thirst more unbearable than hunger. Some had used snow to wash their faces, smearing the grime and soot over parched yellow skin, wiping away the frost with their coat sleeves. Now, they stood shivering, exchanging puzzled, bewildered glances. Even in the worst of the labor camps, there had been real latrines, however primitive. This was too degrading to believe.

"What? You think I can't smell you? You couldn't wait. Now get to it, like the animals you are."

Slowly, the people moved toward the troughs, the men standing shoulder to shoulder, pissing like schoolboys, urine oozing through the cracks, staining the snow in bright patches that steamed briefly, then rapidly froze.

The women shielded each other with their coats and skirts, taking turns a few at a time until the officer shouted, "Faster! *Schnell!* We can't be here all day."

Ksenia spoke up then, mixing Russian words with her poor German. She faced the officer squarely. "We are not animals. We are women. Look, the ones who are finished can cover the others. Soon all will be done."

"What do you think this is? Intermission at the Bolshoi Ballet?" He shoved her in the shoulder with the butt of his pistol. She staggered but did not fall. "Who told you you could talk to me?"

Ilya came to stand next to his wife. "Are we prisoners, then? We came to Dresden on our own. We paid for our tickets with our own money."

"Your own money. Ha! Look, grandpa, as long as you wear this"—he poked a gloved finger, hard, at what remained of the OST patch on Ilya's lapel, a fraying shadow outlined with a few loose threads—"you are *guests* in my country, and you will do what I say." He waved an arm at the pile of corpses near the tracks. "You see those? It would cost me nothing—*nothing*—to add you and your Frau to their number." He pushed them together so their heads lined up, one behind the other. "One bullet."

Galina saw her parents' hands grope instinctively for one another and clasp each other behind the folds of their coats. A tremor rippled across her father's face; her mother stood pale, stony-faced, revealing nothing. Galina broke away from the milling crowd, brushed off Filip's restraining hand. "No!" she screamed. "Mama, Papa! No!"

The officer spun around, raised the pistol over his head, and fired into the air, laughing. "You men—you and you and you two and of course you, *Großvater*," he shouted, pointing at Ilya. "Take these shovels and dig a hole, over there, away from the tracks, for these." He pointed at the corpses with the tip of his boot. "You, *Mutti*, and your brave daughter, strip them. I want all the clothes folded, shoes on top, rings and jewelry inside the shoes. Their papers you will give to me. The rest of you, fill these stinking troughs with snow. Nobody wants to see your shit." When they hesitated, looking around for more shovels, he yelled, "What? You have hands. And five minutes."

It was hard work. Some of the corpses were, like them, wearing several layers of clothes. Galina's fingers trembled, fumbling with icy buttons, tugging at sleeves encasing unyielding arms. "Don't you cry," Ksenia mumbled. "Don't you dare cry. Empty your mind, or say a prayer." They worked quickly, adding to the growing pile of skirts, trousers, sweaters, coats, shirts, dresses, laying children's clothes on top, along with caps and scarves, tossing wedding rings and earrings into a shoe. Neither said another word.

When they were finished, Ksenia walked the shaking Galina to a tree, holding her while she retched, doubled over, wiping the thin stream of greenish slime from the corner of her mouth. Just then the child moved and Galina groaned, both hands on her belly; a bit of color returned to her pallid cheeks. *Thank God*, Ksenia thought. *At least this one is still alive.*

The others scrambled, picking up snow and frigid mud with numbed hands, snow that melted as soon as it hit the reeking, steaming mess; but they kept at it until the ground within a few yards was bare and the troughs filled to overflowing, a light carapace of ice forming over the cooled surface.

The men digging the grave hacked at the frozen ground, making little headway. They were at some distance from the others, with a single guard a few feet away. "There are only six of them," someone said quietly, "and many of us."

"So? We have shovels. They have guns. Even if we get their weapons, where will we go?"

"Anywhere. But the women, the children . . ."

"That's the problem. Best to wait. Something seems different, as if they've lost direction, or the will to fight. They could have shot us," Ilya said, "but they didn't."

It proved impossible to work the frozen earth, even with a pickax; the time required was more than the transport could finally afford to take. Already, they could see people in the forward wagons returning to their places, the signal to resume the journey shouted down along the length of the train. The bodies were left in the shallow trench, covered with bare twigs and heaped with snow. Ilya, working rapidly with a bit of wire, fashioned a rough cross and laid it on top.

Back on the train, the refugees gathered up their things and arranged themselves for the rest of the trip. The transport stopped several more times in the next few days, but everyone was ordered to stay on board.

Some had managed to fill whatever cup or vessel they had with snow, against the implacable thirst; there was no food. Only now, there was a little more room.

Fresh troops were waiting at Plattling, with a convoy of open-bed trucks lined up along the road leading away from the station. Two men took up positions at each wagon door; no one could disembark until given permission. Inside, the people waited, as they had for the end less hours of what should have been a short journey, through detours, rerouting, and many unexplained delays, the train standing idle in open country for hours at a time. After nearly a week on board, they were hungry, filthy, dispirited, and crazed with thirst.

The jolt of the stop woke Galina. She was wedged between Filip and Ksenia, the curve of her stomach pressed against her mother's back, one hand resting on Ksenia's shoulder.

"I was dreaming," she said. "Mama, you had given me some cloth scraps—I recognized one from a dress you made for me when I was little, white with red dots. I loved that dress." Her voice took on a dreamy storytelling cadence. "My doll Masha lay naked on the table, arms at her sides, her blue eyes closed. I was sewing her a dress with my shiny new needle, singing a little song. I was so happy.

"May there always be blue skies, may there always be sunshine. May there always be Mama, may there always be me." She sang in a melodious whisper, raising her chin a little, oblivious to the curious glances from those who overheard.

Ksenia bowed her head. Was it possible Galina had forgotten? Had her mind erased the harrowing details of their ordeal so completely that all she was left with was this innocent child's version? *Lord have mercy. Gospodi pomiluy,* she thought, reaching up to squeeze her daughter's hand. *May you never remember.*

Each car was emptied with model efficiency, the local police working with the soldiers, forming men and teenaged boys into an orderly line and loading them onto the waiting trucks.

The trucks began to move. The women pulled their children closer, buzzing with consternation. Armed guards prevented them from running alongside the convoy but could not keep them from calling out to the departing husbands and brothers, fathers and friends. "Stay strong." "Don't despair." Alyosha, Nikola, Andrei, Sashok.

"Send word, Ilya." Ksenia's voice rose above the others. "I will find you."

They watched the last of the trucks disappear down the road, then turned as one to face the soldiers and police. "Why have you taken them? Where are they going? What happens to us?" they demanded.

"You? March. Single file. Hold your *Kinder* by the hand. Any child who runs will be shot."

PART V

The Women

1

THEIR DESTINATION WAS a deserted summer camp. No military barracks, just several rustic dormitories and a roofed open-sided dining pavilion. The lavatory had a dozen sinks against one wall, several open showers, and a huge oblong bathtub against the other.

Galina could easily imagine this tub filled with squealing, happy children getting washed in batches of ten or twelve, their bodies slick with soap, their heads full of impressions from a day at the lake, the woods, or a farm visit. Soap! What a luxury that was. Would she ever be clean again? How long would it take to scrub away the grayish tint from her skin, or to lose the stale odor that, like a badge of their lowly status, they hardly even noticed on each other?

The overseer noticed, and ordered an immediate disinfection. "Strip, before you carry your lice and filth into our bedding. Put your clothes in the bathtub. Everything," she shouted at the women reluctant to remove their undergarments.

They showered several at a time, scouring their bodies with harsh brown laundry soap that left their skin dry as sandpaper, with raw red patches in the crooks of their elbows, behind the knees, under their breasts, between their thighs. Still wet, they were led from the lavatory across the compound to the infirmary, prevented from concealing their nakedness or sheltering the youngest among them by walking single file, the February wind biting at their skin. All the camp guards, including the women, turned out to see the parade, some hooting or whistling or making crude remarks, others watching in enigmatic silence.

A thin, impassive barber shaved their heads. An emaciated woman of indeterminate age swept the falling hair into sacks; her shabby dress and weary expression suggested she was an inmate like themselves. "They say the hair is disinfected and sold to wig makers," she told them later, her own head covered with a blue-and-white-striped rag tied at the nape of her neck. "Nothing is wasted here."

One by one, the women were admitted into the "treatment room," where a doctor examined them and doused them with disinfectant. Those waiting were silent. All their questions had been ignored. No one knew where the men had been taken, or why. They were still completely at their captors' mercy. There was nothing to say.

The women came out, each one's head yellow with a foul-smelling liquid, each clenching her teeth at the stinging pain of the cuts and scrapes on her freshly shaved scalp and pubis. Some had tear-stained faces; some looked enraged or strangely relieved. Some were in the room longer than others.

When a girl of twelve or thirteen went in, hunched over as if trying to conceal her newly formed breasts, hands cupped in front of her groin in a touching display of modesty, a collective sigh went through the crowd, more eloquent than any words of warning or encouragement. The doctor kept her at least a quarter of an hour. When she emerged, hands at her sides, her face flushed but stony, she, like the others, said nothing. An older woman who stepped out of the line, reached for the child, and spoke her name, received a sharp reprimand and a baton blow across her back, which sent her gasping against the wall. The girl looked at her, then turned away. She went to stand with the "clean" women, waiting with them for whatever came next.

The two in the group who were clearly pregnant gravitated toward each other almost in spite of themselves, as if their nudity exposed more than they might otherwise choose to reveal.

"Galya, from Yalta," Galina said when they found themselves next to one another.

"Marfa, Korovkino. It's near Odessa," the other replied. They looked at each other knowingly, nodded, and smiled.

Later, dressed in their fumigated clothing, which stank strongly of rotten eggs and harshly of ammonia, they sat together on a bench in the dining pavilion, watching the sun sink through the trees. Galina spoke first. "Did he pinch . . . ?"

"Pinch and slap," Marfa confirmed.

"And stroke . . . ?" Galina touched her breast.

"Oh, yes."

"That disinfectant." Both women shuddered, each feeling again the doctor's brush paint their stubbled heads, linger over their private parts longer than necessary, the putrid substance spreading in a stinging yellow stain over their tender skin.

"And the worst part . . ." Marfa looked away.

"'Bend over,'" they said in unison, not daring to look at each other, as if to do so would somehow make them complicit in their own ordeal. The coarse, thickly gloved fingers probing in merciless glee for no good reason except humiliation. It was unspeakable, but they knew no woman in the camp was likely to have escaped that same violation.

"I went in after you," Galina broke the silence that had fallen between them. "Do you know what he said? 'Another pregnant cow.' He looked so disgusted I didn't know whether to laugh or spit in his face."

"What nerve." Marfa pulled at her sweater, which had shrunk in the disinfection, the sleeves now hugging her arms just below the elbows. "And him with those hairs in his ears, like big furry spiders, and that black caterpillar eyebrow across his face. Maybe he fell from the sky, or came out of some hole in the ground. I can't imagine any woman giving birth to such an *urod*. What a freak." They both laughed, and then talked of other things.

2

WHEN IT WAS OVER, when the hot waves had finally stopped ravaging her body, Galina had looked at the attending nurse, her eyes clouded with indelible knowledge. *Is this the secret?* she'd thought. *This thing that only women know, this ripping for which there is no preparation, every fear of which is completely justified? Does every life claw its way toward the light this way? And why?*

The German nurse had held out a squalling red-skinned bundle. "Your daughter," she'd said, all business. "Her name?"

"Katya. Katyusha. Ekaterina for the birth certificate," Galina had immediately replied. Out of nowhere, a scrap of song had echoed in her head. *Katyusha, who walks along the riverbank, sending her message of love and remembrance to her soldier, her sweetheart; she will guard their love while he defends their country. Katyusha.*

"Good." The nurse had nodded as if her approval were needed. "Take the child, please. I must fill out the forms."

"Give her to my mother," Galina had sighed in profound exhaustion.

Ksenia had taken the infant and walked up to the bedside. "No. She is your child. She needs you."

"Oh, Mama. I only want to sleep," Galina had protested. "I am so, so tired. Put her in the basket, then. I will hold her when I wake up." She'd started to turn on her side, away from the early spring light filtering through the filmy curtain covering the ward's single small window.

Ksenia had been adamant. "You must feed her, or she will die. Then you can sleep."

Galina had taken the child, winced when the prehensile mouth attached to her breast and began to suck. She'd examined the strange face with equanimity—the eyes squinted shut, the barely there nose, a fuzz of dark hair haloing the head, a thread of vein throbbing across the skull. *A piglet*, she'd thought. *She looks like nothing if not a piglet.*

She had felt a stirring of affection at the comparison. Vague scenes, impressions, really, from her early childhood floated up: a wooden three-room *izba* in the country, chickens roosting under the eaves, a pig in a fenced enclosure, the smell of earth, hay, manure, and flowers in bloom blending into an unforgettable rustic perfume. She'd felt overwhelmed with nostalgia for this uncomplicated happiness. Would there ever be anything as good as this remembered life, this life before famine, before city tenements, before fear?

Galina had felt her mother's hand on her arm, looked up as Ksenia wiped away the tears she had not been aware of with a corner of the sheet. "Now the other breast," Ksenia had said softly. "Then you both can sleep."

Galina had switched the infant to the other side, detaching the pink mouth with an instinctive pinch of her fingers against her breast, surprising herself with her grasp of this bit of primal knowledge. "*Kto t'y?* Who are you?" she'd said out loud, watching the child ease into her rhythm, walnut-sized fists clenched as if ready for battle.

"*Bist du* . . ." The evening nurse said something Galina did not understand. Are you comfortable? Well? Warm? The nurse smiled vaguely and settled the freshly bathed, diapered, and swaddled infant in Galina's arms. "She is hungry now, then sleep. For you, too." That was clear enough. Again, she used the informal *du* form, addressing the young mother as if she were a child or a servant or a member of the family, though she herself was only a few years older.

Was it just women's solidarity, a tacit admission into the universal club of mothers? Galina thought she'd heard an underlying hint of superiority, a touch of derision, but could not be sure. The four other women in the half-filled ward spoke easily among themselves, ignoring the Russian stranger in their midst, admiring each other's babies, their bright laughter impermeable as a wall of stone.

She wondered where they would be going, these women, in a few days. She imagined their homes, kitchens stocked with household necessities, parlors, no matter how small, filled with furniture. Pictures on the walls, figurines on a shelf, maybe a rug on the floor. Bedrooms with blankets and pillows. Doors between rooms, to open or close. Windows giving a view onto dormant gardens ready to receive the seeds of a new harvest, waiting for spring flowers. *Flowers don't recognize war*, she thought. *Give them rain and sun, and they bloom.*

She wanted to ask the women: Where will your baby sleep when you go home? Is there a crib, a soft embroidered coverlet, fresh diapers, little shirts and gowns and slippers? Toys? But no one looked at her, and anyway, she didn't have the words.

Galina looked at her baby's tiny face, its tightly shut eyes, the lips nearly translucent with the effort of sucking. Single-minded—or no, not minded at all, she realized, just surrendering with a ferocious tenacity to the instinctive act that made the difference between tentative life and certain death.

Soon Mama will come, she thought, *and we can talk about what to do.* Maybe she would have answers to some of the questions that continued to plague Galina, even in her sleep. *Where can I live with my baby? How can I work to keep us alive? Where are Papa and Filip?*

Galina rested her head on the pillow, her mind thick with drowsiness but crowded with recollections. She could still hear the clattering train packed with human cargo, its whistle stilled by wartime regulations, speeding into the abyss of a night made darker by the glow of Dresden burning behind them. The puzzling journey, marked by unexplained delays, the train stopped for hours between stations without food or water, and only the heat of their massed bodies to keep them from freezing. The persistent glimmer of hope, unredeemed by any reasonable evidence, that somehow the worst was now behind them. They had lived through internment in a succession of labor camps, endured myriad humiliations; they had wandered blindly in a hostile, unfamiliar land as vagrants and, occasionally, thieves. They had lost nearly all their pitiful possessions.

And then Plattling, in a dawn light colorless as melting snow, where they were greeted with new orders barked in hoarse voices. Why had the men been taken away? Were they alive? How could she and her mother find them?

In the women's camp, no one had known what was happening. They could feel a gradual slackening of discipline. Not compassion for their sorry plight, no, but a loss of focus, as if their captors had lost interest in the game, no longer cared about maintaining the daily regimen of meaningless tasks and duties. One day, with no explanation, the sentries had been removed, the gates opened. Go.

Was it over? Rumors flew, colliding, multiplying, dissolving into the charged air of speculation. The Red Army, advancing from the east, bent on extracting bloody vengeance on the German nation, was to be feared; those who had fled their homeland could expect no mercy from the Soviets, no matter what the level of abuse they had already endured. Hitler was dead. No, he was in hiding, or traveling in secret to Paris, gathering his forces for one last decisive battle, still obsessed with proving the truth of his insane ideas. The women did not know what to believe.

They had set out on foot, as before, a loose band held together by a common purpose: to find their men and, somehow, to live. Someone had heard of a high-level meeting—America's Roosevelt, Britain's Churchill, and the despised Stalin segmenting Germany like an orange, creating zones of influence and administration while they began to dismantle the Nazi regime. It was up to them now, the women, to discover where these zones lay, and to determine where they might be safe.

When Galina's pregnancy was near term, she and her mother had first heard the word *asylum*. It was balm to their dispirited souls, a source of strength they could draw on to dispel the perpetual weariness with which they moved their feet along the road. Keeping the Danube on their right, they tramped ever south, scavenging or begging for food and shelter from the chilly spring nights, their efforts met with hostility or indifference as often as with acts of ordinary kindness. Bread. A boiled potato. A cup of milk.

Little by little, in ones and twos, the other women fell away, each following her own path, whether by guesswork or calculation, to the rest of her life. By the time they reached the outskirts of Regensburg, they were alone. It was time to stop for the birth of the child.

Ksenia found work in a beer hall kitchen, scrubbing pots and washing dishes. "My daughter, she can also help in the kitchen," she ventured cautiously, eyes lowered, knowing she might compromise her own job by asking for more.

"We have enough cooks now," the beer hall woman, middle-aged, red faced, her complexion chapped by a chronic skin condition, snapped. "She can clean the guest rooms and help with the laundry. One meal a day, no pay, and she can share your room until the baby comes. Then, *raus*. No screaming baby in my house."

The room was an unheated garret space with sloping walls that revealed rough aged roof beams. The women took turns sleeping on the narrow cot, using their coats on top of their own thin blanket for warmth. It was more than acceptable. They had shelter and food, and work, not charity. They were in a town filled with activity, people coming and going, busy rebuilding their world, trading information. And they were near the hospital.

*

"*Bist du . . . ?*" The nurse repeated her question, to which Galina, still uncomprehending, offered a puzzled smile. The nurse turned on her heel and walked away.

"*Du. Ty*, as we say," Ksenia, who had just arrived, echoed. She sat down on a straight-backed wooden chair near the bed. "Such a simple word. And yet . . ."

Galina passed a finger over the baby's downy head, as if exploring a curious new object. "We're less than nobody here. Did you think they would address us any other way? *Vy* or *Sie*, as if we were respectable strangers? Why do you bring it up?"

"Because it's changing. After the revolution, anyone could approach you on the street and address you rudely, the way landowners once spoke to their serfs of any age as if they were children." She took a pair of knitting needles from her cloth satchel, the wood rubbed to a dark sheen by years of handling. "But there's more to it than that."

"What are you talking about?" Galina yawned. *Who cares?* she almost said. *We have more urgent things to worry about.*

Ksenia picked up her knitting, winding the pumpkin-colored yarn around her fingers to even out the tension, working the little sweater sideways, all in one piece. "When I was a young woman," she began, in a tone that promised a story, her voice soft, as if eroded around the edges by the passage of time, taking her back to the clear center of a reminiscence. "I was only a few years married. Your brother was a baby, not two years old, and you were not yet born. We lived in Simferopol, where your father worked as a clerk in a shipping office and practiced his craft at every opportunity. If he had a day or two free from his job, he traveled to nearby towns, following the mountain tourist trade, selling his pins and carvings. He made a decent living, and I was busy with the house—the garden, the hens, my little child."

"I wish we had a better color for Katyusha's first sweater," Galina interrupted.

"We use what we have, my dear. It's soft and clean, and I'm grateful to Frau Herzen for giving me her old vest to rework, and for allowing me to rent her room. She is a good woman, gruff but not unkind. Just today she told me of a room nearby for you and Katya. She agreed to pay you a little for working mornings while I watch the baby."

"Oh, Mama. Thank you." Galina sighed, her body relaxed as if eased of a crushing burden; the worry lines around her mouth smoothed out. "Thank you." She looked up with renewed attention, captivated by her mother's narrative in spite of herself, caught up in the description of bygone times. "Weren't you lonely then, with Papa away?"

Ksenia picked up the thread of her story. "Sometimes, yes, I may have been lonely. Maybe so. I did not think about my life that way. We were young; so much had happened. Your father had suffered gas poisoning in the war, so we had made our way south, for the mild climate and healing waters."

"And the revolution? That had just happened?"

"Yes. Who knew what would come next? We wanted no part of it, just wanted to live in peace. Bolsheviks, Mensheviks, they were all scoundrels, angling for power, using the people's suffering as a way to advance their own ambitions. We just wanted to live, and to worship in freedom."

Galina began to see where this was going. She didn't remember those early years, before Stalin ordered most churches closed and services outlawed. Her parents had refused to participate, would not join the Communist Party, and had paid for that decision: precarious employment, sporadic pay, lower food and clothing rations—these were part of the cost of standing with their beliefs. But if there was a church, they found it, and the icons in their own home had always remained defiantly on view.

Katyusha finished nursing and slept. Galina settled the baby in her basket and laid her own head back against the pillow. "What does all this have to do with *t'y* and *v'y*?" she asked. "We were talking about forms of address and how conventions were changing."

"I remember. How impatient you are! A few years before, when we wanted to marry, we lived in Kostroma. It was too far north; we

needed to be closer to the sanatoriums where your father could begin
treatment for his condition. We had filed our civil marriage papers
already, but it was unthinkable to travel together unless we were man
and wife in the eyes of the Church. Do you see?"

No, Galina thought, but kept silent.

"My Ilya went to see Father Matvei, the new priest assigned to
the one church left open in our part of the city. It was early spring,
I remember, but still cold, with snow on the ground.

"'You must wait another month,' the priest said. 'It is Lent now;
no weddings are permitted without dispensation from the bishop.' He
was our age, recently ordained and married according to our Orthodox
rules; his *matushka* was expecting their first child.

"'Even now, in these times?' Ilya protested.

"'Especially now. If we let ourselves stray from the right path,
ignore the laws set down by our holy fathers, then we are no different from the atheists.'

"Then your father did the unthinkable: he told a lie. 'Father Matvei,'
he said. 'We are believers, Ksenia and I. We live by Church law as
much as we can. But, you see, it is important to Ksenia that we marry
now.' And he cast his eyes down, unable, as he told me later, to continue in his deception. Clearly, he did not think he could convince the
priest that our immediate need to travel together was enough reason
to bend the rules.

"'Have you two sinned?' The young priest sighed. 'Well then, I'll
see what I can do.' In truth, we had only allowed ourselves the briefest
of intimacies—a chaste kiss, a quick embrace—but Ilya admitted to
me that he was not free of lustful thoughts and that, too, was a sin,
if only of a lower order. So we were married, with my brother and
his wife as witnesses."

Galina stretched, her fingers loosely curled, arms resting on the pillow behind her head as if in imitation of her daughter's sleeping pose.
She smiled to herself at having used the same excuse to expedite her
own marriage, the stranger on a Yalta street using almost exactly the

same words—*Have you two sinned?*—before accepting their bribe. But her mother did not need to know. "I just can't imagine you or Papa telling a lie, for any reason," she said instead.

"Was it really a lie? Perhaps in the strictest sense. It was a bad time, civil war. And he was sick, my Ilya. I was afraid that if we parted, if one of us went on ahead, we might not see each other again. We were in love." Ksenia put down her knitting to unwind some more yarn for the baby's sweater.

"But you wouldn't travel together unless you were married? What difference could that have made to anyone?"

"It made a difference to me. As it was, I suffered over the suggestion of impropriety. I worried that Father Matvei assumed I had lapsed into irreparable sin, like so many others had done."

"Oh, Mama. Even Mary Magdalene was forgiven, wasn't she? Besides, you were leaving the area. You wouldn't see this priest again."

"So I thought." Ksenia took up her needles and resumed knitting, the little garment taking shape beneath her fingers. "So I thought."

"Tell me then, before Katyusha wakes up. I need a nap, too."

"We had settled in Kislovodsk. The air was pure, the sun warm, the water rich with healing minerals. Your father's health had improved. Things had settled down somewhat. Life was tolerable. The years of famine and terror were still to come. We found a little house with a garden, fruit trees—plums, cherries, figs. Your brother was nearly two. I was happy. The only thing missing was a church."

"Then Father Matvei turned up?" Galina prompted, eager to move the story along.

"Yes. A woman told me about a basement meeting place where a priest, newly arrived from the north, held services. I took little Maksim and went. It was such a relief to have him properly baptized!"

"Did the priest remember you?"

"Oh, yes. And Ilya, too. Given a choice, we might have gone to worship elsewhere, but there was nowhere to go." She paused. "And he was a righteous man, Father Matvei, an attentive shepherd. He took his calling to heart, at a time when practicing it put him in grave danger. There was no mediocrity in the priesthood then, only devoted servants of the Lord or Communist spies. Nothing in between."

"What did he look like?"

"What a question! He looked like a priest. Thin, with long reddish hair and beard. He did have unusual eyes, gentle and dreamy, as if he saw things closed to the rest of us. When he prayed with us, we felt comforted, uplifted, and safe."

Something happened, or you wouldn't be telling me this, Galina thought. She turned on her side, facing her mother, one hand tucked under her cheek. The baby whimpered. "*Sha,* little one. Sleep," she whispered, rocking the basket with her other hand.

"After mass a few of us women would stay. Father Matvei talked to us, explaining the finer points of the day's scripture reading. He was educated; we knew he read Hebrew and Greek and was well versed in the writings of eminent scholars. But he carried his knowledge lightly, giving us lessons we could take with us, to fortify us for the hard times."

"What lessons?"

"Humility. Charity. Compassion. Love. But also resistance to evil. He admonished us to refrain from *kleveta*—gossip, renunciation of our neighbors."

"And that was dangerous! It still is."

"Yes. One day he approached me after the others had gone. It was my turn to wipe down the icons and sweep the floor.

"'Ksenia.' There was something sad and tender about the way he spoke my name; it thrilled and alarmed me. 'They will come for me soon.' I put the broom down and looked at him. 'Surely not. You are a good—' but he cut me off.

"'The woman who stands near the door, you have noticed her? She does not sing the Lord's Prayer with us, and never takes Communion.'

"'The one who does not cross herself? We thought she was just ignorant of our customs. But she stays for your talks, and asks many questions.'

"He nodded. 'I am not afraid. I'm doing the work I was meant to do. But before I go . . .' He stopped speaking and closed his eyes. I felt a chill of apprehension; I had never seen him so agitated. When he opened his eyes, they seemed to glow with a dark light, like a fire he was struggling to keep under control. We were completely alone in the basement of an empty building. Surely he didn't think I was, I could be . . . no." Ksenia stopped, her face a mask of pain at the vivid recollection.

"Oh, Mama." Galina said, her eyes wide. "You trusted him. How could he take advantage of you that way? Like a common—"

"Wait," Ksenia resumed. "Let me finish. I found the strength to challenge him, young as I was. Hadn't we all been trained to guard our virtue, as girls growing up in Tsarist times? 'You think I was compromised before my wedding,' I said, looking right at him. 'But it is not true. Ilya is an honorable man. I was untouched.' His already pale face blanched completely, then reddened in mottled patches that bloomed on his cheeks like fever. He raised both hands in denial.

"'No. No! Your husband spoke in a vague way. He never said . . . and it was not my place to draw conclusions. It's just—' he raked a hand through his hair.

"'But that is what you did. Draw conclusions.'

"'Ksenia. I am a man of God, bound by my own marriage vows. But I am still a man. I cherish your presence, admire your beauty.'

"'I am not beautiful,' I interrupted. 'I have never been beautiful. I am plain as a clay pot.'" Ksenia pulled, with a rueful expression, at her thin, cropped hair, now dishwater gray, tucked behind large ears, which framed her round face. It was a face that spoke of Ukrainian peasant roots, with a hint of high cheekbones and a barely noticeable slant to her gray eyes suggesting a mixing, generations ago, with Tatar blood. "My nose is like a potato, my eyes are too close together, my teeth uneven."

"You look beautiful to me," Galina protested.

"So he said, too. 'When I look at you, I see your fortitude and the sweetness of your character, the kindness in your eyes. I see how tenderly you care for little Maksim, how conscientiously you carry your work burden.'

"I shook my head, refusing to accept this embarrassment of praise. 'We are all strong, we women. We love our children. We do our work.'

"His voice dropped to nearly a whisper. 'Love is a mystery God has not given us the power to understand. I ask nothing improper of you. I only ask, Ksenia, say *t'y* to me. Just once.' I was struck dumb. It was the last thing I could have imagined, the most unlikely request he could have made.

"'I? To you?' I finally stammered. '*Vam?*' I was careful to say, formally, not daring to lapse into the familiar for even a moment. 'That can never be. Never. You are my confessor, the keeper of my soul. Your ordained hands perform the holy sacraments. You have knowledge and profound understanding of the scriptures that we ordinary people can never achieve.'

"'Ksenia—' he started to say, but I would hear no more.

"'Father Matvei, if I did as you ask, if I dared address you in this way, even once, it would be an unforgiveable transgression. To elevate myself to your level, or bring you down to mine, would be a vulgar vanity. Please forgive me.'"

Galina covered her mouth, trying to stifle the yawn that would no longer be suppressed. *Is that all?* she wanted to say. *Are we not all equal before God? Only you would make so much of this chastity of spirit, this earthly protocol.* "Were you tempted, though?" she asked instead.

Ksenia looked out the window at the barren yard, her knitting loose in her lap. A pair of trees swayed almost imperceptibly in the faint breeze, their bare limbs studded with buds, refusing to be fooled by the caressing sun into untimely bloom. Birds flitted about, engaged in the urgent business of their own survival. Finally, she spoke.

"There was an instant, when we parted, of hesitation. Later, sleepless, I thought, *Why not? What difference would it make to anyone if I did this simple, harmless thing that might touch a man's troubled soul with a spark of joy?* I knew his *matushka*, of course, the small kerchiefed priest's wife who sang the responses and read the prayers during services, but I knew nothing about his life."

She picked up the knitting and worked a few stitches, then put it down again, stroking the half-finished garment with the palm of her hand. "But it does matter. We are not all the same. Even with the new forms of address—comrade this and citizen that—some get more than others: better apartments, more rations, travel permits. If we give in, if we strip away all the conventions of order and respect, then they, the Communists, will have defeated us. We will be nothing but cogs in their new social order, keeping the machinery working for the benefit of a few thugs at the top. We'll be a nation of serfs again, faceless, nameless, and poor."

She worked to the end of the row, turned the piece, and gave a quiet, bemused laugh. "What am I saying? I care nothing for politics. These thoughts came to me later, after Father Matvei was gone. They did come for him, within the week. He had not asked me to commit a political act, to play along with the new fashion of equalization. He wanted a moment of intimacy, a clean, brief heart-to-heart connection. *Ty.* Such a simple word, meaning nothing and everything. I could not do it, Galya. Not then, and probably not now. Do you see?"

Galina, her face pillowed on one arm, mouth slightly open, slept.

3

AND STILL IT RAINED.

How many days now? Four? Six? It hardly mattered. In the rough camp of tented blankets and fallen-branch lean-tos, no spot sheltered enough for a cooking fire remained, or the wood dry enough to light one. The refugees huddled in morose silence, waiting, gnawing raw potatoes, swallowing moldy bread, if they had any.

They were on their own. The war was over, the Nazi labor camps plundered and closed down. Somewhere, victorious Allied commanders were deciding who would rule which piece of Germany, rolling out maps and plans, shifting the now destitute homeless workers about like pawns on a cratered chessboard.

Galina and Marfa found each other again purely by chance. When their eyes locked across a sea of faces, they rushed forward, embraced in joyful silence followed by a torrent of words. How are you? Where did you go? Where are you going? Let me see your baby.

Now they sat, their bodies touching to conserve warmth, each holding her wrapped infant close to her own skin. The babies, miraculously, slept.

"The heavens weep," Marfa said, "for our sins and misdeeds."

"Our sins? What could we possibly have done to deserve this endless rain? And what kind of God would drown the innocent along with the sinners?" Under the tented blanket, Galina moved slightly, out of the line of droplets dripping rapidly onto her neck. "You, for instance. How can you be to blame for anything that happened?"

"I was not unwilling. He said he needed me, he would help me. He called me lovely. Can you imagine? I believed. I wanted to believe."

Marfa lifted her head. Galina looked at her heart-shaped face, with its pointed chin, small close-set eyes, and wide mouth, framed with brittle unruly hair the color of flaking rust. Lovely? More like a cruel joke, nature at play, falling just short of sketching in her features in pleasing proportions. Her character, too, that self-effacing meekness that worked against her, provoking, if she was noticed at all, a kind of fury that led to abuse from men. Marfa had told her how her own widowed father could not help browbeating her, while also enjoying the domestic labor of her hands; neither, it seemed, could the aging Fascist who had fathered her child.

"You were deceived! And anyway, you said he was a high-ranking officer, used to command, older and stronger than you. He didn't have to wait for you to make up your mind. You in his rooms all the time, cleaning, serving his food. It was only a matter of time. The sin is on his head, not yours."

Galina fell silent, her head troubled with memories. If she had worked for Franz, if she had washed his shirts and cooked his meals, the way Marfa had served her officer, how would her life have turned out? How brave she had been, and how foolish. Walking away from him and his marriage proposal, trusting that he would not pursue, not insist, not shoot her down right there in the street. And knowing, in her heart of hearts, that she, too, could have been "willing." She shuddered, not from the cold and damp but from the burden of her secret, the tinge of guilt that lay like a shadow, light but undeniable, across her soul. Unlike Marfa, she had not succumbed, and yet . . . *You are right; we are all sinners*, she thought, and squeezed her friend's hand.

"At least you have a husband. Your Katya has a father, somewhere. My Tolik, my own little boy, he is a . . ." Marfa hesitated, unable to say the word. "He is alone in the world."

"He has us." Ksenia declared, opening the sodden flap that served as a door to their shelter. "As long as we stay together." She sat down heavily on the trampled grass. "I have bread, and news."

She produced the quarter loaf she had kept nearly dry beneath her sweater, tore it in uneven thirds, handed the young women the larger share. "We can't stay here," she began, leaning in to keep the rain from running down her back. "The locals are impatient to have us gone, and who can blame them? They have enough on their hands without having to deal with bands of impoverished vagrants. Food is short. Destruction is everywhere—"

"Yes, yes, Mama," Galina cut in. "We know. But where can we go? Three women with two babies, wearing nothing but these soggy clothes and carrying a few shabby things, our men who knows where."

As if on cue, both infants woke and wailed while thunder rolled like punctuation in the distance; the lightning that followed lit the circle of worried faces, then plunged them back into the dusk.

"I heard there would be refugee camps," Marfa's thin, high voice offered. She ducked her head as if she had spoken out of turn in class.

"Where did you hear this?" Galina demanded. "You didn't tell me."

"Some women talking." She busied herself with the baby at her breast, stroking his cheek, pulling her sweater close around his shivering body.

"It's true," Ksenia nodded. "They're calling us DPs now—displaced persons. The British and Americans—the French, too, I heard—are dividing Germany into zones and setting up processing centers."

"Another labor camp," Galina sniffed. She tucked Katyusha's smooth warm head under the bodice of her dress to finish feeding. "Haven't we had enough of those?"

They sat quietly for a while, rain falling through the newly leafed trees, sheeting down the sides of their tent, carving rivulets around the fledgling grass. The babies suckled, making throaty little noises, sighs and barely audible moans, skin to skin with their mothers, each radiating and absorbing the other's warmth.

Even Ksenia was still, caught in the contentment of the moment, sharing in the miracle.

"It will be better," she said. "We are not prisoners. Our side won the war." She watched each mother take a clean square of cloth from inside her dress and, laying the infant on her lap, quickly change the diaper and return the child to the shelter of the shawl tied across her body. *How fast we learn,* she thought. *How much we know.* Stepping outside, she draped the soiled diapers over a bush, where the rain would wash them clean.

"It will be better," she repeated, settled back inside the cramped dampness of the tent. "They want to help us settle. But first we have to cross the river." She said it casually, as if it was as simple as taking a trolley to town to do the shopping.

Galina's mouth fell open. She glanced at Marfa, who, still busy with Tolik, did not see. "Cross the river? The Danube? Mama, why? The bridge . . ."

"It was bombed, yes. But it still stands. And it leads to the American sector. Here, on this side, we are at the mercy of England and France."

"What does it matter? We can't go home." Marfa's voice was expressionless.

Ksenia explained: "The French cannot be trusted. Everyone knows they collaborated with the Fascists, some say eagerly. The British have their own country to rebuild after the bombing they endured. The last thing they need is more refugees, especially women and children. And Comrade Stalin wants us back. *All is forgiven! Your motherland needs you!*

"But we can't go back. Like it or not, we worked for the enemy. Returning is certain death, or Siberian hard labor." She paused to survey her audience as if measuring the effect of her words. "Only the Americans are strong enough to stand up for us," she finished. "Their cities are not scarred by bombs. Now that the war is over, they don't need Stalin's goodwill." She raised a hand to stop Galina's protest. "We can't wait for clear weather. We go tonight."

*

It was true. The bridge had been bombed but remained standing, as it had since Roman times. Word of the exodus spread rapidly along the shore; well over a hundred women milled about, forming into groups. They sorted their remaining things and tied them into bundles they could carry more easily in the wind and rain.

Ksenia, Galina, and Marfa joined a circle that had gathered around two German women, nurses returning home from their shift at the hospital. "The *Strudel* are very strong, with so much rain," one of them was saying. "Very dangerous."

Strudel? What Strudel? Galina thought. *What's so dangerous about pastry?*

Sensing the confusion, the woman explained. "Strong currents that go around, like this," she made a stirring motion with one hand. "Some very deep. Bad for boats and people. Our Danube is famous for this."

"Whirlpools," a voice in the crowd said, and the word traveled from mouth to ear like a flame through dry brush. From their position at the foot of the bridge, some peered toward the river, hoping to see this phenomenon, but by now a nearly impenetrable darkness had obscured the boundaries between water and sky.

"We're not planning to swim across," someone shouted. "Let's go." They surged toward the bridge, to be stopped almost immediately by a pair of British soldiers.

This bridge was for military vehicles only. Their crowd was too large. "Go back and wait," one guard suggested. "Your camp will be ready when the rain lets up."

The refugees fell back, angry, disappointed, feeling helpless once again in the face of authoritarian commands spoken in a language not their own. Ksenia raised her face to the rain. "So we just stay here and do nothing, wait to be sent back to die? No. We are not under anyone's rule just now! There must be another way."

"There is another bridge two or three kilometers from here," the German nurse said. "But it is damaged, no good for trucks. It would be risky."

*

They set off, walking in small groups to avoid looking like a mob. Some, especially those with small children, decided to stay and wait for better weather. Inevitably, more women left the ranks as the marching became difficult, choosing to take their chances with whatever nation was to determine their fates rather than stake their future on an uncertain venture that had begun to seem risky and perhaps unnecessarily desperate.

But a small column, with Ksenia in the lead, persevered. They marched, driven by her tireless energy, plodding step by painful step along the washed-out road, their feet sinking into ankle-deep mud that sucked at their shoes and clung to their legs like a clammy second skin.

And still it rained.

High above, in a sinister sky, a full moon shone dimly through breaks in sooty clouds, then disappeared, drawing a celestial curtain on the scene below, as if ashamed of its part in the human misery.

They reached the second bridge well after midnight. Unlike the stone bridge, which rose majestically high above the water, this one was narrow, the wooden bed spanning the Danube where the river ran straight for several kilometers, with no visible obstacle to its fluid progress.

The women stopped, their heavy breathing after the exertion of the last five hours' walking drowned out by the noise of the rushing river. They looked at the bridge, its span curving slightly upward toward the center before falling away into the murky distance of the far shore. Numbingly cold waves lapped at their feet in an ominous parody of playfulness.

Galina stepped onto the walkway. She felt the wood shift under her tread; a sudden gust of wind pushed at her skirt, forcing her to grasp the handrail for balance. "Mama. Tell me again why we need to get to the other side. Tonight."

"For our protection. For our children. How do you think Katyusha will do in a Siberian labor camp, or a Soviet orphanage? We must reach the American sector because they believe in liberty. *Svoboda.*" She pronounced the word softly, then repeated it with greater emphasis. "*Svoboda*. Tonight because tomorrow, when the sky clears, it may be too late."

The rain-swollen river ran dark only a handsbreadth beneath the slippery planks, its notorious swirls and eddies outlined with black iridescent foam, the bubbles bursting only to form new clusters downstream. The bridge swayed perceptibly, the wooden slats and handrails creaking against slender steel girders, reminding them that somewhere in the gloom, beyond the visible distance, there was bomb damage whose extent they would not know until they reached it.

Some lightened their loads yet again, leaving abandoned belongings on the shore: blankets, a square pillow, a small rolled rug, a broken doll. Ignoring Katyusha's frightened wailing, Ksenia wrapped the child in her own shawl and tied her to Galina's back, knotting the crossed ends securely across her daughter's chest. She turned to Marfa to do the same with Tolik.

"No." Marfa clutched her child and took a step back, her feet sinking in riverbank mud.

"He'll be safer that way," Ksenia explained. "You'll need your hands free for the crossing."

"No!" Marfa shouted. "Do you think I can't protect him? My own child, my treasure?" She pressed the infant closer while he squirmed in protest at the tightness of her grasp. "He will be safe here, next to my heart." Her voice broke and dropped to a whisper. In the end, she allowed Ksenia to tie the ends of her shawl at her back, for some measure of security.

They set off, walking close together, keeping to the sides near the handrails, bowing their heads into the wind, which intensified as they moved into the open, away from the shelter of the keening trees. It was slow going, the incline toward the center of the structure made steeper by the rain, the planks slick as newly formed ice, the wind's howling reaching satanic proportions in its intensity.

At the crest, they stopped to rest, waiting for the women at the end of the queue to catch up. "Mother of God," someone exclaimed, while the rest surveyed the scene before them in stupefied silence. The bridge fell away toward the shore, the downhill incline mirroring the climb they had just completed. It fell away, then disappeared under black, roiling water, coming up again at the far end onto the riverbank.

"Wait here," Ksenia said, though no one was prepared to move. She edged along the rail toward the submerged section, so close that Galina cried out, "Mama, come back! Please, Mama, come back!"

"The bridge is still there, only part of it underwater, with a rope rail across the damaged section. People must have crossed here to the other side," Ksenia announced on her return. "I think we can do it."

Galina held the back of one hand to her mouth, gripped the slippery rail with the other. "I am afraid," she said softly, so the other women would not hear, but Marfa heard and grasped her by the elbow in silent solidarity.

Ksenia had heard, too. Eyes blazing, she turned on her daughter. "The men who took your father and your husband were headed south," she hissed. "Remember? The camps on this side are deserted. We will find them over there, in the American sector. And I intend to go."

Galina was not alone in her fear. A few women went back to shore, holding children close, preferring to take their chances with human bureaucracy rather than risk defeat by the forces of nature. She watched them go, a huddle of retreating backs dissolving into the stormy night. *Bozhe moi*, she thought. *My God. What will happen to them? To us?*

"Leave anything you don't need," Ksenia instructed. "Anything that can weigh you down. Tie down anything you take. When we get to the rope, you will need both hands." She glared at Marfa, who still held Tolik in her arms, read the obstinacy in her face, and said nothing more. To lead by example, she tossed their last cooking pot into the river. Soon a variety of objects rained down from the bridge: boxes, baskets, bedding. All floated for a moment on the simmering surface before they sank or disappeared downstream. A teakettle bobbed gaily, then passed under the bridge, adding a note of incongruous cheer no one was prepared to appreciate.

"Maybe someone will find this and wonder about us," Marfa murmured, letting a baby pillow embroidered with lavender flowers slip from her fingers.

"Maybe," Galina replied. "Or maybe it will just be so much trash littering the banks of the beautiful blue Danube." *No one cares about us,* she wanted to scream into the wind. *Don't you know that?*

The planks began to sink almost immediately beneath their weight. Twenty intrepid women peered into the gloom ahead and inched along. Twenty determined hands grasped the iron rail like so many birds on a wire. Soon they were wading, as the incline steepened and the creaking bridge fell away into the water. Someone started a chant—*Gospodi pomilui,* Lord have mercy—and others took it up, accompanied by the wind's sustained howling, the staccato drumming of rain. Little Katyusha cried fitfully, her voice muffled against her mother's back. Tolik, his face loosely covered by Marfa's wrap, though wide awake, made no sound.

When they reached the broken section, Ksenia stopped. "Hold the rope with both hands and don't let go. I can see the shore. God willing, we'll soon be safe." A murmur rose up from the women, already up to their knees in water that swirled rapidly around their skirts.

They moved in, Ksenia in the lead, then Galina and Marfa, with the others close behind. Almost at once, they were waist-deep, shuffling their numbed feet to find the broken timbers, scrambling for balance. "Keep moving," Ksenia called over her shoulder. "Hold the rope and keep moving!"

There was no going back. The river seethed and rolled around them, a frigid boiling thing that took the breath from their lungs and emptied their minds of all thought. The end of the bridge rose out of the water just a short distance ahead, but who could look up to see it? Under the surface, they felt the whirling currents pull at their bodies, twisting their clothing as if demanding ransom for the passage. *I am stronger than you,* the river proclaimed. *Just let go*—while Ksenia exhorted them to hold on, hold on and keep moving.

She had reached the end, grasped the knot that unknown helping hands had tied to the remaining iron rail. Turning to the others, she started to say, *"Vot.* Be strong. We are here," when Marfa, with a wind-piercing scream, let go of the rope.

Galina and Ksenia, each holding the rope with one hand, reached instinctively for her, clawing at the ends of her coat, taking her back while she struggled, arms extended toward the rapidly receding bundle the river had wrenched from her side. Marfa roared and yelped like an animal while little Tolik bounced a few times on the crest of a wave and disappeared under the water, his wrap trailing along the surface like false hope before a whirling eddy took it, spinning, into the deep.

The rain stopped at dawn. A shameless sun, concealed behind rapidly receding clouds, burst through their cover, rising as if nothing had happened, its light reflected by countless quivering droplets that clung to every surface before vanishing into steamy air. The river ran as cold and blue as its celebrated popular image.

The other women moved off, busied themselves with their own concerns, hiding their relief at their own successful crossing, reluctant to share a stranger's trouble. The day wore on, warming with spring's promise. Sparrows pecked at the damp ground, chirping; a pair of squirrels chased each other around the base of a tree, then disappeared, chattering, into the upper branches.

Marfa said nothing. She sat down on a fallen tree, her back to the group. She made no attempt to dry her clothes or comb her hair. She sat straight-backed, head bent, staring vacantly dry-eyed at her shoes.

Galina and Ksenia glanced at one another. What was there to say? What comfort can anyone offer for the senseless death of a child? As if the death of this child, the pitiful bundle rocking on the river, spinning in a sinister game, the flash of one tiny hand outlined against the vortex like the veins of a leaf—as if that could be anything but senseless.

It was past midday when Marfa spoke. She rose from her seat and confronted her stunned companions. "Why did you make me come?" Her voice was as flat as her face was blank. "I have no man to find. No husband, no father. No one. In my village there is an auntie. She is old and sick and childless. We could have helped each other, raised my little—" Marfa stopped, unable to utter her son's name. She raised her hands to push away any argument. "*Znayu.* I know, I know. How could I be sure I would return to my village? Well, why not? Who would stop me? I am nobody." She looked up, her eyes wide. "Nobody. *Nikto.*"

"If only you had . . . ," Ksenia started to say, stopped, tried again. "It didn't have to . . . You could have . . ."

"Tied my baby to my back, like you said, like she did," she pointed to Galina, with no hint of the warmth they had so recently shared. "Well, haven't I listened enough to you already?" Marfa shouted, so loud that some of the other women stopped wringing out their clothing and looked at them, though none dared approach or intervene.

It was a desperate outcry, spoken with the rage of a child cornered by her own helplessness and guilt, a child left with nothing but feral instinct, snarling and gnashing her teeth in her own defense. Marfa went back to the seclusion of her log, shaking in wrathful tearless silence.

It was Galina who could not stop weeping. She held her own infant close, ignoring the child's squirming. "Katyusha," she whispered, tears spilling from her eyes in an endless stream, coursing down her swollen cheeks. "Katyusha."

She paced like an animal marking out territory, careful to keep her back to the unforgiven river; her footsteps soon wore a path in the newly sprouted grass, from tree to budding tree. *River of death*, she accused. Her heart filled with hate for its heedless sparkling beauty, hate and frustration that brought on ever more copious tears.

After her outburst, Marfa remained silent, her eyes stone dead, her mouth a thin grim line in a face pale as chalk. The other women had gathered in groups, talking and even laughing among themselves, speculating about the future and its unknown possibilities. "When they rebuild the factories they will need workers . . ." "I know a family in Antwerp . . ." "My godfather's son lives in New York . . ."

"Why won't they talk to us, Mama? It's been two days since we crossed," Galina whined. She lifted a restless Katya up to her shoulder to stop her rooting at Galina's clothing, the child's mouth an O of insatiable appetite.

"Feed her," Ksenia instructed. "As for the women, I don't know. Maybe they think grief is contagious."

Galina collapsed in a fresh torrent of tears. "I fed her. I have no more"—she hiccupped loudly, catching her breath as each explosion left her chest—"no more milk."

Ksenia took the baby and walked with her. "*Nu, nu,* little one. Sleep now," she crooned, offering the tip of her finger, dipped in water, to suck. "*Dochenka,* my daughter, you must temper your grief. Stop crying. God has taken Tolik. We must accept the tragedy and care for the living."

Marfa's head snapped up at the sound of her son's name. Her back stiffened; the disheveled halo of her hair stirred in the breeze. After a few minutes, she rose and approached them. Her dress, distended by engorged breasts, was damp, the leaking milk staining her bodice in dark irregular patches, like rings around a submerged stone. Without a word, she took Katyusha from Ksenia's arms and went back to her log. The baby resisted at first, then hunger won out and she gave in, gulping the strange milk in large mouthfuls, waving one small fist in the air as a last bastion of defiance.

"God had nothing to do with it," Marfa said without turning around. "It was my fault. Only mine."

PART VI

The Men

1

ON LEAVING THE TRAIN at Plattling the men were trucked several kilometers to an abandoned farmhouse, already widely encircled with barbed wire and occupied by several hundred laborers. They were put to work building additional barracks and watchtowers.

"*Schnell*," the guards prodded. "The sooner you finish, the sooner you sleep inside." They worked steadily, unloading materials, sawing boards, pounding nails, tarring roofs, and hanging doors. No one was permitted to use the new buildings until four of the six were finished. The men slept outdoors, huddled together, each with only a thin camp-issue blanket and his own clothing to protect him from the late February cold. Some never got to use the beds they made; they succumbed to the milder but still wintry weather, their own persistent assortment of ailments made worse by low spirits and malnutrition.

The barn had been converted into a dormitory for the guards. Meals were dispensed behind the house, at the kitchen door; each man took his portion and did his best to find a place to eat it, leaning against a wall or squatting on the ground in the yard. Taking food into the barracks was forbidden.

"Why are we here? What do they want with us?" someone grumbled.

"Who knows? Maybe they have a new plan. At least we have something to do."

Filip's knowledge of German saved him, again, from the heaviest labor. He was assigned to the camp supervisor's staff as interpreter, but slept in the barracks with the others, working with them when he wasn't needed in the office.

The German staff numbered only two dozen or so and did not seem to care how the barracks were built. If the roof leaked or the walls were not straight, it made no difference; the shelters were for Slavs, who deserved no better. There were enough men among the newcomers who knew about building; to his surprise, Filip enjoyed working with them. Watching a pile of lumber and a bucket of nails become a house, however simple, was fascinating, as long as he didn't have to swing a hammer all day.

As to their questions—Why are we here? At whose command? Are we prisoners? What happens when we finish the barracks? Where are our women and children?—no answers were forthcoming in any language.

Two weeks into their captivity, Filip met Ilya in the yard at dinnertime. Squatting next to the older man without looking at him, he said, "I found out."

"What?" Ilya, also looking straight ahead, asked softly.

"Why we're here and the women are not." Filip stirred his soup, pushing the turnip bits around, skimming the rapidly congealing fat, what there was of it, onto his spoon. He rubbed the fat onto his bread and chewed.

Finally, Ilya lost patience. "*Nu?* Well?" he exclaimed, far louder than he intended.

"The Reds are on the move, sweeping in from the east, making gains every day against the Nazis. The Germans are afraid we'll join forces with them and give away what we've learned of the land, the enemy positions."

"How do you know this?"

"I overheard two guards complaining. Building these barracks is fool's work. We should slow down. They're just waiting for orders to shoot us when we're done, so they don't have to keep feeding us."

"That's stupid. Why waste the materials? Why not shoot us now? We could be useful yet, for reconstruction projects, or a prisoner exchange when this war ends. And that will be soon. I feel it." Ilya tipped the rest of his broth into his mouth. "What I wouldn't give for a plate—no, just a spoonful—of my Ksenia's cooking." He closed his eyes, resting his head against the wall. There were signs of early spring in the air, a hint of mildness, the sun spreading a welcoming warmth on his upturned face. "You're sure about this? About the Reds?"

"I know what I heard." Filip bristled, startled from his own reminiscence: Galina's body nestled against him, her honey hair parted to reveal the back of her neck, her rhythmic breathing like the whisper of receding waves on the pebbled beach of the Black Sea.

Ilya grunted. "If our boys start liberating the camps, we're all dead men, tainted with the stain of collaboration whether we've worked with the Fascists or not. You know that, don't you?"

"Maybe." *But they might need interpreters, too,* he thought. "Here comes Grisha. We know what's on his mind."

"*Nu, parni, kak dela?* How goes it, fellows?" Grisha, his soup bowl empty, towered over the two men from his considerable height. Though only in his midforties, he was nearly bald, with eyes round as billiard balls looking large behind thick wire-rimmed glasses. "Are you ready to join us?"

Ilya stood up. "Yes. I am. But I'm no fighter. I had enough of it in the last war."

"Times have changed, old man. We have better weapons now, no more mustard gas. And we need numbers, a show of force. I've spoken with the camp commander." He glanced at Filip as if to say, *You're not the only one who speaks German here.* "They will back us up, provide uniforms, and help with training."

"Huh." Filip, still squatting, rolled a cigarette, careful not to spill a speck of the precious leaf. He licked the edge of the paper and pinched the ends closed. "They'll say anything now to keep us from going to the Reds."

Marina Antropow Cramer_

"Oh, you young ones," Grisha exclaimed with evident frustration. "You've never known anything but Communism. With our passion and Hitler's manpower, we can unseat Stalin and his cronies, loosen their grip on our country. It is the ultimate act of patriotism. Just say it—'Russkaya Osvoboditel'naya Armiya, Russian Liberation Army'—and you can be part of it."

"I know what ROA stands for." Filip stood up. Shorter than the older man, he had to tilt his head back to look him in the eye. "And let's say this insane plot succeeds. Then what? Who will form the new government? How do you know the people will support you? Are you counting on the monarchists to bring the surviving Romanovs out of hiding? What if you start another civil war?" He rolled the cigarette gently between fingers and thumb. "I don't see a plan here. What if you win and the Germans choose to stay?"

"Andrei Andreevich Vlasov is perfectly able to form a government. He is a decorated general with many years of Red Army experience, and used to command. He was instrumental in the defense of Moscow, turning the enemy back within sight of the city limits." Grisha closed his eyes, as if explaining a self-evident concept to an obtuse student. "And the monarchists will follow anyone who can replace the Bolsheviks. Isn't that so, Ilya Nikolaevich?"

"Command!" Filip interrupted before Ilya could reply. "That's fine for military operations, but can it make good government? Command? If so, we should stay with what we have."

"We can argue the finer points forever," Grisha said, his voice betraying a trace of impatience. "The truth is, we have no time. The movement is well under way, with over a million men signed up in Germany, Italy, Czechoslovakia, ready to fight. The time is now. Will you join us?"

In the end, after a few more heated recruiting efforts, they joined the ROA. Ilya, with the wholehearted enthusiasm of the newly converted, believing that not all monarchists were out of touch with modern times, kept his hopes to himself. *Look at England or Sweden or Holland*, he thought. *Are they not proof enough that constitutional monarchy is not only possible but also good for people and rulers alike?*

Filip overcame his reluctance more gradually. A million men? He doubted there could be that many. He could understand if refugees and POWs signed up, eager to band together for any hope of stability in their fractured lives. The promise of a hot daily meal and a good coat, plus a measure of protection from the capricious brutality of camp overseers—men had sold their souls for less.

So perhaps a million recruits. But if they were holed up throughout Europe, how would they ever mass together to mount a meaningful offensive? And how many among them were fit for battle? He didn't know if he himself had the discipline or the stamina to be a soldier. Or the courage.

But he could see that holding out labeled him as a Red among men who had ceased to believe in the great Socialist experiment. *It could work*, he thought. Stalin was an anomaly. Remove the dictator; return power to the people—the principles were sound, weren't they? But he also believed that the Reds, together with the Allies, would defeat the Nazis. When that happened, they, his countrymen, would see him as a traitor, no matter what he did now.

He joined so as not to draw attention to himself among these sheep bleating platitudes of a new kind, which he doubted many of them understood. As events heated up, there was bound to be confusion; he had only to watch for an opportunity to escape to the West. He would be vigilant. In the meantime, as a member of the resistance army, he might get to carry a gun—a possibility he found as exciting as it was unsettling.

They sewed the ROA patches on the sleeves of their German-issue uniforms, fingering the fine gray wool with positively sensual pleasure, glad to exchange their tattered jackets and mud-splattered trousers for this superior clothing. They mended the tears and patched the occasional bullet holes with care.

"I wonder which one of our boys shot this poor bastard," Filip asked, holding up the jacket he had been issued. An oblong hole in the upper chest area lined up neatly with a similar one in the left sleeve. He wiggled his fingers through the holes.

"*Nu,*" one of the men remonstrated, as if correcting a foolish child. "No need for such talk."

For the next month or so the new recruits were permitted to drill and even engage in some target practice, using wax bullets aimed at a plywood board bolstered with hay. There were not enough guns to go around. After the first day, when the men rushed from all sides at the pile of weapons laid out on a trestle table, as if playing a grimly comical version of musical chairs, the corporal in charge established a strict rotation, giving each trainee more or less equal shooting time.

Ilya, though not yet fifty, was deemed too old for combat due to his persistent cough, and assigned to the rear guard; his job would be to feed the troops, manage supplies, and care for the wounded. "That suits me," he told his son-in-law. He was glad to be of use but not on the front lines.

Filip was hopelessly inept with a rifle, but liked the heft of a pistol in his hand, and was able to hit the target with a passable degree of accuracy. *As long as it's a bale of hay,* he thought, *and the gun holds blanks,* not at all sure that shooting a man would yield the same kind of satisfaction.

His resolve was tested in a combat exercise that matched the trainees against each other in pairs. Filip's opponent, though larger and stronger, was unarmed. They circled each other for a few minutes, Filip ducking or sidestepping most of the other man's blows, though landing none of his own. Then the larger man moved in and caught Filip in a clinch. They grappled awkwardly, grunting and wheezing, Filip's chin wedged into the other man's shoulder, his buckling knees forcing them to fall to the ground.

A small crowd had gathered around the two men rolling in the dust. Filip was only dimly aware of their jeers—"*Durak!* Use your gun, fool!"—drowned out by the blood roaring in his ears, his only thought to escape his opponent's viselike embrace.

And then the man sneezed. Filip took advantage of his loosened grip, rolled away, and lay facedown, barely breathing, his left arm pinned under his body, the right covering his head in a childlike pose of submission. "Get up!" the men yelled. "Get up! Use your gun!"

Filip didn't hear them. He was only aware of his opponent kneeling over him, pressing the barrel of Filip's own gun against his temple. Then nothing.

"Let's go, *malysh*." Two men were lifting him off the ground, their tone both derisive and strangely affectionate. "They can use you in the kitchen." *Malysh*. Little one. His gorge started to rise at the insult, but he was too embarrassed to take serious offense.

"*Ach, ja,*" he heard one of the German guards remark, laughing, to another when he limped past. "Send that one to fight for Comrade Stalin. We have nothing to fear from such a soldier."

Let them laugh, he thought. When it came time to talk or decipher documents, no one in this camp knew both languages better than he. *I'll show them yet. All of them.*

The kitchen assignment didn't last. Filip proved as useless at peeling potatoes as he was at hand-to-hand combat, and soon returned to his clerical duties.

Among the German camp personnel, after the initial taunts, no one mentioned his ignominious failure, at least in his hearing. Did they expect no more from a Slav, a member of a race they considered inferior beyond contempt? *But I am not all Slav*, he argued, addressing an imaginary interlocutor. *My mother is Greek. They gave the world some epic warriors, in their day. Also scientists, mathematicians. Thinkers. That's part of my legacy, too.*

The only one to mention the incident was Becker, the young lieutenant in charge of office administration. Not much older than Filip,
he treated him with something close enough to respect to put them at
ease with each other. "A man can't know his limits until he is faced
with the thing he cannot do," Becker said a few days after the training episode. "I asked for you. I know this is work you can do well."
He gestured around the office, the desks, files, typewriter—even the
telephone Filip was not permitted to touch. "Here. I got two letters
from home last week. Do you want the stamps?"

"Thank you. *Danke.*" Filip felt the blood rise to his face. He was
touched by the officer's candid remark. *Maybe I can't fight, but surely we
can get along with Germans like these, work together toward ending this war?* Maybe
joining the ROA was not such a bad idea.

He was truly grateful for the stamps. Since leaving home, adding
to his collection had become nearly impossible. What should have
been a bounty of exemplars from many more countries than ever
before became the source of a nagging frustration. Whether traveling
with Galina's family or cooped up in barracks with other detainees,
he was never alone, never able to sort the collection he carried so
faithfully from one place to the next. There was never any money for
new stamps, or time to pore over the exquisite miniature images, to
wish or to daydream.

He missed the faraway days of his boyhood, the hours spent reading
catalogs, sorting, pasting, admiring his stamps, laying aside duplicates
to trade for wonderful new acquisitions. He knew now that in those
moments, with his mother nearby offering fresh pastry, he had been
completely happy. Why was it when others suffered shortages and
derivations, she always had a bit of sugar for his tea?

Of course, he understood; his father was a Party member. His
position in the postal service gave him privileges, like higher rations
for everything from bread to shoes. He wasn't sure why his mother
chose to drink her tea unsweetened. It must have been her religion,
which he knew to be based on sacrifice, atonement, self-denial, full of

saints and martyrs and a strict moral code driven by guilt, with good behavior receiving its sweet reward in some mystical promised land.

She had insisted on having him baptized. It was, as far as he knew, her single act of defiance against his father. It was 1925, the fervor of the revolution still fresh enough to those who could feel its benefits in their own lives. "Would you deny your son the possibility of divine protection?" she had argued. "Are you sure the Party can save his soul?" And his father had assented, defeated, perhaps, by some deeply buried seed of doubt, and by his love for his young wife. Or so the story had come down to Filip, who felt no need of celestial mercy but loved his mother even more for her fierce demands on his behalf. *How are you, Mama?* he wondered. *How are things with you now?*

2

THEN ONE MORNING in late April, the Germans were gone. The most glaring sign, aside from the missing sentry at the gate, was the absence of trucks.

"They must have rolled them out without starting the engines," someone speculated, "or we would have heard them."

It was a clean sweep. Every piece of Nazi correspondence, down to supply requisitions and copies of weekly reports, was gone. A quick look around confirmed they had taken everything easily portable, including the civilian cook and all the provisions. What had happened? Why the stealthy disappearance?

Some men did not wait to find out. They gathered up their things and set out of the camp gates without a backward glance. "It could be a trick." Grisha removed his glasses and polished the lenses on his shirtsleeve. "They could be waiting to pick us off around a bend in the road."

"Why?" Filip argued. "They could have starved or beaten us right here, without wasting bullets. No one would know what happened, not for a long time. This makes no sense. We should go."

"We promised them our support," Ilya, sitting on a bench in the kitchen, rested his arms on his knees. "An army does not kill its own soldiers."

"We accepted *their* support in *our* struggle," Grisha corrected. "It's not the same thing. We're fighting not for Fascism but against the tyranny in our own homeland. So we need to stay together as a unit. We're no good to anyone spread out over the countryside."

"No one but ourselves. And I don't see anyone doing any fighting." Filip walked around, peering into sacks and boxes, opening cupboards, rummaging in drawers. "What's for breakfast?"

They managed to cook up a porridge from whatever edible remnants they found—a grayish unappetizing sludge of which each man had to eat, thankfully, only a small portion.

For the rest of that day and the next, Grisha organized some training exercises and the men went along, for the most part for lack of anything better to do. Others went out to scavenge for food. They came back with several rabbits and a scrawny rooster; no mean feat for hunters armed with sticks and a hastily improvised slingshot. The Germans, of course, had taken all the guns.

A foray into the darkest recesses of the root cellar turned up half a sack of seed potatoes. "We should plant some, now that it's spring," Ilya suggested. But the hungry men ignored him.

"We won't be here long enough to harvest them. Use them sparingly, though," Grisha decreed. " Make them last a few days." The resulting stew, seasoned with wild onions and the first early dandelion greens, was palatable enough.

"What happens when we run out of rabbits?" someone asked, giving voice to the general concern. "I doubt the locals will want to feed us."

"How many are we?" Grisha looked around, took a rough count. "Fifty, give or take a few." More men had left that afternoon, but some who had gone earlier had come back to the relative safety of the camp. "Once I make contact with a larger unit, we can combine forces, go where we're needed."

Filip couldn't imagine where that might be. If Stalin had succeeded in driving the Fascists from Soviet soil, it seemed absurd to fight the Reds in Germany. What if they were captured? Were these old men so deluded by, whatever, idealism or nostalgia, that they couldn't see the only possible outcome? There would be no trial, no repatriation or gulag sentence. He could see them now, each stripped of any usable clothing, lined up to receive a bullet in the head. Field justice.

He was seized with panic. If the Germans had lost—and why else would they abandon the camp?—then the Reds could be anywhere, drunk with victory and eager to exact revenge on those who had attacked their homeland. "We're sitting ducks here," he said. "Don't you see? We have no weapons, no food, no supplies. Not even a radio. Count me out." His fingers gripped the edge of the ROA patch, ready to rip it off his sleeve.

"Wait!" Ilya held Filip's wrist. "Grisha sent some men out to get news. We owe him that much."

"We owe him nothing. Or I don't, anyway." Filip was suddenly aware of everything that irritated him about his father-in-law: the calm benevolence, the senseless piety, the infuriating patience of the man, even the careful way he crafted his useless decorative pieces. "You do what you want."

"Filip. Wait. We have to stay together, you and I. How else can we hope to find my Ksenia and Galya? Your wife and newborn child?" Ilya dropped his hands to his sides and looked at the younger man with a pleading expression of such reasonableness it made Filip's blood boil.

"Fifty men. Fifty men armed with slingshots will liberate the Soviet Union. Bah! You're all crazy." Filip turned with a dismissive wave of the hand and headed toward the barracks, the offending patch hanging from his sleeve by a few loose threads.

And then they heard the trucks.

3

THEY DROVE IN SLOWLY, as if on parade—four open trucks overflowing with American soldiers, waving and cheering like big unruly children. These were followed by a half dozen covered vehicles holding wounded men in various stages of recuperation.

"The war is over. Hitler is dead," the fair-haired sergeant told the assembled inmates, his words rendered into heavily accented but adequate Russian by a soldier Filip's age.

"What's that I hear, Grisha? That sound . . . ," Filip, standing a few feet behind, asked in a voice loud enough to carry over the murmuring crowd.

Grisha gave his head a quarter turn, as if listening. "What sound?"

"The sound of a door slamming. The door to our home. Every man here wearing this damn patch can hear it clearly." He tore the loose ROA insignia off his sleeve and jammed it into his pocket.

The sergeant held up a hand for silence. "All right. You are to stay in this camp as DPs while we process your documents. Your status is 'stateless' unless you have valid papers to the contrary, in which case you will be repatriated as soon as we receive the go-ahead." He scanned the hollow-cheeked faces, unshaven and sallow and mostly expressionless, though some registered anxiety, and some relief. "The processing will begin at once, followed by a visit to Corporal Dominick Macaluso, also known as Nick the

Barber. You'll report to your assigned work detail in the morning. That's all."

Two men brought the kitchen table outside. The sergeant himself did the questioning, filling out the forms in large rounded letters that looked fresh and innocent after the precisely etched German script they had become used to.

Processing was rapid; the registration line snaked around the yard but moved at a good pace, the sergeant assisted by an enlisted man who knew a little Russian. Name, age, place of birth, occupation. Luggage search for hidden weapons or contraband. Barrack assignment, work detail.

"Tell them Yugoslavia," Ilya, standing behind his son-in-law, whispered in his ear.

"What? Why?" Filip protested.

"I'll explain later."

That left Filip in a quandary. If the old man was right about the need to conceal their true origins, how could he, Filip, claim to be an interpreter with knowledge of German and Russian? On the other hand, why would they need one? He knew as much English as he did Serbian—none at all.

"Occupation?"

Filip hesitated. Student? Ridiculous. Interpreter? Too risky. Carpenter? Patently untrue. Then he remembered stringing lights at the amateur theater, splicing brittle wires together, which, with a little instinct and a lot of luck, had lit the stage for their plays. "Electrician," he said bravely, hoping his poor skills would not be tested.

"Place of birth?"

"Yugoslavia." The sergeant kept writing.

"What city?"

"Belgrade. But I've been in school in Germany for several years," he added.

"Papers?"

"Lost in the fire, in Dresden."

"Huh. Right. Stateless. Barrack three. Be ready for work in the morning."

Stepping aside, Filip heard Ilya say, "Yugoslavia."

The man looked up. "Another one. How do you say bread?"

"*Pogacha*," Ilya replied, to Filip's surprise.

"Occupation?"

"Craftsman."

"That's not an occupation. What work can you do?"

"I can make beautiful things out of simple materials," Ilya protested, "with my tools." He pointed to his toolbox, which lay open on the table between them.

"Lovely. We've been looking for someone like you, no doubt. In the meantime, you can push a broom and empty bedpans in the infirmary." He snapped the lid shut and slid the box toward its owner. "Stateless. Barrack three."

A dozen men were sent to clean out the barn. The rest were put to work making a barbed-wire enclosure in one corner of the camp, with a shallow ditch at one end.

"I wonder if they're bringing in animals. Cows or sheep. Maybe dogs?" Filip speculated, wrapping rags around his bleeding fingers. "Damn, this hurts."

"Then why use barbed wire? And why the ditch? Animals would fall in, break a leg. And there's no roof, no shelter from the weather," another man replied. "Here, hold this end steady while I fix the door." The "door" was a flap of the same merciless material, hinged to the enclosure with loops of heavy wire. "That should do it," the man said, giving each loop one last twist with his pliers. "Isn't that your father? What's he doing?"

"He's not my father." They stood a moment and watched Ilya walk around the enclosure, his eyes fixed on the ground.

"What treasure are you finding there, Ilya Nikolaevich?" the man called out.

Ilya stooped to pick something up. "Treasure it is, boys. Treasure it is." Smiling, he showed them several scraps of wire, each no more than a few centimeters, glinting in the palm of his hand.

Filip walked away, heading for the farmhouse headquarters to report the job finished. *The old man's losing his wits*, he thought. *What now?*

Nothing much happened in the next few days. Some lumber appeared—used boards with rusted nails and peeling paint, and each barracks' occupants were permitted to build a table and benches. Grisha organized a morning exercise routine. Participation was voluntary, but most men came. There wasn't much else to do.

"Reminds me of home," one of the men said while waiting his turn to wash at the rain barrel outside the kitchen door. "Doing exercises to the radio before breakfast."

"Reminds me of school," Filip answered. "And the Pioneers. Keep your body clean and strong for your country." *At least it's not combat training*, he thought. *I've had enough of those games.*

Ilya spent his free time at the newly built table, pounding his wire scraps with a little mallet from his toolbox. He was cordial with anyone who came by to watch, whether fellow detainee or American soldier, keeping up a steady pace, ignoring their amused expressions. Under his single-minded efforts, the wire bits grew longer and thinner and more pliable. He twisted them together end to end with infinite care, in nearly invisible joins. Soon he was ready for business.

They paid him with anything they had: cigarettes, crackers, Hershey bars, a few German coins, stamps from the letters every soldier carried in his breast pocket. He accepted everything and kept working, turning out pin after pin, learning the unfamiliar names. Nancy. Evelyn. Rosemary. Molly. Edith.

He worked carefully, without haste, twisting the wire into a fluid rendition of each name. Sometimes Filip sat nearby, watching. Not helping; he had neither the skill nor the inclination. He considered his father-in-law's craft to be not much better than a parlor trick, like those bazaar artists who will sketch your likeness for a few pennies, making you look just like anyone else. He liked the chocolate, though, and cherished the American stamps that came his way.

The day Filip saw Sergeant Evans standing at Ilya's table, he leaned the broom he'd been using to sweep the yard against the barracks wall and sauntered over. He sat down on an upturned crate and muttered, "This has to be the cleanest piece of ground in all Germany."

"We'll have work for you soon," Evans said curtly, nodding at the broom. "The road needs repair, and there's cleanup building projects in the area." He spoke in a curious blend of languages, German and English words tripping over each other. "Lots of work. Just waiting for orders." He turned to Ilya. "Can you do Priscilla?"

"Write it for me." Ilya slid a notepad and pencil across the table.

"And Gary. Do Gary, too."

"Pri . . . sci . . . lla." Ilya studied the name, sounding out the letters. "Your wife?"

"My little girl, not quite two years old." He took a photograph from his wallet. A plump, sweet-faced toddler clutching a stuffed rabbit gazed at them with wide, serious eyes. "She doesn't know her daddy yet. And Gary." He pointed to himself. "That's me."

When the pins were done, Evans rewarded Ilya with a small coil of fine-gauge copper wire. "Better than money," Ilya said. "Thank you."

"I have a little girl, too." The German words fell from Filip's mouth almost before he thought them.

"Where? Near here?" Evans held the name pins in his hand, rubbing his thumb gently over the graceful letters.

"I don't know. We were taken away before she was born."

"So how do you know?"

"Men who arrived after us said one of their wives had seen her at the hospital," Ilya put in.

"The grapevine," Evans muttered in English, pocketing his pins.

"Pardon?" Filip threw Ilya an annoyed glare. Why did he always have to interfere?

"Grapevine," Evans repeated. Then in broken German, "Gossip telegraph. Never mind. Come to me in the morning; I'll find you some work."

When Evans had gone, Filip turned on Ilya. "Why couldn't you stay out of it? Why tell them how we know? It doesn't concern you." He felt the foolishness of his words at once, but the damage was done.

"The birth of my first grandchild and the welfare of the two people who mean more to me than anyone in the world? Could anything concern me more?" Ilya gathered up his files and pliers and placed them into his toolbox. "These people are not the enemy. Maybe they can help us." He closed the lid, secured the latch, and walked off with the box under his arm.

"Not while we're cooped up here!" Filip shot back.

He found a quiet shady spot behind one of the barracks. A little way off, some of the men were playing a game, kicking a ball around. A ball—a bundle of rags wrapped around a handful of stones; he had watched them fashion the thing last night, with much joking, intent on their project as if making a Christmas present for a child. *A child*, he thought, the image faceless, silent, vague. *My child.*

He lowered himself to his haunches, back against the sun-warmed wall, and rolled a cigarette. His eye caught a movement in the newly grown grass. Three fledgling birds hopped around, pecking at the ground, their movements swift but jerky, as if unpracticed. They were tiny, with the familiar markings of the breed, miniature copies of the full-grown sparrows they would soon be, but with the endearingly disheveled look of all animal young. His memory brought up the image of the baby elephant in Dresden, the spiky tuft on its smooth head, the little trunk flailing in the air. Galina's hand extended, unable to reach it, the chagrin on her face. He shook his head, as if to clear his mind. When he looked again, the birds were gone.

The next day, he was assigned to a new work detail: finishing the barn for use as an infirmary. And he met Anneliese.

4

FILIP DID NOT KNOW how long she'd been standing just inside the doorway, watching him and two other men unload portable cots from the truck. She was pretty, with short reddish hair and laughing eyes. She wore men's trousers and a shirt that had once been red, the rolled-up sleeves revealing firm, lightly freckled arms. Older than his own twenty years, he was sure, but possessed of a radiance that made it all but impossible to guess her age.

"Oh." He nearly dropped the cots he was carrying, one under each arm.

"*Guten Tag*," she addressed him in German. "I am looking for the sergeant?" He had heard it before, the lilt that seemed to make a question out of every utterance, but never before had it struck him as charming.

"He is . . . somewhere. I'll find him for you," he offered, but made no move to leave.

"Wait—you are German, *nicht wahr*? Isn't that so?"

"No, Russian." He stopped, flustered, forgetting he was passing for Yugoslav these days, but still wore the German clothes. "The uniform. I can explain. But it's a long story."

"Everybody has a story. Everybody who is still alive." She looked grave for a moment, then lit up with a brilliant smile. "This will be a hospital, yes? With sheets?"

"Yes, with sheets. I mean, I think so." *Americans have everything,* he thought. *Why not sheets?*

"So. I live in the town. I can wash the sheets, and other things. Shirts, other things. My sister helps me."

"Stay right there." Filip put down the cots and ran out into the compound. "I'll get Sergeant Evans."

He had only seen a woman in trousers in the movies, or on the patriotic posters showing farm and factory workers toiling cheerfully for the good of the people. Anneliese didn't look like them; she had neither the self-conscious smugness of the workers nor the slick risqué elegance of the movie stars. She simply looked comfortable.

She came twice a week, exchanged clean linens for soiled ones, and picked up shirts and underwear from her growing list of laundry clients. Everybody liked her—the easy manner that stopped just short of flirting, the careful way she delivered each man's bundle, tied with string and marked with his initials.

Her clients were all Americans. None of the refugees could afford the luxury, nor did they have much to wash. When she came, breezing past the sentry at the gate with a friendly greeting, they would stop to watch her lean her bicycle against the fence, hoist the basket onto her shoulder, and make her way to the building where the officers were housed.

Filip was sweeping out one of the empty barracks that the American wounded had occupied while the infirmary was being prepared. Someone was whistling. He stopped and listened; it was definitely a Mozart tune. *Don Giovanni?* He couldn't be sure of the opera, but in his head, he could almost hear the words. His mother would know the lyrics, fill in the story, nodding her head in time to the music, the crochet hook moving swiftly through the work in her hands.

He started sweeping again. The whistling came closer, and Anneliese stepped in, setting her empty basket down on the nearest bunk. "I come for the sheets. Where are the sick ones?"

"We moved them to the infirmary yesterday."

"*Ach, ja.*" She picked up her basket and turned to go.

"That song you were whistling—Mozart, yes? What is it called?"

"The song? Oh, I wouldn't know. My father played the violin. Some of the tunes stay in my head. So."

"My mother has many opera records," he said, suddenly desperate to keep Anneliese from leaving. "She plays them all the time. Not here. Home, in Russia. Yalta." He forced himself to stop babbling, overcome with sadness and yearning, but for what, exactly, he could not say.

"You are a sweet boy." Anneliese laid a hand on his cheek. He covered it with his own, then embraced her. The broom clattered to the ground. He closed his eyes, his senses filled with the bittersweet aroma of her hair.

She pulled away, looking wistful. With the slightest possible touch of one finger, she stroked the thin brass band on his right hand. "And married?"

"Yes." His voice caught in his throat. "Yes. Married."

———————

Sergeant Evans gave Grisha permission to use one of the empty barracks as a common room, where the men could gather to talk and eat their meals, smoke, and play cards. They were sometimes joined by off-duty soldiers whose naive friendliness enlivened the gatherings with their poor command of European languages and their infectious laughter.

Someone had etched a rough checkerboard into the tabletop, using a pocket knife to scratch in the lines and charcoal to color the dark squares; acorn caps and pebbles made good playing pieces. Soon a tournament was under way, Grisha keeping track as man after man sat down at the board to vie for the championship. For the winner, Ilya fashioned a wire pin to wear until defeated by a cleverer, or luckier, opponent.

They spent the better part of an hour, one evening, deciding what the pin should look like. A lily—too French; a star—too provocative; a rose—too complicated. "Make it a daisy," someone suggested. "Simple, and not political." And so it was; everyone in the camp could recognize the reigning checkers champion by the innocent wire flower pinned to his collar.

Some afternoons, Anneliese would join them. She would stand, the basket of soiled laundry balanced on her hip, and watch the men play, her expression attentive and amused. Eventually, they convinced her to try her hand. "We need a new challenger! By now, we all know each other's tricks."

"I have not played since I was a girl," she protested. "When my brothers were still at home."

She proceeded to beat Grisha, the current champion, in a game that started slowly, then picked up speed, rushing to its merciless conclusion in record time. "When I play against my brothers," Anneliese confessed with a wicked smile, "I always win."

Watching Grisha pin the daisy to Anneliese's shirt, then stoop to kiss her ceremonially on both cheeks, Filip felt distinctly uneasy. Why did it bother him to see Grisha's big hands on her shoulders, holding her while his lips grazed her face? *A German woman who does the laundry. She is nothing to me. Nothing more than a passing friendship.*

Filip did not join in the games. Like the others, he did his assigned work. He amused himself by sketching in a notebook Anneliese had bought for him at his request—buildings, mostly. He strained to remember details he had seen, roofs and cornices, the contours of windows, arches, and doorways. He drew imaginary interiors, drafting elaborate floor plans with staircases, adding balconies, terraces, gardens landscaped with trees and shrubs. He knew they were crude, these dream-house drawings of his untutored hand, and showed them to no one.

The decision to have Anneliese keep the daisy pin was unanimous. "A memento of our time together here. May our nations always be friends," Grisha, carried away into flights of rhetoric, intoned.

She pressed her lips together as if considering her reply, then raised her chin and spoke clearly. "How can our nations be friends when your Red Army comrades are behaving like animals? They hurt our women, humiliate our men. This cage you made"—she pointed in the direction of the empty barbed-wire enclosure—"is it not for German prisoners? We have lost the war, but we still have our pride." She unpinned the daisy and laid it on the table, next to the checkerboard. "I, Anneliese, can be a friend to you. But not on behalf of my country."

After this, the men continued to play, but much of the joy, the childish enthusiasm, went out of their games.

Assigned to clean out the shelves of the farmhouse cellar, Filip discovered a box of chess pieces the Germans had left behind. He was tempted to hide them away, keep them for himself, but thought better of it and showed Evans his find.

"Keep it." The American waved him away. "I'm pretty sure our boys won't know what to do with it."

Using a discarded cupboard door and some scrap wood, Filip hammered together a table small enough to carry easily into the yard, away from the noisy checker players. He drew another board, replaced three missing pawns with white stones and the black queen with a spent shell casing. He found a few willing partners among the detainees, but playing chess required concentration and more time than any of them were willing to spare. Often, he sat at the table alone, trying to remember the classic openings and strategies outlined in the chess books he had left behind in Dresden.

Anneliese came up behind him one such early evening. "My father played this game with his friends," she said, setting her basket on the ground. "I did not know you could do it by yourself."

Filip looked up, surprised but not displeased at the interruption. "You can't, unless you can think like two people." The sun, low in the sky, outlined her form so that he could not see her face. "I wish Borya was here."

Anneliese sat down, placed her elbows on the table. "So. Show me how to play."

———————————

The ache in his ear came on gradually, like a woodwind note in a Beethoven symphony, picked up and repeated by the other sections, building to an insistent crescendo that thrummed and crashed, filling his head with pain. Filip stumbled into the infirmary, where the medic was finishing the paperwork for the most recent batch of wounded Americans patched up well enough to be sent home.

"Help me," Filip said through gritted teeth. "My ear . . ."

The medic examined him. "I have no glycerin for the ear, but I can give you some aspirin to knock this fever down. You may as well lie down." He waved at the empty room. "Plenty of beds."

Filip understood the gesture, if not the words. He unlaced his boots and collapsed on the nearest cot. "Thank you," he said, enunciating the English syllables with care. "Thank. You."

The fever came down a bit, then shot back up within the hour when the aspirin wore off. "Buck up, man," the medic said. "I've got no more morphine until supplies come in. You'll be all right."

Filip understood only *no morphine* and moaned, surrendering to the fresh waves of agony inside his head. Through the hot red haze of fever and pain, he thought he saw Anneliese talking to the medic. Then she was gone.

He didn't know how long he tossed on the narrow cot; shaking his head was worse, so he tried to lie still, the room spinning behind his burning eyes. Someone was turning him onto his side; something cool dripped into his inflamed ear, and suddenly the pain receded. Not gone, no, but reduced to a dull, throbbing pattern, like timpani winding down for the concert finale, the kettle drums still reverberating but softer now, ever softer.

Anneliese sat next to the bed, arms folded in her lap. When she saw his eyes open, she smiled. "Better? Good. I put a little cooking oil in; it helps with the pain until the infection passes. My grandmother taught me."

He tried to raise himself on his elbows, but fell back, weak with the fever still wracking his body. "Anneliese," he said, "you are an angel."

"Pfft. Angels are for babies." She leaned forward, wiped his face with a damp cloth. "Who is Borya? Your brother? A friend for chess?"

"Borya? How do you know Borya?"

"You say his name, when you are sick. And before, you mention. When we play chess."

He told her everything. The wedding registry, the lucky green tie, the firewood, the mushrooms. The white shirt dripping with red paint. Matted blond hair falling over Borya's lifeless face. The bare feet. The drone of SS threats like distant thunder, a storm from which there is no escape. Everything. Even the things he could not put into words.

Anneliese was silent, her head lowered, one hand over her eyes.

"Was it me?" Filip whispered. "Did I do it?"

She rose, pushed another cot up to his and lay down. She held him while he wept, her body pressed against his back, her arms wrapped around his chest, her head nestled into his neck.

He woke alone. On the desk near the door, a single lamp sent feeble rays of light into the dark room. The fever was gone.

5

THE PRISONERS WERE SINGING. In the May twilight, the day's heat abating with the setting sun, the compound empty of all but the sentry at the gate, their voices floated over the camp. More than a few men, whether Russian refugees or American troops, raised their heads to listen. Energetic martial tunes gave way to slower, sadder songs that echoed each man's own longing for home, peace, and loved ones, no matter what the language or the words.

They had been brought in a few at a time, arriving in trucks, hands tied, sometimes at night. They were searched, stripped of all belongings but their uniforms, and registered in the POW logbook: name, rank, serial number. Hometown, date, and place of capture.

It was odd, wearing the same uniforms as the captured enemy. Filip thought it wise to sew the now meaningless ROA patch back on his sleeve, so there would be no mistaking his allegiance. There was no question now of mounting any kind of resistance movement; General Vlasov was himself in captivity in the Soviet Union and likely to be shot or hanged as a traitor. But until Filip could find other clothes, it seemed a necessary precaution.

The enclosure had filled up quickly. Within a few days, there was no room for anyone to lie down. The men stood, or squatted back-to-back to avoid leaning against the barbed wire. Food was dispensed through a chest-high opening in the fence. Each man received his bowl and spoon, moving in a line around the inside perimeter, a soldier counting off the empty vessels and utensils as they were returned.

"It's not right," Ilya observed, watching the line snake around in a spiral, unwinding like a grim dance, those in the center working their way to the periphery to receive their portion. "They are not animals."

"I'm not so sure about that," Sergeant Evans, standing nearby to oversee the meal, shot back. "I've seen the German prison camps."

"The men can't even lie down. These barracks"—Ilya gestured to the buildings—"are standing empty." His voice was hard, steely, as if uncoiling from a spring of anger in his chest. Filip had never seen his father-in-law so angry.

"Waiting for orders to move them out," the sergeant growled. "Anyway, it's not your concern."

"I am a Wehrmacht officer." They all turned toward the next man in line to receive his dinner. His voice, too, had a sharp edge, pitched higher than Ilya's. It rang out like that of a man used to command. "These men need protection from the sun and rain, and boards to cover the latrine. Geneva Conventions."

"Becker." Filip recognized the lieutenant. He was unshaven and his coat was stained, with a long gash in one sleeve. At the sound of his name, he turned, his back perceptibly straighter, and ran a hand through his dirty hair. He and Filip locked eyes.

"Keep moving. I'll get back to you." Evans turned on his heel and walked off toward the house.

Geneva Conventions. Rules for the humane treatment of prisoners. Filip thought of the thousand small humiliations he had witnessed and endured at the hands of German overseers—the gleeful way one would slather rancid butter on stale bread, then scrape all but the lightest coating off with his knife before tossing it on the detainee's plate; the endless taunts and insults—*idiot, half-wit, swine*; days filled with pointless degrading tasks invented for the Nazis' amusement.

Filip shuddered at the memory of Ilya and Ksenia facing imminent execution, when no Conventions stopped the action but the reluctance to waste a bullet. And for prisoners, no doubt, it had been many times worse. *What must it be like for women,* he wondered, *living in constant fear of being assaulted by almost anyone?*

Yet he admired Becker's courage, his commitment to the welfare of men of lower rank who were not even under his command. And he remembered the civility, the lieutenant treating him with something that bordered on respect. Hadn't Becker shared his stamps with him, expecting nothing in return?

That evening, Filip waited for a moment when no one was paying attention. He found the officer dozing at the edge of the enclosure, his back wedged in the corner, the wires digging into the cloth of his coat. "Becker," Filip whispered. "No, don't move," he advised when the man shuddered awake and tried to rise. Filip took a chunk of bread from his pocket, tore it in pieces small enough to fit through the space between barbs.

"*Danke,*" Becker's voice was hoarse, as if he'd been shouting for hours, but his eyes were clear and alert. "We need more water, also. To wash."

Filip nodded and moved away. He had no sway with the Americans, no power to persuade the leadership to do anything for the prisoners. Evans had given them two water buckets, some planks to cover the latrine, plus a daily sprinkling of lime to control the stench. Even so, the ditch teemed with flies. *No wonder they sing,* he thought. *That endless buzzing would drive anyone insane.*

What would happen to these men? Their clothes, after several cycles of sun and rain and the inescapable rubbing against the wire enclosure, were starting to look as bedraggled as the refugees'; their unshaven faces were streaked with dirt and sweat. People were waiting for them, somewhere, like Ksenia had waited for her son, wondering when they might return. Were they hurt, or missing limbs, like Maksim, their lives shattered? Were they alive? *My own mother doesn't know where I am,* he thought. *What might she imagine has happened to me?* He resolved to write to her as soon as they left the camp, by whatever means. It was unwise to write now and betray their Russian origins until the Americans had decided their fate.

"Sergeant Evans," Becker addressed the noncommissioned officer with barely suppressed contempt. "My men need water, to wash." He was still a few paces from the food dispensing window. "Water. To wash."

"I heard you." Evans, standing at the fence, took a last drag on his cigarette. "Damn Kraut," he muttered, crushing the butt with his boot. "Go to hell."

"Geneva Conventions," Becker called out. "Your country signed—"

"Shut up! Just shut the hell up!" He turned his back on the Germans still moving in the food line behind the fence. Filip, on his way to his own breakfast, glanced up just in time to see Becker's arm shoot out of the opening and encircle the sergeant's neck, pulling him up against the fence in a tight clinch. Before anyone could react, he whipped a length of cord from his other hand and passed it under Evans's chin, pulling the ends tight. The other prisoners tried to back away, but there was little free room in the cage; they stood silent.

In the compound everyone moved at once. The cook dropped the sack of bread he had been distributing. Evans reached for his pistol. Several soldiers rushed forward, but Filip got there first, took the pistol out of the sergeant's weakened grasp and held it up to Becker's forehead, while two of the Germans tried to loosen the lieutenant's grip and pull him away from the fence.

The cord around the sergeant's neck snapped just as Filip pulled the trigger. Evans slumped forward into the arms of several of his men. Becker staggered against the crush of prisoners at his back. Filip stood, dumbfounded, and let the gun slip through his fingers to the ground. In the melee, someone had jostled his arm; the bullet had missed its mark, grazing the top of Becker's head, where a thread of blood now trickled down his temple.

Filip watched, spellbound, as it ran down the side of the German's neck and oozed into the collar of his shirt. In the dust at his feet, he saw a piece of the would-be strangler's cord. He picked it up. It was made of threads pulled from woven cloth—shirts, fraying coat sleeves, and the like, he guessed—braided together in many strands and twisted into a thicker length. *Strong enough to strangle a man,* Filip thought, not without admiration for the painstaking work, the patience, the ingenuity. *Almost.* Like Ilya and his bits of wire, making something out of nothing, fighting with all his wits for a shred of human dignity.

In the evening, the Russians gathered around the stove in the common room, not for the heat but for the "coffee" brewed from toasted acorns the cook had ground for them in his spare time. It was bitter and earthy, but no one complained.

"I still don't understand why they won't let the Germans use the empty barracks." Ilya's hands were busy, as always, with his pliers and wire. From time to time, he glanced at the scrap of paper where his new customers had written out their orders: Duluth. Chicago. Syracuse. Philadelphia. Nashville. Also Peace, and Love. "It's cruel to keep them caged like that. One could easily go mad."

"And it's in violation of the international rules for treatment of prisoners," Grisha agreed. "Becker's right about that. He's an officer; he shouldn't even be in there, with the enlisted men. But the Americans don't have enough guards to watch them. This is only meant to be a transit stop on the way to larger facilities."

"How do you know?" Filip squinted at the older man through a haze of cigarette smoke.

"I had some English at university." Grisha packed his pipe and lit it with a burning brand from the stove. "I paid attention."

The next morning, Becker was gone. Not even Grisha could learn what had happened to him. "Maybe he's been transferred to another camp, with facilities for officers." Filip stirred his oatmeal.

"Or maybe he had an accident along the way," Grisha growled. "Move along. You're holding up the line."

After their own breakfast, the German prisoners were taken in groups of three or four to wash under the camp's cold-water shower, and issued clean underwear from the Americans' own supplies. Anneliese offered to launder for them without pay. "Every person should have clean clothes, *ja?*" she cajoled a reluctant Sergeant Evans with her disarming smile. "Your men can check their *Unterhosen* for secret messages, if you want."

In supply, they also found two large canvas tarpaulins. Half a dozen refugees were put to work climbing the barbed wire to stretch them across the top of the enclosure. Filip was spared this task, leaving it to others to cut their hands and arms to shelter the very men who had so recently been their own captors. *War is strange,* he thought. *It could have been the other way around. We could be the ones inside the cage.*

He found Evans in the far corner of the compound, as far from the prisoners as it was possible to be. "Filip." The sergeant shook a cigarette from his pack. Filip took it, tucked it into his shirt pocket to savor later. "You saved my neck, buddy. I owe you one. That SOB would have strung me up for sure."

Filip strained to understand the unfamiliar words. He could read the American's easy, friendly delivery and pleasant expression, but the language, the words, remained shrouded in mystery.

"I'm assigning you and Ilya to the road repair project. You'll be able to come and go at will, pretty much. What else can I do for you?"

That, for the most part, Filip understood. "Teach me English," he said.

6

FILIP WAS AN EAGER STUDENT, even if Evans, preoccupied with his administrative duties, was a haphazard teacher. Evans gave him old copies of *Stars and Stripes* for practice. "Just underline the words you don't know. You can ask me or one of the boys what they mean." He reached into a desk drawer. "Better yet, use this dictionary. It's English to German. That should help you out."

The new project occupied all of Filip's spare time. He found *Stars and Stripes*, with its personal accounts of the American experience of the war, entirely accessible; he especially enjoyed the poems, humorous anecdotes, and cartoons. Soon he was reading independently, calling on the sergeant only to clarify some colloquial expressions not found in his dictionary.

Before long, he had exhausted the camp's stock of back issues. "Are there any books? Anything, just so long as it's in English."

Evans raised an eyebrow at the young Russian's temerity. And surely he was Russian; that Yugoslav designation was an obvious self-preserving lie. "You think this is a library?" He wavered between respect for Filip's thirst for knowledge and annoyance at his presumption. Did this bold fellow think he could have anything he wanted?

And yet. Here was a man facing the future with nothing to depend on but his wits. The years when he should have been meeting girls, studying at university, learning a trade, going out with friends, had been stolen from him without even the compensation of fighting for his country. Who knew what scars he carried under that arrogant facade, after being kicked around from camp to camp like a goddam football? Who knew what he had seen?

Evans sighed. "I'll ask the boys, see if they can lend you something. But you can start with this." He handed Filip a pocket-sized army-issue Bible. "It's been through a lot with me. I want it back. By the way, if you want to find your family, start with your churches. It's where a lot of people go when they're in trouble."

Filip wasn't sure he could use that advice, even if it made a certain kind of sense. He wasn't in the habit of visiting churches, had no idea how to start looking for one. He was glad to lay the Bible aside and return it almost unread when one of the men came up with a battered copy of *David Copperfield*. He had read a great deal of Dickens at home, in translation; the Soviets approved of the social criticism in his works and honored the author's self-made status. Here was a chance to read a real book, in its original language. It helped that he already knew the story and could focus on learning scores of new words.

"Be careful with it, man," the soldier had said. "I picked it up in London, for my kids back home." Filip nodded and smiled, already immersed in the first paragraph. *Whether I shall turn out to be the hero of my own life . . .*

He carried the book everywhere, stopping to read whenever he had the time. It was slow going, its pages full of words he did not yet know, but he resisted using his dictionary so as not to interrupt the flow of the lively tale, picking up meaning from the context of each scene. *How can people live without books?* he thought. *What kind of life is that?*

The road project involved clearing debris from a section that had been heavily bombed. "Throw the loose stuff into the craters and pack dirt on top," Evans instructed. "Pack it good. We won't be paving here anytime soon."

They were issued a pass and permitted to work without supervision. "I wonder why." Filip leaned on his shovel and brushed the sweat out of his eyes.

"Who wants to watch a couple of men shovel rocks into a pit?" Ilya straightened, stretching his back. "They have their hands full with those prisoners."

After another hour or so they sat down in the shade of an old oak. Ilya rolled a cigarette. A squirrel chattered overhead. Ilya craned his neck in time to see it disappear into a hole in the trunk, with an angry flick of its puffed-out tail, its mouth full of leaves and twigs. *Nesting*, he thought. *Making a home.*

"I wonder where our women are," he said. He coughed and blew a stream of smoke into the clear May air. "Don't you want to know? To see your child?"

"Of course I want to know," Filip answered with half-closed eyes. "Pass me the tobacco. I'm out of American smokes."

They smoked a while in silence, the squirrel, resigned to their intrusive presence, going on about its business overhead. Filip took a chocolate bar out of his pocket, took a bite.

"I heard the Americans talking the other day, through an open window. I couldn't understand everything, but it sounded like they don't know what to do with us."

"What did they say?" Ilya waved his hand, refusing the last of the treat his son-in-law belatedly offered to share.

"Something like 'We're supposed to start sending them back, but their papers are a mess. I can't figure out who goes where.'"

"What else?"

"One said, 'These ROA guys, you know they're DOA. They won't get a hero's welcome.' And the other one said, 'Stupid bastards. Why do they keep coming back?'"

"What does DOA mean?"

"I asked a soldier later. It means 'dead when you get there.'"

It couldn't be more obvious. If the Americans started following orders to the letter, the repatriation would begin. It wouldn't matter what anyone's papers said; there was no guarantee their stateless status would protect them. Sergeant Evans had given them a clear chance to get away, and they had nearly squandered it.

Ilya stood up. "Get your things together, Filip. We're leaving."

"What, now? But we haven't finished. It's still early—"

"Not the road. The camp. Tomorrow morning."

In the morning, just after breakfast, they simply walked away. Outside the gate they met Anneliese. She pedaled slowly, her basket balanced on the handlebars. Her knowing glance took in the rucksack Ilya carried, but she said nothing, pausing to follow them with her eyes before entering the compound to deliver the laundry.

Once they put the camp behind them and it was clear there would be no pursuit, the men picked up the pace, moving into the trees when the sun rose higher in the sky.

"Good thing we're in the American sector." Ilya shifted the rucksack to his other shoulder. "I've heard the British are sending all ROA back to the Soviet Union, even if they were only auxiliaries or sympathizers."

"Why? Aren't we all refugees? My feet hurt. Can we stop now?"

Ilya ignored his son-in-law's complaint. "They see us as enemy combatants."

"Combatants? That's ridiculous. The Allies were never our enemies." *And I never wanted anything to do with this stupid idea. I never wanted to fight anyone.*

"The British are a cold people, logical. They can't see how anyone wearing a German uniform can be anything but the enemy. Americans are more practical. They can use our hands to help rebuild the country they destroyed."

"So why did they let us go? The sentry must have seen us." Filip slowed down to demonstrate his growing fatigue.

"They are not disciplined. Do you remember how they rolled into camp, handing out chocolate, laughing and waving? Their people feel secure between the oceans, they know nothing of living with war or the harsh realities of military occupation."

Filip sat down defiantly on a fallen tree trunk. "Where are we, anyway?"

"South of Berlin, southwest of Dresden." Ilya swung the rucksack to the ground and rubbed his shoulder where the canvas strap had bitten into the cloth of his coat.

"I know that." Did the old man think him stupid? "But where exactly are we going?"

"To find my wife, and yours." Ilya rested against a boulder, drank deeply from his water flask.

"Where? How?" Filip's voice rose in exasperation. "Who will help us? The Germans hate us because we're Russians. The Russians see us as traitors. So we can't go back, and we can't stay here. We left our passports and working papers, false though they are, at the American camp. So we can't leave the country, either." He stopped ranting and turned his face away. "And don't say, 'God will help us.'"

"We must keep moving," Ilya said with conviction. "There are others like us, many others. When we find them, we will find our strength, and get information about our family, too, I'm certain." He leaned the rucksack in Filip's direction. "You take this for a while."

Filip winced when the frayed strap settled onto his shoulder. "What did you put in here to make it so damn heavy?"

"My toolbox. A rusty hatchet head the Americans threw away; we can easily make a new handle for it. The boots you won in last week's card game. A little food. Extra underclothes and socks. What we don't have, and need, is a change of clothes."

Filip grunted. He kept a few paces behind Ilya on the forested path, walking parallel to the road. He knew the toolbox alone made up most of the weight. It was made of wood panels several centimeters thick, filled with awls and files and chisels, flat polished disks of ivory and horn ready for carving, cutters and pliers and spools of wire.

It was a mystery to Filip how the old man had managed to hold on to his precious box since leaving Yalta. Time and again, it had been confiscated by guards and camp officials, only to reappear in his possession a day or two later with no explanation. Even in the pandemonium of Dresden, Ilya had refused to leave his toolbox with the piles of carefully labeled luggage on the railroad platform, as if he knew it would only be safe in his own hands, like a cherished child.

PART VII

Family

1

THE OLD MAN was still sleeping when Filip got back. The sun was already high in the sky, the walls of the dilapidated shed pierced by its rays. Filip hated sheltering like this, moving with the stealth of escaped criminals, hiding in barns and outbuildings, scrounging for food, sleeping, as often as not, in the woods. *But we are criminals,* he thought grimly. *Turncoats and traitors.* And now Ilya was sick, very sick, Filip guessed, looking at the face and neck flushed with fever, the dull, sweat-soaked hair. He had never known his father-in-law to sleep so late.

At home, in Yalta, Ilya was always up at first light, bent over his worktable, tapping and scraping at one of his brooches before leaving for his job at the shipping office or the market, depending on the day of the week. This steadfast industriousness, along with the innate goodness of the man, the quiet, unswerving moral certitude, was what Filip found unspeakably irritating.

Filip would lie in bed, listening to Ilya's and Ksenia's voices in the kitchen, his a low, calming counterpoint to her higher, more agitated tone. He would wait for them to finish their breakfast tea, consciously avoiding the silent reproach he was sure he saw in Ilya's eyes, evading, too, the unspoken questions about his own lack of occupation or thought about his future.

That was all long ago, or seemed like it. Before the flight from their homeland, where, he felt, it had been possible to live in relative safety, not like this furtive animal existence. He had come to terms with the German presence, had learned their language. But no, they had to go right into the thick of it, shunted from labor camp to work detail, not knowing whether the bombs they dodged were Russian, German, American, or British. He was sick of it—the hunger, filth, humiliation, disease—and through it all, the peculiar numbing boredom, and the stupid perpetual discomfort.

"I should have stayed in Yalta," Filip muttered. "Taken my chances." But the family had insisted on leaving and Galya was going with them, carrying his child.

He stepped outside and sat down on a tree stump. His head hurt from too much cheap wine, but at least the Fräulein had been a fine one, resting her plump arms on his shoulders, whirling with him, faster and faster, propelled by the driving polka tempo. *What was her name?*

Gretchen? No, they can't all be Gretchens, just as we are not all Ivans. Anna? Sophie? No matter. There were others. The tavern had been full, the dancers spilling out into the yard, where it was cool and lit only by the lamplight streaming out the open door. It had been a relatively calm night, with only two or three fights breaking out over who got which girl, none of the fights involving him. There were enough girls.

Still, he hated not remembering her name. After Anneliese, whose mute kindness had left a permanent imprint on his heart, there had been others. Hilda of the dancing eyes, her mouth hungry for kisses and chocolate; plain, serious Stella, whose cool hands took him into new realms of previously unimagined pleasure. Barely twenty years old and now free of camp restrictions, he was full of restless energy. Whenever he could detach himself from Ilya, he was his own man.

These stops in his personal odyssey were more memorable to him than the nameless towns, the places they had passed through since leaving the American camp; stops leading him back to Galya, of course. Of course to Galya, his wife.

And who knew where she was? The country was awash with bands of wandering refugees prompted to keep moving by hastily enacted municipal decrees: you may stay within the village limits only forty-eight hours or a day or, in rare cases, one week. Filip chafed under the obligation to stay with Ilya, but had to admire the older man's survival instinct, his ability to earn a little money and find food, while quietly gathering information. He knew it was better to stay together, that finding one person would require an extraordinary stroke of luck. *Two people*, he reminded himself, *not one*. Galina and Ksenia were certainly together; nothing short of death could make Ksenia abandon her daughter, of that he was sure. Two women, then, and a newborn child.

Well, this was what happened in war. Galina must understand. He was not a monk. Should they find each other again, he would come to her a full-grown man, free of nervous boyish fumbling, of the false starts and abrupt endings that had marked their intimacy, such as it was, since their clumsy wedding night. He smiled to remember that innocent shame and trepidation, that perfect ignorance.

He tried to imagine Galina's eyes clouded with desire, like Stella's, her head thrown back in abandon, or giggling with mischief, like Hilda. He hadn't known women could be so different one from another, so surprising. Now he knew.

He heard Ilya cough inside the shed and call to him. Filip stubbed his cigarette out carefully on the sole of his shoe, dropped the butt into his shirt pocket, and went in. The older man was sitting on his blanket, his legs stretched out in front of him in a childlike pose; the cuffs of his ill-fitting pants revealed a swath of pasty skin above his bunched socks. Desperate to lose the conspicuous German uniforms, they had settled gladly for the first pieces of clothing that came to hand, even if Filip's new shirt had been liberated from an unattended clothesline, the two good wool uniforms left, neatly folded, on the ground in exchange.

Ilya's face was ashen except for two clownish spots of fever on his cheeks. "Is there any water left?"

Filip checked the flask, emptied the contents into a tin cup, and watched Ilya drink with infuriating slowness. *My God, how much longer until we find someone, anyone? How long do I have to carry this old man?*

"Where is your ring?" Ilya cut into his thoughts, pointing to the wedding band on his own hand. Filip stared at him in momentary confusion, recovered his wits, and reached into his pants pocket. How stupid not to have taken it out of his wallet and put it back on his finger after the dance. How careless.

He felt around, thrusting his hand deep into first one pocket, then the other, expecting to find his horseshoe-shaped leather pouch within the folds. The wallet was not there. "*Chort voz'mi,*" he swore. "Devil take it. I put it here . . ."

"Did you sell it? Are we out of money?"

"No, I did not sell it." Filip, sounding like a petulant boy, discarded without thinking the only reasonable excuse for taking the ring off his finger. "Stay here," he said. He snatched up the flask and walked back toward the road. "There's a couple of potatoes left from last night, maybe a little cheese. I'll be back soon with more water." He turned and ran, not caring who saw him, back toward the village, the tavern, hoping to remember the way to the plump girl's house.

Her name, it suddenly struck him, was Krista.

Approaching the village, he replayed the previous evening's events. This was the road, these the farms, some with freshly ploughed patches among the charred fields. This idyllic section of Bavarian countryside had received its share of Allied bombing, evidenced by cratered roads and the rubble of destroyed buildings. Yet something was growing, the green shoots vivid and vulnerable amid the stubble of burned crops. He knew nothing of agriculture, could not guess if these were wheat, rye, or ordinary meadow grass. Still, it was a sign, if one believed in signs.

Soon the houses came thickly, some standing apart, with fenced yards and fruit trees, others attached each to the next in rows of five or six, each unit set off from its neighbor by a different shade of pastel paint—sky blue, beige, pink, yellow, peach—all under identical green tile roofs. Signs of bomb damage were everywhere, but it was clear that repairs had begun: boarded windows, yards swept clean of debris and broken tiles, usable bricks, glass, and timber in neat stacks at irregular intervals. He didn't know if these materials were communal property, available to anyone who needed them, or closely guarded private reserves for sale or trade. It looked like local pride and the work of willing hands would soon restore the village to its peacetime appearance. All the better to welcome their injured returning fighters, and bury their dead, he mused. The war was over for everyone.

What he had needed yesterday was an apothecary. He felt he would never sleep again if the old man didn't stop coughing. Ilya could not work until his fever came down and his hands stopped shaking. Filip was amazed that, even now, people would buy a wire pin or bracelet, paying with a little cash or food.

The apothecary, when he found it, was closed. Filip had stood outside its shuttered window. What to do now? Honey. Honey would help, if he could find some. Standing outside the shop, he had swayed slightly, giving in to the wave of nostalgia that, for several excruciating moments, took him home, his mother ministering to his boyhood illnesses with tenderness and honeyed tea. And music. She would play her favorite records for him, singing along in a light falsetto, slightly off-key, making him laugh. He could hear it now, Strauss operettas, *Onegin*, *Aida*. Yes, especially *Aida*, the drums, the trumpets . . .

But this was no reverie. There really was a trumpet. He had followed the direction of its blare, pulled along the dusk-darkened streets by its resounding timbre. Approaching the tavern, he had heard other instruments, too—an accordion and then, closer still, a guitar. He had ducked in through the open doorway and listened, watching the trio at the far end of the room, the boy trumpeter full of joyous energy, accompanied by a sprightly white-haired accordion player. The guitarist, perched on a tall stool, beat out the tempo with his wooden leg.

They had made a fine noise, those three, the sounds from their unlikely ensemble clean and bright and lively. The old accordionist seemed to lead, his yellowed fingers bent to the chipped keys with easy familiarity, followed by the guitar player, who picked and strummed a scarred instrument crisscrossed with scratches. The trumpet, too, had seen better days, the horn surface pocked and dinged, the finish dulled, but the sound, when the young musician closed his eyes and blew, was thrilling, reverberating in the hot crowded room like a call to freedom.

Filip had threaded his way between the dancing couples. He'd scanned the room for Red Army uniforms and found none. He signaled a serving girl for a glass of beer and slipped his wedding ring into his coin purse. *Just a glass or two. What's the harm?* He would find honey or medicine in the morning. It felt good to be young and free, with money in his pocket, even if the money was, strictly speaking, not his own, and the freedom illusory.

After the second glass, he was dancing with a succession of nameless smiling girls. And weren't they all pretty in their short-sleeved cotton dresses, moving easily into his arms and out again, their low-heeled shoes skimming the creaking floorboards, bare legs flashing in the dim light? He had not danced in such a long time; he gave himself up to it with no thought at all, letting go of obligations, promises, memories, and caution.

When the band stopped playing, he noticed the girl he'd been dancing with, and realized he had partnered her several times in the last hour. She looked up at him, her round, open face blooming with freshness and glowing with sweat. "*Ein Bier?*" he said, pointing the way to a vacant table near the back door.

"*Nein,*" she smiled. "*Wein, bitte.*" He paid for the unlabeled bottle, pushing his ring out of sight with his little finger while he counted out nearly all his remaining coins. The wine was sharp, young, and bitter, but they drank it willingly, thirsty for a good time. They had talked, their heads nearly touching, Filip intoxicated with her fine russet curls, her vulnerable, perfectly formed ears. He poured the last

of the wine into his glass—she had only drunk a little—and asked
her name.

"Krista," she said. She had pulled him to his feet, taking him out
of the crowded room, into the yard, where they danced under a sky
filled with threads of dark clouds before retreating into the shadows,
away from other couples. "Krista," he repeated, pressing her back
against a tree. "Krista."

And the honey? He had remembered Ilya's cough, remembered asking her where he could get some honey when all the shops were closed.

"Come with me," she said. "We have honey at home, not far from
here."

The walk to her house was a vague memory. Had they turned this
corner, passed this pond? It was a farmhouse, of that he was sure, but
which one? Stumbling in the dark, one arm draped around Krista's
neck, his head buzzing, he had paid little attention to his surroundings.
And what had happened to the honey? He could clearly see Krista
lifting the crock out of the cupboard, doling several large spoonfuls
into a jar, giving him her fingers to lick, one by one. And then all
was muddled, the girl pushing him out the door, answering a voice
from upstairs, an unseen presence descending slowly, with heavy tread,
down the steps.

Filip remembered walking along the road—this road? The early
morning sun had found him sitting under a tree, with a sore head
and stiff legs, a foul taste on his desiccated tongue, his head hammering a dull relentless rhythm. He had found his way back to the
shed without much difficulty; it stood some distance from the road,
in a yard fringed with apple trees, behind an abandoned cottage with
a ragged hole in the roof.

Now he needed to find Krista's house, his wallet, and his ring.

It was hopeless. The half dozen small farms he passed all looked
very much the same: the same green tile roof, same painted gate, same
flower trellis outside the same sturdy door. Even the lace curtains that

billowed out the open windows looked identical. There were differ-
ences, individual details that marked each house distinctly from its
neighbors, but nothing he would have noticed in the dark, his head
thick with drink, all his senses trained on an amorous conquest he
still did not know if he had achieved. He leaned against a boulder
at the side of the road and lit the stub of his cigarette. What to do?

He watched a lone figure come into view in the distance, a woman
on a bicycle just rounding the curve in the road. *Guess I'll have to ask,*
he told himself. *Can't sit here all day.*

He had already stepped into the road, raising his arm to get the
woman's attention, when he heard the sound of an automobile engine
and retreated, instinctively, into the shelter of the trees.

The country was overrun with military personnel: British, American,
Soviet—all waiting for instructions on how the newly brokered peace
was to be administered. Most private cars had been commandeered
by one unit or another. But who could be trusted? Not these men.
Judging by the Russian catcalls, they were Red Army, and that could
only mean trouble for him.

Filip heard the car slow down just short of his hiding place. He
heard a door slam and the woman's bicycle fall to the ground.

"Sashka, we have no time! The colonel wants his brandy," one of
the men called out.

"You just had one, anyway." Another voice, deeper, older. "Let
this one go."

"That was two hours ago, and she was ugly. This one's not bad.
Horosha. Look how smooth and ripe she is. Who can resist? The colonel
can wait five minutes." This voice was young, brash, and confident.

Careful not to disturb the foliage concealing him, Filip peered out.
A young soldier had the woman by both arms, pinned against the car.
She turned her head from side to side, struggling, kicking at him with
short, desperate thrusts of her small feet.

Sashka moved her arms behind her back, easily grasping both wrists
in one hand while he yanked at the neck of her dress with the other.

He laughed. "What? You don't like it here in the road? Excuse me, comrades, we need a little privacy." He spun the girl around and pushed her, still holding her wrists, toward the woods.

Filip froze. *Krista.* He almost said the name out loud, catching himself just in time. He moved silently deeper among the trees, ducking behind a wide oak for cover. He should do something, but what?

He had no papers. He could impersonate a German, but that would get him, at the very least, a severe beating. If they found out he was Russian, it would most certainly be worse. Out of uniform, without papers, he could expect arrest, deportation, exile, even death. Krista was a nice girl, but he did not know how far things had gone between them after the dance, or how many such encounters she may already have survived. The young stud was sure to take exception to having his fun interrupted. *If I had a gun,* Filip thought, *maybe I could be brave.* But what good were his bare hands against three armed men? It was unthinkable. Maybe something would happen. Maybe she would get away.

He listened with growing apprehension to the pair's approaching footsteps. Krista must have stumbled; he heard her cry out and fall. He heard Sashka curse, pull her up, and slam her back against the oak. "Hold on there, Fräulein, let's just tie those pretty hands together, shall we? That's better."

Filip caught his breath when he heard Krista spit at the soldier and unleash an unintelligible stream of invective, a hysterical mix of pleading, cursing, and sobs. "*Molchi, dura,*" the soldier said, muffling her protests with a hand over her mouth. "Shut up, you fool. *Ai!* This one's a biter!" he called out to his waiting companions.

"Sashka, you animal. *Dovol'no.* Enough. Let's go," the older one replied.

"Mama," Filip whispered while the soldier raped the girl, quickly and efficiently, on the other side of the tree. "Why is this happening to me again?"

He was back in Yalta, three years ago, frozen with fear and indecision, unable to defend Galya, his dearest friend, from an attack that seemed, at the time, as imminent as this one. The attack had not come; she had walked away unhurt. He could not remember why. But the paralyzing inertia, the complete inability, like now, to move or speak—that came back to him so intensely he had to dig his fingers into the bark of the tree to keep from falling.

When he recovered his senses, the men were gone, leaving an echo of bawdy soldiers' ditties reverberating on the placid afternoon air. The sounds of heedless birdsong, of crickets chirping and the humming of bees seemed like an obscenity; surely, the only appropriate response to what had just happened here, at the side of the road, in daylight, was silence.

He considered his options. Should he wait until she collected herself and left? No one would ever know he had been there. No one but himself. No, that was wrong. She might need help after her ordeal; he was not made of stone. And there was still the matter of the missing wallet.

"Krista," he said, coming around to her side of the oak. He glanced furtively at her disheveled hair, noticed the imprint around her mouth where the brutal dirty hand had pressed against her face. "Krista, I . . ." He averted his eyes from her crumpled dress and its missing buttons, the angry bruises on her neck and breast.

"You! How long . . . Did you know . . . Why are you here?" She looked up at him with red-rimmed but tearless eyes. Crouched at the base of the tree she looked small, feral.

"I could not . . . could not . . ." It was too much to explain. "You don't understand."

She struggled to get to her feet, ignoring his extended arm, pushing herself up from the ground with both hands. She rubbed at the fresh tie marks around her wrists. "No, I do not understand. Anyone, a stranger, could have at least made some noise, it might have been

enough to scare them off. But you . . . We danced. We talked together.
I even let you kiss me. And you just stayed there, hiding?"

Filip tried to take her elbow to steady her, but she slapped at his
hand and pushed past him, furious, out of the woods. He saw how
the back of her dress was slashed and torn, bloody from where Sashka
had rammed her against the tree's rough bark. *I am so sorry. I should have
done something,* he thought, but could not say it.

She picked up her bicycle and started walking with it along the
road. "Look what they do," she said, pointing to the wheel twisted
beyond repair. "Your countrymen. Just out of malice. Why did you
come, anyway? To collect your honey? For your sick *Vater?*"

"Honey?" He had forgotten all that, forgotten about Ilya and all
those other complications yet to be faced. "No. I . . . last night . . .
I lost my wallet."

She kept walking, one hand holding the front of her dress closed,
the other steering the bicycle along its crooked course. Filip followed
a few steps behind, not really knowing why.

"Well, I am very sorry you lost your wallet," she said finally, turning to face him. "I thought you were a decent person, intelligent and
kind. But you are only a coward. Even if I had your wallet, I would
not return it to you." She walked on, limping a little, struggling to
keep the bicycle's good wheel on the road.

Filip stood a while, watching her stiff gashed back recede slowly,
then turned back in the direction of the shed. "He's not my *Vater.*
My father does not sell trinkets in the street. My father would know
what to do," he muttered, kicking at a stone in his path, feeling his
anger and frustration rise.

The stone arced, bounced once, and rolled into the weeds at the
side of the road. Filip bent down, picked it up. It was an ordinary gray-
brown stone, hot from the sun; it fit perfectly in his hand. He looked
at it, studied it, as if intent on deciphering a cryptic message carved
into its crevices and striations. He pulled his arm back and threw the
stone into the woods, nearly falling over with the force of the effort.

He stooped, picked up another and another, flinging each one with all his strength, running along the road, giving in to the frenzy with a mindless, mirthless obsessiveness fed by dumb fury.

When he stopped, bent over, panting, hands on his knees, his shirt plastered to his skin with foul-smelling perspiration, he felt empty, his mind mercifully blank. Filip passed a gritty hand over his face and laughed, picturing what he must look like: a crazed man with a dirt-streaked face, in unwashed clothing, stumbling along a country road with nothing to his name but his name. He heard a car approaching and hid in the woods, sitting motionless behind a clump of blackberry bushes until the sound of the motor died away in the distance.

2

FILIP SAT IN the woods a long time, long after the noise of the motor faded away and the air filled with bird sounds and the conspiratorial stirring of leaves above his head. He watched a trio of crows follow one another from tree to tree, their iridescent feathers glinting in filtered sunlight, looking for—who knew what crows looked for? Food, or smaller birds to intimidate with their shameless audacity. All the trees seemed alike to him, and maybe the crows thought so, too. They rested only a moment before lifting off for the next perch, stopping now and then for a brief raspy consultation. All at once, they were gone, taking to the sky above the treetops with raucous cawing cacophony. *So we creep from one hiding place to the next,* he thought, *each one identical to the last, meaningless, and no closer to the answers we need. How will we know when the end of the road is in sight?*

It was hunger that finally got him moving; he had eaten nothing since the night before and knew that their own supplies were probably depleted. He got up, stretched, stamped his feet to ease the stiffness in his legs. It looked like midafternoon, the sun still high but starting to arc westward, the way he needed to go to rejoin Ilya. *Time to move on,* he thought. No point staying here, wherever here was. Regensburg lay to the northwest, a city, with a chance to meet more refugees, hear the gossip, find out how others were managing to survive. If he could only get his father-in-law back on his feet.

Avoiding the road, he followed an overgrown footpath, weaving between stands of evergreens interspersed with large deciduous trees. He found a stream, washed the grime from his face and neck, drank deeply with cupped hands. He remembered to fill the flask, wiped it on his shirt before returning it to his pants pocket. It would not last them more than the night, with Ilya's feverish state, but the country was verdant and water was easily found.

More easily than food.

He had no money and nothing to barter but the offer of work. And what could he do? His experience building scenery for the theater group seemed like a lifetime ago; it was of no practical use to him now. Woefully clumsy at repairs, reluctant to get his hands dirty, uneasy around farm animals, he had little to offer in exchange for a meal. Unlike Ilya, who was resourceful, skilled with tools. And humble. Filip had watched him go, cap in hand, approach a farmhouse and come away a short time later with a piece of bread, some cheese, an egg, or a capful of apples. "I nailed up the shutters," he would say, or, "The henhouse roof had a hole in it," or, now and then, "Some people are just kind. They wanted nothing done, so I made them a pin with their son's name. He is still missing."

Filip had no aptitude for this kind of work. The few times he had tried, stuttering idiotically at the hard-eyed woman who answered the door, he was sent away like the vagrant he was, shamed and angry.

He followed the stream until it disappeared underground, reduced to a burbling trickle. Keeping the sun straight ahead, he found the footpath again, leading him ever westward. His feet ached. He thought about returning to the stream; he could almost feel the cool fresh water soothe away the fatigue of so much hiking, but it was getting late; he had to press on.

The path meandered through green fairy-tale woods. Any thicket could hide a wolf, a bear; entering a clearing ringed with tender saplings and huge old trees, he half-expected to see Baba Yaga's dilapidated hut on its spindly chicken legs, foul-smelling smoke hanging in the air as witness to her cannibalistic proclivities. Or maybe he would meet Mayne Reid's headless horseman, his black cloak floating like a curse around his emaciated body, while his severed head scattered drops of blood along the trail. Shunning these horrors, and to divert himself from the gnawing in his gut, he imagined himself as James Fenimore Cooper's pathfinder, sure-footed and vigilant, or a latter-day Robinson Crusoe, fashioning a new life from the shipwrecked remnants of the past.

He was not entirely alone. Deep in the woods, he heard children's voices calling and laughing, sounding like all children everywhere. When the path led him closer to the road, he glimpsed a sturdy woman herding a reluctant cow; occasionally, he was aware of the blur of a cyclist, or an ominous speeding automobile. Once, he saw a group of people, two women, a teenaged girl, a small boy, an old man—walking slowly single file along the very edge of the road, turning to talk to one another as they went. What language were they speaking? He strained to make it out, but they were too far away, their voices muted, the words indistinguishable. He soon left them behind.

All of it struck him as familiar, bucolic and unexceptional, yet also inescapably strange. *I am a refugee. Bezhenets.* The word haunted him, the designation frightening in its paradoxically permanent transience. *I am a man with no home.*

Abruptly, the woods ended and Filip found himself in a large clearing facing the back of a midsized wooden structure, the sharply gabled roof topped with what looked like a small bell tower. Not surprisingly, there was no bell; all metal would have been melted down for the war effort. The building stood in a pool of gravel, wildflowers and grass reclaiming their place among the finely crushed rocks. He walked around to the front and saw a wide tree-lined alley leading back to the main road.

So this was the church. Ilya had said something about rumors of a refugee community, people who had received temporary residence permits in exchange for work on reconstruction projects. But that was north of here, closer to the cities, he was sure, where the damage was greater and the need for extra hands more urgent. And the old man was in the grip of fever, his words unreliable. He might have misheard, or simply dreamed the whole thing, the idea planted in his mind by the same earnest desire for reunion with his family that gave his life purpose.

Yet here it was, with the Orthodox cross over the doors. "Like a target," Filip said with a smirk. "Easy for the Soviets to find us, round us up in groups rather than catch us one by one." No, there must be more to this; something he didn't know. People on the run did not foolishly expose themselves to risk this way. Or did they? He thought of Sergeant Evans lending him his Bible to practice English, saying, *If you want to find your family, start with the churches. It's where a lot of people go when they're in trouble.* What if it was true?

Filip stood outside the building, noted its small windows and completely unremarkable exterior. It was built atop broad stone stairs leading to wide double doors. How had they managed this? With the nearly total lack of building materials and the refugees' universally impoverished state, he could not help but be impressed. Where did these people get their determination, their strength?

He mounted the steps, noting how deeply cracked the stones were, pitted and chipped as if they had withstood a battle. Closer to the doors, he saw that the walls looked recently erected, the wood scarred with burn marks, deep gouges in some of the mismatched planks. The doors, while solid, showed traces of bullet holes and heavy wear. He pulled, and found them unlocked.

Inside, the church was dark, lit only with a few candles near the iconostasis at the front, a small glass votive candle—just a wick immersed in fragrant oil—glowing before each icon. *Lampada,* he told himself, remembering the word from his childhood, before his mother stopped taking him to church in Yalta. He recognized some of the likenesses represented on the icons: Christ on the right, his mother Mary on the left. John the Baptist. How had he known that? When had he paid attention? Two archangels, he didn't know which ones, but you could tell by the wings and the solid virility of their stance. Michael? Gabriel? Some of the other saints looked vaguely familiar, but he didn't know their names, or their importance.

Where had these icons come from, and at what cost? Even he knew you couldn't just paint one; it was an art with specific traditions, strict rules, and rigorous training. Living with Ksenia and Ilya, he had felt some of that passionate spirit, that bullheaded stubbornness that did not admit defeat no matter what the difficulty. But this, this effort was extraordinary. "Miraculous," he said with a sardonic smile.

His ears caught a sound, no more than the softest swish coming from the depths of the empty interior. A gaunt stick of a man emerged, his pale face and graying beard floating toward Filip as if on air, black robes blending into the surrounding gloom. The man spoke, his voice a gravelly basso profundo, in a language Filip recognized as Slavic but did not understand.

Filip shrugged, shook his head. "*Po Russki?*"

"*Horosho.* Very well." The man smiled, his face creasing into deep folds around his eyes and mouth. "Are you here for vespers? We start at six o'clock, but you may wait there." He pointed to a row of wooden chairs along the back wall, his Russian confident but lightly accented.

"No. Vespers? No. Is that the evening prayer service? I'm looking for my wife. This tall"—he raised his hand level with his own head—"blonde, with a . . . a baby." He stopped, put his hand down. He didn't know how else to describe the person whose features were so clear in his mind. "She is beautiful."

The man nodded as if in recognition. "We see new people almost every day. Many move on, but a growing number are receiving work permits and starting to build a small community—Russian, Ukrainian, Serbian, like me. Stay for vespers, or come tomorrow, Sunday. There will be more people. You can ask them about your family."

Before Filip could answer, the door creaked open, letting in a welcome shaft of light and some people. Filip recognized the group he had glimpsed through the trees, walking along the road. They greeted the cleric and spread out, each intent on what seemed to be assigned duties. The old man cranked open the windows. He stepped behind a low counter near the door and set out a tray of slender candles, a stack of notepaper, and a few pencils. The boy busied himself with the incense burner, stirring the cooled embers, adding a few fresh crystals to the plain metal cup, touching them with a straw lit from a burning candle. Carefully, he lowered the ornate slotted lid onto the rim of the cup.

Almost at once, the church filled with the aroma of frankincense, familiar even to Filip. He breathed it in, his mind reeling with confusion. He had no attachment to these rituals. None. He disdained his mother's unquestioning reliance on ancient traditions, mocked her belief in miracles and benevolent spiritual protection, considered himself a thoroughly modern man who embraced rational thinking and the advances of science. He did not believe in God. And yet something pulled at him. *Nostalgia*, he told himself. *That's all.*

He stood awkwardly in the room. The woman and the teenaged girl, kerchiefs tied over their hair, swept the rough, age-stained floor, wiped down the painted icons, collected the burnt-out candle stubs and wax drippings into a large pickle jar, talking quietly among themselves. How often had his mother taken him to church? Had she, too, performed these homely tasks? In that time long ago, the time before conscious memory, had he formed impressions, stored in some recess of his mind; impressions that now, nudged by the sight of candle flames undulating before doleful Byzantine faces and, even more, by the scent that reached directly back into an intimate place completely unknown to him?

Filip shook his head to clear away the bewildering thoughts. "Just hungry," he muttered, then louder, "Thank you, Father . . ."

"Stefan," the man answered. "I am only a deacon. I can lead prayers and Bible reading but am not authorized to perform the Mass. Once a month, we have a priest come from the city to conduct a proper service, along with baptisms and weddings. Burial services I can do, of necessity; they cannot wait. I also bake the church bread for Communion." With a hand on Filip's elbow, he led him toward the counter near the door. "Write the names, first names only, of your loved ones, living and dead, in separate columns. We will add them to our prayers. Leave a coin, if you can, to help us buy flour and oil. If not, God bless."

Well, what can it hurt? Maybe someone would recognize the names, grouped together like that. The paper was rough, with an ochre discoloration around the edges, an Orthodox cross hand-drawn at the top. In the column headed *zdravie* (long life), he entered "Zoya, Vadim, Ksenia, Ilya, Galina, and child," realizing he did not know his child's name. Under *za upokoi* (in memory), he wrote "Maksim," and, after a moment's pause, "Boris."

Father Stefan stood by his side, combing the fingers of his left hand through his grizzled beard. With his right, he reached across the counter and extracted a diminutive loaf, no bigger than a small apple, composed of a flattened circle topped with a smaller disk of dough, stamped with a cross, the whole thing pasty white and hard to the touch. "It is only flour, water, and salt, unleavened as indicated in the Bible," the deacon said, placing the bread in Filip's hand. "And it is not consecrated, since that can only be done during Mass. But it will feed you, body and soul, if you will let it." He turned and walked toward the iconostasis, crossed himself broadly, touched his lips to Christ's image, and disappeared into the altar area, closing the door soundlessly behind him.

Filip knew he should save the bread for Ilya, but hunger got the better of him. He broke off a piece and ate it, almost without chewing, to quiet the relentless ache in his gut. The bread came apart in his hands, the two layers separating with only the slightest pressure from his fingers. He ate the bottom piece, saving the smaller disk, the one with the Orthodox cross etched into its surface, for Ilya. *The old man would care about something like that,* he told himself, neglecting to acknowledge that he had eaten the larger of the two pieces.

Back on the road, he walked rapidly, the late summer dusk gathering around him, gradually obscuring the landscape, painting the sky in shades of indigo and mauve. He had gone only a short distance when he glimpsed an object lying partially concealed in roadside weeds. His wallet.

He picked it up, turned it, felt the familiar horseshoe shape in his hands. When he opened it, after a minute's hesitation, he was not surprised to find it empty. No money. No ring.

He felt nothing. No loss, no anger, not even disappointment. Nothing.

Filip quickened his pace, anxious to reach the shed and confront Ilya with the words that were forming in his mind. *We can't continue this way. If you can walk, let's go. If you're too sick, we must find help. I found the church. We can go there and talk to people, figure out what to do.* He rehearsed his speech, his stride becoming purposeful, his will strong and clear. *It's time to stop hiding like rabbits, scurrying from hole to hole. Time to do something, find a way to live. If not here, then somewhere else.* "And we need papers," he said aloud, pulling hard on the door of the shed, dislodging one of its shaky planks. He kicked it aside and peered into the dim interior.

3

THE SHED WAS EMPTY. The smell of stale sweat and urine, unwashed bodies and soiled clothing, mixed in his nostrils with half-rotted hay, hard-packed dirt, a whiff of animal musk. How had they endured it, thinking themselves fortunate to find such a good resting place? And where was the old man?

Filip stared at the spot where he had last seen his father-in-law, as if willing him to materialize on the tamped-down hay that still held the contours of his body. Nothing there, only the faint, surreptitious rustling of mice in dark corners.

Nothing but the rucksack. It had been moved, dragged, judging by the track in the dirt, toward the door, but it was still there. So Ilya must be nearby. Maybe he felt better and decided to try to find some food or went out looking for water.

Filip picked up the rucksack and immediately noticed how light it felt. Thieves? But why not take the whole thing? He took a quick inventory: hatchet, boots, an extra shirt, socks, matches, his sketchbook and stamp albums, the shovel they had taken from the American camp. It was all there. The only thing missing was Ilya's workbox, with its cutting patterns, sketches, half-finished pieces, scavenged wire, and materials.

Had the old man gone completely out of his mind? He was in no condition to work; his hands could not be steady enough, after days of fever, to cut, carve, or shape anything successfully. Something was wrong here, something that filled Filip with dread, a premonition compounded with the strong possibility that whatever had happened, it was once again his fault.

He slung the rucksack onto his shoulder, grateful, in spite of his alarm, for its lighter weight. He stepped out of the shed and stood looking around, immobilized by indecision. Which way would Ilya have gone? Did it make sense to look for him now, or should he wait until morning?

No, he needed to go now, before whatever trail there was grew cold. He adjusted the strap on his burden, felt it slip into the groove it had worn in his shoulder during these weeks of tramping, and set off toward the nearest farmhouse. He approached it from the front, but seeing light at the back of the house, he went around and knocked on the kitchen door.

The woman who answered eyed him with suspicion, holding the door open just enough to see him. It was enough for him to see, too; he glimpsed a bowl of boiled potatoes steaming on a painted wooden table, inhaled the incomparable aroma of cabbage and bacon cooking on the stove. For a long moment, hunger rendered him mute.

"Well?" the woman said, with no hint of welcome. "What is it? I have no work for you."

Filip gathered his wits, forced himself to look away from the food and into her questioning face. She was handsome, he saw, in the sturdy way of some middle-aged women, blue eyes set off by tanned, lightly freckled skin.

"I . . . no . . . I'm looking for my . . . friend. An older man, dark-haired, a little gray. He is sick. I must find him."

"We saw no one," the woman replied firmly. "We were in the field." She waved her hand toward the outside, opening the door a little wider as she did so. Filip could see several children, ranging in age from a gangly teenaged boy to a small girl of five or six with big blue eyes and short yellow hair.

"I saw a man, *Mutti*, when I came back for water," she declared loudly. "He was walking like this," she demonstrated, weaving comically around the room. "He was drunk, *ja?*"

"Hush, child," the woman said quickly. "You talk nonsense."

Filip squatted down to the girl's level and looked at her seriously. "Was the man carrying something? Did you see? Where did he go?"

"I don't know. He had a box. A big green ugly box." The girl, suddenly timid from so much attention, ran out of the room.

Filip stood up. He felt the blood drain from the rapid movement, leaving him light-headed; he reached out to grasp the door frame to steady himself until the faintness passed.

"*Ach*, you people. Why don't you go home?" The woman turned away but did not close the door. A moment later, she handed him a small bowl filled with potatoes and cabbage. She stood watching, arms folded across her chest, while he devoured the food. Filip gave her the empty bowl, licking the fork one last time. "*Danke*," he said, backing away from the house. "Thank you."

Back on the road, now in near-total moonless darkness, he went on, refreshed by the simple food and energized by fresh information. Cabbage and potatoes. Peasant food. Had anything ever tasted so good? His mouth relived the profound satisfaction of boiled potatoes, the rich surprise of crisped bacon slivers flavoring shredded cooked cabbage. He was not blind to the woman's act of gratuitous kindness; with all those children to feed, she could have closed the door on him, and no one would have blamed her. She did not. Maybe it was a mother's instinct or plain human compassion, but she had responded to a stranger's unspoken need instinctively and without fanfare. Would he have done the same?

"*Ach, ja*, the man with the box." The woman in a house farther down the road nodded. She pulled her sweater close around her body. "*Ja*. My Otto found him, near the road. So sick, so much fever!"

"I thought he was dead." A man, presumably Otto, came to stand next to the woman. They were the same height, equally thin and gray-haired, with deeply creased weathered faces and large, work-rough hands. "But when I tried to take the box from him, to look inside, you know, in case there was a gun . . ."

"Pah!" the woman exclaimed. "How you talk!"

"Anyway. He came alive quick, holding that box like it had treasure in it." The man shook his head from side to side.

Filip did not bother to explain about the toolbox. "Where is he? Do you have him here?" He had all but given up, his search taking him from house to house until, due to the lateness of the hour, people stopped opening their doors to his knock.

"Here? No. We took him, and the box, too, in the wagon, to the Sisters of Perpetual Mercy. They have a small infirmary. They helped many people in the war."

"Is it far?"

"Not far. But it is late now. You will not see the road. Go in the morning. We will tell you the way." Otto had one hand on the door.

"Wait," the woman said. She peered up at Filip as if appraising the risk of helping him. "You have eaten?"

"A little," he admitted, which was true enough.

She disappeared into the house, came back with a piece of cheese and a wedge of coarse bread. "Sleep in the barn," she said, handing him the food wrapped in a cloth. "We are up with the chickens."

In the morning, the woman gave him milk and porridge, letting him sit at the kitchen table while she went about her work. He was well aware of the trust she displayed by allowing him, a vagrant, to enter her house. He repaid her by telling a little of his story, of the wife and child—had she seen them?—he was eager to find. She had not, at least from the sketchy description he gave, but she told him of her own wartime experience: a son felled in Berlin, a daughter perished in a fire caused by Allied bombing, their farm raided first by retreating German troops, then by marauding Soviet soldiers on a spree. "But they left me enough chickens to start again, and did not burn the field. Now the Americans are here. They leave us alone. Otto and I, we work hard. We will survive," she said without emotion, setting a pan of dried beans to soak at the back of the stove.

4

THE INFIRMARY OCCUPIED one wing of the convent's main building; the rest of the one-story structure held a chapel, laundry, administrative office, kitchen, and dining hall. A separate house, surrounded by vegetable and flower gardens studded with beehives, was set back against a screen of poplars and birches. Filip assumed this served as the sisters' residence. There were signs of recent damage here, too, but, just as in the village, things were clearly in the process of being repaired. Nearly everything, from spotless louvered windows to freshly whitewashed walls, seemed to sparkle in the morning sun.

A tall nun greeted him at the door. Her face, smooth as a baby's, hinted at maturity with a fine web of wrinkles around the eyes and mouth. A stiff wimple concealed her hair.

"Yes, he is here, your friend. Ilya is his name, yes?" She led him past a long room with white iron beds arranged dormitory style, a few of them occupied by reclining or seated patients. Across the hall, he saw a similar room; this one had several cribs along one wall and bassinets next to some of the beds. The wail of an infant and a muffled cough punctured the otherwise total silence.

The air here was clean. A fresh breeze from several open windows mingled with the scent of starched linen, taking him home again, his mother ironing sheets, making up his cot, plumping his pillow for him, her hands smelling of rosewater. What was her life like? Would he see her again?

The nun stopped outside a closed door, her hand on the handle. "Your friend is very sick," she said, looking at him gravely. "The doctor only comes on Friday, but in the meantime we put Ilya in this room, alone. We think it might be tuberculosis. When he coughs, there is blood."

"Wait." Filip leaned against the wall, his stomach gripped by cold fear, his head aflame. Who had decided he could manage this responsibility? He wanted to turn and run, to be anywhere but here, far from this developing melodrama. He wanted to lose himself in a crowd, to walk a city street, to think about nothing but which café was likely to have a chess game going, what film was playing at the movie theater. It was all too much, the specter of this illness, the search for his wife and child, the past a montage of memories, the future a blank. He could not do this. He wanted his life back.

And yet. This man had, in so many wise decisions, so many seemingly small ways, saved his life. He was the father of Galya, *his* Galya, who loved her father beyond imagining. Ilya could be unyielding in his insistent judgments; his goodness was unquestionably annoying, his stolid habits boring in the extreme. Even his craftsman's work, fine as it was, was predictably routine. But if this moment was not the very definition of duty, then what was? Duty was not some high-flown patriotic principle, as he had been taught in school. It was this—a hand extended to one in need, an honorable carrying through of human obligation.

He was not at all sure he could do it. "He is not my friend. He is my father-in-law. We have been traveling together for many weeks, looking for the rest of the family. His wife and his daughter, my wife. And our child."

The nun looked at him expectantly. He hesitated, covered his eyes with his hand. "I think I know where I might find them." He turned and walked rapidly back down the hall, past the men's and women's wards, ignoring the sounds of food preparation drifting out the open kitchen door, scarcely aware of the sisters going about their tasks. He only heard the echo of Father Stefan's words: *Come tomorrow. There will be more people.* He didn't dare hope, but he had to see.

The Sunday Mass was a long service, interminable when he was small, attending with Zoya, surrounded by kerchiefed women in dark dresses, thin candles filling the room with a smoky hypnotic haze, the priest chanting ancient Slavonic words he could not understand. He didn't know what time it was, but surely, if he hurried, he could reach the church before the service ended.

The church doors were wide open. Filip ran up, panting, and stood outside listening while his breathing returned to normal. He heard singing, the high female voices underlaid with a single harmonizing bass line, the man's voice so deep it seemed to ignite a reciprocal resonance in his own body. How could these people, who had lost everything, still sing?

It was a modest gathering, thirty or so people, most of them women. All were thin, shabbily dressed, their heads covered with a variety of simple scarves or kerchiefs. The few children he saw looked scrawny, legs protruding from their short pants and dresses like twigs on a sapling. It struck Filip for the first time that refugee life must be impossibly difficult for children, whose small bodies and need for care made them especially vulnerable. It seemed miraculous that any of them survived at all.

On the men's side, to the right, he saw just four, three of them bent with age, standing with caps in hand in nearly identical reverential poses. The younger man was on crutches. There had been many younger men in the camps, both in the German *Arbeitslager* and in the American DP facilities. Were they still wandering, like himself, looking for loved ones, for a way to start a new life in a strange place? How many had gone back, willingly or by force? Maybe they were lying low, afraid to tempt fate by drawing unwanted attention to themselves, or maybe, among the young ones who had grown up in Soviet Russia, church was simply not a place they would go. *What would bring me here but the hope of finding my family?* he thought.

He scanned the women's backs. Some were stooped, many heads bent low. They crowded in; their small number did not fill the available space. They stood like wary animals, gazelles ready to flee or defend one another from attack by banding together. Their motley clothing—flowered dresses, skirts in shades of blue, gray, or brown, dingy white blouse collars, frayed sweaters—made them look pitiful and, without seeing the faces, indistinguishable from one another. Their feet were a study in how much footwear can fall apart before becoming completely unwearable.

One woman did stand out. Taller than the rest, she wore a long black coat, her short hair covered with a gauzy beige scarf. When she turned halfway, as if in response to his questioning gaze, he recognized Ksenia's stern profile.

Filip stepped back outside. The sight of his mother-in-law, the knowledge of her presence there, just a few steps away, filled him with relief. He could relinquish his responsibility for Ilya. He would soon be reunited with Galina. At the same time, he was anxious; there would be a reckoning, and he would fall short of everybody's expectations. His life was about to undergo another monumental change, a bend in the road around which he could see nothing but impenetrable fog.

Ksenia was among the last to leave the church. Filip, from his vantage point at the bottom of the stone stairs, scanned the women's faces filing past him for the one he wanted to see. The women glanced at him, some curious, others expressionless; they talked to each other in low voices or walked alone, silent and self-absorbed. How weary they looked, how plain! He looked for Galya's quick lively eye, anticipated her ready smile, hungered for her loveliness. She was not there.

At last, his mother-in-law emerged, in conversation with a short, bearded man in a worn black cassock; on his chest, he wore a carved wood Orthodox cross suspended from a heavy brass chain. *The visiting priest,* Filip guessed, *here on his monthly circuit.* Father Stefan, the deacon, followed close behind, his own robes unadorned, and locked the doors.

Ksenia looked up when Filip stepped forward. He stood tongue-tied, uncertain what to say or do. So much had happened since February, since their separation, since Dresden. The usual pleasantries seemed insultingly banal. The fact that each of them was alive and standing was proof enough of their relative well-being. Embracing was completely out of the question.

Ksenia recovered first. "Filip," she said. She removed her scarf and dropped her arms to her sides. "I am glad to see you." She used the familiar *t'y* form of address.

"And I you, Ksenia Semyonovna," he replied, taking refuge in formality with an uneasy smile. "We have been looking for you, you and Galina, that is. How fortunate . . ." He trailed off, losing all confidence under her steady gaze.

"She is not here. Katya, the baby, was awake most of the night, teething." She volunteered nothing more, stood waiting for him to speak. Filip's mind flooded with questions: *How did you survive? What did you endure? Where are you staying, how do you live, what does my daughter look like?*

Instead, he blurted out, remembering his mission and his burden, "Ah, you must come, Ksenia Semyonovna. Ilya Nikolaevich is very sick. I don't know what to do." He sketched out the symptoms, told her about the infirmary.

"I have heard of this infirmary. Galina and I will meet you there this afternoon." Ksenia nodded and turned away, striding toward the main road.

Filip stood rooted. What had he expected? With his own mother, there would have been tears and kisses, sympathetic exclamations, tender solicitude. Comfort. This woman, the grandmother of his child, froze him with her hardness, her stoic endurance as incomprehensible to him as Ilya's infernal optimism. But things had never been warm between them and were not likely to change. Galina, and curiosity about Katya, were the only reasons he did not now walk away, strike out on his own in the other direction.

He headed back to the infirmary, his conflicted mind a jumble of relief, anticipation, and dread.

GALINA WAS BONE THIN. When they embraced, Filip could feel her ribs under his fingers through the cloth of her loose dress. He closed his eyes, absorbing the warmth of her, her hips hard as stone against his own diminished body. Her face, framed by a fringe of rough-cut hair, was exquisite in an ethereal way, the cheekbones sculpted, the eyes large and serious, ringed with fatigue but luminous and alive. "You are so beautiful," he whispered, echoing the words spoken just a few years ago, both of them schoolchildren showered with spray from the breaking waves of the Black Sea, cocooned in the purity of their innocence.

She wept, silently, intensely, without sobbing. With a visible effort, she pulled herself together and stepped away from him, wiping at the damp spot on his shirt with a fragile-looking hand. "I left Katya with my friend Marfa," she said, before he could ask about the child. "She finally fell asleep and I didn't want to wake her. Where is my father?"

"Yes." Ksenia, standing a few paces away, moved closer to the young couple. She held a small cloth-wrapped bundle. "Where is Ilya?"

The tall nun recognized Filip. "He drank a little broth yesterday. Nothing today, only water. If only the doctor could come sooner . . ." She opened the door and stood aside while they filed into the room. "There may be some danger of contagion, we believe. Please be careful."

"Papa!" Galina exclaimed, too loud for the small, neat room. She knelt by the bed, pressing her cheek to Ilya's dry hand. "*Papochka*," she said, softly now. "I have missed you so."

Ilya stirred, turned his head in her direction. "Galya," he breathed. "*Dochenka*. My daughter. Don't cry." Gently, he freed his hand and placed it on her head, stroking her hair, barely aware of his own tears. "And your mother?"

He raised his eyes. Ksenia moved to the other side of the narrow bed, wiped his face gently with the back of her hand. He smiled. "My family. I was afraid I would not see you again. I was afraid for you. But you have come? This is not a dream?" He tried to raise himself on one elbow but fell back heavily, his breath catching in his throat.

When the coughing began, Ksenia reached instinctively for the basin on the floor next to the bedside table, raising Ilya to a sitting position. She supported his back with one arm while he surrendered to wave after wave of spasmodic hacking, spitting bloody mucus into the waiting receptacle. Galina stepped back to stand near the window with Filip, her hand to her mouth in horror. Filip stood awkwardly, one arm around his wife's waist, his eyes fixed distractedly on a line of geese moving across the sky in precise geometric formation.

The nun came in with fresh water, bathed the patient's face and hands when the episode subsided and he lay exhausted, eyes closed, his breathing rapid and shallow. "*Schwester*," Ksenia began, her German hesitant, "sister . . . Tell her, Filip. I brought a clean shirt and some shaving soap. Also bread and fruit. Plums. I cannot pay. Tell her."

"God will provide. We are grateful for your kindness," the nun replied, accepting the bundle with her free hand. "The soap, yes. We will shave him. But I don't know what your husband can eat."

"Give it to someone else, then, or use it yourselves. I will try to bring more tomorrow."

"Papa." Galina sat on the edge of the bedside chair, her knees touching the mattress. "Can you hear me?"

Ilya made a throaty sound, but did not speak.

"I heard a new song, just yesterday, in the beer hall where Mama and I work."

"What song?" Ksenia cut in. "I heard no song."

"You were in the kitchen. It was a busy night, remember? I was helping at the bar." Galina frowned, annoyed at the interruption. "Anyway. A young Russian soldier was singing. He was so young! Really just a boy, with a beautiful tenor voice that made me want to cry."

"Your father is tired, Galya. He needs to rest," Ksenia said softly.

Galina raised a protesting hand. *If I keep talking to him, he will not die,* she thought, and fervently believed. "It's a war song, but not about glory or pride. It's about men, people far from home; about danger and loss. About not knowing what will happen next, where the road leads."

"Like us," Filip said unexpectedly, moving from the window to stand at her back.

Ilya looked at his daughter with clouded eyes, the lids coming down as if of their own leaden weight. "The song?" he whispered.

"I don't know all the verses, but I have the tune and the refrain. Shall I sing it for you?" She took his hand, warming it between her palms.

Ilya nodded.

"*Ekh, dorogi . . . pyl' da tuman,*" she began, her voice wavering a little. "Oh, roads . . . dust and fog," she sang, gaining confidence, filling the room with images of snow and wind, of flame and battle and brotherhood. She sang of homesickness and longing for loved ones, and of remembrance.

The echo of the melancholy melody lingered when she was done, each person in the room alone with their thoughts and feelings, beyond the reach of speech.

They started toward the door. Ilya's breathing had evened out to a sleeper's rhythm. When first his daughter, then his wife, kissed his forehead, he stirred but did not open his eyes. In the hall, with the door nearly closed, they heard him call out weakly, "Filip."

"Thank you for finding my family." Ilya's voice was a hoarse whisper, his pale face once more painted with fever on both cheeks.

"I did nothing. It just happened," Filip replied, ashamed at the truth of it, uneasy with the undeserved gratitude. But the old man was asleep, and did not hear him.

6

"WE PRAYED FOR HIM," the young nun said solemnly. "But the Lord in his wisdom chose to end his suffering."

"No." Galina was firm. "Look, I have brought his granddaughter for him to see, if only through the window. He must see her. He must," she insisted, ignoring Ksenia's sharp glance. "I made a bookmark for his birthday. It was last month, but we were separated then." She took a narrow strip of cloth from her sweater pocket, thrust it at the implacable sister. The faded scrap of shiny fabric, which Galina had embroidered with leaves and flowers using threads she had pulled from her own clothing, trembled in her hand.

"He sees us all, child." The nun placed a cool hand on Galina's arm. "Hold your father in your heart, and teach your daughter to know and love him."

Galina turned away, repelled by the sanctimonious words and the woman's air of meek superiority. What did she know? She had most likely lived out the war in hushed seclusion, protected from its daily horrors by her usefulness to all sides.

Galina spun around when Filip approached her and cupped her elbow with his hand. "Why is everyone touching me?" she demanded. "And you—were you not with him? Did you not see he needed help? After we opened our home to you—" She broke off, swiping angrily at her eyes with her free hand.

"I tried! The apothecary was closed." His own anger rose to mirror hers. He could never admit to what had really happened, how he had abandoned his search and gone dancing. But he had paid for that with the guilt that gnawed at his remaining confidence, burdened by the knowledge of his own inadequacy.

Still, hadn't all those unfortunate events led him here, where help was available even if it came too late? Where he had found the people Ilya loved and given them all at least a little time together, no matter how brief? No, he was not to blame for everything. "He wanted to just rest awhile, until he felt better. He did not want a doctor."

"And you believed him! Here," she said, thrusting Katya into his arms. "Meet your daughter." Galina turned and followed her mother into the sparsely furnished room that served as the convent's office.

Filip held the child gingerly, her head cradled in the crook of his elbow, as he imagined babies were to be held. When she squirmed in protest, he tightened his grip, afraid both of hurting her and of letting her fall. Somehow, he managed to raise her to a sitting position, perched on his arm, his free hand supporting her back. He held her away and looked at her.

Katya was thinner than he thought a baby should be, but not emaciated. Her perfectly round head was covered with a dark corona of impossibly fine hair that slipped between his fingers like dandelion fluff. She studied him, her large brown eyes—his mother's eyes, he saw—reflected an unnerving calm, shining with life.

Talking with Galina the day before, he had learned something of their ordeal since the forced separation seven months ago. Something, but not much. Too much had happened in that short time to tell in a single emotional afternoon; it would take years to recount the stories of camp life, of the Danube crossing, of the weeks of tramping, which, though not unlike his own, held additional dangers when the refugees were women.

Filip and Katya regarded each other. For a moment, it looked as if she might cry but decided not to, the quivering of her plump lower lip subsiding into a cryptic bemused expression. *"Shto?"* he finally said. "What do you want from me?" He moved his arm in closer to his body, uncomfortable with the child's steady stare. She let out a shuddering sigh and laid her head against his shoulder.

What, indeed? Until this meeting, his child had been an abstraction, linked to him, but only as an idea, a principle. Now here she was, breathing peaceably in his arms; he could feel the warmth of her head pulsing against his neck.

"Katya." He tried out the name, aware, all at once, of the life in his hands, the concrete thread connecting him now to Galina in a whole new way. And to her family, to Ksenia, the new grandmother, and to Maksim and Ilya, who would never know this child, but whose legacy she embodied simply by being born.

She was not an idea. She was a person. A person who would soon outgrow the little hand-knit sweater that even now looked short on her thin arms. She would need food and a safe place to sleep and protection from all the dangers of the universe. *Books,* he thought. *Where will I get books to teach her about the wonders of the world when I don't even have a place to live?*

He thought again about the previous evening, Ksenia having gone to get Katya from Galina's friend Marfa, leaving Galina to ask—no, to beg—her landlady for permission to let him stay the night in their already cramped basement room.

"He is my husband, my baby's father," she had insisted, her eyes filled with frustrated tears.

"Today this one is the father. Tomorrow it will be another one. You girls have no pride. Bad enough we put up with the crying and your constant coming and going until late at night." Before either of them could protest, they were facing a firmly closed door.

"She cries very little, our Katya," Galina had said, shaking her head and stepping with him into the street. She told him that she cleaned guest rooms in the mornings; Ksenia worked afternoons and well into the evening hours in the tavern kitchen. "We arranged it so that one of us is always here. But sometimes Marfa, who is Katya's godmother, helps us out, too."

The burial took place on the third day. Ilya, washed and dressed in his freshly laundered clothes, lay in a plain coffin of new pine. The box, still redolent of aromatic resin, balanced on two chairs in the center of the church. People approached the casket to pay their respects to this man, a stranger yet one of them, a fellow traveler, a brother they had never known. They studied his pale face, the waxy skin now nearly colorless, as if at any moment it could melt away and reveal the bones underneath.

When the family came in, the small crowd parted to let them pass. They were dressed like everyone else, in the same travel-worn clothing as the day before, but were somehow different, marked by a dignity born of grief.

Filip recalled how that dignity had cracked two days ago, outside the infirmary. The women had made arrangements for the removal of the body, having first secured permission to wash and dress Ilya before moving him to the church. Payment, such as it was, had been settled. Through it all, they had maintained a detached reserve; he had been relieved at their businesslike demeanor, but suspected the emotional storm was yet to come.

And come it did. Once outside the convent gates, mother and daughter had collapsed into each other's arms. Wailing and keening, they had stumbled along the road like a pair of drunks, giving in to a sorrow beyond words. The sounds they had made were unearthly, like the howling of wolves or the cries of shrouded night birds, morbid, timeless, and raw. Filip had stood apart, still holding his now sleeping child, speechless at the wrenching evidence of their dark suffering. He had felt like an intruder, a reluctant witness to something so private that it had left him shaken, his own mind filled with something like shame.

Now Ksenia appeared composed. She looked stately in her long black coat, her hair concealed under a dark-blue kerchief. Galina came in dry-eyed, but succumbed to silent weeping at the sight of her father. She handed little Katya to the ever-present Marfa and leaned heavily on Filip's arm.

The service passed over him in a blur of monotonous prayers and repetitive incantations, the little church closing in on him in a haze of candle glow and incense. Filip's mind wandered to contemplation. Why have funeral rites? Was it really imperative to gather like this, even among strangers, to speed the soul along to its mysterious destination? He saw again the dead piled near the railroad tracks, nameless and unmourned. Savko on the cement factory floor, his mouth filled with stone dust, his body consigned to cold-blooded incineration in the factory furnace. Borya, his remains tossed, no doubt, into a mass unmarked grave.

What was a soul? Was it more than the life force, that light in the eyes extinguished at the moment of death? Did a bear, a shrew, an ant have a soul, or was it coupled with a higher awareness, an ability to show mercy and compassion? He had sampled the works of philosophers, but wasn't schooled enough to puzzle out these ponderous questions. He shifted his weight from one foot to the other and, to his own embarrassment, yawned.

Father Stefan's sonorous basso cut through Filip's fruitless ruminations. In a voice both louder and brighter than before, the deacon intoned the words *vechnyi pokoi*, eternal peace, for the departed. Filip closed his eyes and heard the congregation join in the singing of the final words, in a rising minor motif of such mournful beauty that even he felt the pricking of tears behind his eyelids. Beside him, Galina's clear voice rose above the others, then broke down, the last "*Vechnaya Pamyat'*" no more than a hoarse whisper between her barely stifled sobs. Eternal Memory.

Two men approached to secure the coffin lid. Ksenia held them back; with a swift, smooth gesture, she removed her wedding ring and slipped it onto her husband's finger, the two slim bands resting against each other on his shapely hand. Someone gasped. "Mama . . .," Galina whispered, but Ksenia silenced her, her steely face unreadable. Ksenia ignored all questioning glances and nodded to the men, who hammered nails into the soft wood with merciless finality.

Ilya was buried in the small but growing graveyard behind the church. Each person accepted a spoonful of Ksenia's *kutya*, recognizing the traditional funeral dish of bulgur wheat sweetened with raisins and honey, and went on his or her way, leaving the family group huddled at the grave, while the sound of clodded earth hitting the casket echoed coldly in the late summer air.

7

IT WAS MARFA who resolved their housing dilemma.

"Why not take my room, Filip Vadimovich?" she suggested politely. "I think the owners would not mind. And I could stay with Ksenia Simyonovna, if she will have me." Her gaze fluttered over the assembled group, like a bee among blossoms, flitting from one to another but lighting on none.

Filip found her strange, her presence ghostly; he did not yet know her story. She looked even more angular and plain next to Galina's beauty. Her small, dark, close-set eyes seemed to absorb the light rather than reflect it; there was no life in them. But the women were kind to her, and her attachment to Katya seemed genuine, so he said nothing about her constant presence. Soon, when there was time to talk, he might learn the reasons.

The solution pleased everyone, not least the two landladies—one who would be rid of the child's crying, and the other who could offer the little family an adjoining alcove in addition to their attic room, at double the rent.

"You will need new papers, too, whether you look for work here or decide to move on." Ksenia stood in the windowless alcove, her head bent sideways to keep from hitting the slanted ceiling. Filip and Galina sat at either end of a small table, sipping tea they had been permitted to brew in the kitchen.

"We are all Yugoslav now," Galina explained, setting Katya on her lap. "Comrade Stalin wants us back, but the Americans don't ask for much proof of citizenship. Learn a few words of Serbian, tell them your things were destroyed in Dresden, and you will have your state-less passport. That's what we did." She dipped a crust of bread into her cup and fed it to the child.

"I know." Filip nodded. He was a collector; he had kept the worth-less claim stub from the Dresden train station. Now this piece of personal memorabilia could help verify his story. He and Ilya had burned their Soviet passports in the woods after escaping the American DP camp, leaving nothing behind to identify them as Russian citizens, but they had left without their false papers. *Time to make myself a new history. Why not?*

It was even easier than the first time. The young GI at the American processing center for displaced persons barely glanced at him, his head bent low over the single-page application form. Filip had practiced several useful Serbian phrases, but need not have worried; the soldier was no linguist. He conducted the interview in English larded with bits of bad German. Clearly, this boy knew nothing of Slavic languages, and his superiors seemed to have little interest in cooperating with Stalin's repatriation orders.

At the line for occupation, he had his answer ready. "Electrician," he said, with barely a tremor at the lie. The soldier wrote it down. Within a week Filip had a temporary work permit to go with his new passport.

What he needed now was the work.

It was harder to come by than he had expected. Even with the wandering and hiding days behind them, refugees performed only the most menial jobs. Filip soon realized that his lack of reliable electrical knowledge would not be put to the test; those in a position to hire skilled workers gave overwhelming preference to citizens of their own country. What could he do? He couldn't continue to depend on his wife and mother-in-law for support.

But even without a useful trade he felt at home, here in Germany, on Regensburg's medieval streets. Home, he now understood, was the space you created around yourself, filled with people who wished you well. A sheltering place from which came strength, confidence, endurance. Galina, returning from her morning's cleaning work, would pick up Katya. Marfa insisted on looking after the child, letting Ksenia rest, while Filip looked for work. It was a comfortable routine, practical and predictable, serving everyone's needs without placing an undue burden on any one person.

Sometimes they ate a meal of leftovers from the tavern, reheated on the tiny wood stove in their room. More often they walked to the edge of town, their daughter bouncing happily in her cast-off baby carriage with the bent wheels, to the cafeteria where Ksenia now worked, where the food was hot, simple, cheap, and good. No more scavenged scraps or frostbitten vegetables. No begging or bartering. They put their coins down like everyone else and received soup, bread, tea.

More than just a dining hall, the restaurant was at the heart of Regensburg's refugee community; part social club, part meeting hall, it had become a vital hub in the rapidly expanding communication network that helped people find work, housing, and news of loved ones. It was owned by a prerevolutionary Russian émigré couple in their sixties, with German citizenship, who had operated their modest establishment since well before the war, serving traditional Russian dishes to nostalgic expatriates and their Bavarian neighbors.

Filip grew increasingly curious about Marfa. "Why is she so . . . so absent?" he asked Galina. It was a Sunday afternoon in October. They had left Katya with her grandmother and walked into town, enjoying the chill in the air softened by brilliant sunshine, strolling with no special purpose. "It's impossible to have a conversation with her, the way her eyes are always somewhere else. The only one she really looks at is Katya. What happened? Was she violated?"

"Not raped, no. Seduced and abandoned, by a Nazi officer." *Someone like Franz*, they both thought, but neither spoke the words out loud. "There was a baby. Tolik."

"Where is the baby now?" Filip stood in front of a bookshop window and looked longingly at the tidy shelves visible in the darkened interior. When was the last time he had read anything more than a newspaper? He had a bit of money in his pocket, but Regensburg was a Catholic city and took the Lord's day seriously. The shop was closed.

"She lost him in the Danube crossing. Poor little Tolik. Marfa tried to rescue him, but the currents were too strong. She almost drowned. We held her back, Mama and I, pulled her out half-dead herself." Galina spoke without emotion, as if recounting the passing of an ordinary day. But she stared at the books stacked on a counter just inside the shop door with unseeing eyes.

Filip was silent. He had heard about the Danube crossing from Ksenia and Galina; the moonless night, the wild stormy weather, the merciless river currents that spun and roiled around people desperate enough to take a chance on death by drowning, just to be free. Why had they not mentioned Marfa's child? Either they thought him completely insensitive or the subject was still too painful, the memory too raw.

He reached for Galina's hand; they continued down the main street, walking in step with one another. "Listen," Galina exclaimed, as if eager to move on to other topics. "Mama says the restaurant owners have received news of work. Many men are needed."

"What kind of work?" Filip asked cautiously. If many were needed, it could not be especially desirable. "Where?"

"In Belgium, just across the border. The men are to go first, start working, and get settled. The families are to follow in a separate transport a few weeks later." She gave a little skip, catching up to his longer stride.

"In Brussels? That sounds like construction work. I'm not much good at that, but there may be other opportunities, in a city . . ."

He envisioned himself at a desk or drafting table, apprenticed to an engineer, an architect. He would need to learn French, but that was not a problem.

"Not Brussels. In the country, with housing provided. Anyone can sign up, as long as he's able-bodied."

"I'm not able-bodied; I'm able-minded." Filip smiled ruefully at her. "Able-minded but undereducated, therefore completely useless."

"Don't say that!" She freed her hand from his, grasped both his arms at the elbows, and shook him like a disobedient child. "Everything is changing. We must take what we can, for now. Soon we will have choices. I just know it! You can go to university, find a good starting position, be what you want to be." She spoke earnestly, her voice wavering on the verge of tears.

Galina's hands slid down his coat sleeves, found his, and held them, her fingers warm against his smooth palms. Filip looked at his wife. She had inherited her father's optimism and her mother's practicality, he realized, blended with a sweetness all her own and a seemingly inexhaustible reserve of hope. He loved her.

They crossed the street, Galina's hand tucked under his arm, and headed back toward their lodging. "Mama says we should try to get as far as possible from the Soviets," she continued in a calmer tone. "That's why I brought up the work in Belgium."

Filip could not deny the logic of such a plan. "What kind of work is it, then?"

She bent her head, studied their feet moving along the cobbled street as if absorbed in counting their steps. "Coal mining."

8

HE WAS STILL as handsome as Satan, his sunken cheeks accentuating the flashing eyes, the tawny warmth of his smoothly shaved face set off by shoulder-length hair slick as raven's feathers.

They met him by chance, in the cafeteria. He looked a little less scruffy than the others, his unrumpled clothes less dusty, the one tear in his shirt neatly patched. Standing behind him in the soup line, they recognized his profile when he removed his leather cap and ran a hand through his hair, scanning the room as if looking for someone.

Filip, holding his daughter, was first to speak. "Musa?"

Musa faced them, treating them to the full dazzle of his smile. "Filip. Galina. How good to see you again. I guess we all come here sooner or later." He gestured around the dining hall. "Our home away from home."

Filip handed Katya to Galina and clasped Musa's extended hand, the mixed emotions of their parting forgotten in the pleasure of seeing a familiar face.

"Let's sit outside," Musa suggested. "Enjoy the last of this autumn sunshine."

The men talked while Galina fed the child, helping her dip bread crusts into her soup, spooning carrot slices and bits of meat into her mouth. "What are you doing now," she heard Filip ask, "with the war over?"

Musa shrugged. "I . . . procure things."

"Things?" Filip scraped the last of his buckwheat kasha onto his fork and offered it to Katya, who leaned forward to receive it.

"Whatever's needed. Papers. Clothing. Rooms. Promises of work. I get by."

They went on like this, the men engaged in conversation that Galina followed only sporadically. Katya, seated on her lap, was absorbed in following the single-minded progress of an ant across the table's uneven surface, her finger tracing its stops and starts, her mouth opening to accept bites of cooked apple as if on cue.

Finally, aggravated by the mindless topics, Galina could stand it no longer. "Dresden," she interrupted. "How did you survive?"

Musa stopped in midsentence. "I soaked a blanket at a burst water pipe, threw it over my head, and ran."

"Ran? Ran where?"

"Ha! To the zoo. Remember the zoo?"

"Wasn't that burning, too?"

"Of course. But with more open space and all that concrete, it didn't go up quite as fast."

"Musa"—Galina took a deep breath—"what happened to the animals?"

"The animals. Most of them roasted in their cages. The keepers did what they could; they opened some of the cages to give the captive beasts a chance to escape, but I doubt any survived. What's a giraffe to do, loose in a city savaged by bombs, fire everywhere, pandemonium rampant? There were rumors of a leopard on the prowl in the hills outside the city, but I never saw it, and don't know anyone who did."

He stopped talking, laid a hand on the table for Katya to explore. She patted his palm with a squeal of delight, then lost interest and went back to tracking the ant's industrious wanderings.

"Honestly," Musa resumed. "No one was thinking about the animals. People were dying everywhere, screaming in agony. Parents, their own clothing on fire, ran with charred, lifeless children in their arms.

Others lay crushed under the rubble of collapsing buildings, with no hope of rescue."

He pulled deeply on his cigarette, blew a plume of smoke over Galina's head. "I saw one house, the outer wall demolished, the rooms exposed like a child's dollhouse—beds, dining tables, sofas crashing through the floors to apartments below, the occupants mere darting shadows backlit by burning draperies and exploding glass."

"How horrible . . . ," she started to say, but he went on gravely, with none of the carefree arrogance she remembered from their previous encounter.

"Death. Death was everywhere. The air, thick with gritty smoke, filled my mouth and burned my eyes; my lungs felt too big for my chest, hot against my ribs. I ran blindly, tripping over bodies, fearing the open spaces as much as the flaming houses."

"Why?" Filip asked. "Wouldn't you be a little safer out in the open, away from the falling buildings?"

"They came back, our allies. After the first wave of bombing, there was another. I learned later they targeted the hospital, intent on killing wounded soldiers and medical personnel, along with incidental sick women and old people. Then, before leaving the area, the planes turned, flying low, and strafed the visible survivors with machine guns—people who had crowded into parks and outlying areas, believing they might have escaped the worst, mowed down like ducks in a carnival shooting gallery. Or so I heard."

They sat, Filip and Galina unable to speak, or even to look at each other, their own travails receding into irrelevance. "Ababalalalammm," the child babbled, her expression as serious as the adults around her.

"*Sha*," Galina whispered. "Katyusha, hush."

"I thought about you," Musa said after a while. "I wondered what happened, whether you got away. Whether I could have helped you."

Katya's ant had found a bread crumb and disappeared with its treasure into a crack between two boards. The child squirmed and pushed against her mother, her feet planted on the table's edge. She let out a wail. Galina rose to walk with her, past the dining hall's open door, to the end of the row of weatherworn tables and their mismatched chairs.

She came back as Musa was saying, "Maybe I can help you now. What do you need?"

Filip thought a moment. "Galina earns a little money. We have new papers, clothes, this cafeteria, and a room . . ."

"Work." Galina faced Musa, holding Katya's head against her shoulder, rocking the child to quiet her crying. "My husband needs work."

"What can you do, Filip?"

"Nothing." Filip spread his hands, then dropped them into his lap. What wouldn't he do to avoid the filthy subterranean entombment of coal mining? He caught Galina's sharp glance and sighed. "Anything."

What, really, could he do? Germany's factories were still in shambles; there might be salvage work, but there were many German hands to do it, and to fill the jobs once the reconstruction was done. *As it should be*, he thought. *It's their country.*

He had no trade, not enough education, none of the credentials needed to gain entry into the professional world for which he felt destined. His book of sketches, his knowledge of literature and languages, his inclination toward art—all these amounted to nothing that could be turned into a way to support himself and his family in a country reeling from defeat and destruction.

So, yes, he would take anything for now, until he found the door leading to the future, where his tools would be a sharp pencil, a T square, India ink, and the imaginative capacity of his own mind.

Musa did not find any better prospects. He advised Filip to sign up for Belgium. "It's dirty work, but steady," he said. "And you'll be safer there than in Germany. Once you and your family settle in, you can see what else turns up."

Filip's heart sank. Another derailment, his life's course again controlled by others with only their own benefit in mind. He felt trapped;

he might as well already be underground, struggling to breathe foul, thin air, his skin and clothes grimy with coal dust, with no relief from the ache in his muscles and bones. "What about America?" he asked, desperate for any alternative.

"Be patient, old man," Musa sighed. "This war was bigger than any catastrophe we've ever known. So much chaos, so many impoverished displaced people. It will take time to return to any kind of normal life. I don't know what you've heard, but so far the American relief effort is focused on food and clothing. Cornflakes and powdered milk. Go to Belgium. Take your wife and child—"

"And my mother-in-law," Filip interrupted.

"Of course. The grandmother. She can be a big help. Don't look at me like that. Just keep your ear to the ground." He twisted a corner of his mouth in a rueful grin at Filip's stricken expression. "Sorry. You know what I mean. You're a smart boy."

9

"WILL YOU TAKE THESE?" Galina rested her hand on the stamp albums lying on the table. Everything else—his shirts, pants, shaving brush, and other essentials—was already packed.

Filip reached for the albums, pulled them closer. "My father gave me these when I was ten," he said. "The red one for Russia and Europe, the blue for the rest of the world. When did I last open them? I haven't had much to add." He fingered the cracked covers, touched the corners worn through the faded leather to the cardboard beneath. "I can hardly believe they've come through the war with me."

"Will you take them?" Galina repeated. "It's getting late, and you leave early tomorrow."

Filip sighed. "No. You may as well keep them for me. Musa said families are to follow us to the mining villages within a month or so."

He opened the blue album, turned its glossy pages one by one, pausing to study the few stamps displayed among the gaps of missing exemplars. "So many places," he said. "Galya, imagine going to all these places, seeing these buildings and monuments, these plants and animals, learning about these people."

Galina shook her head and smiled. "You're such a dreamer. I've seen enough places for now. Katya and I need a home." Katya, on her cot next to the bed, slept.

Filip glanced at his wife, saw no sign of anger or irritation, and continued turning pages. Galina rose to hang freshly laundered diapers and shirts on the clothesline near the stove. "You could bring me a little coal before you go. But no, there won't be time. I'll go with Marfa after work."

Filip wasn't listening. "Galya, look. Look what I found." He pushed his chair back from the table and faced her, a pencil box in his hand. "It was between the pages. I thought I had lost it."

Galina stared at him, watched joy and sadness chase each other across his face in quick succession. He looked as if he might cry. "What?"

"My pencil box. The one Avram—you remember Avram, the gro-cer?—he gave it to me on my seventh birthday. Look, here's the Gull's Nest Sanatorium painted on the lid." He passed the box from hand to hand, slid the lid back in its grooves to expose several smooth brown pencils, their points dulled by the friction of many months' travel within the box.

They could have fallen overboard in the barge crossing, those pen-cils, and washed up somewhere on the rocky coast of the Black Sea. They could have burned in Dresden, their ashes mingled with the detritus of wanton destruction. They could have ended up in hostile hands, helping the enemy complete sordid nefarious projects. But here they were, scuffed and scarred, but intact. Ready.

Filip, unable to say any of that, looked at the floor. "It was my birthday. Mama baked me a cake."

Galina left the laundry in its basin. She knelt in front of Filip, took the box from him, and laid it on the table. She held his hands in her cool ones, still damp from the washing. "Have you heard from them, your parents?"

"No. I send a postcard every week, but—no. Months ago I heard a rumor that they might have left Yalta. But I don't know. They could be anywhere."

"We'll find them"

"It would be a miracle." Filip raised his head and looked at her with troubled eyes.

"We found each other. The war is over. We'll find them, too."

She got to her feet and sat down in the other chair. For some minutes, neither spoke; they listened to Katya's breathing rise and fall like water lapping gently against wet sand.

Filip picked up the pencil box and held it out to his wife. "I want Katya to have this." He stood abruptly and paced the little room. "I want her to have everything. Books and dolls and puzzles and music lessons." He covered the space between bed and table in three strides, waved his arms in the air, one hand barely missing the clothesline. "I want her to sing like you and dance and laugh, to learn poems and to always, always have hope." He took a deep breath. "I want her to have enough."

Galina smiled. "All in good time. Now go to bed, or you'll miss the transport in the morning. I need to finish hanging the washing."

10

"DO YOU LOVE ME?" Filip lay on his back, the pulsating glow of the cigarette cradled on his chest the only light in the room. Did she? He suddenly needed to know.

Had he imagined the expression of mournful understanding on her face the first time they had made love after their reunion? She had said nothing, neither questioning nor accusing. The Galina he knew, the spirited girl who looked at life's realities with a spark of humor, might have teased him about his new confidence. Gone was the awkward innocence of their newlywed encounters and the desperate urgency of camp coupling. If she had noticed, or enjoyed, the smoother way he used his hands, his mouth, she gave no sign.

She had been silent, rising quickly to tend to her women's business, showing that she, too, had learned something in the intervening months. This was no time to have another child.

She was silent now, too. Filip grew uneasy. It was not a question that required much reflection, to his mind, and her hesitation was surely a bad omen. Was she sleeping? He glanced in her direction, admiring again the smooth planes of her face, the tendrils of loose hair, which appeared white in the darkness, her open eyes directed at the ceiling. He coughed, put out the cigarette, and considered whether to risk asking again.

"I was walking with my mother the other day," she said, her voice soft and low so as not to wake the baby sleeping in her cot alongside their bed. "You were out. I had finished my job early, and Mama's shift did not begin for another hour or so. We were going to a farmhouse just out of town to buy eggs and milk."

Filip was puzzled. What was the point of this storytelling? Why not just answer the question? No, he did not understand women, after all.

"On the way, at the side of the road, we saw a pair of gray geese. They were the common wild ones, the kind you see everywhere, flying in formation, or flocking at lakes and ponds: grayish-brown feathers, pink feet, speckled bellies. Nothing unusual." She tugged at the blanket, pulling it up to her neck against the chill in the room. She angled her head slightly away from him, watching the sky fill with storm clouds, their menacing shapes rolling past the small square window like film scenes in a movie theater.

"Geese? You saw geese? And what?"

"I will tell you what. One of the geese was lying on the ground, its wing sticking up strangely, broken, the breeze ruffling the feathers into ragged tufts. It was dead, or dying. The other goose stood next to its partner, its neck stretched out full length, orange beak pointing to the sky, wings partly spread. It also was not moving. You know that geese stay together for life. I don't believe that animals don't suffer. It was heartbreaking."

Filip turned to his wife, his annoyance arrested by the edge of sadness in her voice. She wiped a tear sliding down her cheek, using the edge of the blanket.

"My mother said, 'I am this goose. In leaving me now, my Ilya has taken a piece of my soul.'"

"Is that why . . . the ring . . . she was going with him," Filip said.

"Yes. I didn't know what to say to her."

"Because it was so personal?"

"Because I do not understand that kind of love. Not because I'm young; they married young, too, and lived through some terrifying years together." She paused while the thought unwound in her head: *My parents shared something wider and deeper, something eternal that I doubt I will ever know. I have seen love, and while I can't say I know what it is, I know that it is not what I feel for you.*

They lay together, not touching, listening to Katya's quick, shallow breathing.

"So I'm not sure how to answer your question," Galina went on after a while. Katya stirred, whimpered, but did not wake. "When we were apart, I was frightened and anxious. I missed you and wondered what was happening to you, how you were getting on. Of course, I suffered. But I did not lose a piece of my soul."

Filip lit another cigarette, just to quiet the restlessness stirred up by Galina's unexpected confession. It had seemed a simple question, a question he would never have asked if he had any idea it would unleash such an intimate response, such complicated thoughts.

But he was in it now, and needed to know. The work transport was leaving in the morning, taking him to unimagined unpleasant, and dangerous, experiences. Who knew how long this separation would last?

"So then," he prompted.

It had begun to snow. Galina turned away again, watching large feathery flakes drift on the night air, buffeted by invisible currents into a dance that was as timeless as it was new.

"Yes." She spoke without facing him, suppressing more words she could not say aloud: *Now, here, in this place, after all that has happened to us. Yes. If love means forgetting some things and forgiving others, not asking questions to which the answer is better left unsaid.* "Yes, I love you. Now go to sleep. You'll wake the baby."

Filip extinguished his half-smoked cigarette, taking care to leave the butt unbroken. How had he wandered into such hazardous territory? Did she know about, or guess at, his infidelities? Did it matter? In using the word *love* she clearly was admitting to a lesser form, separate from the bedrock of her parents' bond—a serene, abiding emotion for which there seemed to be no verbal expression. Where did this leave him? His head ached from the unexpected intensity of this conversation; he knew less now than he did before.

He knew, too, that it was not a question he would ask again. He drifted off, grateful for the mind-numbing onset of sleep.

Sometime later he woke, sensing Galina's movement on their narrow bed. He raised himself on one elbow. She sat motionless on the very edge, holding Katya asleep on her lap, one hand stroking the child's hair, her form a hazy outline against the window now trimmed with geometric frost patterns.

Outside, the snow had thickened. It fell and swirled, blanketing the roofs of Regensburg as far as the eye could see, the Danube a black ribbon shimmering in the far distance. The tall evergreen whose branches brushed against the house was adorned with dazzling picture-postcard mounds, pulling the laden limbs toward the ground below.

Filip stretched out to touch her shoulder in the thin flannel of her winter gown, then withdrew his hand. She was beyond his reach just now, inhabiting a secret place that was hers alone. "What are you doing?" he whispered.

Galina remained still, her back straight, eyes fixed on the other-worldly scene before her. "I'm looking at the snow."

AUTHOR'S NOTE

How did this book happen? The truth is, of course, that it did not happen. A book never does; a book is built. It emerges from elements as surprising as they are banal: an overheard remark dropped by a passing stranger, a random thought, the seed of an idea, a memory.

This book is built of stories—the ones I started collecting, unawares, as a child growing up among Russian expatriates in a community that sheltered its members while they learned how to live in a postwar world that would never again be the same. Like refugees and displaced people everywhere, they carried their mementos, their recipes, their customs and beliefs, their language and music wherever they went. These were the tools with which they began to carve out a home among baffling and sometimes hostile strangers.

Some of the stories were given to me, passed on as heritage. Others I absorbed whenever friends and newcomers gathered around the table, affirming the bittersweet victory of survival through shared recollections, covering their scars with deep melancholy as often as with laughter and song. Among these people, there were those who said nothing at all. Their enigmatic silence carried, for me, its own mysterious eloquence.

Some narratives I surmised for myself. I pieced them together from scraps hinting at an ordeal too painful to recall in its entirety, an ordeal that nagged at the mind or troubled the heart, refusing to be completely forgotten.

I grew older; people aged. Some died, leaving a trail of memories that started to seem less reliable. The stories had changed in the retelling, tinged by nostalgia. There were omissions, contradictions, discrepancies. The people who had made those journeys, endured those terrors, were the survivors; they had buried the fallen and searched for the lost. But the picture was starting to blur. If I was going to tell the tale, I needed facts.

There were books to read and maps to study, Internet sources and firsthand narratives to evaluate and absorb. It was not enough. I had to go, to see some of the places where these things had happened. It would all be different now, after so much time had passed. But I had to go.

I traveled to Russia, Belgium, Germany. I saw the Elbe at Dresden, sailed down the Danube from Regensburg. Trains carried me through the Bavarian countryside and its legendary forest, past villages with tile-roofed houses, and into teeming cities. Waiting on the platform for a connecting train to my last destination, I heard the conductor announce, "Plattling, Track Two." Plattling. It was not on my itinerary, but it was in my story. I had the time.

And what would I see there? Barbed wire around weathered barracks, watchtowers, a labor camp museum, a commemorative plaque? Or a housing development, a shopping mall, every trace of the grim history obliterated under concrete and steel? Which would be worse?

I didn't go to Plattling. After visiting Dresden, I went home. I had a solid historical framework on which to hang the stories, fresh impressions of people, customs, outlook, and language. And I had a landscape through which to move the composite characters I had created, following them as they embarked on a journey I would now begin to imagine and describe. Already, images, plot points, and lines of dialogue were taking shape in my mind. The work had begun. It was time to build the book.

Clearly, I did not travel the long road to placing this work in readers' hands alone. I thank my editor, Lindsey Schauer, without whose skilled effort to clarify every narrative and grammatical detail these pages would lack much of any polish or cohesiveness they might possess. Of the fellow writers who accompanied me along the way, I single out these: Roselee Blooston, who was the first to take me seriously and to give public exposure to my fledgling work; Steve Otlowski, who gave no quarter when it came to historical accuracy and read an early draft of this book in one exhausting sitting; and Rosa Soy, for her keen ear, her stalwart friendship, and her unflinching confidence in my ability to see this project through to its completion.

Many others listened to the emerging work. I thank them for their attention, for their focused criticism and cogent questions, for suffering through my moments of self-doubt and patches of bad writing. I cannot name them all, for fear of leaving out anyone important; each was important in his or her own way, and to each of them, I am grateful.